PENGUIN BOOKS

THE MAGICIANS

LEV GROSSMAN is the book critic for *Time* magazine and author of the international bestseller *Codex*. He lives in Brooklyn, New York.

Praise for *The Magicians*

"*The Magicians* is to Harry Potter as a shot of Irish whiskey is to a glass of weak tea. Solidly rooted in the traditions of both fantasy and mainstream literary fiction, the novel tips its hat to Oz and Narnia as well as to Harry, but don't mistake this for a children's book. Grossman's sensibilities are thoroughly adult, his narrative dark and dangerous and full of twists. Hogwarts was never like this."
—George R. R. Martin, bestselling author of *A Game of Thrones*

"*The Magicians* ought to be required reading for anyone who has ever fallen in love with a fantasy series, or wished that they went to a school for wizards. Lev Grossman has written a terrific, at times almost painfully perceptive novel of the fantastic that brings to mind both Jay McInerney and J. K. Rowling."
—Kelly Link, author of *Magic for Beginners* and *Stranger Things Happen*

"Anyone who grew up reading about magical wardrobes and unicorns and talking trees before graduating to *Less Than Zero* and *The Secret History* and *Bright Lights, Big City* will immediately feel right at home with this smart, beautifully written book by Lev Grossman. *The Magicians* is fantastic, in all senses of the word. It's strange, fanciful, extravagant, eccentric, and truly remarkable—a great story, masterfully told."
—Scott Smith, bestselling author of *The Ruins* and *A Simple Plan*

"*The Magicians* is a spellbinding, fast-moving, dark fantasy book for grown-ups that feels like an instant classic. I read it in a niffin-blue blaze of page turning, enthralled by Grossman's verbal and imaginative wizardry, his complex characters, and, most of all, his superb, brilliant inquiry into the wondrous, dangerous world of magic."
—Kate Christensen, PEN/Faulkner Award–winning author of
The Great Man and *The Epicure's Lament*

"Remember the last time you ran home to finish a book? This is it, folks. *The Magicians* is the most dazzling, erudite, and thoughtful fantasy novel to date. You'll be bedazzled by the magic but also brought short by what it has to say about the world we live in."
—Gary Shteyngart, author of *Absurdistan* and *The Russian Debutante's Handbook*

"*The Magicians* brilliantly explores the hidden underbelly of fantasy and easy magic, taking what's simple on the surface and turning it over to show us the complicated writhing mess beneath. It's like seeing the worlds of Narnia and Harry Potter through a 3-D magnifying glass." —Naomi Novik, author of *His Majesty's Dragon*

"Fresh and compelling . . . *The Magicians* is a great fairy tale, written for grown-ups but appealing to our most basic desires for stories to bring about some re-enchantment with the world, where monsters lurk but where a young man with a little magic may prevail." —*The Washington Post*

"*The Magicians* is original . . . slyly funny." —*USA Today*

"Lev Grossman's playful fantasy novel *The Magicians* pays homage to a variety of sources . . . with such verve and ease that you quickly forget the references and lose yourself in the story." —*O, The Oprah Magazine*

"I felt like I was poppin' peyote buttons with J. K. Rowling when I was reading Lev Grossman's new novel *The Magicians* . . . couldn't put it down." —Mickey Rapkin, *GQ*

"The novel manages a literary magic trick: it's both an enchantingly written fantasy and a moving deconstruction of enchantingly realized fantasies." —*Los Angeles Times*

"Intriguing, coming-of-age fantasy." —*The Boston Globe* (Pick of the Week)

"*The Magicians* by Lev Grossman is a very entertaining book; one of those summer page-turners that you wish went on for another six volumes. Grossman takes a good number of the best childhood fantasy books from the last seventy-five years and distills their ability to fascinate into the fan-boy mind of his protagonist, Quentin Coldwater. . . . There is no doubt that this book is inventive storytelling and Grossman is at the height of his powers." —*Chicago Sun-Times*

"Entertaining." —*People*

"Lev Grossman's novel *The Magicians* may just be the most subversive, gripping, and enchanting fantasy novel I've read this century. . . . Grossman is a hell of a pacer, and the book rips along, whole seasons tossed out in a single sentence, all the boring mortar ground off the bricks, so that the book comes across as a sheer, seamless face that you can't stop yourself from tumbling down once you launch yourself off the first page. This isn't just an exercise in exploring what we love about fantasy and the lies we tell ourselves about it—it's a shit-kicking, gripping, tightly plotted novel that makes you want to take the afternoon off work to finish it." —Cory Doctorow, Boing Boing

"An irresistible storytelling momentum makes *The Magicians* a great summer book, both thoughtful and enchanting." —Salon.com

"Grossman skillfully moves us through four years of school and a postgraduate adventure, never letting the pace slacken . . . beguiling." —*The Seattle Times*

"Through sheer storytelling grace and imaginative power, Lev Grossman [creates] an adventure that's both enthralling and mature." —*Details*

"Mixing the magic of the most beloved children's fantasy classics (from Narnia and Oz to Harry Potter and Earthsea) with the sex, excess, angst, and anticlimax of life in college and beyond, Lev Grossman's *The Magicians* reimagines modern-day fantasy for grown-ups. [It] breathes life into a cast of characters you want to know . . . and does what [some] claim books never really manage to do: 'get you out, really out, of where you were and into somewhere better.' Or if not better, at least a heck of a lot more interesting." —*The Courier-Journal* (Louisville)

"This gripping novel draws on the conventions of contemporary and classic fantasy novels in order to upend them, and tell a darkly cunning story about the power of imagination itself. [*The Magicians* is] an unexpectedly moving coming-of-age story." —*The New Yorker*

"Fantasy fans can't afford to miss the darkly comic and unforgettably queasy experience of reading this book—and be glad for reality." —*Booklist* (starred review)

"This is a book for grown-up fans of children's fantasy and would appeal to those who loved Donna Tartt's *The Secret History*. Highly recommended." —*Library Journal* (starred review)

"Very dark and very scary, with no simple answers provided—fantasy for grown-ups, in other words, and very satisfying indeed." —*Kirkus Reviews*

"Stirring, complex, adventurous . . . from the life of Quentin Coldwater, his slacker Park Slope Harry Potter, Lev Grossman delivers superb coming-of-age fantasy." —Junot Díaz, Pulitzer Prize–winning author of *The Brief Wondrous Life of Oscar Wao*

ALSO BY LEV GROSSMAN

Codex
The Magician King
The Magician's Land

THE MAGICIANS

A Novel

LEV GROSSMAN

PENGUIN BOOKS

PENGUIN BOOKS
An imprint of Penguin Random House LLC
375 Hudson Street
New York, New York 10014
penguin.com

First published in the United States of America by Viking,
an imprint of Penguin Random House LLC, 2009
Published by Plume, an imprint of Penguin Random House LLC, 2010
Published in Penguin Books 2016

The illustrated map of Fillory was created by Roland Chambers.

THE LIBRARY OF CONGRESS HAS CATALOGED THE HARDCOVER EDITION AS FOLLOWS:
Grossman, Lev.
The magicians : a novel / Lev Grossman.
p.   cm.
ISBN 978-0-670-02055-3 (hc.)
ISBN 978-0-452-29629-9 (pbk.)
1. College students—Fiction.   2. College graduates—Fiction.   3. Magic—Fiction.
4. Psychological Fiction.   I. Title.
PS3557.R6725M34   2009
813'.54—dc22   2008055900

Printed in the United States of America
40 39 38 37 36 35 34 33 32

Original hardcover design by Nancy Resnick

FOR LILY

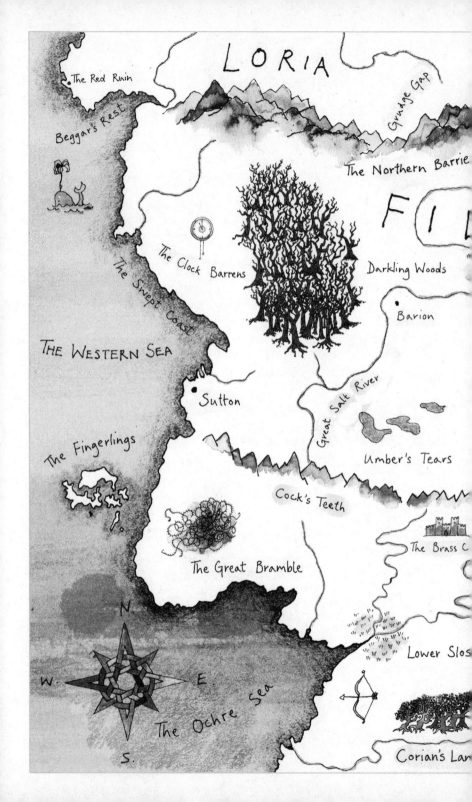

I'll break my staff,
Bury it certain fathoms in the earth,
And deeper than did ever plummet sound
I'll drown my book.

—William Shakespeare, *The Tempest*

BOOK I

BROOKLYN

Quentin did a magic trick. Nobody noticed.

They picked their way along the cold, uneven sidewalk together: James, Julia, and Quentin. James and Julia held hands. That's how things were now. The sidewalk wasn't quite wide enough, so Quentin trailed after them, like a sulky child. He would rather have been alone with Julia, or just alone period, but you couldn't have everything. Or at least the available evidence pointed overwhelmingly to that conclusion.

"Okay!" James said over his shoulder. "Q. Let's talk strategy."

James seemed to have a sixth sense for when Quentin was starting to feel sorry for himself. Quentin's interview was in seven minutes. James was right after him.

"Nice firm handshake. Lots of eye contact. Then when he's feeling comfortable, you hit him with a chair and I'll break his password and e-mail Princeton."

"Just be yourself, Q," Julia said.

Her dark hair was pulled back in a wavy bunch. Somehow it made it worse that she was always so nice to him.

"How is that different from what I said?"

Quentin did the magic trick again. It was a very small trick, a basic one-handed sleight with a nickel. He did it in his coat pocket where nobody could see. He did it again, then he did it backward.

"I have one guess for his password," James said. *"Password."*

It was kind of incredible how long this had been going on, Quentin thought. They were only seventeen, but he felt like he'd known James and

Julia forever. The school systems in Brooklyn sorted out the gifted ones and shoved them together, then separated the ridiculously brilliant ones from the merely gifted ones and shoved *them* together, and as a result they'd been bumping into each other in the same speaking contests and regional Latin exams and tiny, specially convened ultra-advanced math classes since elementary school. The nerdiest of the nerds. By now, their senior year, Quentin knew James and Julia better than he knew anybody else in the world, not excluding his parents, and they knew him. Everybody knew what everybody else was going to say before they said it. Everybody who was going to sleep with anybody else had already done it. Julia—pale, freckled, dreamy Julia, who played the oboe and knew even more physics than he did—was never going to sleep with Quentin.

Quentin was thin and tall, though he habitually hunched his shoulders in a vain attempt to brace himself against whatever blow was coming from the heavens, and which would logically hit the tall people first. His shoulder-length hair was freezing in clumps. He should have stuck around to dry it after gym, especially with his interview today, but for some reason—maybe he was in a self-sabotaging mood—he hadn't. The low gray sky threatened snow. It seemed to Quentin like the world was offering up special little tableaux of misery just for him: crows perched on power lines, stepped-in dog shit, windblown trash, the corpses of innumerable wet oak leaves being desecrated in innumerable ways by innumerable vehicles and pedestrians.

"God, I'm full," James said. "I ate too much. Why do I always eat too much?"

"Because you're a greedy pig?" Julia said brightly. "Because you're tired of being able to see your feet? Because you're trying to make your stomach touch your penis?"

James put his hands behind his head, his fingers in his wavy chestnut hair, his camel cashmere coat wide open to the November cold, and belched mightily. Cold never bothered him. Quentin felt cold all the time, like he was trapped in his own private individual winter.

James sang, to a tune somewhere between "Good King Wenceslas" and "Bingo":

> *In olden times there was a boy*
> *Young and strong and brave-o*

He wore a sword and rode a horse
And his name was Dave-o . . .

"God!" Julia shrieked. "Stop!"

James had written this song five years ago for a middle-school talent show skit. He still liked to sing it; by now they all knew it by heart. Julia shoved him, still singing, into a garbage can, and when that didn't work she snatched off his watch cap and started beating him over the head with it.

"My hair! My beautiful interview hair!"

King James, Quentin thought. *Le roi s'amuse.*

"I hate to break up the party," he said, "but we've got like two minutes."

"Oh dear, oh dear!" Julia twittered. "The duchess! We shall be quite late!"

I should be happy, Quentin thought. I'm young and alive and healthy. I have good friends. I have two reasonably intact parents—viz., Dad, an editor of medical textbooks, and Mom, a commercial illustrator with ambitions, thwarted, of being a painter. I am a solid member of the middle-middle class. My GPA is a number higher than most people even realize it is possible for a GPA to be.

But walking along Fifth Avenue in Brooklyn, in his black overcoat and his gray interview suit, Quentin knew he wasn't happy. Why not? He had painstakingly assembled all the ingredients of happiness. He had performed all the necessary rituals, spoken the words, lit the candles, made the sacrifices. But happiness, like a disobedient spirit, refused to come. He couldn't think what else to do.

He followed James and Julia past bodegas, laundromats, hipster boutiques, cell-phone stores limned with neon piping, past a bar where old people were already drinking at three forty-five in the afternoon, past a brown-brick Veterans of Foreign Wars hall with plastic patio furniture on the sidewalk in front of it. All of it just confirmed his belief that his real life, the life he should be living, had been mislaid through some clerical error by the cosmic bureaucracy. This couldn't be it. It had been diverted somewhere else, to somebody else, and he'd been issued this shitty substitute *faux* life instead.

Maybe his real life would turn up in Princeton. He did the trick with the nickel in his pocket again.

"Are you playing with your wang, Quentin?" James asked.

Quentin blushed.

"I am not playing with my wang."

"Nothing to be ashamed of." James clapped him on the shoulder. "Clears the mind."

The wind bit through the thin material of Quentin's interview suit, but he refused to button his overcoat. He let the cold blow through it. It didn't matter, he wasn't really there anyway.

He was in Fillory.

Christopher Plover's *Fillory and Further* is a series of five novels published in England in the 1930s. They describe the adventures of the five Chatwin children in a magical land that they discover while on holiday in the countryside with their eccentric aunt and uncle. They aren't really on holiday, of course—their father is up to his hips in mud and blood at Passchendaele, and their mother has been hospitalized with a mysterious illness that is probably psychological in nature, which is why they've been hastily packed off to the country for safekeeping.

But all that unhappiness takes place far in the background. In the foreground, every summer for three years, the children leave their various boarding schools and return to Cornwall, and each time they do they find their way into the secret world of Fillory, where they have adventures and explore magical lands and defend the gentle creatures who live there against the various forces that menace them. The strangest and most persistent of those enemies is a veiled figure known only as the Watcherwoman, whose horological enchantments threaten to stall time itself, trapping all of Fillory at five o'clock on a particularly dreary, drizzly afternoon in late September.

Like most people Quentin read the Fillory books in grade school. Unlike most people—unlike James and Julia—he never got over them. They were where he went when he couldn't deal with the real world, which was a lot. (The Fillory books were both a consolation for Julia not loving him and also probably a major reason why she didn't.) And it was true, there was a strong whiff of the English nursery about them, and he felt secretly embarrassed when he got to the parts about the Cozy Horse, an enormous, affectionate equine creature who trots around Fillory by night on velvet hooves, and whose back is so broad you can sleep on it.

But there was a more seductive, more dangerous truth to Fillory that Quentin couldn't let go of. It was almost like the Fillory books—especially the first one, *The World in the Walls*—were about reading itself. When the oldest Chatwin, melancholy Martin, opens the cabinet of the grandfather clock that stands in a dark, narrow back hallway in his aunt's house and slips through into Fillory (Quentin always pictured him awkwardly pushing aside the pendulum, like the uvula of a monstrous throat), it's like he's opening the covers of a book, but a book that did what books always promised to do and never actually quite did: get you out, really out, of where you were and into somewhere better.

The world Martin discovers in the walls of his aunt's house is a world of magical twilight, a landscape as black and white and stark as a printed page, with prickly stubblefields and rolling hills crisscrossed by old stone walls. In Fillory there's an eclipse every day at noon, and seasons can last for a hundred years. Bare trees scratch at the sky. Pale green seas lap at narrow white beaches made of broken shells. In Fillory things mattered in a way they didn't in this world. In Fillory you felt the appropriate emotions when things happened. Happiness was a real, actual, achievable possibility. It came when you called. Or no, it never left you in the first place.

They stood on the sidewalk in front of the house. The neighborhood was fancier here, with wide sidewalks and overhanging trees. The house was brick, the only unattached residential structure in a neighborhood of row houses and brownstones. It was locally famous for having played a role in the bloody, costly Battle of Brooklyn. It seemed to gently reproach the cars and streetlights around it with memories of its gracious Old Dutch past.

If this were a Fillory novel—Quentin thought, just for the record— the house would contain a secret gateway to another world. The old man who lived there would be kindly and eccentric and drop cryptic remarks, and then when his back was turned Quentin would stumble on a mysterious cabinet or an enchanted dumbwaiter or whatever, through which he would gaze with wild surmise on the clean breast of another world.

But this wasn't a Fillory novel.

"So," Julia said. "Give 'em Hades."

She wore a blue serge coat with a round collar that made her look like a French schoolgirl.

"See you at the library maybe."

"Cheers."

They bumped fists. She dropped her gaze, embarrassed. She knew how he felt, and he knew she knew, and there was nothing more to say about it. He waited, pretending to be fascinated by a parked car, while she kissed James good-bye—she put a hand on his chest and kicked up her heel like an old-timey starlet—then he and James walked slowly up the cement path to the front door.

James put his arm around Quentin's shoulders.

"I know what you think, Quentin," he said gruffly. Quentin was taller, but James was broader, more solidly built, and he pulled Quentin off balance. "You think nobody understands you. But I do." He squeezed Quentin's shoulder in an almost fatherly way. "I'm the only one who does."

Quentin said nothing. You could envy James, but you couldn't hate him, because along with being handsome and smart he was also, at heart, kind and good. More than anybody else Quentin had ever met, James reminded him of Martin Chatwin. But if James was a Chatwin, what did that make Quentin? The real problem with being around James was that he was always the hero. And what did that make you? Either the sidekick or the villain.

Quentin rang the doorbell. A soft, tinny clatter erupted somewhere in the depths of the darkened house. An old-fashioned, analog ring. He rehearsed a mental list of his extracurriculars, personal goals, etc. He was absolutely prepared for this interview in every possible way, except maybe his incompletely dried hair, but now that the ripened fruit of all that preparation was right in front of him he suddenly lost any desire for it. He wasn't surprised. He was used to this anticlimactic feeling, where by the time you've done all the work to get something you don't even want it anymore. He had it all the time. It was one of the few things he could depend on.

The doorway was guarded by a depressingly ordinary suburban screen door. Orange and purple zinnias were still blooming, against all horticultural logic, in a random scatter pattern in black earth beds on either side of the doorstep. How weird, Quentin thought, with no curiosity at all, that they would still be alive in November. He withdrew his ungloved hands into the sleeves of his coat and placed the ends of the sleeves under his arms. Even though it felt cold enough to snow, somehow it began to rain.

It was still raining five minutes later. Quentin knocked on the door again, then pushed lightly. It opened a crack, and a wave of warm air tumbled out. The warm, fruity smell of a stranger's house.

"Hello?" Quentin called. He and James exchanged glances. He pushed the door all the way open.

"Better give him another minute."

"Who even does this in their spare time?" Quentin said. "I bet he's a pedophile."

The foyer was dark and silent and muffled with Oriental rugs. Still outside, James leaned on the doorbell. No one answered.

"I don't think anybody's here," Quentin said. That James wasn't coming inside suddenly made him want to go inside more. If the interviewer actually turned out to be a gatekeeper to the magical land of Fillory, he thought, it was too bad he wasn't wearing more practical shoes.

A staircase went up. On the left was a stiff, unused-looking dining room, on the right a cozy den with leather armchairs and a carved, man-size wooden cabinet standing by itself in a corner. Interesting. An old nautical map taller than he was took up half of one wall, with an ornately barbed compass rose. He massaged the walls in search of a light switch. There was a cane chair in one corner, but he didn't sit.

All the blinds were drawn. The quality of the darkness was less like a house with the curtains drawn than it was like actual night, as if the sun had set or been eclipsed the moment he crossed the threshold. Quentin slow-motion-walked into the den. He'd go back outside and call. In another minute. He had to at least look. The darkness was like a prickling electric cloud around him.

The cabinet was enormous, so big you could climb into it. He placed his hand on its small, dinged brass knob. It was unlocked. His fingers trembled. *Le roi s'amuse.* He couldn't help himself. It felt like the world was revolving around him, like his whole life had been leading up to this moment.

It was a liquor cabinet. A big one, there was practically a whole bar in there. Quentin reached back past the ranks of softly jingling bottles and felt the dry, scratchy plywood at the back just to make sure. Solid. Nothing magical about it. He closed the door, breathing hard, his face burning in the darkness. It was when he looked around to make absolutely sure that nobody was watching that he saw the dead body on the floor.

Fifteen minutes later the foyer was full of people and activity. Quentin sat in a corner, in the cane chair, like a pallbearer at the funeral of somebody he'd never met. He kept the back of his skull pressed firmly against the cool solid wall like it was his last point of connection to a same reality. James stood next to him. He didn't seem to know where to put his hands. They didn't look at each other.

The old man lay flat on his back on the floor. His stomach was a sizable round hump, his hair a crazy gray Einstein half-noggin. Three paramedics crouched around him, two men and a woman. The woman was disarmingly, almost inappropriately pretty—she looked out of place in that grim scene, miscast. The paramedics were at work, but it wasn't the high-speed clinical blitz of an emergency life-saving treatment. This was the other kind, the obligatory failed resuscitation. They were murmuring in low voices, packing up, ripping off adhesive patches, discarding contaminated sharps in a special container.

With a practiced, muscular movement one of the men de-intubated the corpse. The old man's mouth was open, and Quentin could see his dead gray tongue. He smelled something that he didn't want to admit was the faint, bitter odor of shit.

"This is bad," James said, not for the first time.

"Yes," Quentin said thickly. "Extremely bad." His lips and teeth felt numb.

If he didn't move, nobody could involve him in this any further. He tried to breathe slowly and keep still. He stared straight ahead, refusing to focus his eyes on what was happening in the den. He knew if he looked at James he would only see his own mental state reflected back at him in an infinite corridor of panic that led nowhere. He wondered when it would be all right for them to leave. He couldn't get rid of a feeling of shame that he was the one who went into the house uninvited, as if that had somehow caused the man's death.

"I shouldn't have called him a pedophile," Quentin said out loud. "That was wrong."

"Extremely wrong," James agreed. They spoke slowly, like they were both trying out language for the very first time.

One of the paramedics, the woman, stood up from where she was squatting by the body. Quentin watched her stretch, heels of her hands pressed to her lumbar region, tipping her head one way, then the other. Then she walked over in their direction, stripping off rubber gloves.

"Well," she announced cheerfully, "he's dead!" By her accent she was English.

Quentin cleared his clotted throat. The woman chucked the gloves neatly into the trash from across the room.

"What happened to him?"

"Cerebral hemorrhage. Nice quick way to go, if you have to go. Which he did. He must have been a drinker."

She made the drinky-drinky gesture.

Her cheeks were flushed from crouching down over the body. She might have been twenty-five at most, and she wore a dark blue short-sleeved button-down shirt, neatly pressed, with one button that didn't match: a stewardess on the connecting flight to hell. Quentin wished she weren't so attractive. Unpretty women were so much easier to deal with in some ways—you didn't have to face the pain of their probable unattainability. But she was not unpretty. She was pale and thin and unreasonably lovely, with a broad, ridiculously sexy mouth.

"Well." Quentin didn't know what to say. "I'm sorry."

"Why are you sorry?" she said. "Did you kill him?"

"I'm just here for an interview. He did alumni interviews for Princeton."

"So why do you care?"

Quentin hesitated. He wondered if he'd misunderstood the premise of this conversation. He stood up, which he should have done when she first came over anyway. He was much taller than her. Even under the circumstances, he thought, this person is carrying around a lot of attitude for a paramedic. It's not like she's a real doctor or anything. He wanted to scan her chest for a name tag but didn't want to get caught looking at her breasts.

"I don't actually care about him, personally," Quentin said carefully, "but I do place a certain value on human life in the abstract. So even though I didn't know him, I think I can say that I'm sorry that he's dead."

"What if he was a monster? Maybe he really was a pedophile."

She'd overheard him.

"Maybe. Maybe he was a nice guy. Maybe he was a saint."

"Maybe."

"You must spend a lot of time around dead people." Out of the corner of his eye he was vaguely aware that James was watching this exchange, baffled.

"Well, you're supposed to keep them alive. Or that's what they tell us."

"It must be hard."

"The dead ones are a lot less trouble."

"Quieter."

"Exactly."

The look in her eyes didn't quite match what she was saying. She was studying him.

"Listen," James cut in. "We should probably go."

"What's your hurry?" she said. Her eyes hadn't left Quentin's. Unlike practically everybody, she seemed more interested in him than in James. "Listen, I think this guy might have left something for you."

She picked up two manila envelopes, document-size, off a marble-topped side table. Quentin frowned.

"I don't think so."

"We should probably go," James said.

"You said that already," the paramedic said.

James opened the door. The cold air was a pleasant shock. It felt real. That was what Quentin needed: more reality. Less of this, whatever this was.

"Seriously," the woman said. "I think you should take these. It might be important."

Her eyes wouldn't leave Quentin's face. The day had gone still around them. It was chilly on the stoop, and getting a little damp, and he was roughly ten yards away from a corpse.

"Listen, we're gonna go," James was saying. "Thanks. I'm sure you did everything you could."

The pretty paramedic's dark hair was in two heavy ropes of braid. She wore a shiny yellow enamel ring and some kind of fancy silver antique wristwatch. Her nose and chin were tiny and pointy. She was a pale, skinny, pretty angel of death, and she held two manila envelopes with their names on them in block Magic Marker letters. Probably transcripts, confidential recommendations. For some reason, maybe just because he knew James wouldn't, Quentin took the one with his name on it.

"All right! Good-bye!" the paramedic sang. She twirled back into the house and closed the door. They were alone on the stoop.

"Well," James said. He inhaled through his nose and breathed out firmly.

Quentin nodded, as if he were agreeing with something James had said. Slowly they walked back up the path to the sidewalk. He still felt dazed. He didn't especially want to talk to James.

"Listen," James said. "You probably shouldn't have that."

"I know," Quentin said.

"You could still put it back, you know. I mean, what if they found out?"

"How would they find out?"

"I don't know."

"Who knows what's in here? Could come in useful."

"Yeah, well, lucky thing that guy died then!" James said irritably.

They walked to the end of the block without speaking, annoyed at each other and not wanting to admit it. The slate sidewalk was wet, and the sky was white with rain. Quentin knew he probably shouldn't have taken the envelope. He was pissed at himself for taking it and pissed at James for not taking his.

"Look, I'll see you later," James said. "I gotta go meet Jules at the library."

"Right."

They shook hands formally. It felt strangely final. Quentin walked away slowly down First Street. A man had died in the house he just left. He was still in a dream. He realized—more shame—that underneath it all he was relieved that he didn't have to do his Princeton interview today after all.

The day was darkening. The sun was setting already behind the gray shell of cloud that covered Brooklyn. For the first time in an hour he thought about all the things he had left to do today: physics problem set, history paper, e-mail, dishes, laundry. The weight of them was dragging him back down the gravity well of the ordinary world. He would have to explain to his parents what happened, and they would, in some way he could never grasp, and therefore could never properly rebut, make him feel like it was his fault. It would all go back to normal. He thought of Julia and James meeting at the library. She would be working on her Western Civ paper for Mr. Karras, a six-week project she would complete in two sleepless days and nights. As ardently as he wished that she were his, and not James's, he could never quite imagine how he would win her. In the most plausible of his many fantasies James died, unexpectedly and painlessly, leaving Julia behind to sink softly weeping into his arms.

As he walked Quentin unwound the little red-threaded clasp that held shut the manila envelope. He saw immediately that it wasn't his transcript, or an official document of any kind. The envelope held a notebook. It was old-looking, its corners squashed and rubbed till they were smooth and round, its cover foxed.

The first page, handwritten in ink, read:

The Magicians
Book Six of *Fillory and Further*

The ink had gone brown with age. *The Magicians* was not the name of any book by Christopher Plover that Quentin knew of. And any good nerd knew that there were only five books in the Fillory series.

When he turned the page a piece of white notepaper, folded over once, flew out and slipped away on the wind. It clung to a wrought-iron area fence for a second before the wind whipped it away again.

There was a community garden on the block, a triangular snippet of land too narrow and weirdly shaped to be snapped up by developers. With its ownership a black hole of legal ambiguity, it had been taken over years ago by a collective of enterprising neighbors who had trucked out the acid sand native to Brooklyn and replaced it with rich, fertile loam from upstate. For a while they'd raised pumpkins and tomatoes and spring bulbs and raked out little Japanese serenity gardens, but lately they'd neglected it, and hardy urban weeds had taken root instead. They were running riot and strangling their frailer, more exotic competitors. It was into this tangled thicket that the note flew and disappeared.

This late in the year all the plants were dead or dying, even the weeds, and Quentin waded into them hip-deep, dry stems catching on his pants, his leather shoes crunching brown broken glass. It crossed his mind that the note might just possibly contain the hot paramedic's phone number. The garden was narrow, but it went surprisingly far back. There were three or four sizable trees in it, and the farther in he pushed the darker and more overgrown it got.

He caught a glimpse of the note, up high, plastered against a trellis encrusted with dead vines. It could clear the back fence before he caught up with it. His phone rang: his dad. Quentin ignored it. Out of the corner of his eye he thought he saw something flit past behind the bracken, large and pale, but when he turned his head it was gone. He pushed past the corpses of gladiolas, petunias, shoulder-high sunflowers, rosebushes—brittle, stiff stems and flowers frozen in death into ornate toile patterns.

He would have thought he'd gone all the way through to Seventh Avenue by now. He shoved his way even deeper in, brushing up against who knew what toxic flora. A case of poison fucking ivy, that's all he needed now. It was odd to see that here and there among the dead plants a few vital green stalks still poked up, drawing sustenance from who knew where. He caught a whiff of something sweet in the air.

He stopped. All of a sudden it was quiet. No car horns, no stereos, no sirens. His phone had stopped ringing. It was bitter cold, and his fingers were numb. Turn back or go on? He squeezed farther in through a hedge, closing his eyes and squinching up his face against the scratchy twigs. He stumbled over something, an old stone. He felt suddenly nauseous. He was sweating.

When he opened his eyes again he was standing on the edge of a huge, wide, perfectly level green lawn surrounded by trees. The smell of ripe grass was overpowering. There was hot sun on his face.

The sun was at the wrong angle. And where the hell were the clouds? The sky was a blinding blue. His inner ear spun sickeningly. He held his breath for a few seconds, then expelled freezing winter air from his lungs and breathed in warm summer air in its place. It was thick with floating pollen. He sneezed.

In the middle distance beyond the wide lawn a large house stood, all honey-colored stone and gray slate, adorned with chimneys and gables and towers and roofs and sub-roofs. In the center, over the main house, was a tall, stately clock tower that struck even Quentin as an odd addition to what otherwise looked like a private residence. The clock was in the Venetian style: a single barbed hand circling a face with twenty-four hours marked on it in Roman numerals. Over one wing rose what looked like the green oxidized-copper dome of an observatory. Between house and lawn was a series of inviting landscaped terraces and spinneys and hedges and fountains.

Quentin was pretty sure that if he stood very still for a few seconds everything would snap back to normal. He wondered if he was undergoing some dire neurological event. He looked cautiously back over his shoulder. There was no sign of the garden behind him, just some big leafy oak trees, the advance guard of what looked like a pretty serious forest. A rill of sweat ran down his rib cage from his left armpit. It was hot.

Quentin dropped his bag on the turf and shrugged out of his overcoat. A bird chirped languidly in the silence. Fifty feet away a tall skinny teenager was leaning against a tree, smoking a cigarette and watching him.

He looked about Quentin's age. He wore a button-down shirt with a sharp collar and very thin, very pale pink stripes. He didn't look at Quentin, just dragged on his cigarette and exhaled into the summer air. The heat didn't seem to bother him.

"Hey," Quentin called.

Now he looked over. He raised his chin at Quentin, once, but didn't answer.

Quentin walked over, as nonchalantly as he could. He really didn't want to look like somebody who had no idea what was going on. Even without his coat on he was sweating like a bastard. He felt like an over-dressed English explorer trying to impress a skeptical tropical native. But there was something he had to ask.

"Is this—?" Quentin cleared his throat. "So is this Fillory?" He squinted against the bright sun.

The young man looked at Quentin very seriously. He took another long drag on his cigarette, then he shook his head slowly, blowing out the smoke.

"Nope," he said. "Upstate New York."

H e didn't laugh. Quentin would appreciate that later.

"Upstate?" Quentin said. "What, like Vassar?"

"I saw you come through," the young man said. "Come on, you need to go up to the House."

He snapped the cigarette away and set off across the wide lawn. He didn't look back to see if Quentin was following, which at first Quentin didn't, but then a sudden fear of being left alone in this place got him moving and he trotted to catch up.

The green was enormous, the size of half a dozen football fields. It seemed to take them forever to get across it. The sun beat on the back of Quentin's neck.

"So what's your name?" the young man asked, in a tone that made sure Quentin knew that he had no interest in the answer.

"Quentin."

"Charming. From?"

"Brooklyn."

"How old?"

"Seventeen."

"I'm Eliot. Don't tell me anything else, I don't want to know. Don't want to get attached."

Quentin had to take a couple of double-time steps to keep up with Eliot. There was something off about Eliot's face. His posture was very straight, but his mouth was twisted to one side, in a permanent half grimace that revealed a nest of teeth sticking both in and out at improbable angles. He looked like a child who had been slightly misdelivered, with some subpar forceps handling by the attending.

But despite his odd appearance Eliot had an air of effortless self-possession that made Quentin urgently want to be his friend, or maybe just be him period. He was obviously one of those people who felt at home in the world—he was naturally buoyant, where Quentin felt like he had to dog-paddle constantly, exhaustingly, humiliatingly, just to get one sip of air.

"So what is this place?" Quentin asked. "Do you live here?"

"You mean here at Brakebills?" he said airily. "Yes, I guess I do." They had reached the far side of the grass. "If you can call it living."

Eliot led Quentin through a gap in a tall hedge and into a leafy, shadowy labyrinth. The bushes had been trimmed precisely into narrow, branching, fractally ramifying corridors that periodically opened out onto small shady alcoves and courtyards. The shrubbery was so dense that no light penetrated through it, but here and there a heavy yellow stripe of sun fell across the path from above. They passed a plashing fountain here, a somber, rain-ravaged white stone statue there.

It was a good five minutes before they stepped out of the maze, through an opening flanked by two towering topiary bears reared up on their hind legs, onto a stone terrace in the shadow of the large house Quentin had seen from a distance. A breeze made one of the tall, leafy bears seem to turn its head slightly in his direction.

"The Dean will probably be down to get you in another minute," Eliot said. "Here's my advice. Sit there"—he pointed to a weathered stone bench, like he was telling an overly affectionate dog to stay—"and try to look like you belong here. And if you tell him you saw me smoking, I will banish you to the lowest circle of hell. Which I've never been there, but if even half of what I hear is true it's almost as bad as Brooklyn."

Eliot disappeared back into the hedge maze, and Quentin sat down obediently on the bench. He stared down between his shiny black interview shoes at the gray stone tiles, his backpack and his overcoat in his lap. This is impossible, he thought lucidly; he thought the words in his mind, but they got no purchase on the world around him. He felt like he was having a not-unpleasant drug experience. The tiles were intricately carved with a pattern of twiny vines, or possibly elaborately calligraphic words that had been worn away into illegibility. Little motes and seeds drifted around in the sunlight. If this is a hallucination, he thought, it's pretty damn hi-res.

The silence was the strangest part of it. As hard as he listened he couldn't hear a single car. It felt like he was in a movie where the sound track had abruptly cut out.

A pair of French doors rattled a few times and then opened. A tall, fat man wearing a seersucker suit strode out onto the terrace.

"Good afternoon," he said. "You would be Quentin Coldwater."

He spoke very correctly, as if he wished he had an English accent but wasn't quite pretentious enough to affect one. He had a mild, open face and thin blond hair.

"Yes, sir." Quentin had never called an adult—or anybody else—sir in his life, but it suddenly felt appropriate.

"Welcome to Brakebills College," the man said. "I suppose you've heard of us?"

"Actually no," Quentin said.

"Well, you've been offered a Preliminary Examination here. Do you accept?"

Quentin didn't know what to say. This wasn't one of the questions he'd prepped for when he got up this morning.

"I don't know," he said, blinking. "I mean, I guess I'm not sure."

"Perfectly understandable response, but not an acceptable one, I'm afraid. I need a yes or a no. It's just for the Exam," he added helpfully.

Quentin had a powerful intuition that if he said no, all of this would be over before the syllable was even fully out of his mouth, and he would be left standing in the cold rain and dog shit of First Street wondering why he'd seemed to feel the warmth of the sun on the back of his neck for a second just then. He wasn't ready for that. Not yet.

"Sure, okay," he said, not wanting to sound too eager. "Yeah."

"Splendid." He was one of those superficially jolly people whose jolliness didn't quite reach all the way up to his eyes. "Let's get you Examined. My name is Henry Fogg—no jokes please, I've heard them all—and you may address me as Dean. Follow me. You're the last one to arrive, I think," he added.

No jokes actually came to Quentin's mind. Inside the house it was hushed and cool, and there was a rich, spicy smell in the air of books and

Oriental carpets and old wood and tobacco. The Dean walked ahead of him impatiently. It took Quentin a minute for his eyes to adjust. They hurried through a sitting room hung with murky oil paintings, down a narrow wood-paneled hallway, then up several flights of stairs to a heavy-timbered wooden door.

The instant it opened hundreds of eyes flicked up and fixed themselves on Quentin. The room was long and airy and full of individual wooden desks arranged in rows. At each desk sat a serious-looking teenager. It was a classroom, but not the kind Quentin was used to, where the walls were cinder block and covered with bulletin boards and posters with kittens hanging from branches with HANG IN THERE, BABY under them in balloon letters. The walls of this room were old stone. It was full of sunlight, and it stretched back and back and back. It looked like a trick with mirrors.

Most of the kids were Quentin's age and appeared to occupy his same general stratum of coolness or lack thereof. But not all. There were a few punks with mohawks or shaved heads, and there was a substantial goth contingent and one of those super Jews, a Hasid. A too-tall girl with too-big red-framed glasses beamed goofily at everybody. A few of the younger girls looked like they'd been crying. One kid had no shirt on and green and red tattoos all over his back. Jesus, Quentin thought, whose parents would let them do that? Another was in a motorized wheelchair. Another was missing his left arm. He wore a dark button-down shirt with one sleeve folded up and held closed with a silver clasp.

All the desks were identical, and on each one an ordinary blank blue test booklet was laid out with a very thin, very sharp No. 3 pencil next to it. It was the first thing Quentin had seen here that was familiar. There was one empty seat, toward the back of the room, and he sat down and scooched his chair forward with a deafening screech. He almost thought he saw Julia's face in among the crowd, but she turned away almost immediately, and anyway there was no time. At the front of the room Dean Fogg cleared his throat primly.

"All right," he said. "A few preliminaries. There will be silence during the Examination. You are free to look at other students' papers, but you will find that they appear to you to be blank. Your pencils will not require additional sharpening. If you would like a glass of water, just hold up three fingers above your head, like this." He demonstrated.

"Do not worry about feeling unprepared for the Examination. There is no way to study for it, though it would be equally true to say that you have been preparing for it your whole lives. There are only two possible grades, Pass and Fail. If you pass, you will proceed to the second stage of the Examination. If you fail, and most of you will, you will be returned to your homes with a plausible alibi and very little memory of this entire experience.

"The duration of the test is two and one half hours. Begin."

The Dean turned to the blackboard and drew a clock face on it. Quentin looked down at the blank booklet on his desk. It was no longer blank. It was filling with questions; the letters literally swam into being on the paper as he watched.

The room filled with a collective rustling of paper, like a flock of birds taking off. Heads bowed in unison. Quentin recognized this motion. It was the motion of a bunch of high-powered type-A test killers getting down to their bloody work.

That was all right. He was one of them.

Quentin hadn't planned on spending the rest of his afternoon—or morning, or whatever this was—taking a standardized test on an unknown subject, at an unknown educational institution, in some unknown alternate climatic zone where it was still summer. He was supposed to be in Brooklyn freezing his ass off and being interviewed by some random senior citizen, currently deceased. But the logic of his immediate circumstances was overwhelming his other concerns, however well founded they might be. He had never been one to argue with logic.

A lot of the test was calculus, pretty basic stuff for Quentin, who was so mysteriously good at math that his high school had been forced to outsource that part of his education to Brooklyn College. Nothing more hazardous than some fancy differential geometry and a few linear algebra proofs. But there were more exotic questions, too. Some of them seemed totally pointless. One of them showed him the back of a playing card—not an actual card but a *drawing* of the back of a playing card, mind you, featuring your standard twin angels riding bicycles—and asked him to guess what card it was. How did that make sense?

Or later on the test gave him a passage from *The Tempest,* then asked him to make up a fake language, and then translate the Shakespeare into the made-up language. He was then asked questions about the grammar and orthography of his made-up language, and then—honestly, what was the point?—questions about the made-up geography and culture and society of the made-up country where his made-up language was so fluently spoken. Then he had to translate the original passage from the fake language back into English, paying particular attention to any resulting distortions in grammar, word choice, and meaning. Seriously. He always gave everything he had on tests, but in this case he wasn't totally sure what he was supposed to give.

The test also changed as he took it. The reading-comprehension section showed him a paragraph that vanished as he read it, then quizzed him on its contents. Some new kind of computerized paper—hadn't he read somewhere that somebody was working on that? Digital ink? Amazing resolution, though. He was asked to draw a rabbit that wouldn't keep still as he drew it—as soon as it had paws it scratched itself luxuriously and then went hopping off around the page, nibbling at the other questions, so that he had to chase it with the pencil to finish filling in the fur. He wound up pacifying it with some hastily sketched radishes and then drawing a fence around it to keep it in line.

Soon he forgot about everything else except putting a satisfactory chunk of his neat handwriting next to one question after another, appeasing whatever perverse demands the test made on him. It was an hour before he even looked up from his desk. His ass hurt. He shifted in his chair. The patches of sunlight from the windows had moved.

Something else had changed, too. When he'd started every single desk had been filled, but now there was a sprinkling of empty ones. He hadn't noticed anybody leaving. A cold crystal seed of doubt formed in Quentin's stomach. Jesus, they must have finished already. He wasn't used to being outclassed in the classroom. The palms of his hands prickled with sweat, and he smeared them along his thighs. Who were these people?

When Quentin flipped to the next page of the test booklet it was blank except for a single word in the center of the page: *FIN,* in swirly italic type, like at the end of an old movie.

He sat back in the chair and pressed the heels of his aching hands against his aching eyes. Well, that was two hours of his life he'd never get back. Quentin still hadn't noticed anybody getting up and walking out, but the room was getting seriously depopulated. There were maybe fifty kids left, and more empty desks than full ones. It was like they were softly and silently slipping out of the room every time he turned his head. The punk with the tattoos and no shirt was still there. He must have finished, or given up, because he was dicking around by ordering more and more glasses of water. His desktop was crowded with glasses. Quentin spent the last twenty minutes staring out the window and practicing a spinning trick with his pencil.

The Dean came in again and addressed the room.

"I'm delighted to inform you all that you will be moving on to the next stage of testing," he said. "This stage will be conducted on an individual basis by members of the Brakebills faculty. In the meantime, you may enjoy some refreshment and converse among yourselves."

Quentin counted only twenty-two desks still occupied, maybe a tenth of the original group. Bizarrely, a silent, comically correct butler in white gloves entered and began circulating through the room. He gave each of them a wooden tray with a sandwich—roasted red peppers and very fresh mozzarella on sourdough bread—a lumpy pear, and a thick square of dark, bitter chocolate. He poured each student a glass of something cloudy and fizzy from an individual bottle without a label. It turned out to be grapefruit soda.

Quentin took his lunch and drifted up to the front row, where most of the rest of the test takers were gathering. He felt pathetically relieved to have gotten this far, even though he had no idea why he'd passed and the others had failed, or what he'd get for passing. The butler was patiently loading the clinking, sloshing collection of water glasses from the punk's desk onto a tray. Quentin looked for Julia, but either she hadn't made the cut or she'd never been there in the first place.

"They should have capped it," explained the punk, who said his name was Penny. He had a gentle moony face that was at odds with his otherwise terrifying appearance. "How much water you can ask for. Like maybe five glasses at most. I love finding shit like that, where the system screws itself with its own rules."

He shrugged.

"Anyway, I was bored. The test told me I was done after twenty minutes."

"Twenty minutes?" Quentin was torn between admiration and envy. "Jesus Christ, it took me two hours."

The punk shrugged again and made a face: What the hell do you want me to say?

Among the test takers, camaraderie warred with mistrust. Some of the kids exchanged names and home towns and cautious observations about the test, though the more they compared notes, the more they realized that none of them had taken the same one. They were from all over the country, except for two who turned out to be from the same Inuit reservation in Saskatchewan. They went around the room telling stories about how they'd gotten here. No two were exactly the same, but there was always a certain family resemblance. Somebody went looking for a lost ball in an alley, or a stray goat in a drainage ditch, or followed an inexplicable extra cable in the high school computer room which led to a server closet that had never been there before. And then green grass and summer heat and somebody to take them up to the exam room.

As soon as lunch was over teachers began poking their heads in and calling out the names of candidates. They went alphabetically, so it was only a couple of minutes before a stern woman in her forties with dark shoulder-length hair summoned Quentin Coldwater. He followed her into a narrow wood-paneled room with tall windows that looked out from a surprisingly great height onto the lawn he'd crossed earlier. Chatter from the adjacent exam room cut off abruptly when the door closed. Two chairs faced each other across a worn, hugely thick wooden table.

Quentin felt giddy, like he was watching the whole thing on TV. It was ridiculous. But he forced himself to pay attention. This was a competition, and he dominated competitions. That was what he did, and he sensed that the stakes of this one were rising. The table was bare except for a deck of cards and a stack of about a dozen coins.

"I understand you like magic tricks, Quentin," the woman said. She had a very slight accent, European but otherwise unplaceable. Icelandic? "Why don't you show me some?"

As a matter of fact, Quentin did like magic tricks. His interest in magic had started three years ago, partly inspired by his reading habits but mostly as a way of fattening up his extracurriculars with an activity that wouldn't force him to actually interact with other people. Quentin had spent hundreds of emotionally arid hours with his iPod on palming coins and shuffling cards and producing fake flowers from skinny plastic canes in a trance of boredom. He watched and rewatched grainy, porn-like instructional videotapes in which middle-aged men demonstrated close-up magic passes in front of backdrops made of bedsheets. Magic, Quentin discovered, wasn't romantic at all. It was grim and repetitive and deceptive. And he worked his ass off and became very good at it.

There was a store near Quentin's house that sold magic supplies, along with junk electronics, dusty board games, pet rocks, and fake vomit. Ricky, the man behind the counter, who had a beard and sideburns but no mustache, like an Amish farmer, grudgingly agreed to give Quentin some tips. It wasn't long before the student surpassed the master. At seventeen Quentin knew the Scotch and Soda and the tricky one-handed Charlier cut, and he could juggle the elusive Mills Mess pattern with three balls and sometimes, for short ecstatic flights, with four. He earned a small dividend of popularity at school every time he demonstrated his ability to throw, with a fierce, robotic accuracy, an ordinary playing card sidearm so that from a distance of ten feet it stuck edge-on in one of the flavorless Styrofoamy apples they served in the cafeteria.

Quentin reached for the cards first. He was vain about his shuffling, so he broke out a faro shuffle rather than the standard riffle just in case—fat chance—the woman sitting across from him knew the difference, and how ridiculously hard it was to do a good faro.

He ran through his usual routine, which was already calculated to show off as many different skills as possible: false cuts, false shuffles, lifts, sleights, passes, forces. In between tricks he tossed and waterfalled and avalanched the cards from hand to hand. He had regular patter to go with it, but it sounded clumsy and empty in this quiet, airy, beautiful room, in front of this dignified, handsome older woman. The words trailed off. He performed in silence.

The cards made shushing, snapping noises in the stillness. The woman watched him steadily, obediently choosing a card whenever he asked her to, showing no surprise when he recovered it—against all odds!—from the middle of a thoroughly shuffled deck, or from his shirt pocket, or out of thin air.

He switched to the coins. They were fresh new nickels, nicely milled, good crisp edges. He had no props, no cups or folded handkerchiefs, so he stuck to palms and passes, flourishes and catches. The woman watched him in silence for a minute, then reached across the table and touched his arm.

"Do that one again," she said.

He obediently did that one again. The trick was an old one, the Wandering Nickel, wherein a nickel (actually three nickels) moved mysteriously from hand to hand. He kept showing it to the audience and then cheekily vanishing it again; then he pretended to lose track of it entirely; then he triumphantly produced it again, whereupon it appeared to vanish again straight out of his open palm, in plain sight. It was actually a fairly ordinary, if well-scripted, sequence of steals and drops, with one particularly nervy retention-of-vision vanish.

"Do it again."

He did it again. She stopped him in the middle.

"This part—there is a mistake."

"Where?" He frowned. "That's how you do it."

She pursed her lips and shook her head.

The woman plucked three nickels from the stack and without an instant of hesitation, or anything in her manner that acknowledged that she was doing something special, performed the Wandering Nickel perfectly. Quentin couldn't stop staring at her small, limber brown hands. Her movements were smoother and more precise than any professional's he'd ever seen.

She stopped in the middle.

"See here, where the second coin must go from hand to hand? You need a reverse pass, holding it like so. Here, come around so you can see."

He obediently trotted around to her side of the table and stood behind her, trying not to look down her blouse. Her hands were smaller than his, but the nickel vanished between her fingers like a bird into a thicket. She did the move for him slowly, backward and forward, breaking it down.

"That's what I'm doing," he said.

"Show me."

Now she was openly smiling. She grasped his wrist to stop him mid-pass.

"Now. Where is the second coin?"

He held out his hands, palm up. The coin was . . . but there was no coin. It was gone. He turned his hands over, waggled his fingers, looked on the table, in his lap, on the floor. Nothing. It had disappeared. Did she nick it while he wasn't looking? With those fast hands and that Mona Lisa smile, he couldn't quite put it past her.

"It is what I thought," she said, standing up. "Thank you, Quentin, I will send in the next examiner."

Quentin watched her go, still patting his pockets for the missing coin. For the first time in his life he couldn't tell if he'd passed or failed.

The whole afternoon went like that: professors parading in through one door and out the other. It was like a dream, a long, rambling dream with no obvious meaning. There was an old man with a shaky head who fumbled in his pants pockets and threw a bunch of frayed, yellowed knotted cords on the table, then stood there with a stopwatch as Quentin untied them. A shy, pretty young woman, who looked like she was barely older than Quentin, asked him to draw a map of the House and the grounds based on what he'd seen since he'd been here. A slick fellow with a huge head and who wouldn't or couldn't stop talking challenged him to a weird variant of blitz chess. After a while you couldn't even take it seriously—it felt like it was his credulity that was being tested. A fat man with red hair and a self-important air released a tiny lizard with iridescent humming-bird wings and huge, alert eyes into the room. The man said nothing, just folded his arms and sat on the edge of the table, which creaked unhappily under his weight.

For lack of a better idea Quentin tried to coax the lizard to land on his finger. It flew down and nipped a tiny chunk out of his forearm, drawing a dot of blood, then zipped away and buzzed against the window like a bumblebee. The fat man silently handed Quentin a Band-Aid, collected his lizard, and left.

Finally the door closed and didn't open again. Quentin took a deep breath and rolled his shoulders. Apparently the procession had ended, though nobody bothered to say anything to Quentin. At least he had a few minutes to himself. By now the sun was setting. He couldn't see it from the exam room, but he could see a fountain, and the light reflected in the pool of the fountain was a cool burnt orange. A mist was rising up through the trees. The grounds were deserted.

He rubbed his face with his hands. His head was clearing. It occurred to him, long after it probably should have, to wonder what the hell his parents were thinking. Normally they were pretty indifferent to his comings and goings, but even they had their limits. School had been out for hours now. Maybe they thought his interview had run long, though the chances that they even remembered Quentin was supposed to have had an interview were pretty small. Or if it was summer here, maybe school hadn't even started yet? The giddy haze he'd been lost in all afternoon was starting to dissipate. He wondered exactly how safe he was here. If this was a dream, he was going to have to wake up pretty soon.

Through the closed door he distinctly heard the sound of somebody crying: a boy, and way too old to be crying in front of other people. A teacher was speaking to him quietly and firmly, but the boy either wouldn't or couldn't stop. He ignored it, but it was a dangerous, unmanning sound, a sound that clawed away at the outer layers of Quentin's hard-won teenage sangfroid. Underneath it there was something like fear. The voices faded as the boy was led away. Quentin heard the Dean speaking in icy, clipped tones, trying not to sound angry.

"I'm really not sure I care one way or the other anymore."

There was an answer, something inaudible.

"If we don't have a Quorum we'll simply send them all home and skip a year." Fogg's genteel reserve was decaying. "Nothing would make me happier. We can rebuild the observatory. We can turn the school into a nursing home for senile old professors. God knows we have enough of those."

Inaudible.

"There is a Twentieth, Melanie. We go through this every year, and we will empty every high school and middle school and juvenile detention center till we find him or her or it. And if there isn't I will happily resign, and it will be your problem, and you're welcome to it. Right now I can't think of anything that would make me happier."

The door opened a crack, and for an instant a worried face peered in at him—it was Quentin's first examiner, the dark-haired European lady with the clever fingers. He opened his mouth to ask about a phone—his cell was down to one useless flickering bar—but the door shut again. How annoying. Was it over? Should he just leave? He made a face to himself. He was all for adventures, God knows, but enough was enough. This one was getting old.

The room was almost dark. He looked around for a light switch, but there wasn't one; in fact all the time he'd been here he hadn't seen a single electrical device. No phones, no lights, no clocks. It was a long time since Quentin had had his sandwich and his square of dark chocolate, and he was hungry again. He stood up and went to the window where it was lighter.

The panes of glass were wiggly with age. Was he the last one left? What was taking so long? The sky was a luminous royal blue dome swarming with huge lazy whorls of stars, van Gogh stars that would have been invisible in Brooklyn, drowned in light pollution. He wondered how far upstate they were, and what had happened to the note he'd been chasing and never found. The book he'd left behind with his backpack in the first exam room; now he wished he'd kept it with him. He imagined his parents making dinner together in the kitchen, something steaming on the stove, his dad singing along to something nightmarishly unhip, two glasses of red wine on the counter. He almost missed them.

With no warning the door banged open and the Dean walked in, talking over his shoulder at somebody behind him.

"—a Candidate? Fine," he said sarcastically. "Let's see a Candidate. And bring some Goddamned candles!" He sat down at the table. His shirt was translucent with sweat. It was not impossible that he'd had a drink between now and the last time Quentin had seen him. "Hello, Quentin. Please sit."

He indicated the other chair. Quentin sat, and Fogg rebuttoned his top button and hastily, irritably whipped a tie out of his pocket.

The dark-haired woman followed Fogg into the room, and after her came the old man with the knots, the fat man with the lizard, then the rest of the dozen or so men and women who had paraded through the room this afternoon. They formed lines along the walls, packed themselves into the corners, craning to look at him, whispering to one another. The punk kid with the tattoos was there, too—he slipped in just as the door was closing, unobserved by the faculty.

"Come on, come on." The Dean waved them into the room. "We should really do this in the conservatory next year. Pearl, you come around here." This to the young blond woman who'd made Quentin draw a map.

"Now," he said when they were all inside. "Quentin. Sit, please."

Quentin was already sitting. He scooched in his chair a little farther.

Dean Fogg took out of one pocket a fresh pack of cards, the plastic wrap still on them, and from the other he took a stack of nickels, maybe a dollar's worth, which he put down too emphatically so that they promptly slumped over. They both reached to restack them.

"All right, let's get to it." Fogg clapped his hands and rubbed them together. "Let's see some magic!"

He sat back in his chair and folded his arms.

Hadn't they already done this part? Quentin kept his face studiously calm and unworried, but his mind was in free fall. Slowly he unwrapped the stiff new cards, the plastic crackling deafeningly in the excruciating stillness, and watched from a mental mile away as his hands dutifully riffled and bridged them, riffled and bridged. He searched his brain for a trick he hadn't already done the first time around. Somebody coughed.

He'd barely started his routine when Fogg stopped him.

"No, no-no-no-no." Fogg chuckled, not especially kindly. "Not like that. I want to see some *real magic*."

He knocked twice on the hard tabletop with his knuckles and sat back again. Quentin took a deep breath and searched Fogg's face for the good humor he'd seen there earlier, but Fogg just watched expectantly. His eyes were a pale milky blue, paler than eyes usually were.

"I don't really get what you mean," Quentin said slowly, in the silence, like he'd forgotten his line in the school play and had to ask for it. "What do you mean, real magic?"

"Well, I don't know." Fogg shot a hilarious sideways glance at the other teachers. "I don't know what I mean. You tell me what I mean."

Quentin shuffled a couple more times, stalling. He didn't know what to do. He would do anything if they would just tell him what he was supposed to do. This was it, he thought, he was coming to the end. This is what failure feels like. He looked around the room, but every face was either blank or avoiding his gaze. No one was going to help him. He was going back to Brooklyn. Maddeningly, he could feel tears pooling in his eyes. He blinked them away. He so badly wanted not to care, but he was falling backward, sinking down inside himself, and there was nothing there to catch him. This is it, he thought. This was the test he couldn't pass. It wasn't really all that surprising. He just wondered how long they were going to let it go on.

"Stop fucking with us, Quentin!" Fogg barked. He snapped his fingers. "Come on. Wake up!"

He reached across the table and grabbed Quentin's hands roughly. The contact was a shock. His fingers were strong and strangely dry and hot. He was moving Quentin's fingers, physically forcing them into positions they didn't want to be in.

"Like this," he was saying. "Like *this*. Like *this*."

"Okay, stop," Quentin said. He tried to pull away. "Stop."

But Fogg didn't stop. The audience shifted uncomfortably, and somebody said something. Fogg kept on working Quentin's hands with both of his, kneading them. He bent Quentin's fingers back, stretching them apart so that the webs between his fingers burned. Light seemed to flash between their hands.

"I said, stop it!" Quentin jerked his hands away.

It was surprising how good the anger felt. It was something to grab on to. In the shocked silence that followed he took a deep breath and forced it out through his nose. When it was out he felt like he'd expelled some of his despair with it. He'd had enough of being judged. He'd been sucking it up his whole life, but even he had his limit.

Fogg was talking again, but now Quentin wasn't even listening. He had begun to recite something under his breath, something familiar. It took him a second to realize that the words he was mouthing weren't English; they were from the foreign language he had invented earlier that afternoon. It was an obscure language—he'd decided—indigenous to a single tropical archipelago, a languorous hot-weather paradise, a Gauguin painting, blessed with black sand beaches and breadfruit trees and freshwater springs and endowed with an angry, glowing red volcano god and an oral culture rich in obscene expletives. He spoke this language fluently, with no accent, like a native. The words he spoke were not a prayer, exactly. More of an incantation.

Quentin stopped shuffling the cards. There was no going back. Everything snapped into very slow, slow motion, as if the room had filled up with a viscous but perfectly clear liquid in which everyone and everything floated easily and calmly. Everyone and everything except for Quentin, who moved quickly. With two hands together, as if he were releasing a dove, he tossed the deck of cards lightly up to the ceiling. The deck broke apart and scattered in flight, like a meteorite losing cohesion in the atmosphere, and as the cards fluttered back down to earth they stacked themselves on the tabletop. They formed a house of cards. It was a recognizable, if impressionistic, model of the building they were sitting in. The cards fell as if by chance, but each one perfectly, snapping into place magnetically, edge to edge, one after the other. The last two, the aces of spades and hearts, leaned up against each other to make the roof over the clock tower.

Now the room was absolutely still. Dean Fogg sat as if he were frozen in place. All the hairs were standing up on Quentin's arms, but he knew what he was doing. His fingers left almost imperceptible phosphorescent trails behind them in the air. He definitely felt high. He leaned forward and blew lightly on the card house, and it collapsed back down into a neatly stacked deck. He turned the deck over and fanned it out on the table like a black-jack dealer. Every card was a Queen—all the standard suits, plus other suits that didn't exist, in different colors, green and yellow and blue. The Queen of Horns, the Queen of Clocks, the Queen of Bees, the Queen of Books. Some were clothed, some were shamelessly naked. Some of them had Julia's face. Some of them had the lovely paramedic's.

Dean Fogg watched Quentin intently. Everybody watched him. Watch this: Quentin squared the deck again and with no particular effort ripped it in half and then ripped the halves in half and tossed the resulting confetti at the assembled company, who all flinched except for Fogg.

He stood up. His chair fell over backward.

"Tell me where I am," Quentin said softly. "Tell me what I'm doing here."

He picked up the stack of nickels in his fist, only it was no longer a stack of coins, it was the hilt of a bright, burning sword that he drew easily out of the tabletop, as if it had been left there buried up to the hilt.

"Tell me what's going on here," Quentin said, louder, to the room. "And if this place isn't Fillory, then for fuck's sake will somebody please tell me where the hell I am?"

Quentin let the tip of the sword hover under Fogg's nose for a slow ten-count, then he reversed his grip and stabbed it down into the wood of the table. The point bit deep into the buttery wood and stuck there.

Fogg didn't move. The sword waggled in place. Quentin sniffed involuntarily. The last of the light from the window died. It was night.

"Well now," the Dean said finally. He removed a neatly folded handkerchief from his pocket and patted his forehead. "I think we can all agree that that was a Pass."

Somebody—it was the old guy with the knots—put a reassuring hand on Quentin's back and gently, with surprising strength, drew the sword out of the table and laid it safely on its side. A slow patter of applause arose from the assembled examiners. It quickly turned into an ovation.

ELIOT

Afterward Quentin couldn't remember much of the rest of that night, except that he spent it there at the school. He was exhausted, and weak, like he'd been drugged. His chest felt hollowed out and empty. He wasn't even hungry anymore, just desperate to sleep. It was embarrassing, but nobody seemed to mind. Professor Van der Weghe—it turned out that was the dark-haired woman's name—told him it was perfectly natural to be tired because he had just cast his first Minor Incantation, whatever that was, and that would wear anybody out. She further promised him that matters had been squared with his parents. They wouldn't be worried. By that point Quentin barely cared, he just wanted to pass out.

He let her half lead, half carry him up approximately ten thousand flights of stairs to a small, neat room containing a very, very soft featherbed with cool white sheets. He lay down on it with his shoes still on. Ms. Van der Weghe took them off for him—it made him feel like a little kid to have somebody untie his shoes for him. She covered him up, and he was asleep before she closed the door.

The next morning it took him a long, confused minute to figure out where he was. He lay in bed, slowly piecing together his memories of the day before. It was a Friday, and by rights he should be in school now. Instead he was waking up in an unfamiliar bedroom wearing yesterday's clothes. He felt vaguely confused and regretful, like he'd drunk too much at a party with people he didn't know very well and fallen asleep in the host's spare bedroom. He even had a trace of what felt like a hangover.

What exactly had happened last night? What had he done? His memories were all wrong. The events were like a dream—they had to be—but they didn't feel like a dream. And this room wasn't a dream. A crow cawed loudly outside and immediately stopped, as if it were embarrassed. There was no other sound.

From where he lay he took stock of the room he was in. The walls were curved—the room was in the shape of a section of a circle. The outer wall was stone; the inner was taken up with dark wooden cabinets and cubbies. There was a Victorian-looking writing desk and a dresser and a mirror. His bed was tucked into a wooden alcove. There were small vertical windows all along the outer wall. He had to admit it was a highly satisfactory room. No danger signs yet. Maybe this wasn't a complete disaster. At any rate it was time to get up. Time to get it over with and find out what was going on.

He got up and padded over to a window. The stone floor was cool on his bare feet. It was early, a misty dawn, and he was very high up, higher than the tops of the highest trees. He had slept for ten hours. He looked down on the green lawn. It was silent and empty. He saw the crow: it drifted by below him on glossy blue-black wings.

A note on the desk informed him that he would be having breakfast with Dean Fogg at his earliest convenience. Quentin discovered a dormitory-style bathroom on the floor below, with shower stalls and rows of capacious white porcelain sinks and stacks of neatly folded scratchy white institutional towels. He washed up—the water was hot and strong, and he let it blast him till he felt clean and calm. He took a long pent-up acid-yellow piss in the shower and watched it spiral down the drain. It felt deeply weird not to be in school, to be on an adventure somewhere new, however dubious. It felt good. A mental meter in his brain was totting up the damage that his absence would be wreaking at home in Brooklyn; so far it was still within acceptable limits. He made himself as presentable as possible in his day-old, slept-in interview suit and walked downstairs.

The place was completely deserted. He hadn't expected a formal reception, exactly, but he had to wander around for twenty minutes, through empty hallways and drawing rooms and classrooms and out onto terraces, before the white-gloved butler who'd served him his sandwich yesterday finally found him and deposited him in the Dean's office, which was surprisingly small and mostly taken up by a presidential desk the size of a panzer tank. The walls were lined with an assortment of books and old-looking brass instruments.

The Dean arrived a minute later wearing a light green linen suit and a yellow tie. He was brusque and peppy and showed no sign of embarrassment, or any other emotion, relating to the scene the night before. He had already had breakfast, Fogg explained, but Quentin would eat while they talked.

"Now." He clapped his hands on his knees and quirked his eyebrows. "First things first: magic is real. But you've probably already gotten that far."

Quentin said nothing. He kept his face, his whole body, carefully still in his chair. He looked at a spot over Fogg's shoulder. He was giving nothing away. Certainly it was the simplest possible explanation for what had happened last night. Part of him, the part he trusted least, wanted to leap on this idea like a puppy on a ball. But in light of everything else that had ever happened to him, in his entire life, he checked himself. He'd spent too long being disappointed by the world—he'd spent so many years pining for something like this, some proof that the real world wasn't the only world, and coping with the overwhelming evidence that it in fact was. He wasn't going to be suckered in just like that. It was like finding a clue that somebody you'd buried and mourned wasn't really dead after all.

He let Fogg talk.

"To answer your questions of last night, you are at the Brakebills College for Magical Pedagogy." The butler arrived with a tray crowded with covered dishes, which he busily uncovered, like a room-service waiter. "Based on your performance in the Examination yesterday, we've decided to offer you a place here. Try the bacon, it's very good. Local farm, they raise the pigs on cream and walnuts."

"You want me to go to school here. College."

"Yes. You'd come here instead of matriculating at a conventional university. If you like it, you can even keep the room you stayed in last night."

"But I can't just—" Quentin didn't know exactly how to put everything that was ridiculous about that idea in a single sentence. "I'm sorry, this is a little confusing. So I would put off college?"

"No, Quentin. You wouldn't put off college. You would abandon college. Brakebills would be your college." The Dean had obviously had a lot of practice at this. "There would be no Ivy League for you. You wouldn't go off to school with the rest of your class. You would never make Phi Beta Kappa or be recruited by a hedge fund or a management consultancy. This isn't summer school, Quentin. This is"—he pronounced the phrase precisely, eyes wide—"'the whole shebang.'"

"So it's four years—"

"Five, actually."

"—at the end of which I get what? A bachelor's of magic?" It was actually funny. "I can't believe I'm having this conversation," he said to nobody.

"At the end of which you will be a magician, Quentin. It is not the obvious career path, I know. Your guidance counselor would not approve. No one will know what you're doing here. You would be leaving all that behind. Your friends, whatever career plans you had, everything. You would be losing one world but gaining another. Brakebills would become your world. It's not a decision to be taken lightly."

Well, no, it wasn't. Quentin pushed his plate away and crossed his arms. He stalled.

"So, how did you find me?"

"Oh, we have a device for that, a globe." Fogg indicated a shelf holding a whole menagerie of them: modern globes; blackwater globes; pale lunar globes; glittering midnight-blue celestial globes; dark, smoky, unreadable globes awash with ludicrously inaccurate continents. "It finds young people like yourself who have an aptitude for magic—essentially it senses magic being performed, often inadvertently, by unregistered sorcerers, of which you are one. I suppose it must have picked up that Wandering Nickel trick of yours.

"We have scouts, too," he added. "Your odd friend Ricky with the whiskers is one." He touched his jawline where Ricky's Amish beard was.

"What about that woman I met, with the braids. The paramedic. Was she a scout, too?"

Fogg frowned. "With braids? You saw her?"

"Well, yes. Right before I came here. Didn't you send her?"

Fogg's face became studiously empty.

"In a manner of speaking. She's a special case. Works on an independent basis. Freelance, you might say."

Quentin's mind spun. Maybe he should ask to see a brochure. And no one had said anything about tuition yet. And gift horses and all that notwithstanding, how much did he know about this place? Suppose it really was a school for magic. Was it any good? What if he'd stumbled into some third-tier magic college by accident? He had to think practically. He didn't want to be committing himself to some community college of sorcery when he could have Magic Harvard or whatever.

"Don't you want to see my SATs?"

"I have," Fogg said patiently. "And a lot more than that. But yesterday's Exam was all we really needed. It's very comprehensive. Admission here is quite competitive, you know. I doubt there's a more exclusive school of any kind on the continent. We held six Exams this summer, for twenty places. Only two Passed yesterday, you and another boy, the boy with the tattoos and the hair. Penny, he says his name is. Can't be his real name.

"This is the only magical school in North America," Fogg went on, leaning back behind his desk. He almost seemed to be enjoying Quentin's discomfort. "There's one in the UK, two on the Continent, four in Asia, and so on. One in New Zealand for some reason. People talk a lot of guff about American magic, but I assure you we are quite up to the international standard. In Zurich they still teach phrenology, if you can believe that."

Something small but heavy fell off Fogg's desk with a clunk. He bent to retrieve it: a silver statue of a bird that seemed to be twitching.

"Poor little thing," he said, petting it with his large hands. "Someone tried to change it into a real bird, but it got stuck in between. It thinks it's alive, but it's much too heavy to fly." The metal bird cheeped feebly, a dry clicking noise like an empty pistol. Fogg sighed and put it away in a drawer. "It's always launching itself out of windows and landing in the hedges.

"Now." The Dean leaned forward and steepled his fingers. "Should you choose to matriculate here, we'll do some minor illusion work with your parents. They can't know about Brakebills, of course, but they'll think you've been accepted to a very prestigious private institute—which isn't at all far from the truth—and they'll be very proud. It's painless and quite effective, as long as you don't say anything too obvious.

"Oh, and you'll start right away. The semester begins in two weeks, so you'll have to skip the rest of your senior year. But I really shouldn't be telling you all this before we've done your paperwork."

Fogg took out a pen and a fat sheaf of closely handwritten paper that looked like a treaty between two eighteenth-century nation-states.

"Penny signed yesterday," he said. "Very quick Examination, that boy. What do you say?"

So that was it, that was the sales pitch. Fogg put the papers in front of him and held out the pen. Quentin took it, a fancy-looking metal fountain pen as thick as a cigar. His hand hovered over the page. This was ridiculous. Was he really going to throw everything away? Everything: everybody he knew, James and Julia, whatever college he would have gone to, whatever career he would have had, everything he thought he'd been getting ready for. For this? This bizarre charade, this fever dream, this fancy-dress role-playing game?

He stared out the window. Fogg watched him impassively, just waiting for him to fall for it. If he cared one way or the other, he wasn't letting on. The little floundering metal bird, having escaped its drawer, butted its head industriously against the wainscoting.

And then a vast stony weight suddenly lifted off Quentin's chest. It felt like it had been there his entire life, an invisible albatross, a granite millstone holding him down, and all at once it just dropped away and disappeared without a splash. His chest expanded. He was going to bob up to the ceiling like a balloon. They were going to make him a magician, and all he had to do was sign. Jesus, what the hell was he thinking? Of course he was going to sign. This was everything he'd always wanted, the break he'd given up on years ago. It was right in front of him. He was finally on the other side, down the rabbit hole, through the looking glass. He was going to sign the papers and he was going to be a motherfucking magician. Or what the hell else was he going to do with his life?

"Okay," Quentin said evenly. "All right. On one condition: I want to start now. I want to stay in that room. I don't want to go home."

They didn't make him go home. Instead, his things arrived from home in a collection of duffel bags and rolly suitcases, packed by his parents, who had, as Fogg promised, somehow been squared with the idea that their only child was suddenly matriculating in the middle of the semester at a mysterious educational institution they had never visited or even heard of. Quentin slowly unpacked his clothes and his books and put them away in the cabinets and cubbies in the little curved tower room. He didn't even want to touch them now. They were part of his old self, his old life, the one he was molting away. The only thing missing was the book, the notebook the paramedic gave him. That was nowhere to be found. He'd left it in the exam room on the assumption that he'd be going back there, but when he finally did it was gone. Dean Fogg and the butler pled ignorance.

Sitting there alone in his room, his folded clothes around him on the bed, he thought about James and Julia. God only knew what they were thinking. Did she miss him? Now that he was gone, would she realize she'd had the wrong man all along? He should probably get in touch with them somehow. Though really, what the hell could he say? He wondered what would have happened if James had taken the envelope from the paramedic too. Maybe he would have gotten to take the exam, too. Maybe that was part of the test.

He let himself unclench a little. Just slightly, he stopped bracing for the blow from above, and for the first time he seriously considered the idea that it might not come at all.

With nothing else to do Quentin roamed through the huge house, unsupervised and rudderless. The Dean and the teachers were nice enough when he ran into them, but they had their own work to do and their own problems to deal with. It was like being at a fancy beach resort during the off-season, rattling around in a grand hotel with no guests, just empty rooms and empty gardens and empty, echoing hallways. He ate his meals alone in his room and loitered in the library—naturally they had the complete works of Christopher Plover—and luxuriously contemplated, one by one, in order, each of the problem sets and projects and papers he would never have to finish. Once he found his way up to the clock tower and spent an afternoon watching the huge rusty iron pendulum sway back and forth, following the massive gears and levers and catchments as they turned and meshed, carrying out their mechanical syllogism, until the glow of the setting sun shone through the tremendous backward clock face.

Sometimes he burst out laughing out of nowhere, for no reason. He was experimenting cautiously with the idea of being happy, dipping an uncertain toe into those intoxicatingly carbonated waters. It wasn't some-thing he'd had much practice at. It was just too fucking funny. He was going to learn magic! He was either the greatest genius of all time or the biggest idiot. But at least he was actually curious about what was going to happen to him next. For the first time in he didn't know how long he was actually following the action with interest. In Brooklyn reality had been empty and meaningless—whatever inferior stuff it was made of, meaning had refused to adhere to it. Brakebills was different. It mattered. Meaning—is that what magic was?—was everywhere here. The place was crawling with it. Out there he had been on the edge of serious depression, and worse, he had been in danger of learning to really dislike himself. He was on the verge of incur-ring the kind of inward damage you didn't heal from, ever. But now he felt like Pinocchio, a wooden boy who was made real. Or maybe it was the other way around, he'd been turned from a real boy into something else? Either way the change was for the better. It wasn't Fillory, but it would do.

He didn't spend all his time alone. Once in a while he spotted Eliot from a distance, loping across the empty green or lolling with his long legs folded up in a window seat, staring out the window or leafing distractedly through a book. He had an air of magnificent melancholy sophistication, as if his proper place were elsewhere, somewhere infinitely more compel-ling even than Brakebills, and he'd been confined to his present setting by a grotesque divine oversight, which he tolerated with as much good humor as could be expected.

One day Quentin was walking the edge of the great lawn when he came across Eliot leaning against an oak tree, smoking a cigarette and reading a paperback book. It was more or less the same spot where they first met. Because of the odd way Eliot's jaw was built, the cigarette stuck out at an angle.

"Want one?" Eliot asked politely. He stopped reading and held out a blue-and-white pack of Merit Ultra Lights. They hadn't spoken since Quen-tin's first day at Brakebills.

"They're contraband," he went on, not visibly disappointed that Quen-tin didn't take one. "Chambers buys them for me. I once caught him in the wine cellar drinking a *very* good petite syrah from the Dean's private collection. Stags' Leap, the ninety-six. We came to an understanding. He's really a nice fellow, I shouldn't hold it over his head. Quite a good ama-teur painter, albeit in a sadly outdated realist mode. I let him paint me once—draped, thank you very much. I was holding a Frisbee. I think I was supposed to be Hyacinthus. Chambers is a *pompiste* at heart. Deep down I don't think he believes Impressionism ever happened."

Quentin had never met anybody so staggeringly and unapologetically affected. It was hard to know how to respond. He summoned up all the wisdom he'd accumulated during his entire life in Brooklyn.

"Merits are for pussies," he said.

Eliot looked at him appraisingly.

"Very true. But they're the only cigarette I can stand. Disgusting habit. Come on, smoke one with me."

Quentin accepted the cigarette. He was in unfamiliar territory here. He'd handled cigarettes before—they were common props in close-up magic—but he'd never actually put one in his mouth. He made the cigarette vanish—a basic thumb palm—then snapped his fingers to bring it back.

"I said smoke it, not fondle it," Eliot said curtly.

He muttered something under his breath, then snapped his own fingers. A lighter-size flame sprang into being over the tip of his index finger. Quentin leaned in and inhaled.

It felt like his lungs had been crumpled up and then incinerated. He coughed for five solid minutes without stopping. Eliot laughed so hard he had to sit down. Quentin's face was slick with tears. He forced himself to take another drag and threw up into a hedge.

They spent the rest of that afternoon together. Maybe he felt guilty for giving Quentin the cigarette, or maybe Eliot had decided that the tedium of solitude was ever so slightly greater than the tedium of Quentin's company. Maybe he just needed a straight man. He led Quentin around the campus and lectured him on the underground lore of life at Brakebills.

"The keen-eyed incoming freshman will have noticed the weather, which is uncommonly clement for November. That's because it's still summer here. There are some very old spells on the Brakebills grounds to keep people from spotting it from the river or walking in by accident, that kind of thing. Fine old enchantments. Classic work of their kind. But they're getting eccentric in their old age, and somewhere in the 1950s time started spinning off its axis here. Gets worse every year. Nothing to worry about, in the larger picture, but we're a little behind the mainstream. Two months twenty-eight days, give or take a few hours."

Quentin didn't know whether to act as awestruck as he felt or try to produce an imitation of cool worldly ennui. He changed the subject and asked about the curriculum.

"You won't have any choice about your schedule your first year. Henry"—Eliot only ever referred to Dean Fogg by his first name—"makes everybody do the same thing. Are you smart?"

There was no non-embarrassing answer to this.

"I guess."

"Don't worry about it, everybody here is. If they even brought you in for the Exam you were the smartest person in your school, teachers included. Everyone here was the cleverest little monkey in his or her particular tree. Except now we're all in one tree together. It can be a shock. Not enough coconuts to go round. You'll be dealing with your equals for the first time in your life, and your betters. You won't like it.

"The work is different, too. It's not what you think. You don't just wave a wand and yell some made-up Latin. There's reasons why most people can't do it."

"Which are what?" Quentin asked.

"The reasons why most people can't do magic? Well." Eliot held up a long, thin finger. "One, it's very hard, and they're not smart enough. Two, it's very hard, and they're not obsessive and miserable enough to do all the work you have to do to do it right. Three, they lack the guidance and mentorship provided by the dedicated and startlingly charismatic faculty of the Brakebills College for Magical Pedagogy. And four, they lack the tough, starchy moral fiber necessary to wield awesome magical energies calmly and responsibly.

"And five"—he stuck up his thumb—"some people have all that stuff and they still can't do it. Nobody knows why. They say the words, wave their arms, and nothing happens. Poor bastards. But that's not us. We're the lucky ones. We have it, whatever *it* is."

"I don't know if I have the moral fiber one."

"I don't either. I think that one's optional, actually."

Silent for a while, they walked along a lush, ruler-straight allée of fence trees leading back toward the lawn. Eliot lit another cigarette.

"Listen, I don't want to pry," Quentin said, "but I'm assuming you have some secret magical way of dealing with the negative health effects of all those cigarettes."

"It's kind of you to ask. I sacrifice a virgin schoolgirl every other fortnight by the light of a gibbous moon, using a silver scalpel forged by Swiss albinos. Who are also virgins. Clears my little lungs right up."

After that Quentin saw Eliot most days. Eliot spent one entire afternoon teaching him how to navigate the hedge maze that separated the House— "as everybody calls it"—from the great lawn, which was officially named Seagrave's Lawn after the eighteenth-century Dean who cleared and leveled it, and which "everybody" referred to as the Sea, or sometimes the Grave. There were six fountains scattered throughout the maze (the Maze), and each one had an official name, usually that of a deceased Dean, as well as a nickname generated by the collective unconsciousness of generations of Brakebillian undergraduates. The hedges that made up the Maze were cut in the shape of heavy, slow-thighed beasts—bears and elephants and other less-easily-identifiable creatures. Unlike ordinary topiary they moved: they lumbered along very slowly, almost imperceptibly, wading half submerged in the dark foliage like hippopotami wallowing in an equatorial African river.

On the last day before classes began, Eliot led him around to the front of the House, which looked out on the Hudson. There was a scrim of plane trees between the front terrace and the river and a flight of wide stone steps that led down to a handsome Victorian boathouse. They decided on the spot that they absolutely had to go out on the water, even though neither of them had any practical ideas about how to do it. As Eliot pointed out, they were both certified sorcerer-geniuses, and how hard could it be to row a damn boat?

With a lot of grunting and yelling at each other, they wrestled a long wooden double scull down from the rafters. It was a fabulous object, strangely light, like the husk of a colossal stick insect, wreathed in cobwebs and redolent with the heady smell of wood varnish. Mostly by luck they managed to turn it over and splash it down into the water without injuring it or themselves or getting so pissed off at each other that they had to abandon the whole project. After some early close calls they got it pointed in a plausible direction and settled into a slow, halting rhythm with it, hindered but not daunted by their incompetence and by the fact that Quentin was hopelessly out of shape and Eliot was both out of shape and a heavy smoker.

They got about half a mile upstream before the summer day abruptly vanished around them and became chilly and gray. Quentin thought it was a summer squall until Eliot explained that they'd reached the outer limits of whatever concealment spells had been applied to the Brakebills grounds, and it was November again. They wasted twenty minutes rowing up past the change and then drifting back down again, up and back, watching the sky change color, feeling the temperature drop and then soar and then drop again.

They were too tired to row on the way back, so they drifted with the current. Eliot lay back in the scull and smoked and talked. Because of his air of infallible entitlement Quentin assumed he'd been raised among the wealthy mandarins of Manhattan, but it turned out he'd actually grown up on a farm in eastern Oregon.

"My parents are paid not to grow soybeans," he said. "I have three older brothers. Magnificent physical specimens—kind-hearted, thick-necked, three-sport athletes who drink Schlitz and feel sorry for me. My dad doesn't know what happened. He thinks he chewed too much dip before I was conceived, and that's why I 'di'n't come out reg'lar.'" Eliot stubbed out his Merit in a glass ashtray balanced precariously on the glossy wooden hull and lit another one. "They think I'm at a special school for computer geeks and homosexuals.

"That's why I don't go home in the summertime. Henry doesn't care. I haven't been home since I started here.

"You probably feel sorry for me," he went on airily. He wore a dressing gown over his regular clothes, which gave him a shabby princely look. "You shouldn't, you know. I'm very happy here. Some people need their families to become who they're supposed to be. And there's nothing wrong with that. But there are other ways to do it."

Quentin hadn't realized how hard-won Eliot's air of ludicrously exaggerated insouciance must be. That facade of lofty indifference must be there to hide real problems. Quentin liked to think of himself as a sort of regional champion of unhappiness, but he wondered if Eliot had him outclassed on that score, too.

As they drifted home they were passed by a few other boats, sailboats and cabin cruisers and a hard-charging eight-woman scull out of West Point, which was a few miles upriver. The occupants looked grim and bundled-up against the cold, in gray sweatshirts and sweatpants. They couldn't perceive, or somehow weren't part of, the August heat that Quentin and Eliot were enjoying. They were warm and dry and didn't even know it. The terms of the enchantment locked them out.

MAGIC

"The study of magic is not a science, it is not an art, and it is not a religion. Magic is a craft. When we do magic, we do not wish and we do not pray. We rely upon our will and our knowledge and our skill to make a specific change to the world.

"This is not to say that we understand magic, in the sense that physicists understand why subatomic particles do whatever it is that they do. Or perhaps they don't understand that yet, I can never remember. In any case, we do not and cannot understand what magic is, or where it comes from, any more than a carpenter understands why a tree grows. He doesn't have to. He works with what he has.

"With the caveat that it is much more difficult and much more dangerous and much more interesting to be a magician than it is to be a carpenter."

Delivering this edifying lecture was Professor March, whom Quentin had last seen during his Examination—he was the round, red-haired man with the hungry lizard. Because he was plump and red-faced he looked like he should be jolly and easygoing, but in actuality he was turning out to be kind of a hard-ass.

When Quentin woke up that morning the huge empty House was full of people—yelling, running, noisy people who dragged trunks thunderously up stairs and occasionally banged open his door, looked him over, and then slammed it shut again. It was a rude awakening; he'd gotten used to wandering around the House by himself as its undisputed lord and master, or at least, after Eliot, its senior undersecretary. But as it turned out there were ninety-nine other students enrolled at Brakebills, divided into five classes that corresponded roughly to freshman through first-year graduate student. They had arrived this morning en masse for the first day of the semester, and they were asserting their rights.

They came in clumps, materializing ten at a time on the back terrace, each group with a hillock of trunks and duffle bags and suitcases beside it. Everybody except Quentin was in uniform: striped blazers and ties for the guys, white blouses and dark tartan skirts for the girls. For a college, it all looked a whole lot like a prep school.

"It's jacket and tie at all times except in your room," Fogg explained. "There are more rules; you'll pick them up from the others. Most boys like to choose their own ties. I am inclined to be lenient on that score, but don't test me. Anything too exciting will be confiscated, and you'll be forced to wear the school tie, which I know very little about these things, but I am told is cruelly unfashionable."

When Quentin got back to his room he found a closetful of identical jackets hanging there, dark blue and chocolate brown in inch-wide stripes, paired with white dress shirts. Most of them looked brand new; a few showed signs of incipient sheen at the elbows or fraying around the cuffs and smelled faintly but not unpleasantly of mothballs and tobacco and former occupants. He changed gingerly and looked at himself in the mirror. He knew that he was probably supposed to resent the uniform, but he relished it. If he didn't feel like a magician yet, at least he could look like one.

Each jacket had an embroidered coat of arms on it, a golden bee and a golden key on a black background dotted with tiny silver stars. He would later hear other students call this device the key-and-bee, and once he started looking for it he saw it everywhere, worked into carpets and curtains, carved into stone lintels, pieced into the corners of parquet floors.

Now Quentin sat in a large square lecture hall, a corner room with high, lofty windows on two sides. It contained four rows of elegant wooden desks set on raked steps like an amphitheater, looking down on a large blackboard and a massive stone demonstration table that had been scorched, scratched, scarred, and scathed within an inch of its life. Particles of chalk dust hung in the air. The class had twenty students, all in uniform, all looking like very ordinary teenagers trying very hard to look cooler and smarter than each other. Quentin knew that probably half the Intel Science Talent Search winners and Scripps Spelling Bee champions in the country were in this room. Based on what he had overheard, one of his classmates had placed second in the Putnam Competition, as a high school junior. He knew for a fact that one of the girls had managed to take over the plenary session of the national model UN and push through a motion sanctioning the use of nuclear weapons to protect a critically endangered species of sea turtle. This while representing Lesotho.

Not that any of that stuff mattered anymore, but the air was still thick with nerves. Sitting there in his new-smelling shirt and jacket, Quentin already wished he were back on the river with Eliot.

Professor March paused, refocusing.

"Quentin Coldwater, would you please come up to the front of the class? Why don't you do some of your magic for us?"

March was looking straight at him.

"That's right." His manner was warm and cheery, like he was giving Quentin a prize. "Right here." He indicated a spot next to him. "Here. I'll give you a prop."

Professor March rummaged in his pockets and took out a clear glass marble, somewhat linty, and put it on the table, where it rolled a few inches before it found a hollow to settle in.

The classroom was absolutely still. Quentin knew this wasn't a real test. It was some kind of object-lesson-slash-hazing ritual. An annual thing, probably nothing to worry about, just one more wonderful old Brakebills tradition. But his legs felt like wooden stilts as he made his way down the broad steps to the front of the class. The other students stared at him with the cold indifference of the gratefully spared.

He took his place next to March. The marble looked ordinary, just glass with a few air bubbles in it. About the same circumference as a nickel. Probably about as easy to palm, too, Quentin supposed. With his brand-new school jacket on he could cuff and sleeve it without too much trouble. All right, he thought, if it's magic they want, magic they shall get. Blood thundering in his ears, he produced it from either hand, from his mouth, from his nose. He was rewarded with scattered giggles from the audience.

The tension broke. He hammed it up. He tossed the marble up in the

air, letting it almost brush the high cathedral ceiling, then leaned forward
and caught it neatly balanced in the hollow of the back of his neck. Somebody did a rim shot on his desk. The room broke up.

For his grand finale Quentin pretended to crush the marble with a
heavy iron paperweight, at the last second substituting a mint Lifesaver
he happened to have in his pocket, which made a nice solid crunch and
left behind a forensically convincing spray of white powder. He apolo-
gized profusely to Professor March, winking broadly at the audience, then
asked him if he could borrow his handkerchief. When he reached for the
handkerchief, Professor March discovered the marble in his own jacket
pocket.

Quentin executed a Johnny Carson golf swing. The First Years applauded
wildly. He bowed. Not bad, he thought. Half an hour into his first semester
and he was already a folk hero.

"Thank you, Quentin," Professor March said unctuously, clapping with
the tips of his fingers. "Thank you, that was very enlightening. You may
return to your seat. Alice, what about you? Why don't you show us some
magic."

This remark was addressed to a small, sullen girl with straight dark
hair who'd been huddling in the back row. She showed no surprise at being
picked; she looked like the kind of person who expected the worst at all
times, and why should today be any different? She walked down the wide
steps of the lecture hall to the front of the room—eyes straight ahead, cold-
bloodedly ascending the gallows, looking hideously uncomfortable in her
freshly creased uniform—and mutely accepted her marble from Professor
March. Taking her place behind the demonstration table, which came up
to her chest, she steadied it on the stone tabletop.

Immediately she made a series of rapid, businesslike gestures over the
marble. It looked like she was doing sign language, or assembling a cat's
cradle with invisible string. Her unfussy manner was the opposite of Quentin's slick, show-offy style. Alice stared at the marble intently, expectantly.
Her eyes went a little crossed. Her lips moved, though from where he was
sitting Quentin couldn't hear what she was saying.

The marble began to glow red, then white, becoming opaque, an eye
clouding over with a milky cataract. A slender undulating curl of gray
smoke rose up from the point where it touched the table. Quentin's smug,

triumphant feeling went cold and congealed. She already knew real magic, he thought. My God, I am so far behind.

Alice rubbed her hands together.

"It takes a minute for my fingers to become impervious."

Cautiously, as if she were retrieving a hot dish from an oven, Alice plucked at the glass marble with her fingertips. It was now molten from the heat, and it pulled like taffy. In four quick, sure motions she gave the marble four legs, then added a head. When she took her hands away and blew on it the marble rolled over, shook itself once, and stood up. It had become a tiny, plump glass animal. It began to walk across the table.

This time no one applauded. The chill in the room was palpable. The hair stood up on Quentin's arms. The only sound was the soft *tik-tik-katikkatik* of its pointy glass feet on the stone tabletop.

"Thank you, Alice!" Professor March said, regaining the stage. "For those of you who are wondering, Alice just performed three basic spells." He held up a finger for each one. "Dempsey's Silent Thermogenesis; a lesser Cavalieri animation; and some kind of ward-and-shield that appears to be home-brewed, so maybe we should name it after you, Alice."

Alice looked back at March impassively, waiting for a cue that she could go back to her seat. She wasn't even smug, just impatient to be released. Forgotten, the little glass creature reached the end of the table. Alice made a grab for it, but it fell and smashed on the hard stone floor. She crouched down over it, stricken, but Professor March was already moving on, wrapping up his lecture.

Quentin watched the little drama with a mixture of compassion and rivalrous envy. Such a tender soul, he thought. But she's the one I'll have to beat.

"Tonight please read the first chapter of Le Goff's *Magickal Historie,* in the Lloyd translation," March said, "and the first two chapters of Amelia Popper's *Practical Exercises for Young Magicians,* a book that you will soon come to despise with every fiber of your innocent young beings. I invite you to attempt the first four exercises. Each of you will be performing one of them for the class tomorrow.

"And if you find Lady Popper's rather quaint eighteenth-century English difficult, keep in mind that next month we will be starting Middle

English, Latin, and Old High Dutch, at which time you will look back on Lady Popper's eighteenth-century English with fond nostalgia."

Students began stirring and gathering up their books. Quentin looked down at the notebook in front of him, which was empty except for one anxious zigzaggy line.

"Final thought before you go." March raised his voice over the shuffling clatter. "I urge you again to think of this as a purely practical course, with a minimum of theory. If you find yourself becoming curious about the nature and origins of the magical powers you are slowly and very, very painfully cultivating, remember this famous anecdote about the English philosopher Bertrand Russell.

"Russell once gave a public lecture on the structure of the universe. Afterward he was approached by a woman who told him that he was a very clever young man but much mistaken in his thinking, because everyone knew that the world was flat and sat on the back of a turtle.

"When Russell asked her what the turtle was standing on, she replied, 'You're very clever, young man, very clever. But it's turtles all the way down!'

"The woman was wrong about the world, of course, but she would have been quite right if she'd been talking about magic. Great mages have wasted their lives trying to get at the root of magic. It is a futile pursuit, not much fun and occasionally quite hazardous. Because the farther down you go, the bigger and scalier the turtles get, with sharper and sharper beaks. Until eventually they start looking less like turtles and more like dragons.

"Everyone take a marble, please, as you go."

The very next afternoon March taught them a simple chant to say over their marbles in a crooked gypsy-sounding language that Quentin didn't recognize (later Alice told him it was Estonian), accompanied by a tricky gesture that involved moving the middle and pinky fingers on both hands independently, which is a lot harder than it sounds. Those who completed it successfully could leave early, the rest had to stay until they got it right. How would they know when they got it right? They would know.

Quentin stayed until his voice was hoarse and his fingers were on fire, until the light in the windows had softened and changed color and then sunk away completely, until his empty stomach ached, and dinner had been served and cleared away in the distant dining room. He stayed until his face was warm with shame, and all but four other people had stood up—some of them pumped their fists in the air and said *yesssss!!!*—and left the classroom. Alice had been the first, after about twenty minutes, though she left silently. Finally Quentin said the chant and made the motions—he didn't even know what he did differently this time—and was rewarded by the sight of his marble wobbling, very slightly but unmistakably, of its own volition.

He didn't say anything, just put his head down on his desk, hiding his face in the crook of his elbow, and let the blood in his head throb in the darkness. The wooden desk was cool on his cheek. It hadn't been a fluke, or a hoax, or a joke. He had done it. Magic was real, and he could do it.

And now that he could, my God, there was so much of it to do. That glass marble would be Quentin's constant companion for the rest of the semester. It was the cold, pitiless glass heart of Professor March's approach to magical pedagogy. Every lecture, every exercise, every demonstration was concerned with how to manipulate and transform it using magic. For the next four months Quentin was required to carry his marble everywhere. He fingered his marble under the table at dinner. It nestled in the inside pockets of his Brakebills jacket. When he showered, he tucked it in the soap dish. He took it to bed with him, and on those rare occasions when he slept he dreamed about it.

Quentin learned to cool his marble until it frosted over. He caused it to roll around a table by invisible means. He learned to float his marble in midair. He made it glow from within. Because it was already transparent it was easy to render invisible, upon which he promptly lost it and Professor March had to rematerialize it for him. Quentin made his marble float in water, pass through a wooden barrier, fly through an obstacle course and attract iron filings like a magnet. This was nuts-and-bolts work, ground-level fundamentals. The dramatic spellcasting display Quentin had performed during his exam, however showy and satisfying, he was told, was a well-understood anomaly, a flare-up of accumulated power that often manifested during a sorcerer's first casting. It would be years before he could do anything comparable again.

In the meantime Quentin also studied the history of magic, about which even magicians knew less than he would have thought. It turned out that magic-users had always lived within mainstream society, but apart from it and largely unknown to it. The towering figures of magical history weren't famous at all in the mundane world, and the obvious guesses were way off base. Leonardo, Roger Bacon, Nostradamus, John Dee, Newton—sure, all of them were mages of various stripes, but of relatively modest ability. The fact that they were famous in mainstream circles was just a strike against them. By the standards of magical society they'd fallen at the first hurdle: they hadn't had the basic good sense to keep their shit to themselves.

Quentin's other homework, Popper's *Practical Exercises for Young Magicians,* turned out to be a thin, large-format volume containing a series of hideously complex finger and voice exercises arranged in order of increasing difficulty and painfulness. Much of spellcasting, Quentin gathered, consisted of very precise hand gestures accompanied by incantations to be spoken or chanted or whispered or yelled or sung. Any slight error in the movement or in the incantation would weaken, or negate, or pervert the spell.

This wasn't Fillory. In each of the Fillory novels one or two of the Chatwin children were always taken under the wing of a kindly Fillorian mentor who taught them a skill or a craft. In *The World in the Walls* Martin becomes a master horseman and Helen trains as a kind of forest scout; in *The Flying Forest* Rupert becomes a deadeye archer; in *A Secret Sea* Fiona trains with a master fencer; and so on. The process of learning is a nonstop orgy of wonderment.

Learning magic was nothing like that. It turned out to be about as tedious as it was possible for the study of powerful and mysterious supernatural forces to be. The same way a verb has to agree with its subject, it turned out, even the simplest spell had to be modified and tweaked and inflected to agree with the time of day, the phase of the moon, the intention and purpose and precise circumstances of its casting, and a hundred other factors, all of which were tabulated in volumes of tables and charts and diagrams printed in microscopic jewel type on huge yellowing elephant-folio pages. And half of each page was taken up with footnotes listing the exceptions and irregularities and special cases, all of which had to be committed to memory, too. Magic was a lot wonkier than Quentin thought it would be.

But there was something else to it, too, something beyond all the practicing and memorizing, beyond the dotted *i*'s and crossed *t*'s, something that never came up in March's lectures. Quentin only sensed it, without really being able to talk about it, but there was something else you needed if a spell was going to get any purchase on the world around you. Whenever he tried to think about it he got lost in abstractions. It was something like force of will, a certain intensity of concentration, a clear vision, maybe a dash of artistic brio. If a spell was going to work, then on some gut level you had to mean it.

He couldn't explain it, but Quentin could tell when it was working. He could sense his words and gestures getting traction on the mysterious magical substrate of the universe. He could feel it physically. His fingertips got warm, and they seemed to leave trails in the air. There was a slight resistance, as if the air were getting viscous around him and pushing back against his hands and even against his lips and tongue. His mind buzzed with a caffeine-cocaine fizz. He was at the heart of a large and powerful system, he *was* its heart. When it was working, he knew it. And he liked it.

Now that his friends had come back from vacation Eliot sat with them at meals instead. They were a highly visible clique, always earnestly conferring with each other and having fits of obstreperous public laughter, conspicuously fond of themselves and uninterested in the greater Brakebills populace. There was something different about them, though it was hard to say what. They weren't better-looking or smarter than anybody else. They just seemed to know who they were, and they weren't constantly looking around at everybody else as if they could tell them.

It rankled the way Eliot had dropped Quentin the minute he ceased to be convenient, but then there were the nineteen other First Years to think of. Though they weren't a wildly social bunch. They were quiet and intense, always eyeing each other assessingly, as if they were trying to figure out who—if it came right down to it—would take out who in an intellectual death match. They didn't congregate overmuch—they were always civil but rarely warm. They were used to competing and used to winning. In other words, they were like Quentin, and Quentin wasn't used to being around people like himself.

The one student he and every other First Year at Brakebills was immediately obsessed with was little Alice, of the tiny glass creature, but it quickly became apparent that in spite of being way ahead of the rest of her year academically she was cripplingly shy, to the point where there wasn't much point in trying to talk to her. When approached at meals she answered questions in whispered monosyllables, her gaze dropping to the tablecloth in front of her as if weighed down by some infinite inner shame. She was almost pathologically unable to make eye contact, and she had a way of hiding her face behind her hair that made it clear how agonizing it was for her to be the object of human attention.

Quentin wondered who or what could possibly have convinced somebody with such obvious gifts that she should be frightened of other people. He wanted to keep up a proper head of competitive steam, but instead he felt almost protective of her. The one and only time he saw Alice look genuinely happy was when he watched her, alone and momentarily unselfconscious, successfully skip a pebble across the pool in a fountain and between the legs of a stone nymph.

Life at Brakebills had a hushed, formal, almost theatrical tone to it, and at mealtimes formality was elevated to the level of a fetish. Dinners were served promptly at six thirty; latecomers were denied the privilege of a chair and ate standing. Faculty and students sat together at one interminable table that was swathed in a tablecloth of mystical whiteness and laid with heavy-handled silverware that didn't match. Illumination was provided by battalions of hideous candelabras. The food, contrary to private school tradition, was excellent in an old-fashioned, Frenchified way. Menus tended toward mid-century warhorses like boeuf en daube and lobster thermidor. First Years had the privilege of serving all the other students as waiters, under the stern direction of Chambers, and then eating by themselves when everybody else was done. Third and Fourth Years were allowed one glass of wine with dinner; Fifth Years (or "Finns," as they were called, for no obvious reason) got two. Oddly enough there were only ten Fourth Years, half the usual number, and nobody would explain why. Asking about it just ended the conversation.

All this Quentin picked up with the speed of a sailor cast away on a savage foreign continent, who has no choice but to learn the local language as rapidly as possible or be devoured by those who speak it. His first two months at Brakebills spun by, and soon red and gold leaves were scattering across the Sea, as if they were being pushed by invisible brooms—which possibly they were?—and the flanks of the slow-moving topiary beasts in the Maze showed streaks of color.

Quentin devoted a half hour every day after class to exploring the campus on foot. One blustery afternoon he stumbled onto a pocket vineyard, a postage stamp of earth ruled into straight lines and planted with rows of grapevines strung up on rusty wires and trained into weird vinicultural candelabra shapes. By now the grapes had already been harvested, and those that hadn't had shriveled on the vine into tiny fragrant raisins.

Beyond it, a quarter mile off into the woods, at the end of a narrow path, Quentin discovered a small field neatly divided into a patchwork of squares. Some of the squares were grass, some were stone, some were sand, some were water, and two were made of blackened, silvery metal, elaborately inscribed.

There was no fence or wall to mark the edge of the grounds, or if there was he never found it. There was just the river along one side and woods all around the rest. Even so the faculty seemed to spend an inordinate amount of time maintaining the spells that kept the school invisible and impregnable to outsiders. They were constantly strolling the perimeter, studying things Quentin couldn't see, and pulling one another out of classes to consult about it.

SNOW

One afternoon in late October Professor March asked Quentin to stay behind after Practical Applications. P.A.—as everybody called it—was the part of the day when the students worked on actual spellcasting. They were allowed to attempt only the most basic magic at this stage, under smotheringly close supervision, but still. It was a small practical reward for all those oceans of theory they were navigating.

That particular class had not been a successful one for Quentin. P.A. was held in a room that resembled a college chemistry lab: indestructible gray stone tables; counters mottled with ancient unspeakable stains; deep, capacious sinks. The air was thickly charged with permanent charms and wards installed by generations of Brakebills professors to prevent students from injuring themselves or each other. It carried a whiff of ozone.

Quentin watched his lab partner Surendra dust his hands with a white powder (equal parts flour and beech-wood ash), draw certain invisible sigils in the air with a freshly trimmed willow wand, and then bring the wand softly down on his marble (nickname: Rakshasa!), slicing it neatly in half with one stroke, first try. But when Quentin brought the willow wand down on his marble (nickname: Martin) it burst with a quiet *pop,* like a dying lightbulb, throwing off a spray of glass chunks and powder. Quentin dropped the wand and spun away to shield his eyes; everybody else in the room craned their heads to look. The atmosphere in the P.A. room wasn't particularly collegial.

So Quentin was already in a foul mood when Professor March asked him to stay behind after class. March chatted with stragglers in the hall while Quentin sat on one of the indestructible tables, swinging his legs and thinking black thoughts. He was somewhat reassured that Alice had been asked to stay behind, too. She sat by the window staring dreamily out at the sluggish Hudson. Her marble floated in slow circles around her head, a lazy miniature satellite, sometimes clicking against the glass when she leaned too close. Why did magic come to her so effortlessly? he wondered. Or was it as effortless as it looked? He couldn't believe it was as hard for her as it was for him. Penny was there, too, looking pale and intense and moon-faced as always. He wore the Brakebills uniform, but they'd let him keep his mohawk.

Professor March came back in, followed by Professor Van der Weghe. She didn't mince words.

"We asked you three to stay behind because we are considering advancing you to Second Year for the spring term," she said. "You would have to do some extra work on your own in order to pass your First Year exams in December and then catch up to the Second Years, but I think you're up to it. Am I right?"

She looked around encouragingly. She wasn't really asking them so much as telling them. Quentin and Penny and Alice glanced at one another uneasily and looked away again. From long experience Quentin had learned not to be surprised when his intellectual abilities were rated over other people's, and this mark of favor certainly wiped out the nightmare of his pul-verized marble, with interest. But everybody was acting very solemn and serious about it. It sounded like a lot of work for the privilege of skipping a year at Brakebills, which he wasn't even sure he wanted to do anyway.

"Why?" Penny spoke up. "Why move us up? Are you going to move other students down to make room for us?"

He had a point. It was an immutable fact of life at Brakebills that there were always twenty students per class, no more and no fewer.

"Different students learn at different speeds, Penny," was all she said. "We want to keep everybody where they're most comfortable."

There were no further questions. After a suitable interval Professor Van der Weghe accepted their silence as consent.

"All right then," she said. "Good luck to all of you."

Those words plunged Quentin into a new and darker phase of his life at Brakebills, just when he'd gotten comfortable with the old one. Until then he'd worked hard, but he got in his share of malingering like everybody else. He wandered around campus and killed time with the other First Years in the First Years' lounge, which was a shabby but cozy room with a fireplace and an assortment of critically injured couches and armchairs and embarrassingly lame "educational" board games, basically magical versions of Trivial Pursuit, all warped and stained and missing crucial pieces and cards and spinners. They even had a contraband video-game console set up in a closet, a three-year-old box hooked up to an even older TV. It fuzzed out and rebooted whenever anybody fired up a spell within two hundred yards of it, which was pretty much constantly.

That was before. Now there was no time when Quentin wasn't studying. As often as Eliot had warned him about what he was in for, and as hard as he'd worked up till now, he still somehow imagined that learning magic would turn out to be a delightful journey through a secret garden where he would gaily pluck the heavy fruit of knowledge from conveniently low-hanging branches. Instead every afternoon after P.A. Quentin went straight to the library to rush through his regular homework so he could betake himself after dinner to the library, where his appointed tutor waited for him.

His tutor was Professor Sunderland, the pretty young woman who had asked him to draw maps during his Examination. She looked nothing like a magician was supposed to: she was blond and dimply and distractingly curvy. Professor Sunderland taught mostly upper-level courses, Fourth and Fifth Years, and didn't have much patience for amateurs. She drilled him relentlessly on gestures and incantations and charts and tables, and when he was perfect, that was a start, but she'd like to see Popper etudes No. 7 and No. 13 again, please, slowly, forward and then backward, just to make sure. Her hands did things Quentin couldn't imagine his hands ever doing. It would have been intolerable if Quentin didn't have a ferocious crush on Professor Sunderland.

He almost felt like he was betraying Julia. But what did he owe her? It's not like she even would have cared. And Professor Sunderland was here. He wanted somebody who was part of his new world. Julia had her chance.

Quentin spent a lot more of his time with Alice and Penny now. Brakebills had an eleven-o'clock lights-out policy for First Years, but with their extra workload the three of them had to find a way around it. Fortunately there was a small study off one of the student wings that, according to Brakebills lore, was exempt from whatever monitoring spells the faculty used to enforce curfew. Probably they left it like that deliberately as a loophole for situations like this. It was a leftover space—musty, windowless, and trapezoidal—but it had a couch and a table and chairs, and the faculty never checked it after hours, so that was where Quentin, Alice, and Penny went when the rest of the First Years went to bed.

They made an odd little tribe: Alice sitting hunched over the table; Quentin sprawled on the couch; Penny pacing in circles, or sitting cross-legged on the floor. The odious Popper books were hexed in such a way that you could practice in front of them and they would tell you if you'd screwed up or not by turning green (good) or red (bad), although annoyingly they wouldn't tell you *how* you'd screwed up.

But Alice always knew how you screwed up. Of the three of them she was the prodigy, with preternaturally flexible hands and wrists and a freakish memory. When it came to languages she was omnivorous and insatiable. While her classmates were still wallowing in the shallows of Middle English, she was already plunging into Arabic and Aramaic and Old High Dutch and Old Church Slavonic. She was still painfully shy, but the late nights she spent with Quentin and Penny in the after-hours room wore away some of her reserve, to the point where she would sometimes exchange notes and pointers with the other two. Once in a while she even revealed a sense of humor, though more often than not she made her jokes in Old Church Slavonic.

They probably would have been lost on Penny anyway. He had no sense of humor at all. He practiced by himself, murmuring and watching his pale hands sign and flutter in a massive baroque gilt-framed mirror leaned up against the wall. The mirror had an old, fading, forgotten enchantment on it, so Penny's reflection was sometimes replaced with an image of a treeless green hillside, a smooth grassy curve under an overcast sky. It was like a TV with a poorly installed cable box, picking up a stray image from far away, some other world.

Rather than take a break, Penny would just wait silently and impassively for the image to change back. Secretly the mirror made Quentin nervous, as if something horrible were about to come strolling over the top of that hill, or was buried restlessly underneath it.

"I wonder where it is," Alice said. "In real life."

"I don't know," Quentin said. "Maybe it's in Fillory."

"You could climb through. That's always how it works in the books."

"How great would that be? Think about it: we could go through and study for a month and come back and ace this thing."

"Please don't tell me you're going to go to Fillory so you can get more homework done," Alice said. "Because that would be the saddest thing I've ever heard."

"A little quiet, people," Penny said.

For a punk Penny could be an unbelievable drag.

Winter descended, a deep, bitter-cold Hudson Valley winter. The fountains froze over, and the Maze was traced in white snow, except where the topiary animals shivered and humped up and shook it off. Quentin and Alice and Penny found themselves drawing apart from their classmates, who regarded them with envy and resentment that Quentin didn't have the time or energy to deal with. For the time being they were their own exclusive club within the already closed club of Brakebills.

Quentin was rediscovering his love of work. It wasn't really a thirst for knowledge that kept him going, or any desire to live up to Professor Van der Weghe's belief that he belonged in Second Year. It was mostly just the familiar, perverse satisfaction of repetitive, backbreaking labor, the same masochistic pleasure that had enabled him to master the Mills Mess pattern and the faro shuffle and the Charlier cut and to lay waste to Calculus 2 when he was still in eighth grade.

A few of the older students took pity on the three marathon crammers. They adopted them as mascots the way a class of kindergartners would adopt a family of gerbils. They egged them on and brought them snacks and sodas after hours. Even Eliot condescended to visit, bringing with him a set of illegal charms and talismans for staying awake and reading faster, though it was hard to tell whether they worked or not. They were procured, he said, from a seedy itinerant salesman who turned up at Brakebills once or twice a year in an old wood-paneled station wagon crammed with junk.

December slid by on silent runners, in a sleepless dream of constant toil. The work had lost all connection to whatever goal it was supposed to be accomplishing. Even Quentin's sessions with Professor Sunderland lost their spark. He caught himself staring bleakly at the radiant upper slopes of her achingly full and gropable breasts when he knew he should be devoting himself to far more pressing technical issues like correct thumb position. His crush went from exciting to depressing, as if he'd gone from the first blush of infatuation to the terminal nostalgia of a former lover without even the temporary relief of an actual relationship in between.

Now he floated through Professor March's lectures from the back row, feeling lofty contempt for his classmates, who were only on Popper etude No. 27, when he had already scaled the glorious heights of No. 51 and watched it grow tiny beneath his still-climbing feet. He began to hate the the grungy misshapen room where he and Penny and Alice did their late-night cramming. He hated the bitter, burned smell of the coffee they drank, to the point where he almost felt tempted to try the low-grade speed Penny took as an alternative. He recognized the irritable, unpleasant, unhappy person he was becoming: he looked strangely like the Quentin he thought he'd left behind in Brooklyn.

Quentin didn't do all his studying in the trapezoidal spare room. On weekends he could work wherever he wanted, at least during the daytime. Mostly he stayed in his own room, but sometimes he climbed the long spiral staircase up to the Brakebills observatory, a respectable if antiquated facility at the top of one of the towers. It contained a massive late-nineteenth-century telescope the size of a telephone pole, poking up at an angle through a tarnished copper dome. Somebody on the staff must have been deeply in love with this obsolete instrument, because it floated on an exquisitely complicated array of brass gears and joints that was kept freshly oiled and in a state of high polish.

Quentin liked to read in the observatory because it was high up and well heated and relatively unfrequented: not only was it hard to get to, the telescope was useless during the day. This was usually enough to secure him an afternoon of lofty, wintry solitude. But on one Saturday in late November he discovered that he wasn't the only one who'd figured this out. When Quentin reached the top of the spiral staircase, the trapdoor was already open. He poked his head up into the circular, amber-lit room.

It was like he'd poked his head into another world, an alien planet that looked eerily like his own, but rearranged. The interloper was Eliot. He was kneeling like a supplicant in front of an old orange armchair with ripped upholstery that stood in the middle of the room, in the center of the circular track that the telescope ran on. Quentin always wondered who had gotten the chair up there in the first place and why they'd bothered—magic was obviously involved, since it wouldn't have fit through the trapdoor, or even any of the tiny windows.

Eliot wasn't alone. There was somebody sitting in the chair. The angle was bad, but he thought it was one of the Second Years, an unexceptional, smooth-cheeked kid with straight rust-colored hair. Quentin barely knew him. His name might have been Eric.

"No," Eric said, and then again sharply: "No! Absolutely not." He was smiling. Eliot started to stand up, but the boy held him down playfully by his shoulders. He wasn't especially large. The authority he exercised over Eliot wasn't physical.

"You know the rules," he said, like he was speaking to a child.

"Please? Just this once?" Quentin had never heard Eliot speak in that pleading, wheedling infantile tone before. "Please?" It was not a tone he had ever expected to hear Eliot speak in.

"Absolutely not!" Eric touched the tip of Eliot's long, pale nose with his finger. "Not until you finish all your chores. Every single one. And take off that stupid shirt, it's pathetic."

Quentin got that it was a game they'd played before. He was watching a very private ritual.

"All *right*," Eliot said petulantly. "And there is nothing wrong with this shirt," he muttered.

Eric cut him off with a look. Then he spat, once, a white fleck on Eliot's pristine shirtfront. Quentin saw the fear behind Eric's eyes as he wondered if he'd gone too far. From this angle the armchair might have blocked Quentin's view, but it didn't quite as Eliot fumbled jinglingly with Eric's belt buckle, then his fly, then jerked down his pants, exposing his thin, pale thighs.

"Careful," Eric warned. There wasn't much affection in his playacting, if that's what it was. "Little bitch. You know the rules."

Quentin couldn't have said why he waited an extra minute before he

ducked back down the ladder, back into his staid, predictable home universe, but he couldn't stop watching. He was looking directly at the exposed
wiring of Eliot's emotional machinery. How could he not have known about
this? He wondered if it was an annual thing, maybe Eliot went through a
boy or two a year, anointing them and then discarding them when they
no longer did the trick. Did he really have to hide like this? Even at Brakebills? On some level Quentin was hurt: If this was what Eliot wanted, why
hadn't he come after Quentin? Though as much as he longed for Eliot's
attention, he didn't know if he could have gone through with it. It was
better this way. Eliot wouldn't have forgiven him for refusing.

The desperate hunger with which Eliot regarded the object on which
he would perform his chores was unlike anything Quentin had ever
seen. He was right in Eliot's line of sight, but he never once glanced over
at him.

Quentin decided he would do his reading elsewhere.

He finished Lady Amelia Popper's *Practical Exercises for Young Magicians*,
Vol. 1, at midnight the night before the exam, a Sunday. He carefully
closed the book and sat for a minute staring at the cover. His hands shook.
His head felt spinny and weightless. His body was unnaturally heavy. He
couldn't stay where he was, but he was too wired to go to bed either. He
heaved himself up from the broken-backed couch and announced that
he was going for a walk.

To his surprise Alice offered to come with him. Penny just stared at the
green, overcast landscape in the mirror, waiting for his pale, stoic face to
reappear so he could keep practicing. He didn't look up as they left.

Quentin's idea had been to walk out through the Maze and across the
snowbound Sea to its outer edge, where he had first arrived, and look back
at the hushed hulk of the House and think about why this was turning
out to be so much less fun than it should have been and try to calm down
enough to go to sleep. He supposed he could do that equally well with
Alice as he could alone. He headed for the tall French doors that opened
onto the back terrace.

"Not that way," Alice said.

After hours the French doors were set to trigger a magical alert in the bedroom of whatever faculty member was on call, Infallible Alice explained, to discourage students from breaking curfew. She led him around to a side door he'd never seen before, unalarmed and concealed behind a tapestry, that opened out into a snow-covered hedge. They squeezed themselves through it and into the freezing darkness.

Quentin was easily eight inches taller than Alice, most of it in his legs, but she kept pace with him doggedly. They navigated the Maze together in the moonlight and set out across the frozen Sea. The snow was half a foot deep, and they kicked little spills of it ahead of them as they walked.

"I come out here every night," Alice said, breaking the silence.

In his sleep-deprived state Quentin had almost forgotten she was there. "Every night?" he said stupidly. "You do? Why?"

"Just . . . you know." She sighed. Her breath puffed out white in the moonlight. "To clear my head. It gets noisy in the girls' tower. You can't think. It's quiet out here."

It was strange how normal it felt to be alone with the usually antisocial Alice. "It's cold out here. You think they know you break curfew?"

"Of course. Fogg does, anyway."

"So if he knows, why bother—"

"Why bother taking the side door?" The Sea was like a smooth clean sheet laid out around them, tucked in at the corners. Except for a few deer and wild turkeys, nobody else had been across it since the last snowfall. "I don't think he really cares that much if we sneak out. But he appreciates it if you make an effort."

They reached the edge of the great lawn and turned and looked back toward the House. One light was on, a teacher's bedroom on a lower floor. An owl called. A hazy moon bleached the clouds white above the blocky outline of the roof. The scene was like an unshaken snow globe.

Quentin flashed on a memory from the Fillory books: the part in *The World in the Walls* when Martin and Fiona go wandering through the frozen woods looking for the trees the Watcherwoman has enchanted, each of which has a round ticking clock embedded in its trunk. As villains went the Watcherwoman was an odd specimen, since she rarely did anything particularly evil, or at any rate not where anybody could see her do it. She was usually glimpsed from a distance, rushing around with a book in one hand and an elaborate timepiece in the other; sometimes she drove a terrifyingly elaborate ormolu clock-carriage that ticked loudly as it raced along. She always wore a veil that covered her face. Wherever she passed she planted her signature clock-trees.

Quentin caught himself listening for ticking, but there was no sound except for an occasional frozen crack from deep in the forest, its origin unguessable.

"This is where I came through the first time," he said. "In the summer. I didn't even know what Brakebills was. I thought I was in Fillory."

Alice laughed: a surprising, hilarious shout. Quentin hadn't actually meant it to be quite that funny.

"Sorry," she said. "God, I used to love those books when I was little."

"So where did you come through?"

"Over there." She pointed at an another, identical stretch of trees. "But I didn't come through like you. I mean, through a portal."

They must have had some special, extra-magical form of conveyance for Infallible Alice, he thought. It was hard not to envy her. A phantom toll-booth, or a chariot of fire, probably. Drawn by thestrals.

"When I came, I walked here? I wasn't Invited?" She was talking in questions, with exaggerated casualness, but her voice was suddenly wobbly. "I had a brother who went here. I always wanted to come, too, but they never Invited me. After a while I was getting too old, so I ran away. I'd been waiting and waiting for an Invitation and it never came. I knew I'd already missed the first year. I'm a year older than you, you know."

He hadn't known. She looked younger.

"So I took a bus from Urbana to Poughkeepsie, then taxis from there, as far as I could. Did you ever notice there's no driveway here? No roads either. The nearest one is the state highway." This was the longest speech Quentin had ever heard Alice make. "I had them let me off on the shoulder, in the middle of nowhere. I had to walk the last five miles. I got lost. Slept in the woods."

"You slept in the woods? Like on the ground?"

"I know, I should have brought a tent. Or something. I don't know what I was thinking, I was just hysterical."

"What about your brother? He couldn't let you in?"

"He died."

She offered this neutrally, purely informationally, but it brought Quentin up short. He had never imagined that Alice could have a sibling, let alone a dead one. Or that she led anything other than a charmed life.

"Alice," he said, "this doesn't make any sense. You do realize you're the smartest person in our class?"

She shrugged off the compliment with one shoulder, staring fiercely up at the House.

"So you just walked in? What did they do?"

"They couldn't believe it. Nobody's supposed to be able to find the House by themselves. They thought it was just an accident, but it's so obvious there's old magic here, tons of it. This whole place is wild with it—if you look at it through the right spells, it lights up like a forest fire.

"They must have thought I was a homeless person. I had twigs in my hair. I'd been crying all night. Professor Van der Weghe felt sorry for me. She gave me coffee and let me take the entrance Exam all by myself. Fogg didn't want to let me, but she made him."

"And you passed."

She shrugged again.

"I still don't get it," Quentin said. "Why didn't you get Invited like the rest of us?"

She didn't answer, just stared up angrily at the hazy moon. There were tears on her cheeks. He realized that he had just casually put into words what was probably the overwhelming question of Alice's entire existence at Brakebills. It occurred to him, long after it should have, that he wasn't the only person here who had problems and felt like an outsider. Alice wasn't just the competition, someone whose only purpose in life was to succeed and by doing so subtract from his happiness. She was a person with her own hopes and feelings and history and nightmares. In her own way she was as lost as he was.

They were standing in the shadow of an enormous fir tree, a shaggy blue-gray monster groaning with snow. It made Quentin think of Christmas, and he suddenly realized that they'd missed it. He'd forgotten they were on Brakebills time. Real Christmas, in the rest of the world, had been two months ago, and he hadn't even noticed. His parents had said something about it on the phone, but the dime hadn't dropped. Funny how things like that stopped mattering. He wondered what James and Julia had done for vacation. They'd talked about all of them going up to Lake Placid together. Her parents had a cabin there.

And what did matter? It was starting to snow again, fine particles settling on his eyelashes. What the hell was out there that was worth all this work? What were they doing it for? Power, he supposed, or knowledge. But it was all so ridiculously abstract. The answer should have been obvious. He just couldn't quite name it.

Next to him Alice shuddered from the cold. She hugged herself.

"Well, I'm glad you're here now, however you got here," Quentin said awkwardly. "We all are." He put an arm around her hunched shoulders. If she didn't lean into him, or in any way admit to being comforted, she didn't have a seizure either, which he was half afraid she would. "Come on, let's get back before Fogg really does get pissed. And we've got an exam tomorrow. You don't want to be too tired to enjoy it."

They took the test the next morning, on the Monday of the third week in December. It was two hours of essays and two hours of practical exercises. There wasn't much actual spellcasting. Mostly Quentin sat in a bare classroom while three examiners, two from Brakebills and one external (she had a German accent, or maybe Swiss), listened to him recite Middle English incantations and identify spell forms and watched him try to make perfect circles of different sizes in the empty air, in different directions, with different fingers, while still more powdery snow sifted soundlessly down from the white sky outside. It was almost anticlimactic.

The results were slipped under each of their doors early the following morning, on a piece of thick cream paper that looked like a wedding invitation, folded over once. Quentin had passed, Alice had passed, and Penny had failed.

THE MISSING BOY

Brakebills let out for the last two weeks of December. At first Quentin wasn't sure why he was so terrified of going home until he realized that it wasn't home he was worried about per se. He was worried that if he left Brakebills they'd never let him back in. He would never find his way back again—they would close the secret door to the garden behind him, and lock it, and its outline would be lost forever among the vines and the stonework, and he would be trapped out in the real world forever.

In the end he went home for five days. And for a moment, as he was climbing the front stairs, and the good old familiar home smell descended on him, a lethal enchantment compounded of cooking and paint and Oriental rugs and dust, when he saw his mother's toothy, exasperated smile and his dad's hale, stubbly good humor, he became the person that he used to be around them again, and he felt the gravitational pull of the little kid he once was and in some unswept back corner of his soul always would be. He gave in to the old illusion that he'd been wrong to leave, that this was the life he should be living.

But the spell didn't hold. He couldn't stay. Something about his parents' house was unbearable to him now. After his little curved tower-top room, how could he go back to his dingy old bedroom in Brooklyn with its crumbly white paint and its iron bars on the window and its view of a tiny walled-in dirt patch? He had nothing to say to his well-meaning, politely curious parents. Both their attention and their neglect were equally intolerable. His world had become complicated and interesting and magical.

Theirs was mundane and domestic. They didn't understand that the world they could see wasn't the one that mattered, and they never would.

He came home on a Thursday. On Friday he texted James, and on Saturday morning he met up with James and Julia at an abandoned boat launch on the Gowanus. It was hard to say why they liked this place, except that it was roughly equidistant from their homes and fairly secluded—it was at the end of a dead-end street that butted up against the canal, and you had to climb over a corrugated-metal barrier to get to it. It had the quiet stillness of any place that was close to open water, however stagnant and poisonous that water might be. There was a kind of concrete barricade you could sit on while you troubled the viscous surface of the Gowanus with handfuls of stray gravel. A burnt-out brick warehouse with arched windows loomed over the scene from the opposite bank. Somebody's future luxury condo.

It was good to see James and Julia again, but it was even better to see himself seeing them, and to see how much he had changed. Brakebills had rescued him. He was no longer the shoe-gazing fuck-up he'd been the day he left, James's sidekick and Julia's inconvenient suitor. When he and James exchanged their gruff hellos and cursory handshake-hugs, he didn't feel that instinctive deference he used to feel around James, as if he were the hero of the piece and not Quentin. When he saw Julia, he searched himself for the old love he used to feel for her. It wasn't gone, but it was a dull, distant ache, still there but healed over—just the shrapnel they couldn't remove.

It hadn't occurred to Quentin that they might not be completely glad to see him. He knew he'd left abruptly, without explanation, but he had no idea how hurt and betrayed they would feel. They all sat together, three in a row, looking out at the water, as Quentin extemporized a breezy account of the obscure but still highly selective educational institution that he was for some reason attending. He kept the curriculum as vague as possible. He focused on architectural details. James and Julia huddled together stiffly against the March chill (it was March now in Brooklyn) like an elderly married couple on a park bench. When it was his turn, James rattled on about senior projects, the prom, teachers Quentin hadn't thought about once in six months—it was incredible that all this stuff was still going on, and that James still cared about it, and that he couldn't see how everything had changed. Once magic was real everything else just seemed so unreal.

And Julia—something had happened to his delicate, freckly Julia while he was away. Was it just that he didn't love her anymore? Was he seeing her clearly for the first time? But no, her hair was longer now, and it was flat and lank—she had done something to tamp down the waviness—and there were dark circles under her eyes that hadn't been there before. Before she only ever smoked at parties, but now she lit cigarette after cigarette, one off the other, feeding each one down the end of a hollow steel fencepost when she was done. Even James seemed unnerved by her, tense and protective. She observed them both coolly, her black skirt blowing around her bare knees. Afterward he couldn't have said for sure whether she'd even spoken at all.

That night, already jonesing for a taste of the magical world he'd just left, Quentin rifled through his old paperbacks for a Fillory novel and stayed up till three in the morning rereading *The Flying Forest,* one of the more incidental, less satisfying installments in the series, which featured Rupert, the goofy, feckless Chatwin brother. He and pretty, princessy Fiona find their way into Fillory via the upper branches of Rupert's favorite climbing tree and spend the novel searching for the source of a ticking sound that's keeping their friend Sir Hotspots (he's a leopard, with exceptionally sharp ears) from sleeping.

The culprits turn out to be a tribe of dwarves who have hollowed out an entire mountain of copper-bearing rock and fashioned it into an immense timekeeping device (Quentin had never noticed before how obsessed Plover was with clockwork). In the end Rupert and Fiona enlist a friendly giant to simply bury the clock deeper with his enormous mattock, muffling its monstrous ticking noise, thereby mollifying both Sir Hotspots and the dwarves, who, as cave dwellers, liked being buried. Then they repair to the royal residence, Castle Whitespire, an elegant keep cunningly constructed as a giant clockwork mechanism. Wound by windmills, a great brass mainspring beneath the castle moved and rotated its towers in a slow, stately dance.

Now that he had been to Brakebills and knew something about real magic he could read Plover with a more critical eye. He wanted to know the technical details behind the spells. And why were the dwarves building that giant clock in the first place? And the denouement didn't strike him as especially final—it reminded him too much of "The Tell-Tale Heart." Nothing stays buried forever. And where was the flying forest in *The Flying Forest*? Where were Ember and Umber, the stately twin rams who patrolled Fillory and kept order there? Though they rarely showed up till after the Chatwins had already taken care of things for them. Their real function seemed to be to make sure the Chatwins didn't overstay their welcome—it was Ember and Umber who regularly evicted them and sent them back to England at the end of each book. It was Quentin's least favorite thing about the series. Why couldn't they just let them stay? Would that have been so bad?

It was obvious that Christopher Plover didn't know anything about real magic. He wasn't even really English: according to the flap copy he was an American who'd made a quick fortune in dry goods in the 1920s and moved to Cornwall just ahead of the stock market crash. A confirmed bachelor, as the saying goes, he embraced Anglophilia, began pronouncing his name the English way ("Pluvver"), and set himself up as a country squire in a vast home crammed with staff. (Only an American Anglophile could have created a world as definitively English, more English than England, as Fillory.) Legend had it that there actually was a family of Chatwin children, who lived next door to him. Plover always claimed that the Chatwin children would come over and tell him stories about Fillory, and that he just wrote them down.

But the real mystery of *The Flying Forest*, endlessly analyzed by zealous fans and slumming academics, lay in the final few pages. With the ticking problem taken care of, Rupert and Fiona are settling down to a celebratory feast with Sir Hotspots and his family—including an appealingly slinky leopard bride and any number of adorable fuzzy leopard kittens—when who should turn up but Martin, the eldest Chatwin child, who first discovered Fillory two books ago in *The World in the Walls*.

Martin is thirteen years old by now, a pubescent teenager, almost too old to be adventuring in Fillory. In earlier books he was a changeful character, whose moods swung from cheerful to black without warning. In *The Flying Forest* he's in his depressive phase. It's not long before he picks a fight with the younger, more dependably sunny Rupert. Some very English yelling and wrestling ensues. The Hotspots clan observes the proceedings with amused leopardly coolth. Breaking away, his shirt untucked and missing a button, Martin shouts at his siblings that it was he who had discovered Fillory, and it was *he* and not *they* who should have gotten to go on the adventure. And it wasn't fair: Why did they always have to go home afterward? He was a hero in Fillory and nothing at home. Fiona icily tells him not to behave like a child. Martin stalks away into the dense Darkling Woods, weeping wimpy English schoolboy tears.

And then . . . he never returns. Fillory swallows him whole. Martin is absent from the next two books—*A Secret Sea* and the last book in the series, *The Wandering Dune*—and although his siblings hunt for him diligently, they never find him again. (Now it made Quentin think of poor Alice's brother.) Like most fans Quentin assumed that Plover meant to bring Martin back in the last book of the series, restored and repentant, but Plover died unexpectedly in his fifties while *The Wandering Dune* was still in manuscript, and nothing in his papers ever suggested an answer to the riddle. It was an insoluble literary mystery, like Dickens's unfinished *Mystery of Edwin Drood*. Martin would always remain the boy who vanished into Fillory and never came back.

Quentin thought the answer might have been in the book he'd possessed so briefly, *The Magicians,* but it was long gone. He'd turned the House inside out and interrogated everybody in it, and by this point he'd given up. Someone at Brakebills must have taken it or tidied it up or lost it. But who, and why? Maybe it hadn't even been real.

Quentin woke up early that Sunday morning already in fully fledged flight mode. He was spinning his wheels here. He had his new life to get on with. Feeling only the barest required minimum of guilt, he improvised an elaborate fictional confection for his parents—rich roommate, ski chalet in New Hampshire, I know it's last minute but could he please? More lies, but what could you do, that was how you rolled when you were a secret teenage magician. He packed hurriedly—he'd left most of his clothes at school anyway—and half an hour later he was out on the streets of Brooklyn. He went straight to the old community garden. He walked into the thickest part of it.

He ended up at the back fence, looking through it at the rusting play set in a neighbor's yard. Could it really be this small? He remembered the garden as practically a forest, but now it looked thin and scraggly. For several minutes he tramped around through the rubble and broken weeds and pumpkin corpses frozen in the act of rotting, back and forth, feeling more and more nervous and embarrassed. What did he do last time? Did he need the book? He must be missing something, but he couldn't think what. The magic wasn't happening. He tried to retrace his steps exactly. Maybe it was the wrong time of day.

Quentin went to get a slice of pizza and take stock, praying that nobody he knew would walk by and see him there when he was supposed to be on his way to Mount Alibi in New Hampshire. He didn't know what to do. The trick wasn't working. It was all falling away from him. He sat there in a booth with his bags next to him staring at his reflection in the floor-to-ceiling mirrors—why do all pizzerias have mirrored walls?—and reading the police blotter in the Park Slope free weekly. The walls reflected each other, mirrors on mirrors, an infinite curving gallery. And as he sat there, the long, narrow, busy room became still around him, almost without his knowing it. The mirrors became dark, the light changed, the bare tile became a polished parquet floor, and when he looked up from the paper again he was eating his slice alone in the junior common room at Brakebills.

Abruptly, with no fuss or ceremony, Alice and Quentin were Second Years. Classes met in a semicircular room in a back corner of the House. It was sunny but terrifyingly cold, and the insides of the tall, paneled windows were permanently iced over. In the mornings they were taught by Professor Petitpoids, an ancient and slightly dotty Haitian woman who wore a pointy black hat and made them address her as "Witch" instead of "Professor." Half the time when someone asked her a question, she would just say, "An it harm none, do what you will." But when it came to the practical requirements of working magic, her knobby walnut fingers were even more technically proficient than Professor Sunderland's. In the afternoons, for P.A., they had Professor Heckler, a long-haired, blue-jawed German who was almost seven feet tall.

There was no particular rush to embrace the two newcomers. The promotion had effectively turned Quentin and Alice into a class of two: the First Years resented them and the Second Years ignored them. Alice wasn't the star of the show anymore, the Second Years had stars of their own, principally a loud, bluff, broad-shouldered girl with straight dishwater hair named Amanda Orloff who was regularly called on to demonstrate techniques for the class. The daughter of a five-star Army general, she did magic in a gruff, unshowy, devastatingly competent way with her big, blocky hands, as if she were solving an invisible Rubik's cube. Her thick fingers wrung the magic out of the air by main force.

The other students all assumed Quentin and Alice were friends already, and probably a couple, which in a funny way had the effect of calling into being a bond between them that hadn't really had time to form yet. They were more comfortable with each other since she'd told him the painful secret of her arrival at Brakebills. She seemed to have been liberated by her late-night confession: she didn't seem so fragile all the time—she didn't always speak in that tiny, whispery voice, and he could make fun of her, and with some prompting he could get her to make fun of him, too. He wasn't sure they were friends, exactly, but she was unfolding a little. He felt like a safecracker who—partly by luck—had sussed out the first digit in a lengthy, arduous combination.

One Sunday afternoon, tired of being shunned, Quentin went and found his old lab partner Surendra and dragged him out of the House for a walk. They wound their way out through the Maze in their overcoats, headed nowhere in particular, neither of them very enthusiastically. The sun was out, but it was still painfully cold. The hedges were heavy with melting ice, and snow was still piled up in the shadowy corners. Surendra was the son of an immensely wealthy Bengali-American computer executive from San Diego. His round, beatific face belied the fact that he was the most brutally sarcastic person Quentin had ever met.

Somehow on their way out to the Sea a Second Year girl named Gretchen attached herself to them. Blond and long-legged and slender, she was built like a prima ballerina except for the fact that she had a severe, clunking limp—something congenital having to do with a knee ligament—and walked with a cane.

"Tally ho, boys."

"It's the gimp," Quentin said.

She wasn't embarrassed about her leg. She told anybody who would listen that that's where her power came from, and if she had it surgically corrected she wouldn't be able to do magic anymore. Nobody knew if it was true or not.

They walked together as far as the edge of the grass, the three of them, then stopped. Maybe this had been a mistake, Quentin thought. None of them seemed to know which way to go, or what they were doing there. Gretchen and Surendra barely knew each other anyway. For a few minutes they talked about nothing—gossip, exams, teachers—but Surendra didn't get any of the Second Year references, and every time he missed one his sulk deepened. The afternoon wobbled on its axis. Quentin picked up a wet stone and threw it as far as he could. It bounced silently on the grass. The wet made his ungloved hand even colder.

"Walk this way!" Gretchen said finally, and struck off across the Sea at an angle with her weird, rolling gait, which despite its awkwardness covered a lot of ground. Quentin wasn't sure if he was supposed to laugh or not. They walked down a narrow gravel path, through a thin scrim of leafless poplar trees, and into a small clearing on the very outer fringe of the grounds.

Quentin had been here before. He was looking at a curious Alice-in-Wonderland playing field laid out in squares, with a broad margin of lawn around it. The squares were about a yard on a side, like a giant chessboard, though the grid was longer than it was wide, and the squares were different materials: water, stone, sand, grass, and two squares made of silvery metal.

The grass squares were neatly trimmed, like a putting green. The water squares were dark, glistening pools reflecting the windblown blue sky overhead.

"What is this place?" he asked.

"What do you mean, what is it," Surendra said.

"Do you want to play?" Gretchen walked around to the other side of the checkerboard, skirting the field. A tall white-painted wooden chair stood at midfield, like a lifeguard's chair, or a judge's chair at a tennis match.

"So this is a game?"

Surendra slit his eyes at him.

"Sometimes I really don't get you," he said. It was dawning on him that he knew something Quentin didn't. Gretchen gave Surendra a conspiratorial look of shared pity. She was one of those people who assumed an attitude of instant intimacy with people she barely knew.

"This," she said grandly, "is welters!"

Quentin was pretty much resigned to death by scorn. "So it's a game."

"Oh, it's so much more than a game," Gretchen said.

"It's a passion," Surendra said.

"It's a lifestyle."

"It's a state of mind."

"I can explain it to you, if you have about ten years." Gretchen blew into her hands. "Basically one team stands at one end and one team stands at the other end and you try to capture squares."

"How do you capture a square?"

Gretchen waggled her fingers in the air mysteriously. "With *maaaaagic!*"

"Where's the broomsticks?" Quentin was only half joking.

"No broomsticks. Welters is more like chess. They invented it about fifty million years ago. I think it was originally supposed to be a teaching aid. And some people say it was an alternative to dueling. Students kept killing each other, so they got them playing welters instead."

"Those were the days."

Surendra tried a standing long jump over a water square, but he slipped as he took off, shorted it, and caught one heel in the water.

"Shit!" He looked up at the freezing blue sky. "I hate welters!"

A crow took flight from the top of a winter elm. The sun was subsiding behind the trees in a frozen swirl of pink cirrus.

Surendra walked off the board, swinging his arms.

"I can't feel my fingers. Let's go in."

They walked back down the path in the direction of the Sea, not talking, just blowing on their hands and rubbing them together. It was getting even colder as the sun went down. The trees were already black against the sky. They would have to hurry to change for dinner. A powerful feeling of late-afternoon futility was descending on Quentin. A gang of wild turkeys patrolled the edge of the forest, upright and alert, looking oddly saurian and menacing, like a lost squadron of velociraptors.

As they crossed the lawn Quentin found himself being quizzed about Eliot.

"So are you really friends with that guy?" Surendra said.

"Yeah, how do you even know him?"

"I don't really. He mostly hangs out with his own crowd." Quentin was secretly proud to be connected with Eliot, even if in reality they hardly spoke to each other anymore.

"Yeah, I know," Surendra said. "The Physical Kids. What a bunch of losers."

"What do you mean, Physical Kids?"

"You know, that whole clique. Janet Way and the fat one, Josh Hoberman—those guys. They all do physical magic for their Disciplines."

In the Maze their white breath streamed up against the darkness of the box hedges. Surendra explained that starting with the Third Year students chose a specific magical topic to specialize in, or, more exactly, had it chosen for them by the faculty. Then students were divided into groups based on their specialties.

"It doesn't matter that much, except that Disciplines map loosely to social groups—people tend to hang out mostly with their own kind. Physical's supposed to be the rarest. They're a little snobby about it, I guess. And anyway Eliot, you know about him."

Gretchen raised her eyebrows and leered. His nose was red from having been out in the cold. By now they had reached the terrace, and the pink sunset was smeared anamorphically all over the wavy glass in the French doors.

"No, I don't think I do know," Quentin said stiffly. "Why don't you tell me?"

"You don't know?"

"Oh my God!" In ecstasy Gretchen put her hand on Surendra's arm. "I bet he's one of Eliot's—!"

At that moment the French doors opened and Penny came striding quickly toward them, stiff-legged, his shirt untucked, no jacket on. His pale round face came looming up out of the dusk. His expression was blank and fixed, his walk hyperanimated by a crazy energy. As he got closer he took an extra little skip step, cocked his arm back, and punched Quentin in the face.

Fighting was almost unheard of at Brakebills. Students gossiped and politicked and sabotaged one another's P.A. experiments, but actual physical violence was vanishingly rare. Back in Brooklyn Quentin had seen fights, but he wasn't the kind of guy who got mixed up in them. He wasn't a bully, and his height made it inconvenient for bullies to pick on him. He didn't have any siblings. He hadn't been seriously punched since elementary school.

There was a freeze-frame moment of Penny's fist, close-up and huge, like a comet passing dangerously close to the Earth, and then a flashbulb went off in Quentin's right eye. It was a straight shot, and he half spun away and brought up his hand to touch the spot in the universal gesture of I've-just-been-punched-in-the-face. He was still trying to get his mind around what had just happened when Penny hit him again. This time Quentin ducked enough that he caught it on his ear.

"Ow!" Quentin yelled, scrambling backward. "What the hell?"

Dozens of windows looked out on the terrace from the House, and Quentin had a blurred impression of rows of fascinated faces pressed up against them.

Surendra and Gretchen stared at Quentin in white-faced horror, their mouths open, as if what was happening were his fault. Penny obviously had some theatrical notions about how a fight should go, because he was bouncing on his feet and doing little fake jabs and weaving his head around like boxers in movies.

"What the fuck are you doing?" Quentin shouted at him, more shocked than hurt.

Penny's jaw was clenched, and his breath hissed in and out between his teeth. There was saliva on his chin, and his eyes looked weird—the phrase "fixed and dilated" flashed through Quentin's mind. Penny aimed a big roundhouse punch at Quentin's head, and Quentin flinched away violently, ducking and covering his head with his arms. He recovered enough to grab Penny around the waist while he was still off balance.

They staggered back and forth like a pair of drunken waltzers, leaning on each other for support, then crashed into a shrubbery at the edge of the terrace. It dropped its payload of snow on them. Quentin was a couple of inches taller than Penny, and his arms were longer, but Penny was made of more solid stuff and could throw him around. A low stone bench cut them off at the knees, and they both fell over, Penny on top.

The back of Quentin's head hit the stone terrace hard. Lightning flashed. It hurt, but at the same time it had the effect of sweeping away all of Quentin's fear, and most of his conscious thoughts, like somebody sweeping the dishes off a table with both arms. In their place it substituted blind rage.

They rolled over each other, both trying to get in a punch and grabbing at the other one's arms so he couldn't. There was blood: Penny had cut his forehead open somehow. Quentin wanted to get up so they could box. He wanted to deck Penny, lay him out flat. He was vaguely aware of an enraged Gretchen trying to hit Penny with her stick and hitting him instead.

He was on top and just about had his fist free for a good hard shot when he felt strong arms encircle his chest, almost tenderly, and lift him back and up. With Quentin's weight off him Penny popped up on his toes like an electric toy, breathing hard, red running down his face, but there were people between them now, the crowd had enveloped them, Quentin was being pulled backward. The spell was broken. The fight was over.

The next hour was a jumble of unfamiliar rooms and people leaning down to talk to him earnestly and dab at his face with rough cloths. An older woman with an enormous bosom whom he'd never seen before worked a spell with cedar and thyme that made his face feel better. She put something cold that he couldn't see on the back of his head where it hit the terrace, whispering in an unfamiliar Asian language. The throbbing faded some.

He still felt a little off—he wasn't in pain, but it was like he was wearing deep-sea diving gear, clumping in slow motion through the hallways, heavy and weightless at the same time, brushing past the curious fish that peered at him and then quickly skittered away. The kids his age and younger regarded his battered face with awe—his ear was swollen, and he had a monster black eye. The older kids found the whole thing funny. Quentin decided to roll with the amusement. He did his best to project calm good humor. For a moment Eliot's face swam in front of him with a look of sympathy that made Quentin's eyes flood with hot tears that he viciously suppressed. It turned out it had been Eliot and those very same Physical Kids, speak of the devil, who had broken up the fight. Those powerful, gentle arms that pulled him off Penny belonged to Eliot's friend Josh Hoberman—the fat one.

He'd missed most of dinner, so he sat down as they were serving dessert, which seemed consistent with the backward quality of the whole day. They waived the rule about late arrivals. He couldn't shake the thickheaded feeling—he watched the world through a long-range lens, heard it through a tumbler pressed against a wall. He still hadn't figured out what the fight had been about. Why would Penny hit him? Why would anybody do that? Why come to somewhere like Brakebills just to screw it up by being an asshole?

He figured he should probably eat something, but the first bite of flourless chocolate cake turned to sticky glue in his mouth, and he had to sprint to make it to the bathroom before he threw up. At which point a massive gravitational field gripped him and pressed him roughly and irrevocably down against the grimy bathroom floor, as if a giant had slapped him down with his mighty hand and then, when he was down far enough, leaned on him with all his weight, smooshing him down into the cool, dirty tiles.

Quentin woke up in darkness. He was in bed, but not his own bed. His head hurt.

Woke up might have been putting it too strongly. The focus wasn't sharp, and his brain wasn't completely sure that its integrity was uncompromised. Quentin knew Brakebills had an infirmary, but he'd never been there before. He didn't even know where it was. He'd passed through another secret portal, this time into the world of the sick and injured.

A woman was fussing over him, a pretty woman. He couldn't see what she was doing, but he felt her cool, soft fingertips moving over his skull.

He cleared his throat, tasted something bitter.

"You're the paramedic. You were the paramedic."

"Uh-huh," she said. "Past tense is better, that was a one-time performance. Though I won't say I didn't enjoy myself."

"You were there. The day I came here."

"I was there," she agreed. "I wanted to make sure you made it to the Examination."

"What are you doing here?"

"I come here sometimes."

"I've never seen you here."

"I make a point of not being seen."

A long pause followed, during which he might have slept. But she was still there when he opened his eyes again.

"I like the hair," he said.

She was no longer wearing her paramedic's uniform, and her dark hair was up, held in place with chopsticks, revealing more of her small, jewel-like face. She had seemed so young before, and she didn't look any different now, but he wondered. She had the gravity of a much older woman.

"Those braids were a bit much," she said.

"That man who died—what really happened to him? Why did he die?"

"No special reason." A vertical line appeared between her eyebrows. "He wasn't supposed to, he just did. People do."

"I thought it might have something to do with my being there."

"Well, there's nothing wrong with your sense of self-importance. Turn over on your stomach."

Quentin did, and she dabbed the back of his head with a liquid that smelled sharply and stung.

"So it didn't mean anything?"

"Death always means something. But no, nothing apart from the usual. There, all done. You have to take care of yourself, Quentin. We need you in fighting trim."

He rolled onto his back again. His pillow had grown cool while she worked. He closed his eyes. He knew that a more alert Quentin would be working harder to zero in precisely on who she was, and what part she was playing in his story, or he in hers. But he couldn't.

"That book you gave me," he said. "I think I lost it. I didn't have a chance to read it."

In his depleted, borderline demented state the loss of the Fillory book suddenly seemed very sad, a tragedy beyond all possibility of redemption. A warm tear rolled down his cheek and into his ear.

"Hush," she said. "It wasn't time yet. You'll find it again, if you look hard enough. That much I can promise you."

It was the kind of thing people always said about Fillory. She placed something cool on his burning forehead, and he lost consciousness.

When he woke up again she was gone. But he wasn't alone.

"You had a concussion," somebody said.

It might have been the voice that finally woke him up. It had been calling his name. He recognized it, but he couldn't place it. It was calm and familiar in a way he found comforting.

"Hey, Q. Q? Are you awake? Professor Moretti said you had a concussion."

It was Penny's voice. He could even see the pale oval of Penny's face, propped up on pillows, across the aisle from him and one bed down.

"That's why you threw up. It must have been when we fell over that bench. You hit your head on the ground." All the crazy anger had drained out of Penny. He was positively chatty now.

"Yeah. I know I hit my head," Quentin said slowly, thickly. "It was my head."

"It won't affect your mental functioning, if you're wondering about that. That's what Moretti said. I asked."

"Well that's a relief."

A long silence passed. A clock ticked somewhere. There was a lovely sequence in the last Fillory book, *The Wandering Dune*, when little Jane, the youngest Chatwin, catches a bad cold and spends a week in bed talking to the Drawing Master on board the good ship *Windswept*, attended to by soft, sympathetic bunnies. Quentin had always liked Jane. She was different from the other Chatwins: more thoughtful, with an unpredictable sense of humor and a sharper edge than her slightly saccharine, Dick-and-Jane siblings.

He wondered what time it was.

"What about you?" he said numbly. He wasn't so sure he was willing to make nice just yet. "Did you get hurt?"

"I cut open my forehead on your tooth. And you broke my nose when you head-butted me. They fixed it with a Pulaski's Mending. I've never seen it done like that before, at least not on a human being. She used goat's milk."

"I didn't even know I head-butted you."

Penny was quiet again. Quentin counted thirty ticks of the clock.

"Do you have a black eye?" Penny said. "I can't see."

"Huge one."

"Thought so."

There was a glass of water on the bedside table. Quentin gulped it gratefully and fell back on the pillow. Hot veins of pain flashed through his head. Whatever the paramedic had done, or whoever she was, he still had some healing to do.

"Penny. Why the hell did you hit me like that?"

"Well, I think I had to," Penny said. He sounded a little shocked that Quentin would even ask.

"You had to." Maybe he wasn't too tired after all. "But I didn't do anything."

"You didn't do anything. Oh, that's right. You didn't do anything." Penny chuckled woodenly. His voice was oddly cool, as if he'd rehearsed this speech, his closing argument, many times. Behind it Quentin could hear that weird manic anger ramping back up. "You could have talked to me, Quentin. You could have shown me a little respect. You and your little girlfriend."

Oh, God. Was this really how it was going to be?

"Penny, who are you even talking about? Are you talking about Alice?"

"Oh, come on, Quentin. You sit there, you give each other little looks, you laugh at me. Openly. Would you believe I actually thought it was going to be fun? That we were all going to work together? Would you believe I actually thought that?"

Quentin recognized Penny's aggrieved tone. Once his parents had rented out the parlor floor of their brownstone to an apparently sane little man, an actuary, who had left them increasingly high-handed notes requesting that they stop videotaping him every time he took out the trash.

"Don't be an ass," Quentin said. He didn't see this as a rise-above-it situation. What, was Penny going to come over and give him another concussion? "Do you even know what you look like to the rest of the world? You sit there with your big-ass punk attitude, and you expect people to come around begging to hang out with you?"

Penny was sitting up now.

"That night," he said, "when you and Alice went off together. You didn't apologize, you didn't ask me, didn't say goodbye, you just walked right out. And then, and *then*," he finished triumphantly, "you passed? And I failed? How is that fair? How is that fair? What did you expect me to do?"

So that was it. "That's right, Penny," Quentin said. "You definitely should have hit me in the face because you didn't pass a test. Why don't you go hit Professor Van der Weghe, too?"

"I don't take things lying down, Quentin." Penny's voice was very loud in the empty infirmary. "I don't want trouble. But if you come after me, I swear to you that I will get right back in your face. That's just how it works. You think this is your own private fantasy world? You think you can do whatever you want? You try to walk all over me, Quentin. I'm going to come right back at you!"

They were both talking so loudly that Quentin didn't even notice when the infirmary door opened and Dean Fogg came in, dressed in an exquisitely embroidered silk kimono and a Dickensian nightcap. For a second Quentin thought he was holding a candle before he realized it was Fogg's upraised index finger that was softly glowing.

"That's enough," he said quietly.

"Dean Fogg—" Penny began as if here, finally, was a voice of reason he could appeal to.

"I said that's enough." Quentin had never heard the Dean raise his voice, and he didn't now. Fogg was always a faintly ridiculous figure in the daytime, but now, at night, wreathed in his kimono, in the alien confines of the infirmary, he looked powerful and otherworldly. Wizardly. "You're not going to speak again except to answer my questions. Is that clear?"

Did that count as a question? To be safe Quentin just nodded. His head hurt worse now.

"Yes sir," Penny said promptly.

"I have heard absolutely enough about this. Who instigated this appalling incident?"

"I did," Penny said instantly. "Sir. Quentin didn't do anything, he had nothing to do with it."

Quentin said nothing. That was the funny thing about Penny. He was insane, but he did have his insane principles, and he stuck to them.

"And yet," Fogg said, "somehow your nose found its way into the path of Quentin's forehead. Will it happen again?"

"No, sir."

"No."

"All right." Quentin heard springs chirp as the Dean sat down on an empty bed. He didn't turn his head. "There is only one thing that pleases me about this afternoon's altercation, which is that neither of you resorted to magic to hurt each other. Neither of you is advanced enough in your studies to understand this properly, but in time you will learn that wielding magic means working with enormously powerful energies. And controlling those energies requires a calm and dispassionate mind.

"Use magic in anger, and you will harm yourself much more quickly than you will harm your adversary. There are certain spells . . . if you lose control of them, they will change you. Consume you. Transform you into something not human, a *niffin*, a spirit of raw, uncontrolled magical energy."

Fogg regarded them both with stern composure. Very dramatic. Quentin looked up at the infirmary's pressed-tin ceiling stubbornly. His consciousness was guttering and fading. Where was the part where he told Penny to stop being a dick?

"Listen to me carefully," Fogg was saying. "Most people are blind to magic. They move through a blank and empty world. They're bored with their lives, and there's nothing they can do about it. They're eaten alive by longing, and they're dead before they die.

"But you live in the magical world, and it's a great gift. And if you want to get killed here, you'll find plenty of opportunities without killing each other."

He stood up to go.

"Will we be punished, sir?" Penny asked.

Punished? He must honestly believe they were still in high school. The Dean paused at the door. The light from his finger was almost extinguished.

"Yes, Penny, as a matter of fact you will be. Six weeks of washing dishes, lunch and dinner. If this or anything like it happens again, you're expelled. Quentin—" he stopped to consider. "Just learn to handle yourself better. I don't want any more problems."

The door closed behind him. Quentin exhaled. He closed his eyes, and the room drifted silently off its moorings and out to sea. He wondered, with no special interest either way, whether Penny was in love with Alice.

"Wow," Penny said, apparently unfazed by the prospect of spending the next month and a half with pruny fingertips. He sounded like a little kid.

"I mean, *wow*. Did you hear what he said? About magic consuming you? I didn't know any of that. Did you know any of that stuff?"

"Penny," Quentin said. "One, your hair is stupid. And two, I don't know what it's like where you come from, but if you ever do anything that could get me sent back to Brooklyn again, I won't just break your nose. I will motherfucking kill you."

THE PHYSICAL KIDS

Six months later, in September, Quentin and Alice spent the first day of their Third Year at Brakebills sitting outside a small square Victorian outbuilding about a half mile from the House. It was a piece of pure folly architecture, a miniature house, white with a gray roof, complete with windows and gables, that might at one time have been servants' quarters, or a guest cottage, or a largish garden shed.

There was a weathervane on top, wrought iron and shaped like a pig, that always pointed somewhere other than where the wind was blowing. Quentin couldn't make out anything through the windows, but he thought he heard snatches of conversation coming from inside. The cottage stood on the edge of a wide hayfield.

It was midafternoon. The sky was blue and the early autumn sun was high. The air was silent and still. A rusted-out old piece of farm machinery stood half drowned in the same long grass it used to mow.

"This is bullshit. Knock again."

"You knock," Alice said. She released a convulsive sneeze. "I've been knocking for twenty . . . for twenty . . ."

She sneezed again. She was allergic to pollen.

"Bless you."

"Twenty minutes. Thank you." She blew her nose. "They're in there, they just won't open the door."

"What do you think we should do?"

Quentin thought for a minute.

"I don't know," he said. "Maybe it's a test."

———

Back in June, after finals, all twenty members of the Second Year had been marched through the Practical Applications room one at a time to be assigned their Disciplines. The sessions were scheduled at two-hour intervals, though sometimes it took longer; the entire process lasted three days. It was a circus atmosphere. Most of the students, and probably the faculty, were ambivalent about the whole idea of Disciplines. They were socially divisive, the theory behind them was weak, and everybody ended up studying pretty much the same curriculum anyway, so what was the point? But it was traditional for every student to have one, so a Discipline every student would have. Alice called it her magic bat mitzvah.

The P.A. lab was transformed for the occasion. All the cabinets were open, and every inch of the counters and tabletops was crammed with old instruments made of wood and silver and etched brass and worked glass. There were calipers and bulbs and beakers and clockwork and scales and magnifying glasses and dusty glass bulbs full of wobbling mercury and other less easily identifiable substances. Brakebills was largely dependent on Victorian-era technology. It wasn't an affectation, or not entirely; electronics, Quentin was told, behaved unpredictably in the presence of sorcery.

Professor Sunderland presided over the circus. Quentin had avoided her as much as possible since that horrible, dreamlike period when she tutored him during his first semester. His crush on her had faded to a faint but still pathetic echo of its former self, to the point where he could almost look at her and not want to fill his hands with her hair.

"I'll be with you in just one minute!" she said brightly, busily repacking a set of very fine, sharp-looking silver instruments in a velvet carrying case.

"So." She snapped the case shut and latched it. "Everybody at Brakebills has an aptitude for magic, but there are individual variations—people tend to have an affinity for some specific strain." She delivered this speech by rote, like a stewardess demonstrating in-flight safety procedures. "It's a very personal thing. It has to do with where you were born, and where the moon was, and what the weather was like, and what kind of person you are, plus all kinds of technical stuff that's not worth getting into. There are two hundred or so other factors which Professor March would be happy to list for you. It's one of his specialties. In fact I think Disciplines are his Discipline."

"What's your Discipline?"

"It's related to metallurgy. Any other personal questions?"

"Yes. Why do we have to go through all this testing? Can't you just figure my Discipline out from my birthday and all that stuff you just mentioned?"

"You could. In theory. In practice it would just be a pain in the ass." She smiled and put her blond hair up and secured it with a clip, and a sharp shard of his old yen for her pierced Quentin's heart. "It's much easier to go at it inductively, from the outside in, till we get a hit."

She placed a bronze scarab in each of his hands and asked him to recite the alphabet, first in Greek, then in Hebrew, which he had to be prompted on, while she studied him through what looked like a many-crooked collapsible telescope. He could feel the metal beetles crackling and buzzing with old spells. He had a horrible fear that their little legs would suddenly start wriggling. Occasionally she would stop and have him repeat a letter while she adjusted the instrument by means of protruding screws.

"Mm," she said. "Uh-huh."

She produced a tiny bonsai fir tree and made him stare at it from different angles while it ruffled its tiny needles in response to a wind that wasn't there. Afterward she took the tree aside and conferred with it privately.

"Well, you're not an herbalist!" she said.

Over the next hour she tested him in two dozen different ways, only a few of which he understood the point of. He ran through basic First Year spells while she watched and measured their effectiveness with a battery of instruments. She had him read an incantation while standing next to a large brass clock with seven hands, one of which circled its face backward and with disconcerting speed. She sighed heavily. Several times she took down sagging, overweight volumes from high shelves and consulted them for long, uncomfortable intervals.

"You're an interesting case," she said.

There is really no end to life's little humiliations, Quentin reflected.

He sorted pearl buttons of various sizes and colors into different piles while she studied his reflection in a silver mirror. She tried to get him to take a nap so she could pry into his dreams, but he couldn't fall asleep, so she put him under with one sip of a minty, effervescent potion.

Apparently his dreams didn't tell her anything she didn't already know. She stared at him for a long minute with her hands on her hips.

"Let's try an experiment," she said finally, with forced liveliness. She smiled thinly and tucked a stray strand of hair back behind her ear.

Professor Sunderland walked down the length of the room closing the dusty wooden shutters with a clatter until it was dark. Then she cleared the clutter off a gray slate tabletop and boosted herself up onto it. She yanked her skirt down over her knees and motioned for him to sit facing her on the table opposite.

"Go like this," she said, holding up her hands as if she were about to conduct an invisible orchestra. Unladylike half-moons of sweat bloomed under the arms of her blouse. He went like this.

She led him through a series of gestures familiar to him from Popper, though he'd never seen them put together in quite that combination. She whispered some words he didn't catch.

"Now go like this." She flung her hands up over her head.

When she did it, nothing happened. But when Quentin mirrored her, streams of fat white sparks streamed out of his fingertips. It was amazing—it was like they'd been inside him all his life, just waiting for him to wave his hands the right way. They splashed happily out across the ceiling in the dimness and came floating festively down around him, bouncing a few times when they hit the floor and then finally winking out. His hands felt warm and tingly.

The relief was almost unbearable. He did it again and a few more sparks flew out, weaker this time. He watched them trail down around him. The third time he got only one.

"What does it mean?" he asked.

"I have no idea," Professor Sunderland said. "I'll put you down as Undetermined. We'll try again next year."

"Next year?" Quentin watched with a rising sense of disappointment as she jumped down off the table and started reopening shutters, window by window. He winced at the sunlight flooding in. "What do you mean? What am I going to do till then?"

"Wait," she said. "It happens. People put too much importance on these things. Be a darling and send in the next student, would you? We're already running late, and it's only noon."

The summer dragged by in slow motion. It was really the fall, of course, in the world outside Brakebills, and the Brooklyn Quentin came home to for summer vacation was chilly and gray, the streets plastered with wet brown leaves and mashed ginkgo balls that smelled like vomit.

He haunted his old house like a ghost—it took a special effort to make himself visible to his parents, who always looked vaguely surprised when their phantom son requested their attention. James and Julia were away at college, so Quentin took long walks. He visited the branching, angular Gowanus Canal, its water the green of pooled radiator fluid. He shot baskets on deserted courts with missing nets and rainwater puddles in the corners. The autumn cold gave the ball a dead, inert feel. His world wasn't here, it was elsewhere. He traded desultory e-mails with friends from Brakebills—Alice, Eliot, Surendra, Gretchen—and flipped indifferently through his summer reading, an eighteenth-century *History of Magic* that appeared quite slim from the outside but turned out to contain, by some subtle bibliographical magic, no fewer than 1,832 pages.

In November he received a cream-colored envelope, which turned up tucked by invisible hands into *History of Magic*. It contained a stiff letter-pressed card with an elegant engraving of the Brakebills crest, inviting him to return to school at six in the evening by way of a narrow, never-used alleyway next to the First Lutheran Church ten blocks from his house.

He dutifully presented himself at the correct address at the appointed time. This late in the fall the sun set at four thirty in the afternoon, but it was unseasonably mild out, almost warm. Standing there at the entrance to the passageway, looking around for stray vergers who might charge him with trespassing—or worse, offer him spiritual guidance—cars whooshing by in the street behind him, he had never felt so absolutely sure that he was delusional, that Brooklyn was the only reality there was, and that everything which had happened to him last year was just a fanboy hallucination, proof that the boredom of the real world had finally driven him totally and irreversibly out of his mind. The alley was so skinny he practically had to turn sideways to walk down it, his two overstuffed Brakebills duffel bags—they were midnight blue with dark brown trim, school colors—scraping against the sweating stone walls on either side. He was overwhelmingly certain that in thirty seconds he would be standing at the blank wall at the end of the alley.

But then an impossible breath of warm, sweet, late-summer air came wafting toward him from the far end of the alleyway, accompanied by the chirping of crickets, and he could see the green expanse of the Sea. As heavy as his bags were he ran toward it.

Now it was the first day of the semester, and Quentin and Alice were stranded in a baking hot meadow outside a precious white Victorian bungalow. The bungalow was where the students who did Physical Magic met on Tuesday afternoons for their weekly seminar.

When she was tested, Alice displayed a highly technical Discipline involving light manipulation—phosphoromancy, she said it was called—that placed her in Physical Magic. Quentin was there because Physical was the group that had both the fewest total members and the fewest incoming members, so that seemed like the best place to stash him until he had a Discipline of his own. The first seminar had been scheduled for 12:30, and Quentin and Alice had even gotten there early, but now it was almost five, and they'd been out there all afternoon. They were hot and tired and thirsty and annoyed, but neither of them wanted to give up and go back up to the House. If they were going to be Physical Kids, apparently they would have to prove it by getting in the front door.

They sat under a massive spreading beech tree that stood nearby, coolly indifferent to their plight. They leaned back against the trunk with a fat hard gray root between them.

"So what do you want to do," Quentin said dully. Tiny motes drifted by in the late-afternoon sunlight.

"I don't know." Alice sneezed again. "What do you want to do?"

Quentin plucked at the grass. A burst of faint laughter came from inside the house. If there was a password they hadn't found it. He and Alice had spent an hour looking for hidden writing—they scanned the door in every spectrum they could think of, visible and invisible, infrared to gamma, and tried to strip the paint off to look underneath, but it wouldn't come.

Alice even tried some advanced graphological enchantments on the squiggly grain of the wood itself, but it just stared back at them blankly. They'd sent currents of force twisting into the lock, jiggling the tumblers, but they couldn't pick it. They looked for a fourth-dimensional path around the door. They'd jointly plucked up their nerve and summoned a kind of phantasmal axe—it wasn't *explicitly* against any rule they could think of—but they couldn't even scratch it. For a while Alice was convinced the door was an illusion, that it didn't even exist, but it certainly looked and felt real, and neither of them could find any charms or enchantments to dispel.

"Look at it," Quentin said. "It's like some lame Hansel and Gretel hut. I thought the Physical Kids were supposed to be cool."

"Dinner's in an hour," Alice said.

"I'll skip it."

"It's lamb tonight, with a rosemary crust. Potatoes *au dauphin*." Alice's eidetic memory retained odd details.

"Maybe we should have our own seminar. Out here."

She snorted. "Yeah, that'd show 'em."

The beech tree was on the edge of a field that had just been mown. The giant cinnamon rolls of hay dotting the field cast long shadows.

"You're a what again? A photomancer?"

"Phosphoromancer."

"What can you do?"

"I'm not sure yet. I practiced some things over the summer. Focusing light, refracting it, bending it. If you bend light around something, it turns invisible. But I want to understand the theory of it first."

"Show me something."

Alice turned shy. It didn't take much.

"I can hardly do anything."

"Look, I don't even have a Discipline. I'm a nothingmancer. I'm a squatmancer."

"They just don't know what it is yet. You have your little sparky thing."

"Same difference. And don't make fun of my sparky thing. Now bend me some damn light."

She grimaced, but she got up on her knees on the grass and held up her hand, fingers spread. They were kneeling face-to-face, and he was suddenly aware of her full breasts inside her thin, high-necked blouse.

"Watch the shadow," she snapped.

She did something with her fingers, and the shadow of her hand disappeared. It was simply gone, leaving behind only a few ghostly rainbow highlights.

"Nice."

"It's pathetic, I know." She waved her hand, scrubbing out the magic. "My whole hand is supposed to go invisible, but I can only do the shadow."

There was something here. Quentin felt his sulk starting to dispel. This was a test. Physical magic. They weren't Morris dancing with tree spirits here. This was a brute-force problem.

"What about the other way?" he said slowly. "Could you focus light instead, like a magnifying glass?"

She didn't answer right away, but he could see her nimble mind take hold of the problem and start turning it over.

"Maybe if I . . . hm. I think there's something in Culhwch and Owen. You'd need to stabilize the effect, though. And localize it."

She made a circle with her thumb and forefinger and spoke five long words over it. Quentin could see light bending inside the circle, warping and distorting the leaves and grass visible through it. Then it sharpened and focused to a white dot that burned an afterimage into his retina, and he looked away. She tilted it, and the ground under her hand smoked.

"I will kill you if you get me kicked out of Brakebills. Do you understand me? I'm not joking. I know how to do it. I will literally make you die."

"That's funny, that's exactly what I told Penny after he hit me," Quentin said.

"Except I'll really do it."

They had decided to burn their way through the door. If it was a test, Quentin reasoned, it didn't matter much how they solved it as long as they solved it. They hadn't been given any rules, so they couldn't be breaking any. And if they did burn down the damn house, with Eliot and his smug little friends inside it, serve them right.

They had to work fast, because the sunlight was fading. The sun had already gone dull and coppery, and in another few minutes its lower rim would touch the tops of the trees on the far side of the hayfield. The barest early-fall chill was in the air. Yellow lights were already on inside the house. Quentin heard—did he imagine it?—the pop of a cork being withdrawn from a bottle.

Holding both arms above her head and curved slightly upward, like she was balancing a large invisible basket on her head, Alice had created the magical equivalent of a magnifying glass a dozen yards across—her bent arms defined a small section of the total circumference of a soaring circular lens, the upper edge of which was even with the top of the beech tree, taller than the chimney of the little Victorian bungalow. Quentin could just make out the edge of the lens as a curved distortion in the air. The focal point was too bright to look at.

Alice stood about fifty feet back from the door. Quentin stood closer, to one side, holding out a hand to shield his eyes and shouting out directions:

"Up! Okay, slow! A little more! Keep moving! Okay, now right!"

Quentin could feel the heat from the focused sunlight against his face and smell the savory-sweet smell of wood smoke, along with an acrid tang of seared house paint. The door was definitely vulnerable to heat. They'd been worried that there wouldn't be enough sunlight left, but Alice's spell was cutting a nice deep charred trench in the wood. They'd decided to cut the door in half laterally, and if the trench wasn't penetrating all the way through, it must be pretty close. A bigger problem was Alice's aim, which wasn't good, and in one place she had wandered off the door and burned a groove in the wall.

"I feel stupid!" Alice shouted. "How are we doing?"

"Looking good!"

"My back hurts! Are we almost done?"

"Almost!" he lied.

With a foot to go Alice expanded the spell's radius to compensate for the fading sun. She was whispering, but he wasn't sure if it was an incantation or just obscenities. Quentin realized they were being observed: one of the older professors, a very erect, white-haired man named Brzezinski, who specialized in potions and whose pants were always covered with appalling stains, had interrupted his evening stroll to watch them. In another lifetime he had given Quentin the test involving knots during his Examination. He wore sweater-vests and smoked a pipe and looked like an IBM engineer, circa 1950.

Shit, Quentin thought. They were about to get busted.

But Professor Brzezinski just took his pipe out of his mouth. "Carry on," he said gruffly. He turned and walked back in the direction of the House.

It took only about ten minutes for Alice to make a full lateral cut, then go back across it a second time. The trench glowed red.

When she was finished, Quentin walked back to where she was standing.

"You have ash on your face," she said. She brushed at his forehead with her fingers.

"Maybe we should go across again. You know, just to be sure." If this didn't work, he was out of ideas, and he didn't think he could spend the night out here. He also didn't think he could face going back to the House in defeat.

"There's not enough light." She looked drained. "By the end the lens was probably out to a quarter mile. After that it just loses coherence. Falls apart at the edges."

A quarter mile? Quentin thought. How powerful is she?

His stomach rumbled. It was fully dusk now, and the sky was a luminous blue. They stared at the scarred, blackened door. It looked worse than he thought—Alice's aim had strayed on the second pass, so in places there were two separate trenches. If this was wrong, Eliot was going to kill him.

"Should I try to kick it in?"

Alice pulled her mouth to one side. "What if there's somebody behind it?"

"So what do you suggest?"

"I don't know." She picked at one of the burnt parts that had cooled. "I think we're almost through . . ."

There was an old iron knocker on the door in the shape of a disembodied hand holding an iron ball. It was bolted on.

"Okay," Quentin said. "Stand back."

God, please let this work. He got a good grip on the iron hand, put one foot on the door, uttered a long falsetto martial arts yell, and threw his weight backward. The top half of the door swung open with no resistance whatsoever—it must have been hanging on by a few flakes of ash. He fell down backward on the path.

A girl Quentin recognized as one of the Fourth Years stood in the doorway with warm light streaming out into the twilight around her, holding a glass of dark red wine in one hand. She looked down at him coolly. Alice was leaning against the side of the house laughing so hard that no sound was coming out.

"Dinner's almost ready," the girl said. "Eliot made an amatriciana sauce. We couldn't get any guanciale, but I think bacon works fine. Don't you?"

In spite of the heat a fire popped and flickered in the fireplace.

"Six hours, twelve minutes," said a fat young man with wavy hair sitting in a leather club chair. "That's actually about par."

"Tell them how long it took you, Josh," said the girl who'd met them at the door. Quentin thought her name was Janet.

"Twenty hours, thirty-one minutes. Longest night of my life. Not a record, but pretty close."

"We thought he was trying to starve us out." Janet poured out the rest of a bottle of red wine into two glasses standing on a sideboard and handed them to Quentin and Alice. Two more empty bottles stood on the floor, though the others didn't seem especially drunk.

They were in a shabby but comfortable library lined with threadbare rugs and lit by candles and firelight. Quentin realized that the little house must be larger on the inside than it was on the outside; it was also a lot cooler—the atmosphere was that of a nice, chilly fall evening. Books overflowed the bookcases and stood in wobbly stacks in the corners and even on the mantelpiece. The furniture was distinguished but mismatched, and in places it was severely battered. In between the bookcases the walls were hung with the usual inexplicable artifacts that accumulate in private clubs: African masks, dreary landscape paintings, retired ceremonial daggers, glass cases full of maps and medals and the deteriorating corpses of exotic moths that had presumably been captured at great effort and expense. Quentin felt overheated and underdressed but mostly just relieved to finally be inside.

There were only five of them, counting himself and Alice. Eliot was

there, scanning one of the bookshelves and acting like he hadn't noticed
them yet. He seemed to be trying to make a serious argument about magical theory to somebody, but nobody was listening

"Tinkerbell, we have guests," Janet said. "Please turn around and face
the room." She was lean and animated, with a serious, somewhat anachro-
nistic pageboy haircut. She was the loud one: Quentin had seen her holding
forth to the others on walks through the Maze and making speeches over
dinner in the dining room.

Eliot broke off his monologue and turned around. He was wearing an
apron.

"Hello," he said, not missing a beat. "Glad you could make it. Alice, I
understand you burned our door in half."

"Quentin helped."

"We watched you out the window," Josh said. "You're hella lucky Brzezinski didn't catch you with that axe."

"What's the correct solution?" Alice asked. "I mean, I know it worked,
but there must be a better way."

She took a timid sip of her wine, immediately followed by a less timid
one.

"There isn't one," Janet said. "Or not a good one, anyway. That's part of
the point. This is Physical Magic. It's messy. It's crude. As long as you don't
knock the building down, it counts. And if you did it would probably still
count."

"How did you do it?" Alice asked shyly. "I mean, when it was your
turn?"

"Froze and shattered it. I do a special kind of cold magic, that's my Discipline. Sixty-three minutes. And that *is* a record."

"It used to be you could say 'friend' in Elvish and it would let you in,"
Josh said. "Now too many people have read Tolkien."

"Eliot, darling, I think our dinner must be ready," Janet said. Her attitude toward Eliot was hard to read, a weird combination of tenderness and
contempt. She clapped her hands. "Josh, maybe you could do something
about . . . ?" She gestured in the direction of the half-demolished door.
"The mosquitoes are getting in."

Still dazed, Quentin trailed Eliot into the kitchen, which was, again,
larger and nicer than really seemed plausible from the outside, with white

cabinets up to the high ceiling and soapstone counters and an aerodynamic-looking 1950s refrigerator. Eliot sloshed some wine from his glass into a pan of red sauce on the stove.

"Never cook with a wine you wouldn't drink," he said. "Though I guess that presupposes that there *is* a wine I wouldn't drink."

He didn't seem at all embarrassed by the fact that he'd ignored Quentin for the past year. It was like it never happened.

"So you have this whole place to yourself?" Quentin didn't want to let on how much he wanted to belong here, even now that he did, officially, belong here.

"Pretty much. So do you, now."

"Do all the Disciplines have their own clubhouses?"

"It's not a clubhouse," Eliot said sharply. He dumped a huge clump of fresh pasta into a tall pot of boiling water and stirred it to break it up. "This'll cook in about a minute flat."

"Then what is it?"

"Well, all right, it is a clubhouse. But don't call it that. We call it the Cottage. We have the seminars here, and the library isn't bad. Sometimes Janet paints in the bedroom upstairs. Only we can get in here, you know."

"What about Fogg?"

"Oh, and Fogg, though he never bothers. And Bigby. You know Bigby, right?"

Quentin shook his head.

"I can't believe you don't know Bigby!" Eliot said, chuckling. "God, you're going to love Bigby."

He tasted the sauce, then glugged in a slug of heavy cream and stirred it in in widening circles. The sauce paled and thickened. Eliot had a jaunty, offhanded confidence at the stove.

"All the groups have a place like this. The Naturals have this deeply lame treehouse off in the forest. The Illusionists have a house just like this one, though only they know where it is. You have to find it to get in. Knowledge just has the library, the poor suckers. And Healing has the clinic—"

"Eliot!" Janet's voice came from the other room. "We're starving." Quentin wondered how Alice was faring out there.

"All right, all right! I hope you don't mind pasta," he added, to Quentin. "It's all I made. There's bruschetta out there, or there was. At least there's lots of wine." He drained the pasta in the sink, sending up a huge gout of steam, and dumped it into the pan to finish in the sauce. "God, I love cooking. I think if I weren't a magician, I'd be a chef. It's just such a relief after all that invisible, intangible bullshit, don't you think?

"Richard was the real cook around here. I don't know if you knew him, he graduated last year. Tall. Total grind, made us all look bad in front of Bigby, but at least he could cook. Grab those two bottles there, would you? And the corkscrew?"

With a white tablecloth and two heavy silver candelabras and a wildly eclectic assortment of silverware, some of which bordered on light hand-to-hand weaponry, the table in the library almost looked like somewhere you could eat. The food was simple but not at all bad. He'd forgotten he was starving. Janet performed a trick—Quentin wasn't sure whether it was magical or just mechanical—to shorten the long seminar table into a dinner table.

Janet, Josh, and Eliot gossiped about classes and teachers and who was sleeping with whom and who wanted to sleep with whom. They speculated endlessly about other students' relative strengths as spellcasters. They maneuvered around one another with the absolute confidence of people who had spent huge amounts of time together, who trusted and loved one another and who knew how to show one another off to best advantage and how to curb each other's boring and annoying habits. Quentin let the chatter wash over him. Eating a sophisticated meal, alone in their own private dining room, felt very adult. This was it, he thought. He had been an outsider before, but now he had really entered into the inner life of the school. This was the real Brakebills. He was in the warm secret heart of the secret world.

They were arguing about what they would do after they graduated.

"I imagine I'll retreat to some lonely mountaintop," Eliot said airily. "Become a hermit for a while. I'll grow a long beard and people will come to me for advice, like in cartoons."

"Advice about what?" Josh snorted. "About whether a dark suit counts as black tie?"

"And I'd like to see you *try* to grow a beard," Janet added. "God, you're self-centered. Don't you want to help people?"

Eliot looked puzzled. "People? What people?"

"Poor people! Hungry people! Sick people! People who can't do magic!"

"What have people ever done for me? People don't want my help. People called me a faggot and threw me in a Dumpster at recess when I was in fifth grade because my pants were pressed."

"Well, I hope for your sake there's a wine cellar on your mountaintop," Janet said, annoyed. "Or a full bar. You won't last eight hours without a drink."

"I will brew a crude but potent beverage from local herbs and berries."

"Or dry cleaning."

"Well, that is a problem. You can use magic, but it's never the same. Maybe I'll just live at the Plaza, like Eloise."

"I'm bored!" Josh bellowed. "Let's do Harper's Fire-Shaping."

He went over to a large cabinet full of dozens of tiny drawers, narrow but deep, that turned out to be a kind of miniature twig library. Each drawer bore a tiny handwritten label, starting with Ailanthus in the upper left-hand corner and ending with Zelkova, Japanese, in the lower right. Harper's Fire-Shaping was a useless but extremely entertaining spell for stretching and leading a flame into elaborate calligraphic shapes that flared for a moment in midair and then disappeared. You did it with an aspen twig. The evening devolved into attempts to shape the candle flames into increasingly elaborate or obscene words and shapes, which in turn led, inevitably, to the curtains catching on fire (apparently not for the first time) and having to be extinguished.

A halt was called. Eliot produced a slender, dangerous-looking bottle of grappa. Only two of the candles had survived the fire-shaping, but nobody bothered to replace the others. It was late, after one in the morning. They sat there in the half darkness in contented silence. Janet lay on her back on the carpet staring up at the ceiling, her feet propped up on Eliot's lap. There was a funny physical intimacy between the two of them, especially considering what Quentin knew about Eliot's sexual appetites.

"So this is it? We're full-fledged Physical Kids now?" The grappa was like a fiery seed that had drifted into Quentin's chest and taken root there. The seed gave birth to a hot, glowing sapling, which grew and spread and unfolded into a big warm leafy tree of good feeling. "Don't we have to be hazed or branded or, I don't know, shaved or something?"

"Not unless you want to be," Josh said.

"Somehow I thought there would be more of you," Quentin said. "Of us."

"This is it," Eliot said. "Since Richard and Isabel graduated. There aren't any Fifth Years. Nobody placed in. If we didn't get anybody this year, Fogg was talking about merging us with Natural."

Josh shuddered theatrically.

"What were they like?" Alice asked. "Richard and Isabel?"

"Like fire and ice," Josh said. "Like chocolate and marzipan."

"It's different without them," Eliot said.

"Good riddance," said Janet.

"Oh, they weren't so bad," Josh said. "You remember when Richard thought he could bring the weathervane to life? He was going to make it move around by itself. He must have been up there for three days rubbing it with fish oil and I don't even want to think about what else."

"That was unintentionally funny," Janet said. "Doesn't count."

"You just never got the point of Richard."

Janet snorted.

"I got plenty of Richard," she said, with surprising bitterness.

A tiny hush fell. It was the first false note of the evening.

"But now we have a quorum again," Eliot said quickly, "an eminently respectable quorum. Physical Magic always gets the best ones."

"To the best ones," Josh said.

Quentin raised his glass. He was up in the lofty branches of his fiery tree, swaying in the warm alcoholic breeze.

"The best ones."

They all drank.

THE BEAST

The entire time he'd been at Brakebills, through First Year, the exams, the whole disaster with Penny, right up until the night he joined the Physical Kids, Quentin had been holding his breath without knowing it. He realized only now that he'd been waiting for Brakebills to vanish around him like a daydream. Even aside from the many and varied laws of thermodynamics that were violated there on a regular basis, it was just too good to be true. It was like Fillory that way. Fillory never lasted forever. Ember and Umber promptly kicked the Chatwins out at the end of every book. Deep down Quentin felt like a tourist who at the end of the day would be herded back onto some dirty, lumbering, snorting tour bus—with ripped vinyl seats and overhead TVs and a stinking toilet—and shipped home, clutching a tacky souvenir postcard and watching as the towers and hedges and peaks and gables of Brakebills dwindled in the rearview mirror.

But it hadn't happened. And now he understood, he really got, that it wasn't going to happen. He'd wasted so much time thinking, It's all a dream, and It should have been somebody else, and Nothing lasts forever. It was time he started acting like who he was: a nineteen-year-old student at a secret college for real, actual magic.

Now that he was in among them he had some leisure to observe the Physical Kids up close. When he first met Eliot, Quentin assumed that everyone at Brakebills would be like him, but in fact that wasn't the case at all. For one thing, even in this rarefied setting Eliot's bizarre personal manner set him apart. For another, he was conspicuously brilliant in class—maybe not quite as quick as Alice, but Alice worked her ass off and Eliot didn't even try, or if he did he hid it very, very well. As far as Quentin could tell he never studied at all. The only thing in the world that he would actually cop to caring about was his appearance, especially his expensive shirts, which he wore with cuff links, even though it cost him regular menial punishments for violating the dress code.

Josh always wore the standard school uniform but managed to make it look like he didn't—his jacket never quite fit his wide, round build, it was always twisted or rumpled or too narrow in the shoulders. His whole personality was like an elaborate joke that he never stopped telling. It took Quentin a while to figure out that Josh expected people not to take him seriously, and he enjoyed—not always kindly—the moment when they realized, too late, that they'd underestimated him. Because he wasn't as self-absorbed as Eliot or Janet he was the group's sharpest observer, and he missed very little of what went on around him. He told Quentin that he'd been waiting for Penny to snap for weeks:

"Are you kidding? That guy was a mystery wrapped in an enigma and crudely stapled to a ticking fucking time bomb. He was either going to hit somebody or start a blog. To tell you the truth I'm kind of glad he hit you."

Unlike the other Physical Kids Josh was an undistinguished student, but once he'd mastered a skill he was an exceptionally forceful spellcaster. It was a full six weeks into his first year at Brakebills before he was able to move his marble by magic, but when he finally did—as Eliot told the story—it shot through a classroom window and buried itself six inches in the trunk of a maple tree outside, where it probably still was.

Janet's parents were lawyers, of the high-flying Hollywood-consorting variety, and colossally wealthy. She grew up in L.A. being babysat by various celebrities, whom under duress—but not very much duress—she would name. Quentin supposed that accounted for the vivid, actressy edge to her manner. She was the most visible of the Physical Kids, loud and brusque and always proposing toasts at dinner. She had terrible taste in men—the best that could be said of her endless series of boyfriends is that none of them lasted long. Pretty rather than beautiful, she had a flat, flapperish figure, but she used what she had to maximum advantage—she sent her uniforms back home to be tailored—and there was something vibrantly sexy about her ravenous, too-wide gaze. You wanted to meet it and be devoured by it.

Janet was about as annoying as a person could be and still be your friend, but Quentin was never bored around her. She was passionately loyal, and if she was obnoxious it was only because she was so deeply tender-hearted. It made her easily wounded, and when she was wounded she lashed out. She tortured everybody around her, but only because she was more tortured than anyone.

Even though he was part of the Physical Kids now, Quentin still spent most of his time with the other Third Years: he took his classes with them, and worked with them in P.A., and studied for exams with them, and sat with them at dinner. The Maze had been scrambled and redrawn over the summer—as it was every summer, it turned out—and they spent a week's worth of afternoons relearning it, yelling at one another over the tall hedges when they got lost or found an especially sweet shortcut.

They threw a party in honor of the fall equinox—there was a strong undercurrent of Wiccan sentiment at Brakebills, though hardly anybody took it seriously except the Naturals. They had a bonfire and music and a Wicker Man, and a light show by the Illusionists, and everybody stayed out way too late, their noses running in the cold fall air, their faces hot and red from the fire. Alice and Quentin taught the others the fire-shaping spell, which was a big hit, and Amanda Orloff revealed that she'd been brewing a batch of mead on the sly for the past couple of months. It was sweet and fizzy and disgusting, and they all drank way too much of it and felt like death the next day.

That fall Quentin's studies changed again. There was less rote learning of gestures and arcane languages, though God knows there was plenty of that, and more actual spellcasting. They spent an entire month on low-level architectural magic: spells to strengthen foundations and rain-proof roofs and keep gutters free of rotting leaves, all of which they practiced on a pathetic little shed barely larger than a doghouse. Just one spell, to make a roof resistant to lightning, took Quentin three days to memorize, grinding the gestures in a mirror to get them exactly right, at the proper speed and with the proper angles and emphasis. And then there was the incantation, which was in a corrupt old Bedouin Arabic and very tricky. And then Professor March conjured a little rainstorm which emitted a single lightning bolt that sheared through it in one eye-searing, ego-demolishing instant, while Quentin stood there getting soaked to the skin.

On alternate Tuesdays Quentin worked with Bigby, the Physical Kids' unofficial faculty advisor, who turned out be a small man with large liquid eyes and close-cropped gray hair who dressed neatly, if extremely affectedly, in a long Victorian-looking duster. His posture was slightly hunched, but he didn't seem otherwise frail or crippled. Quentin had the impression that Bigby was a political refugee from somewhere. He was always making vague noises about the conspiracy that had ousted him, and what he would do following his inevitable return to power. He had the stiff, wounded dignity of the deposed intelligentsia.

One afternoon during a seminar—Bigby specialized in ridiculously difficult enchantments that transmuted elements by manipulating their structure on a quantum level—he paused and performed an odd gesture: he reached back behind first one shoulder, then the other, unbuttoning something back there. The movement reminded Quentin of nothing more than a woman unhooking her bra. When Bigby was finished four magnificent insect wings like a dragonfly's, two on each side, sprang out from behind him. He flexed them with a deep, satisfied sigh.

The wings were gauzy and iridescent. They disappeared for a second in a buzz of activity, then reappeared as they became still.

"Sorry," he said. "Couldn't stand it a minute more."

It never stopped, the weirdness of this place. It just went on and on.

"Professor Bigby, are you a—" Quentin stopped. A what? An elf? An angel? He was being rude, but he couldn't help it. "Are you a fairy?"

Bigby smiled a pained smile. His wings made a dry chitinous rattle.

"Pixie, technically," he said.

He seemed a little sensitive about it.

One morning, very early, Professor March was giving a lecture on weather magic and summoning cyclonic wind patterns. For a portly man he was surprisingly spry. Just looking at him bouncing on his toes, with his red ponytail and his red face, made Quentin want to go back to bed. In the mornings Chambers served tarry black espresso which he smelted in a

delicate, gilded-glass exotic Turkish device. But it was all gone by the time
Quentin came down for class.

He closed his eyes. When he opened them again Professor March was
addressing him directly.

". . . between a subtropical cyclone and an extratropical? Quentin? In
the French, please, if you can."

Quentin blinked. He must have drifted off.

"The difference?" he hazarded. "There is no difference?"

There was a long, awkward pause, into which Quentin inserted more
words in an attempt to find out what exactly the question had been, and
to say "baroclinic zones" as many times as possible just in case they were
relevant. People shifted in their chairs. March, having caught the delicious
scent of humiliation, was prepared to wait. Quentin waited, too. There was
something in the reading about this. He'd actually done it, that was the
injustice of it.

The moment stretched on and on. His face was on fire. This wasn't even
magic, it was meteorology.

"I don't understand—" came a voice from the back of the classroom.

"I'm asking Quentin, Amanda."

"But maybe you could clarify something?" It was Amanda Orloff. She
persisted, with the shit-eating blitheness of somebody who had academic
cred to burn. "For the rest of us? Whether these are barotropic cyclones or
not? I find it a little confusing."

"They are all barotropic, Amanda," March said, exasperated. "It's irrel-
evant. All tropical cyclones are barotropic."

"But I thought one was barotropic and one was baroclinic," Alice put in.

The resulting mass wrangle ended up being so inane and time-
consuming that March was forced to abandon Quentin and move on or
lose the entire thread of the lecture. If he could have done so unobtru-
sively, Quentin would have run back to where Amanda Orloff was sitting
and kissed her on her broad, unmoisturized forehead. Instead he settled for
blowing her a kiss when March wasn't looking.

March had segued into a lengthy spell that involved sketching an elaborate mandala-like symbol on the chalkboard. He stopped every thirty seconds and stepped back to the edge of the stage, hands on hips, whispering
to himself, then dove back into the design. The point of the spell was fairly

trivial—it either guaranteed hail or prevented it, one or the other, Quentin wasn't really following, and anyway the principle was the same.

Either way, Professor March was struggling with it. The spell was in a very proper and precise Medieval Dutch that evidently wasn't his forte. It occurred to Quentin that it might be nice if he screwed it up. He hadn't particularly enjoyed being called out on technical minutiae this early in the morning. He would play a tiny prank.

Brakebills classrooms were proofed against most forms of mischief, but it was well known that the podium was any teacher's Achilles' heel. You couldn't do much to it, but the wards on it weren't quite ironclad, and with a lot of effort and some body English you could get it to rock back and forth a little. Maybe that would be enough to throw Professor March (the students called him "Death" March) off his game. Quentin made a few small gestures under his desk, between his knees. The podium stirred, as if it were stretching a kink in its back, then became inert again. Success.

March was reeling off some extra Old High Dutch. His attention flicked down at the podium as he felt it move, and he hesitated but recovered his concentration and forged ahead. It was either that or start the whole spell over.

Quentin was disappointed. But Infallible Alice leaned over.

"Idiot," she whispered. "He dropped the second syllable. He should have said—"

Just then, for an instant, the film of reality slipped off the spokes of its projector. Everything went completely askew and then righted itself again as if nothing had happened. Except that, like a continuity error in a movie, there was now a man standing behind Professor March.

He was a small man, conservatively dressed in a neat gray English suit and a maroon club tie that was fixed in place with a silver crescent-moon pin. Professor March, who was still talking, didn't seem to realize he was there—the man looked out at the Third Years archly, conspiratorially, as if they were sharing a joke at the teacher's expense. There was something odd about the man's appearance—Quentin couldn't seem to make out his face. For a second he couldn't figure out why, and then he realized it was because there was a small leafy branch in front of it that partially obscured his features. The branch came from nowhere. It was attached to nothing. It just hung there in front of the man's face.

Then Professor March stopped speaking and froze in place.

Alice had stopped, too. The room was silent. A chair creaked. Quentin couldn't move either. There was nothing restraining him, but the line between his brain and his body had been cut. Was the man doing this? Who was he? Alice was still leaned over slightly in his direction, and a flyaway wisp of her hair hung in his field of vision. He couldn't see her eyes; the angle was wrong. Everything and everybody was still. The man on the stage was the only thing in the world still in motion.

Quentin's heart started to pound. The man cocked his head and frowned, as if he could hear it. Quentin didn't understand what had happened, but something had gone wrong. Adrenaline poured into his bloodstream, but it had nowhere to go. His brain was boiling in its own juices. The man began strolling around the stage, exploring his new environment. His demeanor was that of a gentleman balloonist who had accidentally touched down in exotic surroundings: inquisitive, amused. With the branch in front of his face his intentions were impossible to read.

He circled Professor March. There was something strange about the way he moved, something too fluid about his gait. When he walked into the light, Quentin saw that he wasn't quite human, or if he had been once he wasn't anymore. Below the cuffs of his white shirt his hands had three or four too many fingers.

Fifteen minutes crawled by, then half an hour. Quentin couldn't turn his head, and the man moved in and out of his field of view. He puttered with Professor March's equipment. He toured the auditorium. He took out a knife and pared his fingernails. Objects stirred and shifted restlessly in place whenever he walked too near them. He picked up an iron rod from March's demonstration table and bent it like a piece of licorice. Once he cast a spell—he spoke too fast for Quentin to catch the details—that made all the dust in the room fly up and whirl crazily in the air before settling down again. It had no other obvious effect. When he cast the spell, the extra fingers on his hands bent sideways and backward.

An hour passed, then another. Quentin's fear came and went and came back in huge sweating rushes, crashing waves. He was sure something very bad was happening, it just wasn't clear yet exactly what. He knew it had something to do with his joke on March. How could he have been so stupid? In a cowardly way he was glad he couldn't move. It spared him from having to attempt something brave.

The man seemed barely aware that he was in a room full of people. There was something grotesquely comic about him—his silence was like that of a mime. He approached a ship's clock that hung at the back of the stage and slowly put his fist through it—he didn't punch it, he forced his hand into its face, breaking the glass and snapping the hands and crushing the mechanism inside until he was satisfied that it was destroyed. It was as if he thought he would hurt it more that way.

Class should have been over ages ago. Somebody on the outside must have noticed by now. Where were they? Where was Fogg? Where the hell was that paramedic-nurse-woman when you really needed her? He wished he knew what Alice was thinking. He wished he could have turned his head just a few degrees more before he'd been frozen, so he could see her face.

Amanda Orloff's voice broke the silence. She must have gotten loose somehow and was chanting a spell, rhythmically and rapidly but calmly. The spell was like nothing Quentin had ever heard, an angry, powerful piece of magic, full of vicious fricatives—it was offensive magic, battle magic, designed to literally rip an opponent to pieces. Quentin wondered how she'd even learned it. Just knowing a spell like that was way off-limits at Brakebills, let alone casting it. But before she could finish her voice became muffled. It went higher and higher, faster and faster, like a tape speeding up, then faded out before she could finish. The silence returned.

Morning turned into afternoon in a fever dream of panic and boredom. Quentin went numb. He heard signs of activity from outside. He could see only one window, and that was out of the very corner of his eye, but something was going on out there, blocking the light. There were sounds of hammering and, very faintly, six or seven voices chanting in unison. A tremendous, silent flash of light burst behind the door to the corridor with such force that the thick wood glowed translucent for an instant. There were rumblings as if somebody were trying to break through the floor from underneath. None of this visibly bothered the man in the gray suit.

In the window a single red leaf flapped crazily in the wind on the end of a bare branch, having hung on longer into the fall than any of its fellows.

Quentin watched it. The wind flailed the leaf back and forth on the end of its stem. It seemed like the most beautiful thing he had ever seen. All he wanted was to go on looking at it for one minute longer. He would give anything for that, just one more minute with his little red leaf.

He must have slipped into a trance, or fallen asleep—he didn't remember. He woke up to the sound of the man on stage singing softly and high under his breath. His voice was surprisingly tender:

> *"Bye, baby Bunting*
> *Daddy's gone a-hunting*
> *Gone to get a rabbit skin*
> *To wrap his baby Bunting in"*

He lapsed into humming. Then, with no warning, he vanished.

It happened so silently and so suddenly that at first Quentin didn't notice he was gone. In any case his departure was upstaged by Professor March, who'd been standing onstage the entire time with his mouth open. The instant the man was gone March crumpled forward bonelessly off the stage and knocked himself cold on the hardwood floor.

Quentin tried to stand up. Instead he slid off his chair, down onto the floor between the rows of seats. His arms, legs, and back were hideously cramped. There was no strength in them. Slowly, lying on the floor in a mixture of agony and relief, he stretched out his legs. Delicious bubbles of pain released in his knees, as if he were finally unbending them after a trans-hemispherical flight in coach. Tears of relief started in his eyes. It was over. The man was finally gone and nothing terrible had happened. Alice was groaning, too. A pair of shoes, probably hers, was in his face. The whole room rocked with moans and sobs.

Afterward Quentin would learn that Fogg had mustered the entire staff almost immediately, as soon as the man had made his appearance. The school's defensive spells detected him instantly, even if they didn't keep him out. By all accounts Fogg made a surprisingly competent battlefield commander: calm, organized, rapid and accurate in his assessment of the situation, skillful in his deployment of the resources at his disposal.

Over the course of the morning an entire temporary scaffold had been constructed around the outside of the tower. Professor Heckler, wearing a welder's helmet to shield his eyes, had nearly set the tower on fire with pyrotechnical attacks. Professor Sunderland had heroically attempted to phase herself through the wall, but to no avail, and anyway it wasn't clear what she would have done if she succeeded. Even Bigby made an appearance, deploying some exotic nonhuman witchcraft that—Quentin got the impression—had made the rest of the faculty a little uncomfortable.

That evening after dinner, after the usual announcements about clubs and events and activities had been sullenly and desultorily attended to, Dean Fogg addressed the student body to try to explain what had happened.

He stood at the head of the long dining room table, looking older than usual, as the candles guttered down and the First Years gloomily cleared the last of the silverware. He fussed with his cuffs and touched his temples where he was losing his thin blond hair.

"It will not come as a surprise to many of you that there are other worlds besides our own," he began. "This is not conjecture, it is fact. I have never been to these worlds, and you will never go there. The art of passing between worlds is an area of magic about which very little is known. But we do know that some of these worlds are inhabited.

"Probably the beast we met today was physically quite vast." ("The Beast" was what Fogg called the thing in the gray suit, and afterward nobody ever referred to it any other way.) "What we saw would have been a small part of it, an extremity it chose to push into our sphere of being, like a toddler groping around in a tide pool. Such phenomena have been observed before. They are known in the literature as Excrescences.

"Its motivations are difficult to guess." He sighed heavily. "To such beings we look like swimmers paddling timidly across the surface of their world, silhouetted against the light from above, sometimes diving a little below the surface but never going very deep. Ordinarily they pay no attention to us. Unfortunately something about Professor March's incantation today caught the Beast's attention. I understand it may have been corrupted or interrupted in some way. That error offered the Beast an opportunity to enter our world."

At this Quentin convulsed inwardly but kept his face composed. It had been him. He had done it. Fogg went on.

"The Beast spiraled up out of the depths, like a deep-water shark intent on seizing a swimmer from below. Its motivations are impossible to imagine, but it did appear as if it was looking for something, or someone. I do not know whether it found what it was looking for. We may never know."

Ordinarily Fogg projected an air of certainty and confidence, tempered by his natural slight ridiculousness, but that night he looked disoriented. He lost his train of thought. He fingered his tie.

"The incident is finished now. The students who witnessed the incident will all be examined, medically and magically, and then cleansed in case the Beast has marked or tagged or tainted them. Tomorrow's classes are canceled."

He stopped there and left the room abruptly. Everybody had thought he would say more.

But all that came much later. Lying on the floor after the attack, the agony fading from his arms and legs and back, Quentin felt only good things. He felt relieved to be alive. Disaster had been averted. He had made a terrible mistake, but everything was all right now. He felt a profound gratitude for the old, splintery wooden underside of the chair he was looking up at. It was fascinating and beautiful. He could have looked at it forever. It was even a little thrilling to have been through something like that and lived to tell about it. In a way he was a hero. He breathed deeply and felt the good solid floor under his back. The first thing he wanted to do, he realized, was to put his hand reassuringly on Alice's warm soft ankle, which was next to his head. He was so grateful to be able to finally look at her again.

He didn't know yet that Amanda Orloff was dead. The Beast had eaten her alive.

LOVELADY

The rest of Quentin's Third Year at Brakebills went by beneath a gray watercolor wash of quasi-military vigilance. In the weeks that followed the attack the school was locked down both physically and magically. Faculty members wandered the grounds retracing the lines of its ancient defensive spells, renewing and strengthening them and casting new ones. Professor Sunderland spent an entire day walking backward all the way around the school's perimeter, scattering colored powders on the snow behind her in carefully braided trails, her plump cheeks turning pink with cold. She was followed by Professor Van der Weghe, who checked her work, and preceded by a gaggle of attentive students who cleared brush and fallen logs out of her path and resupplied her with materiel. It had to be done in one unbroken circuit.

Cleansing the auditorium was just a matter of ringing a few bells and burning sage in the corners, but resetting the school's main wards took a solid week; according to student rumor they were all cinched to an enormous worked-iron totem kept in a secret room at the campus's exact geographical center, wherever that was, but nobody had ever seen it. Professor March, who after his ordeal never quite lost a certain anxious, hunted look, roamed endlessly in and out of the school's many basements and sub-basements and cellars and catacombs, where he obsessively tended and reinforced the foundation spells that secured them against attack from below. The Third Years had made a bonfire at their Equinox party, but now the faculty made a real bonfire, fed with specially prepared cedar logs, dried and peeled and as straight as railroad ties, stacked in an arcane, eye-bending configuration like a giant Chinese puzzle that took Professor Heckler all day to get right. When he finally lit it, using a twist of paper with words scribbled on it in Russian, it burned like magnesium. They were discouraged from looking directly at it.

In a way it was an education in itself, a chance to watch real magic being worked, with real things at stake. But there was no fun in it. There was only silence at dinner, and useless anger, and a new kind of dread. One morning they found the room of a First Year boy cleared out; he'd dropped out and gone home overnight. It was not uncommon to come across conclaves of three or four girls—girls who mere weeks earlier had actively avoided sitting next to Amanda Orloff at dinner—perched together on the stony rim of a fountain in the Maze, weeping and shivering. There were two more fights. As soon as he was satisfied that the foundations were taken care of, Professor March went on sabbatical, and those who claimed to know—i.e., Eliot—put the odds of his ever coming back at approximately zero.

Sometimes Quentin wished he could run away, too. He thought he would be shunned for the little joke he'd played on March with the podium, but the strange thing was that nobody said anything about it. He almost wished they would. He didn't know whether he'd committed the perfect crime or a crime so public and unspeakable that nobody could bring themselves to confront him about it in broad daylight. He was trapped: he couldn't grieve properly for Amanda because he felt like he'd killed her, and he couldn't atone for killing her because he couldn't confess, not even to Alice. He didn't know how. So instead he kept his little particle of shame and filth inside, where it could fester and turn septic.

This was the kind of disaster Quentin thought he'd left behind the day he walked into that garden in Brooklyn. Things like this didn't happen in Fillory: there was conflict, and even violence, but it was always heroic and ennobling, and anybody really good and important who bought it along the way came back to life at the end of the book. Now there was a rip in the corner of his perfect world, and fear and sadness were pouring in like freezing filthy water through a busted dam. Brakebills felt less like a secret garden and more like a fortified encampment. He wasn't in a safe little story where wrongs were automatically righted; he was still in the real world, where bad, bitter things happened for no reason, and people paid for things that weren't their fault.

A week after the incident Amanda Orloff's parents came to collect her things. No special fuss was made over them, at their request, but Quentin happened by one afternoon while they were saying goodbye to the Dean. All of Amanda's belongings fit into one trunk and one pathetically small paisley-fabric suitcase.

Quentin's heart seized up as he watched them. He was sure they could see his guilt; he felt like he was covered in it, sticky with it. But they ignored him. Mr. and Mrs. Orloff looked more like siblings than husband and wife: both six feet tall and broad-shouldered, with dishwater hair, his high and tight, hers in a businesslike shag. They seemed to be walking in a daze—Dean Fogg was guiding them by the elbows around something Quentin couldn't see—and it took him a minute to figure out that they were heavily enchanted, so that even now they wouldn't understand the nature of the school that their daughter had attended.

That August the Physical Kids straggled back from summer vacation early. They spent the week before classes camping out in the Cottage, playing pool and not studying and making a project out of drinking their way jigger by jigger through an old and viscous and thoroughly disgusting decanter of port Eliot had found at the back of a cabinet in the kitchen. But the mood was sober and subdued. Incredibly, Quentin was now a Fourth Year at Brakebills.

"We have to have a welters team," Janet announced one day.

"No," Eliot said, "we don't."

He lay with one arm over his face on an old leather couch. They were in the library in the Cottage, exhausted from having done nothing all day.

"Yes, actually we do, *Eliot.*" She nudged him sharply in the ribs with her foot. "Bigby told me. There's a tournament. Everybody has to play. They just haven't announced it yet."

"Shit," Eliot, Alice, Josh, and Quentin all said in unison.

"I call equipment manager," Alice added.

"Why?" Josh moaned. "Why are they doing this to us? *Why, God?*"

"It's for morale," Janet said. "Fogg says our spirits need elevating after last year. Organized welters is part of a 'return to normalcy.'"

"My morale was fine until a minute ago. Fuck, I can't stand that game.

It's a perversion of good magic. A perversion, I say!" Josh waved a finger at nobody in particular.

"Too bad, it's compulsory. And it's by Discipline, so we're a team. Even Quentin"—she patted his head—"who still doesn't have one."

"Thanks for that."

"I vote Janet captain," Eliot said.

"Of course I'm captain. And as captain it is my happy duty to inform you that your first practice is in fifteen minutes."

Everybody groaned and stirred and then settled themselves more comfortably where they were.

"Janet?" Josh said. "Stop doing this."

"I've never even played," Alice said. "I don't know the rules."

She lay on the rug paging limply through an old atlas. It was full of ancient maps in which the seas were populated with lovingly engraved marginal monsters, though in these maps the proportions were inverted, and the monsters were far larger and more numerous than the continents. Alice had acquired a pair of uncharacteristically hip rectangular glasses over the summer.

"Oh, you'll pick it right up," Eliot said. "Welters is fun—and educational!"

"Don't worry." Janet leaned down and gave the back of Alice's head a maternal kiss. "Nobody really knows the rules."

"Except Janet," Josh said.

"Except me. I'll see you all there at three."

She flounced happily out of the room.

In the end it came down to the fact that none of them had anything better to do, which Janet had clearly been counting on. They reassembled by the welters board looking bedraggled and unpromising in the baking summer heat. It was so bright out you could barely stand to look at the grass. Eliot clutched the sticky decanter of port, the sleeves of his dress shirt rolled up. Just seeing it made Quentin feel dehydrated. Blue summer sky blazed in the water squares. A grasshopper collided with Quentin's pants and clung there.

"So," Janet said, climbing the ladder to the weather-beaten wooden judge's chair in her perilously short skirt. "Who knows how we start?"

Starting, it emerged, involved picking a square and throwing a stone called the globe onto it. The stone was rough marble, bluish in color—it did look a little like a globe—and about the size of a Ping-Pong ball, though it was weirdly heavy. Quentin turned out to be unexpectedly talented at this feat, which was performed at various times during the game. The real trick was to avoid plunking it into a water square, in which case the game was forfeit, plus it was a pain to fish the globe out of the water.

Alice and Eliot were on the same team, facing off against Josh and Quentin, with Janet refereeing. Janet wasn't the most assiduous student of the Physical Kids—that was Alice—or the most naturally gifted—Eliot— but she was ferally competitive, and she'd decided to acquire a total command of the technical intricacies of welters, which really was an amazingly complicated game.

"Without me you people would be lost!" Janet said, and it was true.

The game was half strategy, half spell-casting. You captured squares with magic, or protected them, or recaptured them by superseding an earlier spell. Water squares were the easiest, metal the hardest—they were reserved for summonings and other exotic enchantments. Eventually a player was supposed to step bodily onto the board, becoming in effect a playing piece in his or her own game, and as such vulnerable to direct, personal attacks. As he approached the edge the meadow around Quentin seemed to shrink, and the board expanded, as if it were at the center of a fisheye lens. The trees lost some of their color, becoming dim and silvery.

Things went quickly in the early rounds as both sides captured uncontested squares in a free-for-all land grab. As in chess, there were any number of conventional openings that had been worked out and optimized long ago. But once all the free squares were gone they had to start slugging it out head to head. The afternoon wore on, with long breaks for Janet's highly technical welters tutorials. Eliot disappeared for twenty minutes and came back with six slender bottles of a very dry Finger Lakes Riesling he'd apparently been saving for just such an emergency, in two tin buckets full of melting ice. He hadn't thought to bring any glasses, so they swigged straight from the bottles.

Quentin still didn't have much of a capacity for alcohol, and the more wine he drank the less he could focus on the details of the game, which were getting hellishly complex. Apparently it was legal to transmute squares from one kind to another, and even make them slide around and switch places on the board somehow. By the time the players themselves had stepped onto the board, everybody was so drunk and confused that Janet had to tell them where to stand, which she did with towering condescension.

Not that anybody really cared. The sun drifted down behind the trees, dappling the grass with shadows, and the blue of the sky deepened to a luminous aqua. The air was bathwater warm. Josh fell asleep on the square he was supposed to be defending and sprawled across a whole row. Eliot did his impression of Janet, and Janet pretended to get mad. Alice took off her shoes and dabbled her feet in a temporarily uncontested water square. Their voices drifted up and got lost in the summer leaves. The wine was almost gone, the empty bottles bobbing around in the tin buckets, which were now full of lukewarm water in which a wasp had drowned.

Everyone was pretending to be bored to tears, or maybe they actually were, but Quentin wasn't. He was unexpectedly happy, though he instinctively kept it a secret. In fact he was so full of joy and relief he could barely breathe. Like a receding glacier the ordeal of the Beast had left behind it a changed world, jumbled and scraped and raw, but the earth was finally putting up new green shoots again. Fogg's idiotic welters plan had actually worked. The gray gloom the Beast had cast over the school was retreating. It was all right for them to be teenagers again, at least for a little longer. He felt forgiven, though he didn't even know by whom.

Quentin imagined how they would all look from above. If somebody were to gaze down on them from a low-flying airplane, or a wandering dirigible, five people strewn around the neat little welters board on the grounds of their secret, exclusive magical enclave, their voices soft and unintelligible from a distance, how contented and complete in themselves that observer would believe them all to be. And it was actually true. The observer would be right. It was all real.

"Without me," Janet said again, with fierce glee, blotting tears of laughter with the heel of her hand, "you people would be *lost*."

If welters restored some of Quentin's lost equilibrium, it presented a whole new kind of problem for Josh. They kept on practicing through the first month of the semester, and Quentin gradually got the hang of the game. It wasn't really about knowing the spells, or the strategy, though you did have to know them. It was more about getting spells off perfectly when you had to—it was about that sense of power that lived somewhere in your chest, that made a spell strong and vital. Whatever it was, you had to be able to find it when you needed it.

Josh never knew what he would find. At one practice Quentin watched him go up against Eliot over one of the two metal squares on the board. These were made of a tarnished silvery stuff—one actually was silver, the other was palladium, whatever that was—with fine swirling lines and tiny italic words etched into them.

Eliot had chosen a fairly basic enchantment that created a small, softly glowing orb. Josh attempted a counterspell, muttering it half-heartedly while sketching a few cursory gestures with his large fingers. He always looked embarrassed when he cast spells, as if he never believed they were actually going to work.

But as he finished, the day went slightly faded and sepia toned, the way it might if a cloud drifted in front of the sun, or in the first moments of an eclipse.

"What the hell . . . ?" Janet said, squinting up at the sky.

Josh had successfully defended the square—he'd abolished Eliot's will-o'-the-wisp—but he'd gone too far. Somehow he'd created its inverse, a black hole: he'd punched a drain hole in the afternoon, and the daylight was swirling into it. The five Physical Kids gathered around in the amber light to look, as if it were some unusual and possibly venomous beetle. Quentin had never seen anything quite like it. It was like some heavy-duty appliance had been turned on somewhere, sucking up the energy needed to light the world and causing a local brown-out.

Josh was the only one who didn't seem bothered by this.

"How you like me now?" He did a victorious-chicken dance. "Huh? How do you like Josh now!"

"Wow," Quentin said. He backed away a step. "Josh, what is that thing?"

"I don't know, I just waved my little fingers—" He waggled his fingers in Eliot's face. A soft breeze was kicking up.

"Okay, Josh," Eliot said. "You got me. Shut it down."

"Had enough? Is it too real for you, magic man?"

"Seriously, Josh," Alice said. "Please get rid of that thing, it's creeping us out."

By now the whole field was plunged in deep twilight, even though it was only two in the afternoon. Quentin couldn't look directly at the space above the metal square, but the air around it looked wavy and distorted, the grass behind it distant and smeared. Underneath it, in a perfect circle that could have been ruled by a compass, the blades of grass were standing up perfectly straight, like splinters of green glass. The vortex drifted lazily to one side, toward the edge of the board, and a nearby oak tree leaned toward it with a monstrous creaking sound.

"Josh, don't be an idiot," Eliot snapped. Josh had stopped celebrating. He watched his creation nervously.

The tree groaned and listed ominously. Roots popped underground like muffled rifle shots.

"Josh! Josh!" Janet shouted.

"All right already! All right!" Josh scrubbed out the spell, and the hole in space vanished.

He looked pale but regretful, resentful: they'd pissed on his parade. They stood silent in a half circle around the half-toppled oak. One of its longest branches almost touched the ground.

Dean Fogg arranged an entire tournament schedule of weekend welters matches, culminating in a school championship at the end of the semester. To their surprise the Physical Kids tended to win their games. They even beat the snobby, standoffish Psychic group, who made up for any short-falls in their spellcasting ability with their uncannily prescient strategic instincts. Their run of success continued through October. Their only real rivals were the Natural Magic group, who in spite of their pacifist, sylvan ethos were annoyingly hyper-competitive about welters.

Bit by bit the summer atmosphere of balmy congeniality evaporated as the afternoons got colder and shorter and the demands of the game started to conflict with their already crushing academic workload. After a while welters became a chore just like anything else, except even more meaning-less. As Quentin and the other Physical Kids became less enthusiastic, Janet got shriller and pushier about the game, and her shrill pushiness became less endearing. She couldn't help it, it was just her neurotic need to control everything coming out to play, but that didn't make it any less of a pain in the ass for the rest of them. Theoretically they could have gotten out of it by tanking a match—it would only have taken one—but they didn't. Nobody quite had the heart, or the guts.

But Josh's inconsistency continued to be a problem. On the morning of the final game of the season, he didn't show up at all.

It was a Saturday morning in early November, and they were playing for the school championship—what Fogg had grandly christened the Brakebills Cup, although so far he hadn't produced any actual physical vessel that answered to that name. The grass around the welters field was tricked out with two ranks of grimly festive wooden bleachers that looked like something out of old newsreel footage of college sporting events, and which had probably been lying disassembled in numbered sections in some unimaginably dusty storeroom for decades. There was even a VIP box occupied by Dean Fogg and Professor Van der Weghe, who clutched a coffee cup in her pink-mittened hands.

The sky was gray, and a heavy wind made the leaves seethe in the trees. The gonfalons (in Brakebills blue and brown) strung along the backs of the bleachers fluttered and snapped. The grass was crunchy with frozen dew.

"Where the hell is he?" Quentin jogged in place to keep warm.

"I don't *know!*" Janet had her arms around Eliot's neck, clinging to him for warmth, which Eliot put up with irritably.

"Fuck him, let's start," he said. "I want to get this over with."

"We can't without Josh," Alice said firmly.

"Who says we can't?" Eliot tried to dislodge Janet, who clung to him relentlessly. "We're better off without him anyway."

"I'd rather lose with him," Alice said, "than win without him. Anyway, he's not dead. I saw him just after breakfast."

"If he doesn't show up soon, we're all going to die of exposure. He'll be the only one left alive to carry on our glorious fight."

Josh's absence made Quentin worried, about what he didn't know.

"I'll go find him," Quentin said.

"Don't be ridiculous. He's probably—"

At that moment the officiating faculty member, a hale, brick-colored man named Professor Foxtree, strode up to them wrapped in an ankle-length down parka. Students respected him instinctively because of his easy good humor and because he was tall and Native American.

"What's the holdup?"

"We're short a player, sir," Janet told him. "Josh Hoberman is MIA."

"So?" Professor Foxtree hugged himself vigorously. His long hooked nose had a drop on the end of it. "Let's get this shit-show on the road, I'd like to be back in the senior common room by lunchtime. How many do you have?"

"Four, sir."

"It'll have to do."

"Three, actually," Quentin said. "Sorry, sir, but I have to find Josh. He should be here."

He didn't wait for an answer but set off back toward the House at a jog, his hands in his pockets, his collar turned up around his ears to block out the cold.

"Come on, Q!" he heard Janet say. And then, disgustedly, when it was clear he wasn't coming back: "Shit."

Quentin didn't know whether to be pissed off at Josh or worried about him, so he was both. Foxtree was right: it wasn't like the game actually mattered. Maybe the bastard just overslept, he thought as he half-ran over the hard, frosted turf of the Sea. At least he had his fat to keep him warm. The fat bastard.

But Josh wasn't in his bed. His room was a maelstrom of books and paper and laundry, as usual, some of it floating loosely in midair. Quentin walked down to the sunroom, but its only occupant was the aged Professor Brzezinski, the potions expert, who sat at the window, eyes closed, drenched in sun, his white beard flowing down over a stained old apron. An enormous fly bounced against one of the windowpanes. He looked asleep, but when Quentin was almost out the door he spoke.

"Looking for someone?"

Quentin stopped. "Yes, sir. Josh Hoberman. He's late for welters."

"Hoberman. The fat one."

The old man waved Quentin over with a blue-veined hand and fumbled a colored pencil and a piece of lined paper out of the pocket of his apron. With sure, rapid strokes Professor Brzezinski sketched a rough outline of the Brakebills campus. He muttered a few words in French and made a sign over it with one hand like a compass rose.

He held it up.

"What does this tell you?"

Quentin had expected magical special effects of some kind, but there was nothing. A corner of the map was stained from a coffee spill on the tray.

"Not a lot, sir."

"Really?" The old man studied the paper for himself, looking puzzled. He smelled like ozone, shattered air, as if he had recently been struck by lightning. "But this really is a very good locator spell. Look again."

"I don't see anything."

"That's right. And where on campus does even a very good locator spell not work?"

"I have no idea." Admitting ignorance promptly was the fastest way to get information out of a Brakebills professor.

"Try the library." Professor Brzezinski closed his eyes again, like an old walrus settling back down onto a sunny rock. "There are so many old seek-and-finds on that room, you can't find a Goddamned thing."

Quentin had spent very little time in the Brakebills library. Hardly anybody did if they could help it. Visiting scholars had been so aggressive over the centuries in casting locator spells to find the books they wanted, and spells of concealment to hide those same books from rival scholars, that the entire area was more or less opaque to magic, like a palimpsest that has been scribbled on over and over, past the point of legibility.

To make matters worse, some of the books had actually become migratory. In the nineteenth century Brakebills had appointed a librarian with a highly Romantic imagination who had envisioned a mobile library in which the books fluttered from shelf to shelf like birds, reorganizing themselves spontaneously under their own power in response to searches. For the first few months the effect was said to have been quite dramatic. A painting of the scene survived as a mural behind the circulation desk, with enormous atlases soaring around the place like condors.

But the system turned out to be totally impractical. The wear and tear on the spines alone was too costly, and the books were horribly disobedient. The librarian had imagined he could summon a given book to perch on his hand just by shouting out its call number, but in actuality they were just too willful, and some were actively predatory. The librarian was swiftly deposed, and his successor set about domesticating the books again, but even now there were stragglers, notably in Swiss History and Architecture 300–1399, that stubbornly flapped around near the ceiling. Once in a while an entire sub-sub-category that had long been thought safely dormant would take wing with an indescribable papery susurrus.

So the library was mostly empty, and it wasn't hard to spot Josh in an alcove off the second floor, sitting at a small square table across from a tall, cadaverously thin man with chiseled cheekbones and a pencil mustache. The man wore a black suit that hung on him. He looked like an undertaker.

Quentin recognized the thin man: he was the magical bric-a-brac dealer who turned up once or twice a year at Brakebills in his woodie station wagon, loaded down with a bizarre collection of charms and fetishes and relics. Nobody particularly liked him, but the students tolerated him, if only because he was unintentionally funny and annoyed the faculty, who were always on the verge of banning him permanently. He wasn't a magician himself and couldn't tell the difference between what was genuine and what was junk, but he took himself and his stock extremely seriously. His name was Lovelady.

He'd turned up again shortly after the incident with the Beast, and some of the younger kids bought charms to protect themselves in the event of another attack. But Josh knew better than that. Or Quentin would have thought so.

"Hey," Quentin said, but as he started toward them he knocked his forehead against a hard invisible barrier.

Whatever it was was cool and squeaked like clean glass. It was soundproof, too: he could see their lips moving, but the alcove was silent.

He caught Josh's eye. There was a quick exchange with Lovelady, who peered over his shoulder at Quentin. Lovelady didn't look happy, but he picked up what looked like an ordinary glass tumbler that had been standing upside-down on the table and flipped it over. The barrier vanished.

"Hey," Josh said sullenly. "What's up?" His eyes were red, and the bags under them were dark and bruised-looking. He didn't look especially happy to see Quentin either.

"What's going on?" Quentin ignored Lovelady. "You know we have a match this morning, right?"

"Oh, man. Right. Game time." Josh smeared his right eye blearily with the heel of his hand. Lovelady watched them both, carefully husbanding his dignity. "How long do we have?"

"About negative half an hour."

"Oh, man," he said again. Josh put his forehead down on the table, then looked up suddenly at Lovelady. "Got anything for time travel? Time-turner or something?"

"Not at this time," Lovelady intoned gravely. "But I will make inquiries."

"Awesome." Josh stood up. He saluted smartly. "Send me an owl."

"Come on, they're waiting for us. Fogg is freezing his ass off."

"Good for him. Too much ass on that man anyway."

Quentin got Josh out of the library and heading toward the rear of the House, though he was moving slowly and with a worrying tendency to lurch into door frames and occasionally into Quentin.

He did an abrupt about-face.

"Hang on," he said. "Gotta get my quidditch costume. I mean uniform. I mean welters."

"We don't have uniforms."

"I know that," Josh snapped. "I'm drunk, I'm not delusional. I still need my winter coat."

"Jesus, man. It's not even ten o'clock." Quentin couldn't believe he'd been worried. This was the big mystery?

"Experiment. Thought it might relax me for the big game."

"Yeah?" Quentin said. "Really? How's that working out for you?"

"It was just a little Scotch, for Christ's sake. My parents sent me a bottle of Lagavulin for my birthday. Eliot's the lush around here, not me." Josh looked up at him with his crafty, stubbly monk's face. "Relax, I know what I can handle."

"Yeah, you're handling the hell out of it."

"Oh, who gives a shit!" Josh was turning nasty. If Quentin was going to get mad, he would get madder. "You were probably hoping I wouldn't show up and blow your precious game for you. I just wish you had the balls to admit it. God, you should hear Eliot do you behind your back. You're as much of a cheerleader as Janet is. At least she has the tits for it."

"If I wanted to win," Quentin said coldly, "I would have left you in the library. Everybody else wanted to."

He waited in the doorway, furious, arms folded, while Josh rifled through his clothes. He snatched his coat off the back of a desk chair, causing the chair to fall over. He let it lie there. Quentin wondered if it was true about Eliot. If Josh was trying to hurt him, he certainly knew where to stick the knife in.

They set off down the hall together in silence.

"All right," Josh said finally. He sighed. "Look, you know how I'm kind of a fuck-up, right?"

Quentin said nothing, stone-faced. He didn't feel like playing into Josh's personal drama right now.

"Well, I am. And don't bother with the self-esteem lecture, it's gone so far beyond what you even want to know about. I've always been a smart guy, but I'm a low-grades/high-test-scores kind of smart guy. If it wasn't for Fogg they would have kicked me out after last semester."

"All right."

"Look, all the rest of you can go around playing Peter Perfect, and that's fine, but I have to work my ass off just to stay here! If you saw my grades— you guys don't even know the alphabet goes that high."

"We all have to work at it," Quentin said a little defensively. "Well, except Eliot."

"Yeah, okay, fine. But it's fun for you. You get off on it. That's your thing." Josh shouldered his way through the French doors, out into the late-autumn morning, shrugging his way into his heavy overcoat at the same time. "Fuck, it's cold. Look, I love it here, but I'm not going to make it on my own. I just don't know where it comes from."

With no warning he grabbed the front of Quentin's coat and pushed him up against the wall of the House.

"Don't you get it? I don't know where it comes from! I do a spell, I don't know if it's going work or not!" His normally soft, placid face had worked itself into a mask of anger. "You look for the power, and it's just there! Me, I never know! I never know if it's going to be there when I need it. It comes and it goes and I don't even know why!"

"Okay, okay." Quentin put his hands on Josh's shoulders, trying to calm him down. "Jesus. You're hurting my man-boobs."

Josh let go of him and stalked off in the direction of the Maze. Quentin caught up with him.

"So you thought Lovelady could help."

"I thought he could . . . I don't know." Josh shrugged helplessly. "Give me a little boost. Just make it so I could count on it a little more."

"By selling you some trash he got off eBay."

"You know, he has interesting connections." Just like that Josh was finding his good humor again. He always did. "They act all superior when we're watching, but some of the faculty buy from Lovelady. I heard a couple of years ago Van der Weghe bought an old brass door knocker off him that turned out to be a Hand of Oberon. Chambers uses it to cut down trees around the Sea.

"I thought he could sell me a charm. Something to bring my grades up. I know I act like I don't care, but I want to stay here, Quentin! I don't want to go back out there!"

He pointed off in the general direction of the outside world. The grass was wet and half frozen, and the Sea was misty.

"I want you to stay, too," Quentin said. His anger was going, too. "But Lovelady—Jesus, maybe you are an idiot. Why didn't you just go to Eliot for help?"

"Eliot. He's the last guy I'd talk to. Don't you see how he looks at me in class? A guy like that—okay, he's had it tough, in lots of ways, but this isn't the kind of thing he understands."

"What did Lovelady try to sell you?

"Bunch of old dust bunnies. Bastard told me they were Aleister Crowley's ashes."

"What were you going to do with them anyway? Snort them?"

They pushed their way through the scrim of trees around the field. It was a grim scene. Eliot and Janet were huddled at one end of the board looking bedraggled and thoroughly chilled. Poor Alice was out on the board, squatting on a stone square and hugging herself miserably. The Natural Magic group was at the other end; despite the Physical Kids' shortfall, they had chosen to field the full five players. Not very sportsmanlike. It was hard to see their faces—in an effort to intimidate their opponents they wore hooded druid robes that somebody had sewn together out of a bunch of green velvet curtains. They weren't made to get wet.

The Physical Kids gave a ragged cheer when Josh and Quentin appeared.

"My heroes," Janet said sarcastically. "Where did you find him?"

"Somewhere warm and dry," Josh said.

They were being beaten badly, but Josh's surprise reappearance revived their fighting spirit. On his first turn Josh went for the silver square, and after five solid minutes of Gregorianesque chanting he improbably brought into being a fiery elemental—a slow-moving, woodchuck-size salamander that looked like it was constructed out of glowing orange embers, and which went on to laconically capture two adjacent squares for good measure. It then settled down on its six legs to smolder and watch the rest of the match, raindrops sizzling and skating off its charred scales.

The Physical Kids' comeback had the unfortunate effect of lengthening the game beyond all possibility of enjoyment. It was the longest game they'd played all season; it was shaping up to be the longest welters game anybody could remember. Finally after another hour the handsome, Scandinavian-looking captain of the Natural team—whom Quentin was pretty sure Janet used to date—toed the edge of the sand square he stood on, gathered his wet velvet robe around him regally, and caused an elegantly twisted little olive tree to curl up out of a grass square in the Physicals' home row.

"Suck it!" he said.

"That's the win," Professor Foxtree called from the judge's chair. He was visibly catatonic from boredom. "Unless you Physicals can match it. If not, then this damn game is finally over. Somebody throw the globe."

"Come on, Q," Eliot said. "My fingernails are blue. My lips are probably blue."

"Your balls are probably blue," Quentin said. He picked up the heavy marble from where it rested in a stone bowl by the edge of the board.

He looked around at the strange scene he stood at the center of. They were still in it—they'd been down, but they'd come almost all the way back, and he hardly ever missed with the globe. Mercifully there was no wind, but a mist was gathering, and it was getting hard to see the far end of the board. The afternoon was silent except for the dripping of the trees.

"Quentin!" a boy's voice called hoarsely from the bleachers. "Quen-*tin!*"

The Dean was still up in the VIP box, gamely miming enthusiasm. He blew his nose loudly into a silk handkerchief. The sun was a distant memory.

All at once a pleasant feeling of lightness and warmth came over Quentin—it was so vivid, and so divorced from the freezing cold reality all around him, that he wondered if somebody was doing some surreptitious magic on him; he looked suspiciously at the smoldering salamander, but it loftily ignored him. There was the familiar sense of the world narrowing to the limits of the board, trees and people shrinking and curving away around it, becoming silvery, solarized. Quentin's view took in the miserable Josh, pacing by the edge of the board and taking deep breaths, and Janet, who was clenching her jaw and jutting it at him fiercely, hungrily, her arm through Eliot's, whose eyes were fixed on some invisible scenery in the middle distance.

It all felt very far away. None of it mattered. That was the funny thing—it was incredible that he hadn't seen it before. He would have to try and explain this to Josh. He had done a terrible, stupid thing in the classroom, the day Amanda Orloff had died, and he would never get over it, but he'd figured out how to live with it. You just had to get some idea of what matters and what doesn't, and how much, and try not to be scared of the stuff that doesn't. Put it in perspective. Something like that. Or otherwise what was the point? He didn't know if he could explain it to Josh. But maybe he could show him.

Quentin took off his coat, as if he were sloughing off a scratchy, too-small skin. He rolled his shoulders in the cold air; he knew it would be freezing in a minute, but for the moment it was just refreshing. He sighted on the blond Natural player in his idiotic robe, leaned to one side, and slung the globe sidearm at his knee. It hit the heavy velvet with an audible thump.

"Ow!" The Natural grabbed his knee and looked up at Quentin with an outraged expression. That would bruise. "Foul!"

"Suck it," Quentin said.

He whipped his shirt off over his head. Ignoring the rising yelps of dismay on all sides—it was so easy to ignore people when you understood how little power they really had over you—he walked over to where Alice stood, dumbstruck, on her square. He would probably regret this later, but God it was good to be a magician sometimes. He hoisted her over his shoulder fireman-style and jumped with her into the freezing, cleansing water.

MARIE BYRD LAND

Quentin had been wondering about the mystery of the Fourth Year ever since he got to Brakebills. Everybody did. The basic facts were common knowledge: every year in September half the Fourth Years swiftly and silently disappeared from the House overnight. No one discussed their absence. The vanished Fourth Years reappeared at the end of December looking thin and drawn and generally chewed over, to no particular comment—it was considered fatally bad form to say anything about it. They quietly mixed back into the general Brakebills population, and that was that. The rest of the Fourth Years vanished in January and came back at the end of April.

Now the first semester of Quentin's Fourth Year was almost over, and he had acquired not one single new piece of information about what happened during that interval. The secret of where they went and what they did there, or what was done to them, was improbably well kept. Even students who took nothing else at Brakebills seriously were passionately serious on that one point: "Dude, I'm not even kidding, you so don't want to be asking me about that . . ."

The disaster of the Beast had thrown off the previous year's schedule. The regular contingent of Fourth Years had departed for the first semester—they were gone when it happened—but the second-semester group, which included Eliot, Janet, and Josh, had finished out the year at Brakebills as usual. To the extent that they speculated about it, they called themselves "the Spared." Apparently whatever the faculty had in store for them was nasty enough as it was without the added threat of assault by an interdimensional carnivore.

But now it was back to business as usual. This year half the Fourth Years departed on schedule, along with a handful of the Fifth Years: the ten Spared had been split up between the two semesters, five and five. Whether by accident or by design, the Physical Kids would all be shipping out together in January.

It was a regular topic of conversation around the battered billiard table in the Cottage.

"You know what I bet?" Josh said, one Sunday afternoon in December. They were treating hangovers with glasses of Coke and huge quantities of bacon. "I bet they make us go to normal college. Just some random state school where we have to read *Cannery Row* and debate the Stamp Act. And like the second day Eliot's going to be crying in the bathroom and begging for his foie gras and his malbec while some jock sodomizes him with a lacrosse stick."

"Um, did that just turn into your total gay fantasy halfway through?" Janet asked.

"I have it on good authority"—Eliot attempted to jump the cue ball over the 8 and failed completely, pocketing both, which seemed not to bother him at all—"on the *best* of authority, that the whole Fourth Year enigma is a front. It's all a hoax to scare off the faint of heart. You spend the whole semester on Fogg's private island in the Maldives, contemplating the infinities of the multiverse in grains of fine white beach sand while coolies bring you rum-and-tonics."

"I don't think they have 'coolies' in the Maldives," Alice said quietly. "It's been an independent republic since 1965."

"So how come everybody comes back all skinny?" Quentin asked. Janet and Eliot were playing, the rest of them lay on two beat-up Victorian couches. The room was small enough that they occasionally had to lean to one side to avoid the butt end of a cue.

"That's from all the skinny-dipping."

"Hork hork hork," said Janet.

"Quentin should be good at that," Josh added.

"Your fat ass could use some skinny-dipping."

"I don't want to go," Alice said. "Can't I get a doctor's note or something? Like when they let the Christian kids out of sex ed? Isn't anybody else worried?"

"Oh, I'm terrified." If he was joking, Eliot gave no sign of it. He handed Janet the cue ball. It was decorated with trompe-l'oeil lunar craters to look like the moon. "I'm not strong like the rest of you. I'm weak. I'm a delicate flower."

"Don't worry, delicate flower," Janet said. She made her shot without dropping her gaze, no-look. "Suffering will make you strong."

They came for Quentin one night in January.

He knew it would happen at night—it was always at breakfast that they noticed that the Fourth Years were gone. It must have been two or three in the morning, but he woke up instantly when Professor Van der Weghe knocked on his door. He knew what was going on. The sound of her husky European voice in the darkness reminded him of his first night at Brakebills, when she'd put him to bed after his Examination.

"It's time, Quentin," she called. "We are going up to the roof. Do not bring anything."

He stepped into his slippers. Outside a file of silent, rumpled Brakebills students stood on the stairs.

Nobody spoke as Professor Van der Weghe led them through a door in a stretch of wall that Quentin could have sworn had been blank the day before, between a pair of ten-foot-high oil paintings of clipper ships foundering in heavy seas. They shuffled up the dark wooden stairs without speaking, fifteen of them—ten Fourth Years, five leftover Fifth Years—everyone wearing identical navy blue Brakebills-issue pajamas. Despite Van der Weghe's orders, Gretchen sullenly gripped a worn black teddy bear along with her cane. Up ahead of them Professor Van der Weghe banged open a wooden trapdoor, and they filed out onto the roof.

It was an awkward perch, a long, narrow, windy strip with a shingled drop falling away steeply on either side. A low wrought-iron fence ran along the edge, providing absolutely no protection or reassurance whatsoever; in fact it was the perfect height to take you out at the knees if you accidentally backed into it. The night was bitingly cold, with a lively cross-breeze. The sky was lightly frosted with high, wind-whisked clouds luridly backlit by a gibbous moon.

Quentin hugged himself. Still nobody had said a word; no one even looked at anybody else. It was like they were all still half asleep, and a single word would have shattered the delicate dream in which they walked. Even the other Physical Kids were like strangers.

"Everyone take off your pajamas," Professor Van der Weghe called out.

Weirdly, they did. Everything was so surreal and trancelike already that it made perfect sense that they would all, guys and girls alike, get naked in front of each other in the freezing cold without a hint of self-consciousness. Afterward Quentin even remembered Alice putting a warm hand on his bare shoulder to steady herself as she stepped out of her pajama bottoms. Soon they were naked and shivering, their bare backs and buttocks pale in the moonlight, the starlit campus rolling away far below them, with the dark trees of the forest beyond.

Some of the students clutched their pajamas in both hands, but Professor Van der Weghe instructed them to drop them in a heap at their feet. Quentin's blew away and disappeared over the ledge, but he didn't try to stop them. It didn't matter. She moved down the line, dabbing a generous gob of chalky white paste on each forehead and both shoulders with her thumb as she passed. When she was done, she walked back the other way, lining them up, checking her work, making sure they were standing up straight. Finally she called out a single harsh syllable.

Instantly a huge soft weight pressed down on Quentin, settling on his shoulders, bending him forward. He crouched down, straining against it. He tried to fight it, to lift it. It was crushing him! He bit back panic. It flashed through his brain—the Beast was back!—but this was different. As he doubled over he felt his knees folding up into his belly, *merging* with it. Why wasn't Professor Van der Weghe helping them? Quentin's neck was stretching and stretching out and forward, out of his control. It was grotesque, a horrible dream. He wanted to vomit but couldn't. His toes were melting and flowing together, his fingers were elongating enormously and spreading out, and something soft and warm was bursting out of his arms and chest, covering him completely. His lips pouted grotesquely and hardened. The narrow strip of roof rose up to meet him.

And then the weight was gone. He squatted on the gray slate roof, breathing hard. At least he didn't feel cold anymore. He looked at Alice, and Alice looked back at him. But it wasn't Alice anymore. She had become a large gray goose, and so had he.

Professor Van der Weghe moved down the line again. With both hands she picked up each student in turn and threw him or her bodily off the roof. They all, in spite of the shock or because of it, reflexively spread out their wings and caught the air before they could be snared by the bare, grasping treetops below. One by one they sailed away into the night.

When it was his turn, Quentin honked in protest. Professor Van der Weghe's human hands were hard and scary and burned against his feathers. He shat on her feet in panic. But then he was in the air and tumbling. He spread his wings and beat his way up into the sky, thrashing and punishing the air till it bore him up. It would have been impossible not to.

Quentin's new goose-brain, it emerged, was not much given to reflection. His senses now tracked only a handful of key stimuli, but it tracked those very, very closely. This body was made for either sitting or flying, not much else, and as it happened Quentin was in a mood to fly. In fact, he felt like flying more than he had ever felt like doing anything in his entire life.

With no conscious thought or apparent effort, he and his classmates fell into the classic ragged V formation, with a Fourth Year named Georgia at the apex. Georgia was the daughter of the receptionist at a car dealership in Michigan, and she had come here against her family's will—unlike Quentin, she had confessed fully the nature of Brakebills, and as a reward for her honesty Georgia's parents had tried to have her committed. Thanks to Fogg's subtle spellcraft Georgia's parents believed her to be attending a vocational institute for troubled adults. Now Georgia, whose Discipline was an obscure branch of Healing roughly analogous to endocrinology, and who wore her wiry black hair cinched at the back with a tortoiseshell barrette, was leading them southward, her brand-new wings pumping vigorously.

It was just chance; any one of them could have led the flock. Quentin was vaguely aware that, although he'd lost the lion's share of his cognitive capacity in the transformation, he'd also picked up a couple of new senses. One had to do with air: he could perceive wind speed and direction and air temperature as clearly as whorls of smoke in a wind tunnel. The sky now appeared to him as a three-dimensional map of currents and eddies, friendly rising heat plumes and dense dangerous sinks of cool air. He could feel the prickle of distant cumulus clouds swapping bursts of positive and negative electrical charge. Quentin's sense of direction had sharpened, too, to the point where it felt like he had a finely engineered compass floating in oil, perfectly balanced, at the center of his brain.

He could feel invisible tracks and rails extending away from him through the air in all directions into the blue distance. They were the Earth's lines of magnetic force, and it was along one of these rails that Georgia was leading them. She was taking them south. By dawn they were a mile up and doing sixty miles an hour, overtaking cars on the Hudson Parkway below them.

They passed New York City, a stony encrustation crackling with alien heat and electrical sparks and exuding toxic flatulence. They flew all day, following the coastline, past Trenton and Philadelphia, sometimes over sea, sometimes over frozen fields, surfing the temperature gradients, boosted by updrafts, transferring seamlessly from current to current as one petered out and the next one kicked in. It felt fantastic. Quentin couldn't imagine stopping. He couldn't believe how strong he was, how many wing beats he had stored up in his iron chest muscles. He just couldn't contain himself. He had to talk about it.

"*Honk!*" he yelled. "Honk honk honk honk honk honk *honk!*"

His classmates agreed.

Quentin was shuffled up and down the V in an orderly fashion, in more or less the same way a volleyball team rotates serve. Sometimes they plonked down and rested and fed in a reservoir or a highway median or a badly drained spot on the lawn of a suburban office park (landscaping errors were pure gold to geese). Not infrequently they shared these priceless scraps of real estate with other V's, real geese who, sensing their transformed nature, regarded them with polite amusement.

How long they flew, Quentin couldn't have said. Once in a while he caught sight of a land formation he recognized, and he tried to calculate time and distance—if they flew at such and such a speed, and the Chesapeake Bay was so many miles south of New York City, then X number of days must have passed since . . . what again exactly? The X's and blanks and other equationly such-and-such's stubbornly refused to fill themselves in. They didn't want to do their dance. Quentin's goose-brain didn't have the hardware to handle numbers, nor was it interested in whatever point those numbers were supposed to prove anyway.

They had gone far enough south now that the weather was perceptibly warmer, and then they went farther still. They went south over the Florida Keys, dry, crusty little nubbins barely poking their heads up out of the ceaselessly lapping turquoise, then out over the Caribbean, bypassing Cuba, farther south than any sensible goose had license to go. They overflew the Panama Canal, no doubt causing any bird-watchers who happened to spot them to shake their heads at the lost little V as they dutifully logged it in their bird journals.

Days, weeks, maybe months and years passed. Who knew, or cared? Quentin had never experienced peace and satisfaction like this. He forgot about his human past, about Brakebills and Brooklyn and James and Julia and Penny and Dean Fogg. Why hang on to them? He had no name anymore. He barely had any individual identity, and he didn't want one. What good were such human artifacts? He was an animal. His job was to turn bugs and plants into muscle and fat and feathers and flight and miles logged. He served only his flock-fellows and the wind and the laws of Darwin. And he served whatever force sent him gliding along the invisible magnetic rails, always southward, down the rough, stony coast of Peru, spiny Andes on his port, the sprawling blue Pacific on his starboard. He had never been happier.

Though it was tougher going now. They splashed down more rarely and in more exotic locales, widely spaced way stations that must have been picked out for them in advance. He'd be cruising along a mile and a half up, one eye monitoring the rocky ruff of the Andes, feeling his empty belly and the ache in his chest muscles, when something would twinkle in the forest a hundred miles down the line, and sure enough they'd happen upon a freshly flooded soccer field, or an abandoned swimming pool in some Shining Path warlord's ruined villa, rainwater having diluted almost to nothing the lingering chemical tang of chlorine.

It was getting colder again, after their long tropical interlude. Peru gave way to Chile and the grassy, wind-ruffled Patagonian pampas. They were a lean flock now, their fat reserves depleted, but nobody turned aside or hesitated for a second as they plunged suicidally south from the tip of

Cape Horn out over the terrifying blue chaos of Drake Passage. The invisible highway they rode would brook no swerving.

There was no playful intra-flock honking now. Quentin glanced over once at the other branch of the V to see Janet's black button eye burning with furious determination opposite him. They overnighted on a miraculous barge adrift in deep water and loaded with good things, watercress and alfalfa and clover. When the bleak gray shore of Antarctica heaved up over the horizon, they regarded it not with relief but with collective resignation. This was no respite. There were no goose names for this country because geese didn't come here, or if they did they never came back. He could see magnetic tracks and rails converging in the air here, carving in from far away on either side, like the longitude lines that come crowding together at the bottom of a globe. The Brakebills V flew high, the wrinkled gray swells telescopically clear below them through two miles of dry, salted air.

Instead of a beach a fringe of tumbled boulders crammed with bizarre, unintelligible penguins crept by, then blank white ice, the frozen skull of the Earth. Quentin was tired. The cold tore at his little body through its thin feathery jacket. He no longer knew what was keeping them aloft. If one of them dropped, he knew, they would all give up, just fold their wings and dive for the porcelain white snow, which would happily devour them.

And then the rail they followed dipped like a dowser's rod. It angled them downward, and they slipped and slid gratefully down it, accepting a loss of altitude in exchange for speed and blessed relief from the effort of maintaining height with their burning wings. Quentin could see now that there was a stone house there in the snow, an anomaly in the otherwise featureless plain. It was a place of men, and ordinarily Quentin would have feared it, crapped on it, and then blown by it and forgotten it.

But no, there was no question, their track ended there. It buried itself in one of the stone house's many snowy roofs. They were close enough now that Quentin could see a man standing on one of them, waiting for them, holding a long straight staff. The urge to fly from him was strong, but exhaustion and above all the magnetic logic of the track were stronger.

At the very last second he cupped his stiffened wings and they caught the air like a sail, snatching up the last of his kinetic energy and breaking

his fall. He plopped onto the snow roof and lay there gasping at the thin
atmosphere. His eyes went dull. The human hadn't moved. Well, fuck him.
He could do what he wanted with them, pluck them and gut them and stuff
them and roast them, Quentin didn't care anymore as long as he could just
have one blessed moment of rest for his aching wings.

The man shaped a strange syllable with his fleshy, beakless lips and
tapped the base of his staff on the roof. Fifteen pale, naked human teenagers lay in the snow under the white polar sun.

Quentin woke up in a bare white bedroom. He could not have guessed to
the nearest twenty-four hours how long he'd been asleep. His chest and
arms felt bruised and achy. He looked at his crude, pink, human hands,
with their stubby featherless fingers. He brought them up to touch his face.
He sighed and resigned himself to being a man again.

There was very little in the bedroom, and all of it was white: the bed-
clothes, the whitewashed walls, the coarse drawstring pajamas he wore, the
white-painted iron bedstead, the slippers waiting for him on the cold stone
floor. From the small square window Quentin could see he was on the second floor. His view was of broken snowfields beneath a white sky, stretching out to the horizon, a meaningless abstract white line an unjudgable
distance away. My God. What had he gotten himself into?

Quentin shuffled out into the corridor, still in his pajamas and a thin robe
he'd found hanging on a hook on the back of the door. He found his way
downstairs into a quiet, airy hall with a timbered ceiling; it was identical to
the dining hall at Brakebills, but the vibe was different, more like an Alpine
ski lodge. A long table with benches ran most of the length of the hall.

Quentin sat down. A man sat alone at one end of the table, nursing a
mug of coffee and staring bleakly at the picked-over remains of a lavish
breakfast. He was sandy-haired, tall but round-shouldered, with a weak
chin and the beginnings of a paunch. His dressing gown was much whiter
and fluffier than Quentin's. His eyes were a pale, watery green.

"I let you sleep," he said. "Most of the others are already up."

"Thanks." Quentin scooched down the bench to sit across from him.
He rummaged through the leftover plates and dishes for a clean fork.

"You are at Brakebills South." The man's voice was oddly flat, with a slight Russian accent, and he didn't look directly at Quentin when he talked. "We are about five hundred miles from the South Pole. You flew in over the Bellingshausen Sea on your way in from Chile, over a region called Ellsworth Land. They call this part of Antarctica Marie Byrd Land. Admiral Byrd named it after his wife."

He scratched his tousled hair unself-consciously.

"Where's everybody else?" Quentin asked. There didn't seem to be any point in being formal, since they were both wearing bathrobes. And the cold hash browns were unbelievably good. He hadn't realized how hungry he was.

"I gave them the morning." He waved in no particular direction. "Classes begin in the afternoon."

Quentin nodded, his mouth full.

"What kind of classes?" he managed.

"What kind of classes," the man repeated. "Here at Brakebills South you will begin your education in magic. Or I suppose you thought that was what you were doing with Professor Fogg?"

Questions like that always confused Quentin, so he resorted to honesty.

"Yes, I did think that."

"You are here to internalize the essential mechanisms of magic. You think"—his accent made it *theenk*—"that you have been studying magic." *Medzhik.* "You have practiced your Popper and memorized your conjugations and declensions and modifications. What are the five Tertiary Circumstances?"

It popped out automatically. "Altitude, Age, Position of the Pleiades, Phase of the Moon, Nearest Body of Water."

"Very good," he said sarcastically. "Magnificent. You are a genius."

With an effort Quentin decided not to be stung by this. He was still enjoying the Zen afterglow of having been a goose. And the hash browns.

"Thank you."

"You have been studying magic the way a parrot studies Shakespeare. You recite it like you are saying the Pledge of Allegiance. But you do not understand it."

"I don't?"

"To become a magician you must do something very different," the man said. This was clearly his set piece. "You cannot study magic. You cannot learn it. You must ingest it. Digest it. You must merge *with* it. And it with you.

"When a magician casts a spell, he does not first mentally review the Major, Minor, Tertiary, and Quaternary Circumstances. He does not search his soul to determine the phase of the moon, and the nearest body of water, and the last time he wiped his ass. When he wishes to cast a spell he simply casts it. When he wishes to fly, he simply flies. When he wants the dishes done, they simply are."

The man muttered something, tapped once resonantly on the table, and the dishes began noisily arranging themselves into stacks as if they were magnetized.

"You need to do more than memorize, Quentin. You must learn the principles of magic with more than your head. You must learn them with your bones, with your blood, your liver, your heart, your *deek*." He grabbed his crotch through his dressing gown and gave it a shake. "We are going to submerge the language of spellcasting deep into who you are, so that you have it always, wherever you are, whenever you need it. Not just when you have studied for a test.

"You are not going on a mystical adventure here, Quentin. This process will be long and painful and humiliating and very, *very*"—he practically shouted the word—"boring. It is a task best performed in silence and isolation. That is the reason for your presence here. You will not enjoy the time you spend at Brakebills South. I do not encourage you to try."

Quentin listened to this in silence. He didn't especially like this man, who had just referred to his penis and whose name he still didn't know. He put it out of his mind and focused on cramming starch into his depleted body.

"So how do I do that?" Quentin mumbled. "Learn things in my bones? Or whatever?"

"It is very hard. Not everybody does. Not everybody can."

"Uh-huh. What happens if I can't?"

"Nothing. You go back to Brakebills. You graduate. You spend your life as a second-rate magician. Many do. Probably you never realize it. Even the fact that you failed is beyond your ability to comprehend."

Quentin had no intention of letting that happen to him, though it occurred to him that probably nobody actually set out to have that happen to them, and, statistically speaking, it had to happen to somebody. The hash browns no longer tasted quite so scrumptious. He put his fork down.

"Fogg tells me you are good with your hands," the sandy-haired man said, relenting a little. "Show me."

Quentin's fingers were still stiff and sore from having served as wings, but he picked up a sharp knife that looked decently balanced, carefully cleaned it off with a napkin, and held it between the last two fingers in his left hand. He spun it, finger by finger, as far as his thumb, then he tossed it up almost to the ceiling—still spinning, careful to let it pass between two rafters—with the idea that it would fall and bury itself in the table between the third and fourth fingers of his outstretched left hand. This was best done without looking, maintaining eye contact with his audience for maximum effect.

Quentin's breakfast companion picked up a loaf of bread and stuck it out so that the falling knife speared it. He tossed loaf and knife contemptuously on the table.

"You take stupid risks," the man said stonily. "Go on and join your friends. I think"—*theenk*—"you will find them on the roof of the West Tower." He pointed to a doorway. "We begin in the afternoon."

Okay, Mr. Funnylaffs, Quentin thought. You're the boss.

He stood up. The stranger stood up, too, and shuffled off in another direction. He had the air of a disappointed man.

Stone for stone, board for board, Brakebills South was the same house as the House at Brakebills. Which was reassuring, in a way, but it was incongruous to find what looked like an eighteenth-century English country house planted in the middle of a soaring Antarctic wasteland. The roof of the West Tower was broad and round and paved with smooth flagstones, with a stone wall running around the edge. It was open to the elements, but some kind of magical arrangement kept the air warm and humid and protected it from the wind, or mostly. Quentin imagined he could feel a deep chill lurking underneath the warmth somewhere. The air was tepid, but the floor, the furniture, everything he touched was cool and clammy. It was like being in a warm greenhouse in the dead of winter.

As promised, the rest of the Brakebills group was up there, standing around dazed in threes and fours, staring out at the snowpack and talking in low tones, bathed in the eerie, even Antarctic light. They looked different. Their waists were trimmer, and their shoulders and chests were sturdier, huskier. They'd lost fat and packed on muscle during their flight south. Their jaws and cheekbones were sharply defined. Alice looked lovely and gaunt and lost.

"Honk honk honkonk honk *honk!*" Janet said when she saw Quentin. People laughed, though Quentin had the impression she'd already made that joke a few times.

"Hey, man," Josh said, trying to sound nonchalant. "Is this place fucked up or what?"

"Doesn't seem so bad," Quentin said. "What time is skinny-dipping?"

"I might have been a little off base with that," Eliot said gloomily, also probably not for the first time. "We did all get naked, anyway."

They were all wearing identical white pajamas. Quentin felt like an inmate in an insane asylum. He wondered if Eliot was missing his secret boyfriend of the moment, whoever it was.

"I ran into Nurse Ratched downstairs," he said. The pajamas had no pockets, and Quentin kept looking for somewhere to put his hands. "He gave me a speech about how stupid I am and how miserable he's going to make me."

"You slept through our little meet'n'greet. That's Professor Mayakovsky."

"Mayakovsky. Like Dean Mayakovsky?"

"He's the son," Eliot said. "I always wondered what happened to him. Now we know."

The original Mayakovsky had been the most powerful magician in a wave of international faculty brought in during the 1930s and 1940s. Until then Brakebills taught English and American magic almost exclusively, but in the 1930s a vogue for "multicultural" spellcasting had swept the school. Professors were imported at huge expense from around the world, the more remote the better: skirt-wearing shamans from Micronesian dot-islands; hunch-shouldered, hookah-puffing wizards from inner-city Cairo coffeehouses; blue-faced Tuareg necromancers from southern Morocco. Legend had it that Mayakovsky senior was recruited from a remote Siberian location, a cluster of frozen Soviet blockhouses where local shamanic traditions had hybridized with sophisticated Muscovite practices brought there by gulag inmates.

"I wonder how badly you have to fuck up to get this assignment," Josh mused.

"Maybe he wanted it," Quentin said. "Maybe he likes it here. Dude must be in creepy loner heaven."

"I think you were right, I think I am going to be the first one to crack," Eliot said, as if he were having a different conversation. He felt the fluffy stubble on his cheek. "I don't like it here. This stuff is giving me a rash." He fingered the material of the Brakebills South pajamas. "I think it might have a stain on it."

Janet rubbed his arm comfortingly. "You'll be okay. You survived Oregon. Is this worse than Oregon?"

"Maybe if I ask nicely he'll turn me back into a goose."

"Oh my God!" said Alice. "Never again. Do you realize we ate bugs? We ate bugs!"

"What do you mean, never again? How do you think we're getting back?"

"You know what I liked about being a goose?" Josh said. "Being able to crap wherever I wanted."

"I'm not going back." Eliot threw a white pebble out into the white bleakness, where it became invisible before it hit the ground. "I could fly to Australia from here. Or New Zealand—the vineyards there are really coming along. Some nice sheep farmer will adopt me and feed me sauvignon blanc and turn my liver into a wonderful foie gras."

"Maybe Professor Mayakovsky can turn you into a kiwi bird," Josh said helpfully.

"Kiwi birds can't fly."

"Anyway, he didn't strike me as the kind of guy who's going to do us a lot of favors," Alice said.

"He must spend a lot of time alone," Quentin said. "I wonder if we should we feel bad for him."

Janet snorted.

"Honk honk honk honk honk!"

There was no reliable way to measure time at Brakebills South. There were no clocks, and the sun was a dull white fluorescence permanently thumbtacked half an inch above the white horizon. It made Quentin think of the Watcherwoman, how she was always trying to stop time. She would have loved this place.

That first morning they talked and mingled on the roof of the West Tower for what felt like hours, huddling together to cope with all the strangeness. Nobody felt like going back downstairs, even after they got tired of standing and ran out of things to talk about, so they all sat around the edge of the roof with their backs against the stone wall and just stared off into the pale, hazy distance, bathed in the weird, directionless, all-permeating white light reflecting off the snow.

Quentin leaned his back against the cool stone and closed his eyes. He felt Alice put her head on his shoulder. If nothing else, he could hang on to her. Whatever else changed, she was always the same. They rested.

Later, it might have been minutes or hours or days, he opened his eyes. He tried to say something and discovered that he couldn't talk.

Some of the others were on their feet already. Professor Mayakovsky had appeared at the head of the stairs, his white bathrobe belted over his gut. He cleared his throat.

"I've taken the liberty of depriving you of the power of speech," he said. He tapped his Adam's apple. "There will be no talking at Brakebills South. It is the hardest thing to adjust to, and I find it eases the transition if I simply prevent you from speaking for your first weeks here. You may vocalize for the purposes of spellcasting, but for no other reason."

The class stared at him mutely. Mayakovsky seemed to be more comfortable now that nobody could answer back.

"If you will all follow me downstairs, it is time for your first lesson."

One thing had always confused Quentin about the magic he read about in books: it never seemed especially hard to do. There were lots of furrowed brows and thick books and long white beards and whatnot, but when it came right down to it, you memorized the incantation—or you just read it off the page, if that was too much trouble—you collected the herbs, waved the wand, rubbed the lamp, mixed the potion, said the words—and just like that the forces of the beyond did your bidding. It was like making salad dressing or driving stick or assembling Ikea furniture—just another skill you could learn. It took some time and effort, but compared to doing calculus, say, or playing the oboe—well, there really was no comparison. Any idiot could do magic.

Quentin had been perversely relieved when he learned that there was more to it than that. Talent was part of it—that silent, invisible exertion he felt in his chest every time a spell came out right. But there was also work, hard work, mountains of it. Every spell had to be adjusted and modified in a hundred ways according to the prevailing Circumstances—they adorned the word with a capital letter at Brakebills—under which it was cast. These Circumstances could be just about anything: magic was a complicated, fiddly instrument that had to be calibrated precisely to the context in which it operated. Quentin had committed to memory dozens of pages of closely printed charts and diagrams spelling out the Major Circumstances and how they affected any given enchantment. And then, once you had all that down, there were hundreds of Corollaries and Exceptions to memorize too.

As much as it was like anything, magic was like a language. And like a language, textbooks and teachers treated it as an orderly system for the purposes of teaching it, but in reality it was complex and chaotic and organic. It obeyed rules only to the extent that it felt like it, and there were almost as many special cases and one-time variations as there were rules. These Exceptions were indicated by rows of asterisks and daggers and other more obscure typographical fauna which invited the reader to peruse the many footnotes that cluttered up the margins of magical reference books like Talmudic commentary.

It was Mayakovsky's intention to make them memorize all these minutiae, and not only to memorize them but to absorb and internalize them. The very best spellcasters had talent, he told his captive, silent audience, but they also had unusual under-the-hood mental machinery, the delicate but powerful correlating and cross-checking engines necessary to access and manipulate and manage this vast body of information.

That first afternoon Quentin expected a lecture, but instead, when

Mayakovsky was done jinxing their larynxes, he showed each of them to what looked like a monk's cell, a small stone room with a single high, barred window, a single chair, and a single square wooden table. A shelf of magical reference books was bolted to one wall. It had the clean, industrious air of a room that had just been vigorously swept with a birch-twig broom.

"Sit," Mayakovsky said.

Quentin sat. The professor placed in front of him, one by one, like a man setting up a chessboard, a hammer, a block of wood, a box of nails, a sheet of paper, and a small book bound in pale vellum.

Mayakovsky tapped the paper.

"Hammer Charm of Legrand," he said. "You know it?"

Everybody knew it. It was a standard teaching charm. While simple in theory—all it did was ensure that a hammered nail would go in straight, in one shot—it was extraordinarily persnickety to cast. It existed in literally thousands of permutations, depending on the Circumstances. Casting Legrand was probably harder than just hammering the damn nail in the old-fashioned way, but it came in handy for didactic purposes.

Mayakovsky tapped the book with a thick-nailed finger.

"This book, each page describes a different set of Circumstances. All different. Understand? Place, weather, stars, season—you will see. You turn the page, you cast the spell according to each set of Circumstances. Good practice. I'll come back when you finish book. *Khorosho?*"

Mayakovsky's Russian accent was getting thicker as the day wore on. He was dropping his contractions and definite articles. He closed the door behind him. Quentin opened the book. Somebody not very creative had written ABANDON HOPE ALL YE WHO ENTER HERE on the first page. Something told Quentin that Mayakovsky had noticed the graffiti but let it stand.

Soon Quentin knew Legrand's Hammer Charm better than he wanted to know any spell ever. Page by page the Circumstances listed in the book became more and more esoteric and counterfactual. He cast Legrand's Hammer Charm at noon and at midnight, in summer and winter, on mountaintops and a thousand yards beneath the earth's surface. He cast the spell underwater and on the surface of the moon. He cast it in early evening during a blizzard on a beach on the island of Mangareva, which would almost certainly never happen since Mangareva is part of French Polynesia, in the South Pacific. He cast the spell as a man, as a woman, and once—was this really relevant?—as a hermaphrodite. He cast it in anger, with ambivalence, and with bitter regret.

By then Quentin's mouth was dry. His fingertips were numb. He had pounded his thumb with the hammer four times. The block of wood was now crammed with flattened iron nail heads. Quentin groaned soundlessly and let his head loll back against the hard back of the chair. The door flew open, and Professor Mayakovsky entered carrying a jingling tray.

He set the tray down on the desk. It supported a cup of hot tea, a tumbler of water, a plate with a pat of yeasty European butter and a thick slab of sourdough bread on it, and a glass containing what would turn out to be two fingers of peppery vodka, one finger of which Mayakovsky drank off himself before placing it on the table.

When he was done he slapped Quentin hard across the face.

"That is for doubting yourself," he said.

Quentin stared at him. He lifted a hand to his cheek, thinking: This man is batshit insane. He could do anything to us out here.

Mayakovsky turned the book back to the first page again. He turned the piece of paper with the spell on it over and patted it. On the back was written another spell: Bujold's Sorcerous Nail Extraction.

"Begin again, please."

Wax on, wax off.

When Mayakovsky was gone, Quentin stood up and stretched. Both his knees cracked. Instead of beginning again he went over to the tiny window looking out on the lunar snowfields. The sheer monochromaticity of the landscape was beginning to make him hallucinate colors. The sun had not moved at all.

That was how Quentin's first month at Brakebills South went. The spells changed, and the Circumstances were different, but the room was the same, and the days were always, always, always the same: empty, relentless, interminable wastelands of repetition. Mayakovsky's ominous warnings had been entirely justified, and arguably a little understated. Even during his worst moments at Brakebills, Quentin had always had a niggling suspicion that he was getting away with something by being there, that the sacrifices asked of him by his instructors, however great, were cheap by comparison with the rewards of the life he could look forward to as a magician. At Brakebills South, for the first time, he felt like he was giving value for money.

And he understood why they'd been sent here. What Mayakovsky was asking of them was impossible. The human brain was not meant to ingest these quantities of information. If Fogg had tried to enforce this regimen back at Brakebills, there would have been an insurrection.

It was difficult to gauge how the others were holding up. They met at mealtimes and passed in the hall, but because of the prohibition against speech there was no commiserating, just glances and shrugs and not much of that. Their gazes met bleakly over the breakfast table and turned away. Eliot's eyes were empty, and Quentin supposed his own probably looked the same way. Even Janet's animated features were set and frozen. No notes were exchanged. Whatever enchantment kept them from talking was global: their pens wouldn't write.

Quentin was losing interest in communicating anyway. He should have been ravenous for human contact, but instead he felt himself falling away from the others, deeper inside himself. He shuffled like a prisoner from bedroom to dining room to solitary classroom, down the stone corridors, under the tediously unblinking gaze of the white sun. Once he wandered up to the roof of the West Tower and found one of the others, a gangly extrovert named Dale, putting on a mime show for a listless audience, but it really wasn't worth the effort of turning his head to follow what was going on. His sense of humor had died in the vastness.

Professor Mayakovsky seemed to expect this, as if he'd known it was going to happen. After the first three weeks he announced that he had lifted the spell that kept them from talking. The news was received in silence. Nobody had noticed.

Mayakovsky began to vary the routine. Most days were still devoted to grinding through the Circumstances and their never-ending Exceptions, but once in a while he introduced other exercises. In an empty hall he erected a three-dimensional maze composed of wire rings through which the students would levitate objects at speed, to sharpen their powers of concentration and control. At first they used marbles, then later steel balls only slightly narrower than the rings. When a ball brushed a ring a spark cracked between them, and the spellcaster felt a shock.

Later still they would guide fireflies through the same maze, influencing their tiny insect minds by force of will. They watched one another do this in silence, feeling envy at one another's successes and contempt for one another's failures. The regime had divided them against each other. Janet in particular was bad at it—she tended to overpower her fireflies, to the point where they would crisp up in midair and become puffs of ash. Mayakovsky, stony-faced, just made her start over, while tears of wordless frustration ran down her face. This could and did go on for hours. No one could leave the hall before everyone had completed the exercise. They slept there more than once.

As the weeks went by, and still no one spoke, they plowed deeper and deeper into areas of magic Quentin never thought he'd have the guts to try. They practiced transformations. He learned to unpack and parse the spell that had turned them into geese (much of the trick, it turned out, was in shedding, storing, and then restoring the difference in body mass). They spent a hilarious afternoon as polar bears, wandering clumsily in a herd over the packed snow, swatting harmlessly at each other with giant yellow paws, encased as they were in layers of fur, hide, and fat. Their bear bodies felt clumsy and top heavy, and they kept toppling over sideways onto their backs by accident. More hilarity.

Nobody liked him, but it became apparent that Mayakovsky was no fraud. He could do things Quentin had never seen done at Brakebills, things he didn't think had been done for centuries. One afternoon he demonstrated, but did not allow them to try, a spell that reversed the flow of entropy. He smashed a glass globe and then neatly restored it again, like a film clip run in reverse. He popped a helium balloon and then knitted it back together and refilled it with its original helium atoms, in some cases fishing them from deep inside the lungs of spectators who had inhaled them. He used camphor to smother a spider—he showed no particular remorse about this—and then, frowning with the effort, brought the spider back to life. Quentin watched the poor thing creep around in circles on the tabletop, hopelessly traumatized, making little dazed rushes at nothing and then retreating to a corner, hunched up and twitching, while Mayakovsky moved on to another topic.

One day, about three months into the semester, Mayakovsky announced that they would be transforming into Arctic foxes for the afternoon. It was an odd choice—they'd already done a few mammals, and it was no tougher than becoming a goose. But why quibble? Being an Arctic fox turned out to be a hell of a lot of fun. As soon as the change was in effect Quentin shot out across the snowpack on his four twinkling paws. His little fox body was so fast and light, and his eyes were so close to the ground, that it was like flying a high-performance jet at low altitude. Tiny ridges and crumbs of snow loomed up like mountains and boulders. He leaped over them and dodged around them and crashed through them. When he tried to turn he was going so fast he skidded and wiped out in a huge plume of snow. The rest of the pack gleefully piled on top of him, yipping and yapping and snapping.

It was an amazing outpouring of collective joy. Quentin had forgotten he was capable of that emotion, the way a lost spelunker feels like there never was such a thing as sunlight, that it was just a cruel fiction. They chased one another around in circles, panting and rolling and acting like idiots. It was funny, Quentin thought, with his stupid little miniature fox brain, the way he could automatically recognize everybody as foxes. That was Eliot with the snaggle-teeth. That plump blue-white critter was Josh. That small, silky specimen with the wide eyes was Alice.

Somewhere in the goofing off a game spontaneously evolved. It had something to do with pushing around a chunk of ice with your paws and your nose as fast as possible. Beyond that the point of the game wasn't really clear, but they frantically pounced on the chunk of ice, or pounced on whoever had pounced on it just before them, and pushed it until the next person pounced on them.

An Arctic fox's eyes weren't all that much to brag about, but its nose was unbelievable. Quentin's new nose was a Goddamned sensory masterpiece. Even in the middle of the fray he could recognize classmates by snuffing their fur. Increasingly, Quentin noticed one scent more than the others. It was a sharp, acrid, skunky musk that probably would have smelled like cat piss to a human being, but to a fox it was like a drug. He caught flashes of it in the fray every few minutes, and every time he did it grabbed his attention and jerked him around like a fish on a hook.

Something was happening to the game. It was losing its cohesion. Quentin was still playing, but fewer and fewer of his fellow foxes were playing with him. Eliot lit out in a streak off into the snow dunes. The pack dwindled to ten, then eight. Where were they going? Quentin's fox brain barked. And what the hell was that unbe-fucking-lievable smell he kept stumbling on? There it was again! This time he tackled the source of the smell, buried his snuffling muzzle in her fur, because of course he had known all along, with what was left of his consciousness, that what he was smelling was Alice.

It was totally against the rules, but breaking the rules turned out to be as much fun as obeying them. How had he never figured *that* out before? The others were playing more and more wildly—they weren't even *trying* to go after the chunk of ice anymore—and the game was disintegrating into little knots of tussling foxes, and he was tussling with Alice. Vulpine hormones and instincts were powering up, taking over, manhandling what was left of his rational human mind.

He locked his teeth in the thick fur of her neck. It didn't seem to hurt her any, or at least not in a way that was easily distinguishable from pleasure. Something crazy and urgent was going on, and there was no way to stop it, or probably there was but why would you? Stopping was one of those pointless, life-defeating human impulses for which his merry little fox brain had nothing but contempt.

He caught a glimpse of Alice's wild dark fox's eye rolling with terror and then half shutting with pleasure. Their tiny quick breaths puffed white in the air and mingled and disappeared. Her white fox fur was coarse and smooth at the same time, and she made little yipping snarls every time he pushed himself deeper inside her. He never wanted to stop.

The snow burned underneath them. It glowed hot like a bed of coals. They were on fire, and they let the fire consume them.

To an outside observer breakfast the next day wouldn't have looked much different than it usually did. Everybody shuffled in in their loose-fitting, all-white Brakebills South uniforms, sat down without speaking or looking at one another, and ate what was put in front of them. But Quentin felt like he was walking on the moon. Giant slow-motion steps, ringing silence, vacuum all around him, a television audience of millions. He didn't dare look at anybody else, least of all Alice.

She was sitting across the table and three people down from him, impassive and unperturbed, calmly focused on her oatmeal. He couldn't have guessed within a light-year what she was thinking. Though he knew what was on everybody else's minds. He was sure they all knew what had happened. They'd been right out in the open, for God's sake. Or had they all been doing the same thing? Did everybody pair off? His face felt hot. He didn't even know if she was a virgin. Or, if she had been whether she still was one.

It would all be so much simpler if he even understood what it meant, but he didn't. Could he be in love with Alice? He tried to compare what he felt for her with his remembered feelings for Julia, but the two emotions were worlds apart. Things just got out of control, that's all. It wasn't them, it was their fox bodies. Nobody had to take it too seriously.

Mayakovsky sat at the head of the table looking smug. He had known this was going to happen, Quentin thought furiously, stabbing at his cheese grits with a fork. A bunch of teenagers cooped up in the Fortress of Solitude for two months, then stuck in the bodies of stupid horny animals. Of course we were going to go crazy.

Whatever perverted personal satisfaction Mayakovsky got out of what happened, it became obvious over the next week that it was also a practical piece of personnel management, because Quentin reapplied himself to his magical studies with the laserlike focus of a person desperate to avoid meeting anybody else's eyes or thinking about things that actually mattered, like how he really felt about Alice, and who it was who had had sex with her out on the ice, him or the fox. It was back to the grind, pounding his way through Circumstances and Exceptions and a thousand mnemonics designed to force him to embed a thousand trivial particles of data in the soft tissue of his already supersaturated mind.

They fell into a collective tribal trance. The depleted palette of the Antarctic world hypnotized them. The shifting snows outside briefly revealed a low ridge of dark shale, the only topographical feature in a featureless world, and the students watched it from the roof like television. It reminded him of the desert in *The Wandering Dune*—God, he hadn't thought about Fillory for ages. Quentin wondered if the rest of the world, his life before this, had just been a lurid dream. When he pictured the globe now it was entirely Antarctic, a whole world over which this monochromatic continent had metastasized like an icy cancer.

He went a little insane. They all did, though it took them in different ways. Some of the others became obsessed with sex. Their higher functions were so numb and exhausted they became animals, desperate for any kind of contact that wouldn't ask words of them. Impromptu orgies were not unheard of. Quentin came upon them once or twice in the evenings—they would gather in apparently arbitrary combinations, in an empty classroom or in somebody's bedroom, in semi-anonymous chains, their white uniforms half or all the way off, their eyes glassy and bored as they pulled and stroked and pumped, always in silence. He saw Janet take part once. The display was as much for other people as for themselves, but Quentin never joined in or even watched, just turned away, feeling superior and also strangely angry. Maybe he was just angry that something kept him from jumping in. He was disproportionately relieved that he never saw Alice there.

Time passed, or at least Quentin knew that, according to theory, it pretty much had to be passing, though he didn't personally see much evidence of it, unless you counted the weird menagerie of mustaches and beards he and his male classmates were growing. However much he ate he got thinner and thinner. His state of mind devolved from mesmerized to hallucinatory. Tiny random things became charged with overwhelming significance—a round pebble, a stray straw from a broom, a dark mark on a white wall—that dissipated again minutes later. In the classroom he sometimes saw fantastical creatures mixed in with his classmates—a huge, elegant brown stick insect that clung to the back of a chair; a giant lizard with horny skin and a German accent, whose head burned with white fire—though afterward he could never be sure if he had imagined them. Once he thought he saw the man whose face was hidden by a branch. He couldn't take this much longer.

Then, just like that, one morning over breakfast Mayakovsky announced that there were two weeks remaining in the semester, and it was time they gave serious thought to the final exam. The test was simply this: they would walk from Brakebills South to the South Pole. The distance was on the order of five hundred miles. They would be given no food and no maps and no clothing. They would have to protect and sustain themselves by magic. Flying was out of bounds—they would go on foot or not at all, and in the form of human beings, not as bears or penguins or some other naturally cold-resistant animal. Cooperation between students was prohibited—they could view it as a race, if they liked. There was no time limit. The exam was not mandatory.

Two weeks wasn't quite long enough to prepare properly, but it was more than long enough for the decision to hang over them. Yes or no, in or out? Mayakovsky stressed that safety precautions would be minimal. He would do his best to keep track of them in the field, but there was no guarantee that if they screwed up he'd be able to rescue their sorry, hypothermic asses.

There was a lot to study up on. Would sunburn be a problem? Snow blindness? Should they toughen the soles of their feet or try to create some kind of magical footwear? Was there any way to get mutton fat, which they could need to cast Chkhartishvili's Enveloping Warmth, from the kitchen? And if the test wasn't even mandatory, then what was the point of it? What would happen if they failed? It sounded more like a ritual or a hazing than a final exam.

On the last morning Quentin got up early with the idea of foraging for contraband spell components in the kitchen. He had made up his mind to compete. He had to know if he could do it or not. It was that simple.

Most of the cupboards were locked—he probably wasn't the first student to have thought of it—but he did manage to load up his pockets with flour and a stray silver fork and some old sprouting garlic cloves that might come in handy for something, he didn't know what. He headed downstairs.

Alice was waiting for him on the landing between floors.

"I have to ask you something," she said, her voice full of crisp determination. "Are you in love with me? It's okay if you aren't, I just want to know."

She made it almost all the way through, but she couldn't quite say the last phrase full voice and whispered it instead.

He hadn't even met her eyes since the afternoon they'd been foxes together. Three weeks at least. Now they stood together on the smooth, freezing stone floor, abjectly human. How could a person who hadn't washed or cut her hair in five months be so beautiful?

"I don't know," he said. His voice was scratchy from lack of use. The words felt more frightening than any spell he had ever cast. "I mean, you'd think I would, but I don't. I really don't know."

He tried to make his tone light and conversational, but his body felt heavy. The floor was accelerating rapidly upward with both of them on it. At that moment, when he should have been most lucidly present, he had no idea whether he was lying or telling the truth. With all the time he'd spent studying here, everything he'd learned, why hadn't he learned this one thing? He was failing both of them, himself and Alice.

"It's okay," she said, with a quick little smile that strained the ligaments that held Quentin's heart in his chest. "I didn't think so. I was more wondering whether you would lie about it."

He was lost. "Was I supposed to lie?"

"It's okay, Quentin. It was nice. The sex, I mean. You do realize it's all right to have nice things sometimes, right?"

She saved him from having to answer by standing up on tiptoe and kissing him softly on the lips. Her lips were dry and chapped, but the tip of her tongue was soft and warm. It felt like the last warm thing in the world.

"Try not to die," she said.

She patted his rough cheek and disappeared down the stairs ahead of him in the predawn twilight.

After that ordeal the test was almost an afterthought. They were released separately out onto the snowpack, at intervals, to discourage collaboration. Mayakovsky made Quentin disrobe first—so much for the flour and the garlic and that bent silver fork—and walk naked out beyond the range of the protective spells that kept the temperature bearable at Brakebills South. As he passed through the invisible perimeter the cold hit him face-first, and it was beyond all belief. Quentin's whole body spasmed and contracted. It felt like he'd been dropped into burning kerosene. The air seared his lungs. He bent over, hands jammed in his armpits.

"Happy trails," Mayakovsky called. He tossed Quentin a Ziploc bag full of something gray and greasy. Mutton fat. *"Bog s'vami."*

Whatever. Quentin knew he had only a few seconds before his fingers would be too numb for spellcasting. He tore open the bag and jammed his hands inside and stuttered out Chkhartishvili's Enveloping Warmth. It got easier after that. He layered on the rest of the spells by turns: protection from the wind and the sun, speed, strong legs, toughened feet. He threw up a navigation spell, and a great luminous golden compass wheel that only he could see appeared overhead in the white sky.

Quentin knew the theory behind the spells, but he'd never tested them all together at full strength. He felt like a superhero. He felt bionic. He was in business.

He turned to face the *S* on the compass wheel and trotted off toward the horizon at speed, circling around the building he'd just left, bare feet fluffing silently through bone-dry powder. With the strength spells in place his thighs felt like pneumatic pistons. His calves were steel truck springs. His feet were as tough and numb as Kevlar brake shoes.

Afterward he remembered almost nothing of the week that followed. The whole thing was very clinical. Reduced to its technical essence, it was a problem of resource management, of nurturing and guarding and fanning the little flickering flame of life and consciousness within his body as the entire continent of Antarctica tried to leach away the heat and sugar and water that kept it burning.

He slept lightly and very little. His urine turned a deep amber then ceased to flow entirely. The monotony of the scenery was relentless. Each low crunchy ridge he topped revealed a vista composed of its identical clones, arranged in a pattern of infinite regress. His thoughts went around in circles. He lost track of time. He sang the Oscar Mayer jingle and the *Simpsons* theme song. He talked to James and Julia. Sometimes he confused James with Martin Chatwin and Julia with Jane. The fat melted out of his body; his ribs grew more prominent, tried to push their way out through his skin. He had to be careful. His margin of error was not large. The spells he was using were powerful and highly durable, with a life of their own. He could die out here, and his corpse would probably keep jogging merrily along toward the pole on its own.

Once or twice a day, sometimes more, a lipless blue crevasse would open beneath his feet, and he would have to trot around it or cross it with a magic-assisted leap. Once he stumbled right into one and fell forty feet down into blue-tinted darkness. The ward-and-shield spells around his pale, nude body were so thick that he barely noticed. He just ground to a slow stop, jammed in between two rough ice walls, and then lifted himself back out again, like the Lorax, and kept on running.

Even as his physical strength faded he leaned on the iron magical vigor that his sojourn under Professor Mayakovsky had given him. It no longer felt like a fluke when he worked magic successfully. The worlds of magical and physical reality felt equally real and present to him. He summoned simple spells into being without conscious thought. He reached for the magical force within him as naturally as he would reach for the salt on the dinner table. He had even gained the ability to extemporize a little, to guess at magical Circumstances when he hadn't been drilled on them. The implications of this were stunning: magic wasn't simply random, it had an actual shape—a fractal, chaotic shape, but subconsciously his blindly groping mental fingertips had begun to parse it.

He remembered a lecture Mayakovsky had given a few weeks before, which at the time he hadn't paid much attention to. Now, however, jogging forever south across the frozen, broken plains, it came back to him almost word for word.

"You dislike me," Mayakovsky had begun. "You are sick of the sight of me, *skraelings*." That was what he called them, *skraelings*. Apparently it was a Viking word that meant, roughly, "wretches."

"But if you listen to me only one more time in your lives, listen to me now. Once you reach a certain level of fluency as a spellcaster, you will begin to manipulate reality freely. Not all of you—Dale, I think you in particular are unlikely to cross that Rubicon. But for some of you spells will one day come very easily, almost automatically, with very little in the way of conscious effort.

"When the change comes, I ask only that you know it for what it is, and be aware. For the true magician there is no very clear line between what lies inside the mind and what lies outside it. If you desire something, it will become substance. If you despise it, you will see it destroyed. A master magician is not much different from a child or a madman in that respect. It takes a very clear head and a very strong will to operate once you are in that place. And you will find out very quickly whether or not you have that clarity and that strength."

Mayakovsky stared out at their silent faces a moment longer, with undisguised disgust, then stepped down from the lectern. "Age," Quentin heard him mutter. "It's wasted on the young. Just like youth."

When night finally fell the stars burned shrilly overhead with impossible force and beauty. Quentin jogged with his head up, knees high, no longer feeling anything below his waist, gloriously isolated, lost in the spectacle. He became nothing, a running wraith, a wisp of warm flesh in a silent universe of midnight frost.

Once, for a few minutes, the darkness was disturbed by a flickering on the horizon. He realized it must be another student, another *skraeling* like himself, moving on a parallel path but way off to the east, twenty or thirty miles at least, and ahead of him. He thought about changing course to make contact. But seriously, what was the point? Should he risk getting busted for collaborating, just to say hi? What did he, a wraith, a wisp of warm flesh, need with anybody else?

Whoever it was, he thought dispassionately, was using a different set of spells than he was. He couldn't piece out the magic at this distance, but they were throwing off a whole lot of pale pink-white light.

Inefficient, he thought. Inelegant.

When the sun rose he lost sight of the other student again.

Some immeasurable period of time later, Quentin blinked. He had lost the habit of closing his magically weatherproofed eyes, but something was bothering him. It was a matter for concern, though he could barely formulate why in any conscious, coherent way. There was a black spot in his vision.

The landscape had, if anything, gotten more monotonous. Far behind him were the moments when streaks of dark frozen schist occasionally marred the white snow. Once he'd passed what he was fairly sure was a fallen meteorite stuck in the ice, a lump of something black, like a lost charcoal briquette. But that was a long time ago.

He was far gone. After days without real sleep his mind was a machine for monitoring spells and moving his feet, nothing else. But while he was checking off anomalies, there was something screwy going on with his compass wheel, too. It wobbled erratically, and it was getting kind of distorted. The *N* had grown vast and swollen; it was taking up five-sixths of the circle, and the other directions had withered away to almost nothing. The *S* he was supposed to be following had shrunk to a tiny squiggle in microscopic jewel type.

The black spot was taller than it was wide, and it bobbed up and down with his stride the way an external object would. So it wasn't corneal damage. And it was growing larger and larger, too. It was Mayakovsky, standing by himself in the powdery nothingness, holding a blanket. He must be at the pole. Quentin had completely forgotten where he was going or why.

When he got close enough Mayakovsky caught him. The tall man grunted, wrapping the heavy, scratchy blanket around him, and swung him down to the snow. Quentin's legs kept moving for a few seconds, then he lay still, panting, on his side, twitching like a netted fish. It was the first time in nine days that he'd stopped running. The sky spun. He retched.

Mayakovsky stood over him.

"*Molodyetz,* Quentin. Good man. Good man. You made it. You are going home."

There was something odd in Mayakovsky's voice. The sneer was gone, and it was thick with emotion. A twisted smile revealed for a moment the older wizard's yellow teeth in his unshaven face. He hauled Quentin to his feet with one hand; the other hand he flourished, and a portal appeared in the air. He shoved Quentin unceremoniously through it.

Quentin staggered and fell into a psychedelic riot of green that assaulted him so violently that at first he didn't recognize it as the rear terrace of Brakebills on a hot summer day. After the blankness of the polar ice the campus was a hallucinatory swirl of sound and color and warmth. He squeezed his eyes tight shut. He was home.

He rolled over on his back on the baking smooth stone. Birds sang deafeningly. He opened his eyes. A sight even stranger than the trees and the grass met them: looking back through the portal, he could still see the tall, soft-shouldered magician standing there with Antarctica in the background. Snow kicked up around him. A few stray crystals drifted through and evaporated in midflight. It looked like a painting executed on an oval panel and hung in midair. But the magical window was already closing. He must be preparing himself to go back to his empty polar mansion, Quentin thought. He waved, but Mayakovsky wasn't looking at him. He was looking out at the Maze and the rest of the Brakebills campus. The unguarded longing on his face was so excruciating Quentin had to look away.

Then the portal closed. It was over. It was late May, and the air was full of pollen. After the rarefied atmosphere of Antarctica it tasted hot and thick as soup. It was a lot like that first day he'd come to Brakebills, straight through from that frigid Brooklyn afternoon. The sun beat down. He sneezed.

They were all waiting for him, or almost all: Eliot and Josh and Janet, at least, wearing their old school uniforms, looking fat and happy and relaxed and none the worse for wear, like they'd done nothing for the past six months but sit on their asses and eat grilled cheese sandwiches.

"Welcome back," Eliot said. He was munching a yellow pear. "They only told us ten minutes ago you might be coming through."

"Wow." Josh's eyes were round. "Man, you look skinny. Wizard needs food badly. And also maybe a shower."

Quentin knew he had only a minute or two before he burst into tears and passed out. He still had Mayakovsky's scratchy wool blanket wrapped around him. He looked down at his pale, frozen feet. Nothing looked frostbitten, anyway, though one of his toes was sticking out at an angle. It didn't hurt yet.

It was very, very comfortable, deliriously comfortable, lying on his back on the hot stone like this, with the others looking down at him. He knew he should probably get up, for the sake of politeness if for no other reason, but he didn't feel like moving yet. He thought he might just stay where he was for another minute. He had earned himself a rest.

"Are you all right?" Josh said. "What was it like?"

"Alice kicked your ass," Janet said. "She got back two days ago. She already went home."

"You were out there a week and a half," Eliot said. "We were worried about you."

Why did they keep talking? If he could just gaze up at them in silence, that would be perfect. Just look at them and listen to the chirping birds and feel the warm flagstones holding him up. And maybe somebody could get him a glass of water, he was desperately thirsty. He tried to articulate this last sentiment, but his throat was dry and cracked. He wound up just making a tiny creaking noise.

"Oh, I think he wants to know about us," Janet said. She took a bite of Eliot's pear. "Yeah, nobody else went out but you two. What—you think we're stupid?"

ALICE

Quentin didn't spend any time in Brooklyn that summer because his parents didn't live there anymore. Abruptly and without consulting him, they'd sold off their Park Slope town house for a colossal sum and semiretired to a faux-Colonial McMansion in a placid suburb of Boston called Chesterton, where Quentin's mother could paint full time and his father could do God only knew what.

The shock of being severed from the place he grew up in was all the more surprising because it never really came. Quentin looked for the part of him that should have missed his old neighborhood, but it wasn't there. He supposed he must have been shedding his old identity and his old life all along, without noticing it. This just made the cut cleaner and neater. Really, it was probably easier this way. Not that his parents had made the move out of kindness, or any logic other than the obvious financial one.

The Chesterton house was yellow with green shutters and sat on an acre so aggressively landscaped that it looked like a virtual representation of itself. Though it was trimmed and detailed in a vaguely Colonial style, it was so enormous—bulging in all directions with extra wings and gables and roofs—that it looked like it had been inflated rather than constructed. Huge cement air-conditioning bunkers hummed outside night and day. It was even more unreal than the real world usually was.

When Quentin arrived home for summer vacation—Brakebills summer, September for the rest of the world—his parents were alarmed at his gaunt appearance, his hollow, shell-shocked eyes, his haunted demeanor.

But their curiosity about him was, as always, mild enough to be easily manageable, and he started gaining weight back quickly with the help of their massive, ever-full suburban refrigerator.

At first it was a relief just to be warm all the time, and to sleep in every day, and to be free of Mayakovsky and the Circumstances and that merciless white winter light. But after seventy-two hours Quentin was already bored again. In Antarctica he'd fantasized about having nothing to do except lie on his bed and sleep and stare into space, but now those empty hours were here, and they were getting old amazingly fast. The long silences at Brakebills South had made him impatient with small talk. He had no interest in TV anymore—it looked like an electronic puppet show to him, an artificial version of an imitation world that meant nothing to him anyway. Real life—or was it fantasy life? whichever one Brakebills was—that was what mattered, and that was happening somewhere else.

As he usually did when he was stuck at home, he went on a Fillory binge. The old 1970s-era covers looked more and more dated every time he saw them, with their psychedelic *Yellow Submarine* palette, and on a couple of them the covers had come off completely and been tucked back between the pages as bookmarks. But the world inside the books was as fresh and vital as ever, unfaded and unironized by time. Quentin had never before really appreciated the cleverness of the second book. *The Girl Who Told Time,* in which Rupert and Helen are abruptly shanghaied into Fillory straight out of their respective boarding schools, the only time the Chatwins cross over in winter instead of summer. They end up back in an earlier time period, one that overlaps with the storyline of the first book. With the aid of foreknowledge, Rupert dogs Martin's and Helen's footsteps—the earlier Helen's—as they repeat the action of *The World in the Walls,* note for note. He keeps just out of view, dropping clues and helping them out without their knowledge (the mysterious character known only as the Wood One turns out to have been Rupert in disguise); Quentin wondered if Plover wrote *The Girl Who Told Time* just to shore up all the plot holes in *The World in the Walls.*

Meanwhile Helen embarks on a hunt for the mysterious Questing Beast of Fillory, which according to legend can't be caught, but if you do catch it—all logic aside—it's supposed to give you your heart's desire. The Beast leads her on a tricksy, circuitous chase that somehow winds in and out of the enchanted tapestries that adorn the library of Castle Whitespire. She only ever catches a glimpse of it, peeking coyly out at her from behind an embroidered shrub before vanishing in a flicker of cloven hoofs.

At the end the twin rams Ember and Umber show up as usual, like a pair of sinister ruminant constables. They were a force for good, of course, but there was a slightly Orwellian quality to their oversight of Fillory: they knew everything that went on, and there was no obvious limit to their powers, but they rarely bestirred themselves to actively intervene on behalf of the creatures in their charge. Mostly they just scolded everybody involved for the mess they'd made, finishing each other's sentences, then made everyone renew their vows of fealty before wandering away to crop some luckless farmer's alfalfa fields. They firmly usher Rupert and Helen back into the real world, back into the damp, chilly, dark-wood-paneled halls of their boarding schools, as if they had never left it.

Quentin even plowed through *The Wandering Dune,* the fifth and last book in the series (that is, the last as far as anybody but Quentin knew) and not a fan favorite. It was longer by half than any of the other books and starred Helen and the youngest Chatwin, clever, introverted Jane. The tone of *The Wandering Dune* is different from earlier books: having spent the last two volumes searching fruitlessly for their vanished brother, Martin, the Chatwins' usual cheery English indomitability has been tempered by a wistful mood. On entering Fillory the two girls encounter a mysterious sand dune being blown through the kingdom, all by itself. They climb the dune and find themselves riding it through the green Fillorian countryside and on out into a dreamy desert wasteland in the far south, where they spend most of the rest of the book.

Almost nothing happens. Jane and Helen fill up the pages with interminable conversations about right and wrong and teenage Christian metaphysics and whether their true obligations lie on Earth or in Fillory. Jane is desperately worried about Martin but also, like Quentin, a little jealous: whatever iron law kept the Chatwins from staying in Fillory forever, he had found a loophole, or it had found him. Alive or dead, he had managed to overstay his tourist visa.

But Helen, who has a scoldy streak, heaps scorn on Martin—she thinks he's just hiding in Fillory so he won't have to go home. He's the child who doesn't want to leave the playground, or who won't go to bed. He's Peter Pan. Why can't he grow up and face the real world? She calls him selfish, self-indulgent, "the biggest baby of us all."

In the end the sisters are picked up by a majestic clipper ship that sails through the sand as if it were water. The ship is crewed by large bunnies who would be overly cutesy (the *Wandering Dune*–haters always compared them to Ewoks) if it weren't for their impressively hard-assed attention to the technical details of operating their complex vessel.

The bunnies leave Jane and Helen with a gift, a set of magical buttons they can use to zap themselves from Earth to Fillory and back at will. On returning to England, Helen, in a fit of self-righteousness, promptly hides the buttons and won't tell Jane where they are, upon which Jane excoriates her in fine period vernacular and turns the entire household upside down and inside out. But she never finds the buttons, and on that unsatisfying note the book, and the whole series, ends.

Even if it didn't turn out to be the final book in the series, Quentin wondered where Plover could possibly have gone with the story in *The Magicians*. For one thing he was out of Chatwins: the books always featured two Chatwin children, an older one from the previous book and a new, younger one. But pretty, dark-haired Jane was the last and youngest Chatwin. Would she have gone back to Fillory alone? It broke the pattern.

For another, half of the fun of the books was waiting for the Chatwins to find their way into Fillory, for the magic door that opens for them and them only to appear. You always knew it would, and it always surprised you when it did. But with the buttons you could shuttle back and forth at will. Where was the miracle in that? Maybe that was why Helen hid them. They might as well have built a subway to Fillory.

Quentin's conversations with his parents were so circular and self-defeating, they sounded like experimental theater. In the mornings he lay in bed as long as he could stand it, in an attempt to avoid breakfast with them, but they always waited him out. He couldn't win: they had even less to do than he did. Sometimes he wondered if it was a perverse game they played, that they were in on and he wasn't.

He would come down to find them sitting at a table littered with crusts and crumbs and clementine peels and cereal bowls. While he pretended to be interested in the *Chesterton Chestnut,* he would furiously search for some even remotely plausible topic of conversation:

"So. Are you guys still going on that trip to South America?"

"South America?" His dad looked up, startled, as if he'd forgotten Quentin was there.

"Aren't you going to South America?"

A look passed between Quentin's parents.

"Spain. We're going to Spain and Portugal."

"Oh, Portugal. Right. I was thinking Peru for some reason."

"Spain and Portugal. It's for your mother. There's an artists' exchange with the university in Lisbon. Then we're going to take a boat trip down the Tigris."

"*Tagus,* darling!" Quentin's mother said, with her tinkling I-married-an-idiot! laugh. "The Tagus! The Tigris is in Iraq."

She bit into a piece of raisin toast with her large straight teeth.

"Well, I don't think we'll be sailing down the Tigris anytime soon!" Quentin's father laughed loudly at this, exactly as if it were funny, and then paused for thought. "Darling, do you remember that week we spent in a houseboat on the Volga . . . ?"

An extended Russian reminiscence followed, a duet punctuated by significant silences that Quentin interpreted as allusions to sexual activities that he didn't want to know about. It was enough to make you envy the Chatwins, with Dad in the army and Mum in the madhouse. Mayakovsky would have known what to do with this kind of conversation. He would have silenced it. He wondered how hard that spell was to learn.

By about eleven every morning Quentin would hit his limit and flee the house for the relative safety of Chesterton, which stubbornly refused to reveal even the slightest hint of mystery or intrigue beneath its green, self-satisfied exterior. He had never learned to drive, so he rode his father's white 1970s-era ten-speed, which weighed approximately one metric ton, to the center of town. Out of deference to its glorious Colonial heritage the town was governed by a set of draconian zoning laws that kept everything in a state of permanent unnatural quaintness.

Knowing no one, caring about nothing, Quentin took a tour of the low-ceilinged, heavy-timbered residence of some Revolutionary luminary.

He inspected a boxy white-painted Unitarian church, est. 1766. He surveyed the lush flat lawns where amateur Continental irregulars had faced off against well-drilled, well-armed Redcoats, with predictable results. There was one pleasant surprise, hidden behind the church: a lovely half-vanished seventeenth-century graveyard, a little square glebe of ultra-green grass scattered with wet saffron-colored elm leaves, with a bent wrought-iron fence around it. Inside, it was cool and hushed.

The gravestones were all winged skulls and bad devotional quatrains about whole families carried off by fever, weathered in places into illegibility. Quentin crouched down on the wet grass to try to decipher one very old one, a rectangle of blue slate that had split in half and sunk halfway into the green turf, which rose up to meet it like a wave.

"Quentin."

He straightened up. A woman about his age had come in through the cemetery gate.

"Hi?" he said cautiously. How did she know his name?

"I guess you didn't think I would find you," she said unsteadily. "I guess you didn't think of that."

She walked right up to him. At the last possible moment, too late to do anything about it, he realized that she wasn't going to stop. Without breaking stride she grabbed the front of his barn jacket and marched him stumbling backward over a low footstone right into the aromatic branches of a cypress tree. Her face, pushed right up in front of his, dangerously close, was an angry mask. It had been raining off and on all afternoon, and the needles were damp.

He resisted the impulse to struggle. He wasn't going to be caught fighting a girl in a churchyard.

"Whoa, whoa, whoa!" he said. "Stop. Just stop."

"Now I'm here," she said, clinging precariously to her composure, "now I'm here, and we are going to talk. You are going to deal with me."

Now that he had a closer look at her he could see she was covered in warning signs. Her whole body screamed unbalance. She was too pale and too thin. Her eyes were too wild. Her long dark hair was lank and smelled unwashed. She was dressed in a raggedy goth outfit—her arms were wrapped in what looked like black electrical tape. There were scabby red scratches on the backs of her hands.

He almost didn't recognize her.

"I was there, and you were there," Julia said, locking eyes with him. "Weren't you. In that place. That school, or whatever it was. You got in, didn't you?"

He got it then. She had been at the Exam after all, he hadn't been mistaken, but she hadn't made the cut. They'd culled her in the first round, during the written test.

But this was all wrong. It wasn't supposed to happen, there were safeguards against it. Anybody who flunked the Exam was supposed to have their memory gently, lovingly clouded by a faculty member and then overwritten with a plausible alibi. It wasn't simple, nor was it outrageously ethical, but the spells were humane and well understood. Except in her case they hadn't worked, or not completely.

"Julia," he said. Their faces were very close together. There was nicotine on her breath. "Julia, what are you doing here?"

"Don't pretend with me, don't you *dare* pretend! You go to that school, don't you? The magic school?"

Quentin kept his face blank. It was a basic rule at Brakebills not to discuss the school with outsiders. He could get expelled. But whatever, if Fogg screwed up the memory spells it wasn't Quentin's problem. And this was Julia. Her lovely freckly face, so close to his, looked much older. Her skin was blotchy. She was in agony.

"All right," he said. "Okay. Sure. I go there."

"I knew it!" she shrieked. She stamped her booted foot on the graveyard grass. From her reaction he guessed that she'd been at least halfway bluffing. "I knew it was real, I knew it was real," she said, mostly to herself. "I *knew* it wasn't a dream!" She bent over, with her hands over her face, and one convulsive sob escaped her.

Quentin took a deep breath. He readjusted his jacket.

"Listen," he said gently. She was still doubled over. He bent down, putting a hand on her narrow back. "Julia. You're not supposed to remember any of that stuff. They're supposed to make you forget if you don't get in."

"But I should have!" She straightened up with the flashing red eyes and cold crystal seriousness of the true nutjob. "I was supposed to get in. I know I was. It was a mistake. Believe me, it was." Her large eyes tried to burn into his. "I'm like you, I can do real magic. I'm like you. See? That's why they couldn't make me forget."

Quentin saw. He could see everything. No wonder she'd been so altered the last time he saw her. That one glimpse through the curtain, of the world behind the world, had knocked her completely out of orbit. She'd seen it once, and she couldn't let go. Brakebills had ruined her.

There was a time when he would have done anything for her. And he still would, he just didn't know what to do. Why did he feel so guilty? He took a deep breath.

"But that's not how it works. Even if you really can do magic, that wouldn't make you any more resistant to memory spells than anybody else."

She was staring at him hungrily. Everything he was saying just confirmed what she wanted to believe: that magic was real. He backed away, just to put some distance between them, but she grabbed his sleeve.

"Oh, no-no-no-no-no," she said with a brittle smile. "Q. Please. Wait. No. You're going to help me. That's why I came here."

She had dyed her hair black. It looked dry and burnt.

"Julia, I want to. I just don't know what I can do."

"Just watch this. Watch."

She let go of his arm, reluctantly, as if she expected him to vanish or run away the instant she did. Incredibly, Julia launched into a basically correct version of a simple Basque optical spell called Ugarte's Prismatic Spray.

She must have found it online. Some genuine magical information did circulate in the straight world, mostly on the Internet, though it was buried in so much bogus crap that nobody could tease out the real stuff, even if they could have used it. Quentin had even seen a Brakebills blazer for sale on eBay. It was extremely rare, but not unheard of, for civilians to work up a spell or two on their own, but as far as Quentin knew they never got into anything serious. Real magicians called them hedge witches. A few of them had careers as stage magicians, or set themselves up as cult demi-deities, gathering around themselves congregations of Wiccans and Satanists and oddball Christian outliers.

Julia proclaimed the words of the spell theatrically, overarticulating like she was doing summer-stock Shakespeare. She had no idea what she was doing. Quentin glanced nervously at the doorway at the back of the church.

"Look!" She held up her hand defiantly. The spell had actually worked, sort of. Her bitten-down fingertips left faint radiant rainbow trails in the air. She waved them around, making mystical gestures like an interpretive dancer. Ugarte's Prismatic Spray was a totally useless spell. Quentin felt a pang when he thought about how many months, if not years, it must have cost her to figure it out.

"See?" she demanded, close to tears. "You see it too, right? It's not too late for me. I won't go back to college. Tell them. Tell them I could still come."

"Does James know?"

She shook her head tightly. "He wouldn't understand. I don't see him anymore."

He wanted to help her, but there was no way to. It was far, far too late. Better to be blunt about it. This could have been me, he thought. This was almost me.

"I don't think there's anything I can do," he said. "It's not up to me. I've never heard of them changing their minds—no one ever gets a second Exam."

But Alice got an Exam, he thought, even though she wasn't Invited.

"You could tell them, though. You can't decide, but you can tell them I'm here, right? That I'm still out here? You can at least do that!"

She grabbed his arm again, and he had to mutter a quick counterspell to snuff out the Prismatic Spray. That stuff could eat into fabric.

"Just tell them you saw me," she said urgently, her eyes full of dying hope. "Please. I've been practicing. You can teach me. I'll be your apprentice. I'll do whatever you need. I have an aunt who lives in Winchester, I can live with her.

"Or what do you need, Quentin?" She moved closer to him, just slightly, so that her knee touched his knee. In spite of himself he felt the old electrical field form between them. She hazarded a curvy, sardonic smile, letting the moment hang in the air. "Maybe we can help each other. You used to want my help."

He was angry at himself for being tempted. He was angry at the world for being this way. He wanted to yell obscenities. It would have been terrible to see anybody scrape the bottom like this, but her . . . it should have been anybody but her. She has already seen more unhappiness, Quentin thought, than I will ever see in my life.

"Listen to me," he said. "Julia. If I tell them, they're just going to find you and wipe your memory. For real this time."

"They can try," she snarled, suddenly fierce. "They tried once already."

She breathed hard through pinched white nostrils.

"Just tell me where it is. Where we were. I've been looking for it. Just tell me where the school is, and I'll leave you alone."

Quentin could only imagine the kind of shit he'd be in if Julia showed up at the House hell-bent on matriculating and dropped his name.

"It's in upstate New York. On the Hudson somewhere, I don't know exactly where. I really don't. It's near West Point. They make it invisible. Even I don't know how to find it. But I'll tell them about you, if that's truly what you want."

He was just making it worse. Maybe he should have bluffed her after all, he thought. Tried harder to lie. Too late.

She put her arms around him, as if she were too exhausted by relief and despair to stand anymore, and he held her. There was a time when this was everything he wanted.

"They couldn't make me forget," she whispered into his chest. "Do you understand that? They couldn't make me forget."

He could feel her heart beating, and the word he heard when it beat was *shame, shame, shame.* He wondered why they hadn't taken her. If anybody should have gone to Brakebills, it was her, not him. But they really would wipe her memory, he thought. Fogg would make sure this time. She'd be happier that way anyway. She could get back on track, go back to college, get back together with James, get on with her life. It would all be for the best.

By next morning he was back at Brakebills. The others were already there; they were surprised he'd lasted as long as he did. The most any of them had spent at home was forty-eight hours. Eliot hadn't gone home at all.

It was cool and quiet in the Cottage. Quentin felt safe again. He was back where he belonged. Eliot was in the kitchen with a dozen eggs and a bottle of brandy, trying to make flips, which nobody wanted but which he was determined to make anyway. Josh and Janet were playing an idiotic card game called Push—it was basically the magical equivalent of War—that was wildly popular at Brakebills. Quentin just used it as a chance to show off his card-handling skills, which was why nobody ever wanted to play with him anymore.

While they played Janet told the story of Alice's Antarctic ordeal, despite the fact that everybody except Quentin had heard it already, and Alice herself was right there in the room, silently paging through an old herbal in the window seat. Quentin didn't know how he would feel about seeing Alice again, after he'd made such a comprehensive mess of their last conversation, but to his amazed relief, and despite every possible reason to the contrary, it wasn't awkward at all. It was perfect. His heart clenched with silent happiness when he saw her.

"And then when Mayakovsky tried to give her the bag of sheep fat, she threw it back in his face!"

"I meant to hand it back to him," Alice said quietly from the window seat. "But it was so cold and I was shaking so badly, I sort of flung it at him. He was all *'chyort vozmi!'*"

"Why didn't you just take it?"

"I don't know." She put the book down. "I'd made all these plans for getting by without it, it just threw me off. Plus I wanted him to stop looking at me naked. And anyway I didn't know he was going to have mutton fat for us. I hadn't even prepared the Chkhartishvili."

That was a white lie. Like Alice couldn't have cast Chkhartishvili cold. He had missed her so much.

"So what did you do for heat?" he said.

"I tried using some of those German thermogenesis charms, but they kept fading away whenever I fell asleep. By the second night I was waking myself up every fifteen minutes just to make sure I was still alive. By the third day I was losing my mind. So I ended up using a tweaked Miller Flare."

"I don't get it." Josh frowned. "How is that supposed to help?"

"If you kind of mangle it a little it becomes inefficient. The extra energy comes out as heat instead of light."

"You know you could have cooked yourself by accident?" Janet said.

"I know. But when I realized the German thing wasn't going to work, I couldn't think of anything else."

"I think I saw you once," Quentin said quietly. "At night."

"You couldn't have missed me. I looked like a road flare."

"A naked road flare," Josh said.

Eliot came in with a tureen full of viscous, unappetizing flip and began ladling it into teacups. Alice picked up her book and headed for the stairs.

"Hang on, I'm coming back with the hot ones!" Eliot called, busily grating nutmeg.

Quentin didn't hang on. He followed Alice.

At first he'd thought everything would be different between him and Alice. Then he thought everything was back to normal. Now he understood that he didn't want things to be back to normal. He couldn't stop looking at her, even after she'd looked at him, seen him looking at her, and looked away in embarrassment again. It was like she'd become charged in some way that drew him to her uncontrollably. He could sense her naked body inside her dress, smell it like a vampire smells blood. Maybe Mayakovsky hadn't quite managed to get all the fox out of him.

He found her in one of the upstairs bedrooms. She was lying on one of a pair of twin beds, on top of the bedspread, reading. It was dim and hot. The roof slanted in at an odd angle. The room was full of odd, old furniture—a wicker chair with a staved-in seat, a dresser with a stuck drawer—and it had deep red wallpaper that didn't match any other room in the house. Quentin yanked up the window halfway—it made an outraged squawk— and flopped down on the other twin bed.

"Can you believe they have these here? It's a full set—they were in the bookcase in the bathroom." She held up the book she was reading. Incredibly, it was an old copy of *The World in the Walls*.

"I had that exact same edition." The cover showed Martin Chatwin halfway through the old grandfather clock, with his feet still in this world and his amazed head poking into Fillory, which was drawn as a groovy 1970s disco winter wonderland.

"I haven't looked at them for years. God, remember the Cozy Horse? That big velvet horse that would just carry you around? I wanted one so badly when I was that age. Did you read them?"

Quentin wasn't sure how much to reveal about his Fillory obsession.

"I may have taken a look."

Alice smirked and went back to the book. "Why is it that you still think you can keep secrets from me?"

Quentin folded his hands behind his head and lay back on the pillow and looked up at the low, tilted ceiling. This wasn't right. There was something brother-sister about it.

"Here. Budge over."

He switched beds and lay down next to Alice, hip-checking her sideways to make room on the narrow bed. She held up the paperback, and they read together silently for a few pages. Their shoulders and upper arms touched. Quentin felt like the bed was on a train moving very fast, and if he looked out the window he'd see the landscape racing past. They were both breathing very carefully.

"I never got it about the Cozy Horse," Quentin said after a while. "First of all, there's only one of it. Is there a whole herd of Cozy Horses somewhere? And then it's too useful. You'd think somebody would have domesticated it by now."

She whacked his head with the spine, not completely gently.

"Somebody *evil*. You can't break the Cozy Horse, the Cozy Horse is a free spirit. Anyway it's too big. I always figured it was mechanical—somebody made it somehow."

"Like who?"

"I don't know. A magician. Somebody in the past. Anyway the Cozy Horse is a girl thing."

Janet stuck her head in. Apparently the exodus downstairs was general.

"Ha!" Janet brayed. "I can't believe you're reading that."

Alice scooched an inch away from him, instinctively, but he didn't move.

"Like you didn't," Quentin said.

"Of course I did! When I was nine I made my family call me 'Fiona' for two weeks."

She vanished, leaving behind a comfortable, echoless silence. The room was cooling down as hot air ascended out through the half-open window. Quentin imagined it rising in an invisible braided plume into the blue summer day.

"Did you know there really was a Chatwin family?" he asked. "In real life? Supposedly they lived next door to Plover."

Alice nodded. She unscooched now that Janet was gone. "It's sad though."

"Sad how."

"Well, do you know what happened to them?"

Quentin shook his head.

"There's a book about it. Most of them grew up to be pretty boring. Housewives and insurance magnates and whatnot. I think one of the boys married an heiress. I know one got killed in World War Two. But you know the thing about Martin?"

Quentin shook his head.

"Well, you know how he disappears in the book? He really did disappear. He ran away or had an accident or something. One day after breakfast he just vanished, and they never saw him again."

"The real Martin?"

"The real Martin."

"God. That is sad."

He tried to imagine it, a big fresh-faced, floppy-haired English family—he pictured them in a sepia-toned family portrait, in tennis whites—suddenly with a gaping hole opening in the middle of it. The somber announcement. The slow, decorous acceptance. The lingering damage.

"It makes me think of my brother," Alice said.

"I know."

At this she looked at him sharply. He looked back. It was true, he did know.

He propped himself up on one elbow so he could look down at her, the air around him whirling with excited dust motes. "When I was little," he said slowly, "and even when I was not so little, I used to envy Martin."

She smiled up at him.

"I know."

"Because I thought he'd finally done it. I know it was supposed to be a tragedy, but to me it was like he broke the bank, beat the system. He got to stay in Fillory forever."

"I know. I get it." She put a restraining hand on his chest. "That's what makes you different from the rest of us, Quentin. You actually still believe in magic. You do realize, right, that nobody else does? I mean, we all know magic is real. But you really believe in it. Don't you."

He felt flustered. "Is that wrong?"

She nodded and smiled even more brightly. "Yes, Quentin. It's wrong."

He kissed her, softly at first. Then he got up and locked the door.

And that's how it started, though of course it had been starting for a long time. At first it was like they were getting away with something, as if they half expected someone or something to stop them. When nothing happened, and there were no consequences, they lost control—they ravenously, roughly pulled each other's clothes off, not just out of desire for each other but out of a pure desire to lose control. It was like a fantasy. The sound of breathing and rustling cloth was thunderous in the little chaste bedroom. God only knew what they could hear downstairs. He wanted to push her, to see if she had it as bad as he did, to see how far she'd go and how far she'd let him go. She didn't stop him. She pushed him ever further. It wasn't his first time, or even his first time with Alice, technically, but this was different. This was real, human sex, and it was so much better just because they weren't animals—because they were civilized and prudish and self-conscious humans who transformed into sweaty, lustful, naked beasts, not through magic but because that's who on some level they really were all along.

They tried to be discreet about it—they barely even discussed it between themselves—but the others knew, and they came up with excuses to leave the two of them alone, and Quentin and Alice took them. Probably they were relieved that the tension between them was finally over. In its way the fact that Alice wanted Quentin as much as he wanted her was as much of a miracle as anything else he'd seen since he came to Brakebills, and no easier to believe, though he had no choice but to believe it. His love for Julia had been a liability, a dangerous force that lashed him to cold, empty Brooklyn. Alice's love was so much more real, and it bound him finally and for good to his new life, his real life, at Brakebills. It fixed him here and nowhere else. It wasn't a fantasy. It was flesh and blood.

And she understood that. She seemed to know everything about Quentin, everything he was thinking and feeling, sometimes before he did, and she wanted him in spite of it—because of it. Together they rudely colonized the upstairs at the Cottage, running back to the dorms only for indispensable personal items, and letting it be known that trespassers would be exposed to displays of mutual affection, verbal and otherwise, and the sight of their scattered underthings.

That wasn't the only miraculous event that summer. Astoundingly, the three older Physical Kids had graduated from Brakebills. Even Josh, with his lousy grades. The official ceremony would happen in another week; it was a private affair to which the rest of the school was not invited. By tradition they would be allowed to stay at Brakebills for the rest of the summer, but after that they would be ushered out into the world.

Quentin was stunned by this turn of events. They all were. It was hard to imagine life at Brakebills without them; it was hard for Quentin to imagine life after Brakebills at all. There hadn't been much discussion of what they were going to do next, or at least not around Quentin.

It wasn't necessarily a cause for alarm. The passage from Brakebills to the outside world was a well-traveled one. There was an extensive network of magicians operating in the wider world, and, being magicians, they were in no danger of starving. They could do more or less whatever they wanted as long as they didn't interfere with one another. The real problem was figuring out to their own satisfaction what that was. Some of the student body went into public service—quietly promoting the success of humanitarian causes, or subtly propping up the balance of various failing ecosystems, or participating in the governance of magical society, such as it was. A lot of people just traveled, or created magical artworks, or staged elaborate sorcerous war games. Others went into research: many magical schools (although not Brakebills) offered programs of post-graduate study, with various advanced degrees conferred at the end. Some students even chose to matriculate at a regular, nonmagical university. The application of conventional science, chemistry especially, to magical techniques was a hot field. Who knew what exotic spells you could create using the new transuranic elements?

"I was thinking of trying to talk to the Thames dragon about it," Eliot said airily one afternoon. They were sitting on the floor in the library. It was too hot for chairs.

"The who?" Quentin said.

"You think he would see you?" Josh asked.

"You never know till you ask."

"Wait a minute," Quentin said. "Who or what is the Thames dragon?"

"The Thames dragon," Eliot said. "You know. The dragon who lives in the Thames. I'm sure he has another name, a dragon name, but I doubt we could pronounce it."

"What are you saying." Quentin looked around for help. "An actual dragon? Are you saying there are real dragons?" He hadn't quite reached the point where he always knew when he was being made fun of.

"Come on, Quentin," Janet scoffed. They'd gotten to the part of Push where they flipped cards across the room into a hat. They were using a mixing bowl from the kitchen.

"I'm not kidding."

"You really don't know? Didn't you read the McCabe?" Alice looked at him incredulously. "It was in Meerck's class."

"No, I did not read the McCabe," Quentin said. He didn't know whether to be angry or excited. "You could have just told me there were real dragons."

She sniffed. "It never came up."

Apparently there really were such things as dragons, though they were rare, and most of them were water dragons, solitary creatures who rarely broke the surface and spent a lot of their time asleep, buried in river mud. There was one—no more—in each of the world's major rivers, and being smart and practically immortal, they tended to stash away all kinds of odd bits of wisdom. The Thames dragon was not as sociable as the Ganges dragon, the Mississippi dragon, or the Neva dragon, but it was said to be much smarter and more interesting. The Hudson River had a dragon of its own—it spent most of its time curled up in a deep, shadowy eddy less than a mile from the Brakebills boathouse. It hadn't been seen for almost a century. The largest and oldest known dragon was a colossal white who lived coiled up inside a huge freshwater aquifer under the Antarctic ice cap, and who had never once in recorded history spoken to anyone, not even its own kind.

"But you really think the Thames dragon is going to give you free career advice?" Josh said.

"Oh, I don't know," Eliot said. "Dragons are so weird about these things. You want to ask them deep, profound questions, like where does magic come from, or are there aliens, or what are the next ten Mersenne primes, and half the time they just want to play Chinese checkers."

"I love Chinese checkers!" Janet said.

"Well, okay, maybe you should go talk to the Thames dragon," Eliot said irritably.

"Maybe I will," she said happily. "I think we'd have a lot to talk about."

———————

Quentin felt like all the Physical Kids were falling in love with each other, not just him and Alice, or at least with who they were when they were around each other. In the mornings they slept late. In the afternoons they played pool and boated on the Hudson and interpreted each other's dreams and debated meaningless points of magical technique. They discussed the varying intensities and timbres of their hangovers. There was an ongoing competition, hotly contested, as to who could make the single most boring observation.

Josh was teaching himself to play the rinky-tink upright piano in the upstairs hallway, and they lay on the grass and listened to his halting rendition of "Heart and Soul," over and over and over again. It should have been annoying, but somehow it wasn't.

By this point they had thoroughly co-opted the butler, Chambers, who regularly furnished them with extra-special bottles from the Brakebills cellars, which were overcrowded anyway and needed to be drunk up. Eliot was the only one with any real sophistication in oenological matters, and he tried to teach the rest of them, but Quentin's tolerance was low, and he refused to spit as a matter of principle, so he just ended up getting drunk every night and forgetting whatever he was supposed to be learning and starting over from scratch the next night. Every morning when he woke up it seemed impossible that he could ever consume another drop of alcohol, but that conviction had always evaporated by five o'clock in the afternoon.

EMILY GREENSTREET

One afternoon all five of them were sitting cross-legged in a circle in the vast empty middle of the Sea. It was a baking hot summer day, and they had gone out there with the intention of attempting a ridiculously elaborate piece of collaborative magic, a five-person spell that, if it worked, would sharpen their vision and hearing and increase their physical strength for a couple of hours. It was Viking magic, battlefield magic designed for a raiding party, and as far as any of them knew it hadn't been tried in roughly a millennium. Josh, who was directing their efforts, confessed that he wasn't completely sure it had ever worked in the first place. Those Viking shamans did a lot of empty boasting.

They had started drinking early, over lunch. Even though Josh said everything was ready at noon—done deal, good to go, let's hook it up—by the time he actually gave them their handouts, spiral-ring pages of Old Norse chants scratched out in ballpoint in Josh's neat, tiny runic script, and prepared the ground by pouring out a weaving, branching knot in black sand on the grass, it was almost four. There was singing involved, and neither Janet nor Quentin could carry a tune, and they kept cracking each other up and having to start over.

Finally they got all the way through it, and they sat around staring at the grass and the sky and the backs of their hands and the clock tower in the distance, trying to tell if anything was different. Quentin jogged to the edge of the forest to pee, and when he got back Janet was talking about somebody named Emily Greenstreet.

"Don't tell me you knew her," Eliot said.

"*I* didn't. But remember I roomed with that cow Emma Curtis during First Year? I was talking to her cousin last week when I was home, she lives near my parents in L.A. She was here then. Told me the whole story."

"*Really.*"

"And now you're going to tell us," Josh said.

"It's all a big secret, though. You can't tell anybody."

"Emma wasn't a cow," Josh said. "Or if she was she was a hot cow. She's like one of those *wagyu* cows. Did she ever pay you back for that dress she threw up on?" He was lying on his back, staring up into the cloudless sky. He didn't seem to care if the spell had worked or not.

"No, she didn't. And now she's gone to Tajikistan or something to save the vanishing Asiatic grasshopper. Or something. Cow."

"Who's Emily Greenstreet?" Alice asked.

"Emily Greenstreet," Janet said grandly, savoring the rich, satisfying piece of gossip she was about to impart, "was the first person to leave Brakebills voluntarily in one hundred fifty years."

Her words floated up and drifted away like cigarette smoke in the warm summer air. It was hot out in the middle of the Sea, with no shade, but they were all too lazy to move.

"She came to Brakebills about eight years ago. I think she was from Connecticut, but not fancy Connecticut, with the money and the Kennedy cousins and the Lyme disease. I think she was from New Haven, or Bridgeport. She was quiet, sort of mousy-looking—"

"How do you know she was mousy-looking?" Josh asked.

"*Sh!*" Alice whacked Josh on the arm. "Don't antagonize her. I want to hear the story." They were all lying on a stripy blanket spread out over the ruins of Josh's sand pattern.

"I know because Emma's cousin told me. Anyway, it's my story, and if I say she was mousy, then she had a tail and she lived on Swiss fucking cheese.

"Emily Greenstreet was one of these girls that nobody ever notices, who are only friends with other girls nobody notices. Nobody likes or dislikes them. They have weak chins or chicken-pox scars, or their glasses are too big. I know I'm being mean. But you know, they're just sort of at the edge of everything.

"She was a good student. She kept busy and got by in her boring little way until her Third Year, when she finally distinguished herself by falling in love with one of her professors.

"Everybody does it, of course. Or at least the girls do, since we all have daddy complexes. But usually it's just a crush, and we get over it and move on to some loser guy our own age. But not our Emily. She was deeply, passionately, delusionally in love. *Wuthering Heights* love. She stood outside his window at night. She drew little pictures of him in class. She looked at the moon and cried. She drew little pictures of the moon in class and cried at them.

"She become moody and depressed. She started wearing black and listening to the Smiths and reading Camus in the original whatever. Her eyes became interestingly pouchy and sunken. She started hanging out at Woof."

All groaned. Woof was a fountain in the Maze; its official name was Van Pelt, after an eighteenth-century Dean, but it depicted Romulus and Remus suckling from a she-wolf with many dangling wolf-boobs, hence Woof. It was the chosen hangout of the goths and the artsy crowd.

"Now she had a Secret, capital *S*, and ironically it made her more attractive to people, because they wanted to know what her Secret was. And sure enough, before long a boy, some deeply unfortunate boy, fell in love with her.

"She didn't love this boy back, since she was savin' all her lovin' for Professor Sexyman, but he made her feel pretty damn good, since nobody had ever been in love with her before. She strung him along and flirted with him in public in the hope that it would make her real love interest jealous.

"Now we turn to the third point in our little triangle of love. By all rights the professor should have been completely impervious to our Emily's charms. He should have had an avuncular little chuckle over it in the Senior Common Room and then forgotten about it. She wasn't even that hot. Maybe he was having a midlife crisis, maybe he thought a liaison with Ms. Greenstreet could restore to him some of his long-vanished youth. Who knows. He was married, too, the idiot.

"We'll never know exactly what happened or how far it went, except that it went too far, and then Professor Sexyman came to his senses, or got what he wanted, and he called it off.

"Needless to say our Emily became even gothier and weepier and more like a Gorey drawing than she already was, and her boy became even more besotted and brought her presents and flowers and was Supportive.

"Maybe you knew this, I don't know, I didn't, but Woof used to be different from the other fountains. That's why the doomers started hanging out there in the first place. You wouldn't notice what was off about it, at first, but after a while you'd realize that when you looked into it, you wouldn't see your own reflection, just empty sky. And maybe if the sky was cloudy on that particular day, the sky in the fountain would be blue, or the other way around. It definitely wasn't a normal reflection. And every once in a while you'd look into it and you'd see other faces looking up at you, looking puzzled, as if they were looking into some other fountain somewhere else and were weirded out because they were seeing your face and not their own. Somebody must have figured out a way to switch the reflections in two fountains, but who did it and why, and how, and why the Dean didn't change them back, I have no idea.

"You have to wonder, too, if it was more than just the reflections—if you could dive down into one pool and come up in the other one, in this world or some other world. There's always been something off about those fountains. Did you know they were here before Brakebills? They built the school to be near them, and not the other way around. Or that's what people say."

Eliot snorted.

"Well that's what people *say,* darling. *Anyway,*" Janet went on, "the thing is, Emily started spending a lot of time at Woof, just smoking and hanging out, and I guess mooning over her little affair. She spent so much time there that she started to recognize one of the faces in the fountain. Somebody like her, who was spending a lot of time at the other fountain, the one in the reflection. Let's call her Doris. After a while Emily and Doris got to noticing each other. They'd acknowledge each other, a little wave, you know, just to be polite. Probably Doris was a little mopey, too. They got to feeling like kindred spirits.

"Emily and Doris worked out a way to communicate. Again, the exact details have eluded your intrepid correspondent. Maybe they held up signs or something. They must have had to be in mirror writing, to make sense as reflections, or am I getting that wrong?

"I don't know how things worked in Woofland, where Doris lived, maybe magic is different there. Or maybe Doris was fucking with our Emily, maybe she was sick of hearing Emily whine about her love life. Maybe there was something really wrong with Doris, maybe she was something genuinely evil. But one day Doris suggested that if Emily wanted her lover back, maybe her appearance was the problem, and she should try changing it?"

A chill settled over the group, where they lay on the sun-warm turf. Even Quentin knew that using magic to alter one's physical appearance never ended well. In the world of magical theory it was a dead spot: something about the inextricable, recursive connection between your face and who you were—your soul, for lack of a better word—made it hellishly difficult and fatally unpredictable. When Quentin had first gotten to Brakebills, he'd wondered why everybody didn't just make themselves ridiculously good-looking. He'd looked at the kids with an obviously flawed feature— like Gretchen with her leg, or Eliot with his twisted jaw—and wondered why they didn't get somebody to fix them up, like Hermione with her teeth in *Harry Potter*. But in reality it always ended in disaster.

"Poor Emily," Janet said. "When she took down the spell that Doris taught her through the fountain, she actually thought she'd found it, the secret technique everybody else had missed. It was elaborate and costly, but it really looked like it might work. After a few weeks of laying the groundwork, she put it together one night by herself in her room.

"How do you think she felt when she looked in the mirror and saw what she'd done to herself?" You could almost hear a note of genuine sympathy in Janet's hard voice. "I can't imagine. I really can't."

It was late enough in the afternoon now that the shadows from the forest had almost stretched out from the western edge of the Sea far enough to lap at the edge of their blanket.

"Must have been she could still talk, because she got word to her boy that she was in trouble, and he came to her room, and after much preliminary whispering through the keyhole she let him in. And we have to give our boy credit. It must have been bad, very bad, but he stuck by her. She wouldn't let him go to the faculty—Dunleavy was still Dean, and she would have kicked Emily out without thinking about it.

"So he told her to stay there, don't move, don't do anything to make it worse, he would go to the library and see what he could find.

"He came back just before dawn, thinking he had it pretty much worked out. You can imagine the scene. They'd both been up all night. They're sitting cross-legged on her little bed, her with her scrambled head, him with about eight books open around him on the covers. He's mixed up a few reagents in cereal bowls from the dining hall. She's leaning what's left of her forehead against the wall, trying to keep cool. The blue in the window is getting brighter and brighter, they've got to take care of this soon. She'd probably gone past panic and regret at this point. But not past hope.

"But then think about his state of mind. In a way, for him, it was the perfect thing to have happen. This is his golden moment, his chance to be the hero, to save her and win her love, or at least some pity sex. It's his chance to be strong for her, which is the only thing he's ever wanted to do.

"But I don't know, I think he'd had enough time at this point, maybe he'd figured out what was really going on. I'm guessing the dime had finally dropped. She'd taken a terrible chance, and he had to know she hadn't done it for him.

"Either way he was in no shape to be doing major wizardry. He was tired and scared and in over his head, and I think his heart must have been broken a little, too. Maybe he just wanted it too badly. He launched into the repair spell, which I happen to know which one it was, it was from the Major Arcana, Renaissance stuff. Big energies. It got away from him in the worst possible way. It took him over, took his body away. Right in front of her eyes, he burned up screaming. Blue fire. He became a *niffin*."

That's what Fogg was talking about that night in the infirmary, Quentin thought. About losing control. Apparently the others knew what the word meant, *niffin*. They stared at Janet like they'd been turned to stone.

"Well. Emily freaked out, I mean *freaked* out. Barricaded the door, wouldn't let anybody in until her beloved professor himself showed up. By that point the whole school was awake. I can only imagine how he felt, since in a way the whole thing was his fault. He can't have been too proud of himself. I suppose he would have had to try to banish the *niffin* if it didn't want to leave. I don't know if even he could have. I don't think those things really have an upper limit.

"Anyway, he kept his head, kept everybody else out of the room. He put her face back, right there on the spot, which cannot have been easy. Whatever else he was he must have been some magician, because that spell that came through the fountain, that was a nasty piece of work. And she probably twisted it up even more in the casting, too. But he parsed it on the fly and made her reasonably presentable, though I hear she's never been quite the way she was. Not like she's deformed or anything, just different. Probably if you hadn't met her you would never know.

"And that's pretty much it. I can't even imagine what they told the boy's parents. I hear he was from a magical family, so they probably got some version of the truth. But, you know, the clean version."

There was a long silence. A bell was clanging far away, a boat on the river. The shadow from the trees had flooded all the way over them, deliciously cool in the late-summer afternoon.

Alice cleared her throat. "What happened to the professor?"

"You haven't figured it out?" Janet didn't bother to conceal her glee. "They gave him a choice: resign in disgrace . . . or transfer to Antarctica. Brakebills South. Guess which one he took."

"Oh my God," Josh said. "It was Mayakovsky."

"That explains a hell of a lot," Quentin said.

"Doesn't it though? Doesn't it just?"

"So what happened to Emily Greenstreet?" Alice asked. "She just left school?" There was a trace of ground steel in her voice. Quentin wasn't totally sure where it was coming from. "What happened to her? Did they send her to a normal school?"

"I hear she does something businessy in Manhattan," Janet said. "They set her up with an easy corporate job, I don't know, management consulting or something. We own part of some big firm. Lots of magic to cover up the fact that she doesn't do anything. She just sits in an office and surfs the Web all day. I think part of her just didn't survive what happened, you know?"

After that even Janet stopped talking. Quentin let himself drift among the clouds. He felt spinny from the wine, like the Earth had come untightened and was wobbling loose on its gimbaled base. Apparently he wasn't the only one, because when Josh stood up after a few minutes he immediately lost his balance and fell over again on the turf. There was scattered applause.

But then he stood up again, steadied himself, did a slow, deep knee bend, and executed a perfect standing backflip. He stuck the landing and straightened up, beaming.

"It worked," he said. "I can't believe it. I take back everything bad I ever said about Viking shamans! It fucking worked!"

The spell had worked, though for some reason Josh was the only one who got anything out of it. As they picked up the picnic things and shook the sand out of the blanket, Josh did laps around the field, whooping and making huge superhero leaps in the fading light.

"I am a Viking warrior! Cower before my might! Cower! The strength of Thor and all his mighty hosts flows through me! And I fucked your mother! I . . . fucked . . . your . . . motherrrrrrrrr!"

"He's so happy," Eliot said dryly. "It's like he cooked something and it came out looking like the picture in the cookbook."

Eventually Josh disappeared in search of other people to show off to, loudly singing "The Battle Hymn of the Republic." Janet and Eliot straggled off in the direction of the Cottage, Alice and Quentin toward the House, sunburnt and sleepy and still half drunk. Quentin had already made up his mind to nap through dinner.

"He's going to hurt somebody," he said. "Probably himself."

"There's some damage resistance built in. Strengthening the skin and the skeleton. He could put his fist through a wall and probably not break anything."

"Probably. If he can, he will."

Alice was even more quiet than usual. It wasn't until they were deep in the twilight alleys of the Maze that Quentin saw that her face was slick with tears. His heart went cold.

"Alice. Alice, sweetheart." He stopped and turned her to face him. "What is it?"

She pressed her face miserably into his shoulder.

"Why did she have to tell that story?" she said. "Why? Why is she like that?"

Quentin immediately felt guilty for having enjoyed it. It *was* a horrible story. But there was something irresistibly gothic about it, too.

"She's just a gossip," he said. "She doesn't mean anything."

"Doesn't she?" She pulled back, fiercely wiping her tears with the backs of her hands. "Doesn't she? I always thought my brother died in a car crash."

"Your brother?" Quentin froze. "I don't understand."

"He was eight years older than me. My parents told me he died in a car crash. But that was him, I'm sure it was."

"I don't understand. You think he was that boy in the story?"

She nodded. "I think he was. I know he was." Her eyes were red and rubbed with rage and hurt.

"Jesus. Look, it's just a story. There's no way she could know."

"She knows." Alice kept walking. "It all works out, the timing of it. And he was like that. Charlie—he was always falling in love with people. He would have tried to save her himself. He would have done that." She shook her head bitterly. "He was stupid that way."

"Maybe she didn't know. Maybe Janet didn't realize it was him."

"That's what she wants everybody to think! So you won't realize what a howling cunt she is!"

Howling was a big word at Brakebills that year. Quentin was about to keep defending Janet when something else clicked.

"That's why you weren't Invited here," he said quietly. "It has to be. Because of what happened to your brother."

She nodded, her eyes unfocused now, her relentless brain chewing away at this wrinkle, fitting other things into the bleak new picture it created.

"They didn't want anything to happen to me. As if it would. God, why is everybody else in the world but us so fucking stupid?"

They stopped a few yards short of the edge of the Maze, in the deep shadow that pooled where the hedges grew close together, as if they couldn't face the daylight again, not quite yet.

"At least now I know," she said. "But why did she tell that story, Q? She knew it would hurt me. Why would she do that?"

He shook his head. The idea of conflict within their little clique made him uncomfortable. He wanted to explain it away. He wanted everything to be perfect.

"She's just bitter," he said finally, "because you're the pretty one."

Alice snorted.

"She's bitter because we're happy," she said, "and she's in love with Eliot. Always has been. And he doesn't love her."

She started walking again.

"What? Wait." Quentin shook his head, as if that would make all the pieces fit together again. "Why would she want Eliot?"

"Because she can't have him?" Alice said bitterly, without looking back at him. "And she has to have everything? I'm surprised she hasn't come after you. What, you think she hasn't slept with Josh?"

They left the Maze and climbed the stairs to the rear terrace, lit by the yellow light coming through the French doors and littered with premature autumn leaves. Alice cleaned herself up as best she could with the heels of her hands. She didn't wear much makeup anyway. Quentin stood by and silently handed her tissues to blow her nose with, adrift in his own thoughts. It never failed to astonish him, then or ever, how much of the world around him was mysterious and hidden from view.

FIFTH YEAR

Then September came, and it was just Quentin and Alice. The others were gone, in a swirl of falling leaves and a crackle of early frost.

It was a shock to see them go, but along with the shock, mixed in with it like the liquor in a cocktail, was an even greater feeling of relief. Quentin wanted things to be good between them, to be better than good, to be perfect. But perfection is a nervy business, because the moment you spot the tiniest flaw it's ruined. Perfection was part of Quentin's mythology of Brakebills, the story he told himself about his life there, a narrative as carefully constructed and reverently maintained as *Fillory and Further*, and he wanted to be able not just to tell it to himself but to believe it. That had been getting progressively more difficult. Pressure was building up in some subterranean holding tank, and right at the end there things had begun to come apart. Even Quentin, with his almost limitless capacity for ignoring the obvious, had begun to pick up on it. Maybe Alice was right, maybe Janet really did hate her and love Eliot. Maybe it was something else, something so glaringly obvious that Quentin couldn't stand to look at it directly. One way or another the bonds that held them together were starting to fray, they were losing their magical ability to effortlessly love one another. Now, even though things would never be the same, even though they'd never be together in the same way, at least he could always remember it the way he wanted to. The memories were safe, sealed forever in amber.

As soon as the semester began Quentin did something he had already put off for much too long: he went to Dean Fogg and told him what had happened to Julia. Fogg just frowned and told him he'd take care of it.

Quentin wanted to climb across the desk and grab Fogg by his natty lapels for what he'd done to her by screwing up the memory spells. He tried to explain to Fogg that he had made Julia suffer in a way that nobody should ever have to suffer. Fogg just watched, neither moved nor unmoved. In the end the best Quentin could do was to make him promise that he would strain whatever the applicable regulations were to the breaking point to make things easier for her. It was all he could think of. He left Fogg's office feeling exactly as bad as he had when he entered it.

Sitting at dinner, or strolling between classes through the dusty hallways full of sideways afternoon light, Quentin began to realize for the first time how cut off from the rest of the school he and Alice had been for the past two years, and how few of the other students he really knew. All the groups were cliques unto themselves, but the Physical Kids had been especially tight, and now he and Alice were all that was left of them. He still had classes with the other Fifth Years, and he chatted with them in a friendly way, but he knew that their loyalties and their attention were elsewhere.

"I bet they think we're horrible snobs," Alice said one day. "The way we keep to ourselves."

They were sitting on the cool stone rim of the fountain known as Sammy, a knockoff of the Laocoön in Rome, serpents strangling the renegade priest and his sons, but with water squirting cheerfully out of everybody's mouths. They had come out to try a piece of messy domestic magic for removing stains from a skirt of Alice's, that was best performed outdoors, but they'd forgotten a key ingredient, turmeric, and weren't ready to face the walk back yet. It was a beautiful fall Saturday morning, or really it was closer to noon, the temperature balanced precariously on the tipping point between warm and chilly.

"You think so?"

"Don't you?"

"No, you're probably right." He sighed. "They probably do. Uncharitable bastards. *They're* the snobs."

Alice tossed an acorn overhand at the fountain. It ticked off one of the dying priest's sturdy knees and into the water.

"Do you think we are? Snobs, I mean?" Quentin asked.

"I don't know. Not necessarily. No, I don't think we are. We have nothing against them."

"Exactly. Some of them are perfectly fine."

"Some of them we hold in the highest esteem."

"Exactly." Quentin dabbled his fingertips in the water. "So what are you saying? We should go out and make friends?"

She shrugged. "They're the only other magicians our age on the continent. They're the only peers we'll ever have."

The sky was burning blue, and the tree branches stood out sharply against it in the clear, shivering reflection in the fountain.

"Okay," Quentin said. "But not with all of them."

"Well, God no. We'll be discriminating. Anyway, who even knows if they'll want to be friends with us?"

"Right. So who?"

"Does it matter?"

"Of course it matters, Vix," Quentin said. "It's not like they're all the same." "Vix" was a term of endearment with them, short for vixen, an allusion to their Antarctic interlude, *vixen* being the word for a female fox.

"So who?"

"Surendra."

"Okay. Sure. Or no, he's going out with that horrible Second Year. You know, with the teeth. She's always trying to make people do madrigals after dinner. What about Georgia?"

"Maybe we're overthinking this. We can't force it. We'll just let it happen naturally."

"Okay." Quentin watched her study her nails with her intense, birdlike focus. Sometimes she looked so beautiful he couldn't believe she had anything to do with him. He could barely believe she existed at all.

"But you have to do it," she said. "If it's me, nothing's going to happen. You know I'm pathetic at that kind of thing."

"I know."

She threw an acorn at him.

"You weren't supposed to agree."

And so, with a concerted effort, they roused themselves from their stupor and embarked on a belated campaign to socialize with the rest of their class, most of whom they'd drifted almost completely out of touch with. In the end it wasn't Surendra or Georgia but Gretchen—the blond girl who walked with a cane—who turned out to be the key. It helped that Alice and Gretchen were both prefects, which was a source of both pride and embarrassment to them. The position carried with it almost no official duties; mostly it was just yet another absurd, infantilizing idea borrowed from the English public school system, a symptom of the Anglophilia that was embedded so deeply in the institutional DNA of Brakebills. Prefectships were given to the four students in the Fourth and Fifth Years with the highest GPA, who then got (or had) to wear a silver pin in the shape of a bee on their jackets. Their actual responsibilities were petty things like regulating access to the single phone on campus, an obsolete rotary monster hidden away in a battle-scarred wooden phone booth that was itself tucked away under a back staircase, which always had a line a dozen students long. In return they had access to the Prefects' Common Room, a special locked lounge on the east side of the House with a high, handsome arched window and a cabinet that was always stocked with sticky-sweet sherry that Quentin and Alice forced themselves to drink.

The Prefects' Common Room was also an excellent place to have sex in, as long as they could square it with the other prefects in advance, but that usually wasn't a problem. Gretchen was sympathetic, since she had a boyfriend of her own, and the third prefect was a popular girl with spiky blond hair named Beatrice, whom nobody had even realized was especially smart before she was named a prefect. She never used the room anyway. The only real trick was avoiding the fourth prefect, because the fourth prefect was, of all people, Penny.

The announcement that Penny was a prefect was so universally, gobsmackingly surprising that nobody talked about anything else for the rest of the day. Quentin had barely spoken to Penny since their infamous altercation, not that he'd gone looking for him. From that day on Penny had become a loner, a ghost, which was not an easy thing to be at a school as small as Brakebills, but he had a talent for it. He walked quickly between classes with a flat, frozen stare on his round frying-pan face, bolted his food at mealtimes, went on long solitary rambles, stayed in his room in the afternoons after class, went to bed early, got up at dawn.

What else he did, nobody knew. When the Brakebills students were sorted into groups by Discipline at the end of second year, Penny wasn't assigned to a group at all. The rumor was that he had tested into a Discipline so arcane and outlandish it couldn't be classified according to any of the conventional schemes. Whether it was true or not, next to his name on the official list Fogg had simply put the word INDEPENDENT. He rarely turned up in class after that, and when he did he lurked silently in the back of the room with his hands shoved in the pockets of his fraying Brakebills blazer, never asking questions, never taking notes. He had an air of knowing things other people didn't. He was sometimes seen in the company of Professor Van der Weghe, under whose guidance he was rumored to be pursuing an intensive independent study.

The Prefects' Common Room was an increasingly important refuge for Quentin and Alice because their old sanctuary, the Cottage, was no longer sacrosanct. Quentin had never really thought about it, but it was pure chance that last year nobody new had been placed in the Physical group, thus preserving the integrity of their little clique. But the drought was bound to come to an end, and it did. At the end of the previous semester no fewer than four rising Third Years had tested into Physical, and now, although it seemed wrong in every possible way, they had as much right to the Cottage as Quentin and Alice did.

They did their best to be good sports about it. On the first day of classes they sat patiently in the library as the new Physical Kids went through the ritual and broke into the Cottage. They'd debated long and earnestly about what to serve the newcomers when they came in, finally settling on a goodish champagne and—not wanting to be selfish, even though that was exactly how they felt—an obscenely expensive array of oysters and caviar with toast points and crème fraîche.

"Cool!" the new Physical Kids said, one after the other, as they made their way inside. They goggled at the oversize interior. They inspected the bric-a-brac and the piano and the cabinet of alphabetized twigs. They looked impossibly young. Quentin and Alice made small talk with them, trying to be witty and knowing, the way they remembered the others having been when they first got there.

Sitting in a row on the couch, the Third Years squirmed and sipped their champagne too quickly, like children waiting to be excused. They asked polite questions about the paintings and the Cottage library. Do the books circulate outside the building? Did they really have a first-edition

Abecedarian Arcana in the hand of Pseudo-Dionysius himself? Really. And when was the Cottage first constructed? Really! Wow. That's old. That's, like, *ancient*.

Then, after a suitable interval, they disappeared en masse into the pool room. They showed no particular desire to be chaperoned there, and Quentin and Alice had no particular desire ever to see them again, so they stayed where they were. As the evening wore on, the sounds of adolescent bonding could be heard. It became apparent to Quentin and Alice that they were relics of an earlier era that had worn out its welcome. They had come full circle. They were outsiders again.

"I feel like an elderly docent," Quentin said.

"I already forget their names," Alice said. "They're like quadruplets."

"We should give them numbers. Tell them it's a tradition."

"And then we could always call them by the wrong number. Freak them out. Or we could call them all the same thing. Alfred or something."

"Even the girls?"

"Especially the girls."

They were sipping tepid leftover champagne. They were getting drunk, but Quentin didn't care. From the pool room came the glittery tinkle of breaking glass—a champagne flute, probably—and then, a little later, the sound of a sash being raised and somebody throwing up, hopefully out the window.

"The problem with growing up," Quentin said, "is that once you're grown up, people who aren't grown up aren't fun anymore."

"We should have burned this place down," Alice said gloomily. They were definitely drunk. "Been the last ones out the door and then torched it."

"Then walked away with it burning behind us in the background, like in a movie."

"End of an era. End of an epoch. Which one? Era or epoch? What's the difference?"

Quentin didn't know. They would have to find something else, he thought mazily. Something new. Couldn't stay here anymore. Couldn't go back. Only forward.

"Do you think we were ever like this?" Quentin asked. "Like these kids?"

"Probably. I bet we were even worse. I don't know how the others put up with us."

"You're right," he said. "You're right. God, they were so much nicer than we are."

That winter Quentin didn't go home for the holidays. Around Christmastime—real-world Christmas—he'd had the usual conversation with his parents about Brakebills' unusual schedule, which he had to remind them about every year, lounging inside the old phone booth under the back stairs with one foot braced up against the folding wooden door. Then by the time Brakebills-calendar Christmas rolled around, it was already March in the real world, and it didn't seem like such a big deal not to go back. If they had asked him—if they'd put it out there for an instant that they were eager to see him, or that they would be disappointed if he didn't come—he might have caved. He would have, in a second. But they were their usual blithe, oblivious, glassine selves. And besides, he got an independent feeling from coolly informing them that he had other plans, thanks very much.

Instead Quentin went home with Alice. It was her idea, though as it got closer to the holidays Quentin wasn't exactly sure why she'd invited him, since the prospect obviously made her suicidally uncomfortable.

"I don't know, I don't know!" she said when he asked her. "It just seemed like the kind of things boyfriends and girlfriends do!"

"Well, whatever, I don't have to come. I'll just stay here. Just say I had a paper to finish or something. I'll see you in January."

"But don't you want to come?" she wailed.

"Of course I do. I want to see where you come from. I want your parents to know who I am. And God knows I'm not taking you back to *my* parents' house."

"All right." She didn't sound any less anxious. "Do you promise to hate my parents as much as I do?"

"Oh, absolutely," Quentin said. "Maybe even more."

The opening of the portals home for vacation was always a complicated and tedious procedure that inevitably led to huge numbers of Brakebillians backed up with all their luggage in a ragged line that wound down the dark, narrow corridor leading to the main living room, where Professor Van der Weghe was in charge of getting people where they needed to go. Everybody was relieved that exams were over, and there was always a lot of giddy pushing and shoving and shrieking and casting of minor pyrotechnic spells. Quentin and Alice waited together in silence with their packed bags, solemnly, side by side, Quentin looking as respectable as he could manage. He hardly had any clothes anymore that weren't part of his Brakebills uniform.

He knew Alice was from Illinois, and he knew Illinois was in the Midwest, but he couldn't have pointed to the precise location of that state within a thousand miles. Apart from a European vacation in junior high he'd barely ever been off the East Coast, and his Brakebills education hadn't done much to improve his grasp of American geography. And as it turned out he hardly saw Illinois anyway, or at least not its exterior.

Professor Van der Weghe set up the portal to open directly into an anteroom inside Alice's parents' house. Stone walls, flat mosaic floors, post-and-lintel doorways on all sides. It was a precise re-creation of a traditional bourgeois Roman residence. Sound echoed in it like a church. It was like stepping past the red velvet rope at a museum. Magic tended to run in families—Quentin was an exception in that respect—and Alice's parents were both magicians. She had never had to sneak around behind their backs the way he had to with his parents.

"Welcome to the house that time forgot to forget," Alice said sulkily, kicking her bags into a corner. She led him by the hand along an alarmingly long, dark corridor to a sunken living room with cushions and hard Roman-style couches strewn around at careless angles and a modest plashing fountain in the middle.

"Daddy changes it all around every few years," she explained. "He mostly does architectural magic. When I was little it was all Baroque, gold knobs on everything. That was almost nice. But then it was Japanese paper screens—you could hear *every*thing. Then it was Fallingwater—Frank Lloyd Wright—until Mom got sick of living in a mildew farm for some reason. And then for a while it was just a big old Iroquois longhouse with a dirt floor. No walls. That was hilarious. We had to beg him to put in a real bathroom. I think he seriously thought we were going to watch him defecate into a pit. I doubt even the Indians did that."

With that she sat down heavily on a hard leather Roman couch, opened a book, and became absorbed in her vacation reading.

Quentin understood that it was sometimes better to wait out Alice's black periods than to try to coax her out of them. Everybody has their own idiopathic reaction to their childhood home. So he spent the next hour wandering around what looked remarkably like an upper-middle-class Pompeian household, complete with pornographic frescoes. It was obsessively authentic except for the bathrooms—a concession had obviously been granted on that score. Even dinner, when it arrived, served by a squad of three-foot-tall animated wooden marionettes who made little *click-clacking* noises as they walked, was revoltingly historical: calf brains, parrot tongues, a roasted moray eel, all peppered beyond the point of edibility, just in case they weren't inedible to begin with. Fortunately, there was plenty of wine.

They had progressed to the third course, the stuffed and roasted uterus of a sow, when a short, portly, round-faced man suddenly appeared in the doorway. He was dressed in a well-worn toga the gray of unlaundered bedsheets. He hadn't shaved for several days, and his dark stubble extended well down his neck, and what hair he had left on his head could have used cutting.

"Ave atque vales!" he proclaimed. He gave an elaborate, made-up-looking Roman salute, which was essentially the same as a Nazi salute. "Welcome to the *domus* of *Danielus!*"

He made a face that implied that it was other people's fault that the joke wasn't funny.

"Hi Dad," Alice said. "Dad, this is my friend Quentin."

"Hi." Quentin stood up. He'd been trying to eat reclining, Roman-style, but it was harder than it looked, and he had a stitch in his side. Alice's father shook his outstretched hand. He seemed to forget he was doing it halfway through, then looked surprised to find a fleshy alien extremity still in his grip.

"Are you really eating that stuff? I had Domino's an hour ago."

"We didn't know there was anything else. Where's Mom?"

"Who knows?" Alice's father said. He bugged his eyes out like it was a wacky mystery. "She was working on one of her compositions downstairs, last I saw."

He jogged the few steps down into the room, sandals slapping the stone tiles, and served himself some wine from a decanter.

"And that was when? November?"

"Don't ask me. I lose track of time in this damn place."

"Why don't you put in some windows, Daddy? It's so dark in here."

"Windows?" He bugged out his eyes again; it appeared to be his signature facial expression. "You speak of some barbarian magic of which we noble Romans know nothing!"

"You've done an amazing job here," Quentin piped up, the soul of obsequiousness. "It looks really authentic."

"Thank you!" Alice's father drained the goblet and poured himself another, then sat down heavily on a couch, spilling a purple track of wine down the front of his toga in the process. His bare calves were plump and bone white; black bristles stood straight out from them in static astonishment. Quentin wondered how his beautiful Alice could possibly share a single base pair of genetic information with this person.

"It took me three years to put it together," he said. "Three years. And you know what? I'm already sick of it after two months. I can't eat the food, there are skid marks on my toga, and I have plantar fasciitis from walking around on these stone floors. What is the point of my life?" He looked at Quentin furiously, as if he actually expected an answer, as if Quentin were concealing it from him. "Would someone tell me that, please? Because I have no idea! None!"

Alice glared at her father like he'd just killed her pet. Quentin stayed perfectly still, as if that meant that Alice's father, like a dinosaur, couldn't see him. They all three sat in awkward silence for a long beat. Then he stood up.

"*Gratias*—and good night!"

He tossed the train of his toga over his shoulder and strode out of the room. The marionettes' feet *clack-clacked* on the stone floor as they mopped up the spilled wine he left behind.

"*That's my dad!*" Alice said loudly, and rolled her eyes as if she expected a laugh track to kick in behind her. None did.

In the midst of this domestic wasteland Alice and Quentin established a workable, even comfortable routine for themselves, invaders staking out a safe perimeter deep in hostile territory. It was weirdly liberating to be in the middle of somebody else's domestic agony—he could see the bad emotional energy radiating out in all directions, sterilizing every available surface with its poisonous particles, but it passed through him harmlessly, like neutrinos. He was like Superman here, he was from off-planet, and that made him immune to any local villainy. But he could see it doing its ruinous work on Alice, and he tried to shield her as best he could. He knew the rules here instinctively, what it meant to have parents who ignored you. The only difference was that his parents did it because they loved each other, Alice's because they hated each other.

If nothing else the house was quiet and well stocked with Roman-style wine, sweet but perfectly drinkable. It was also reasonably private: he and Alice could share a bedroom without her parents caring or even noticing. And there were the baths: Alice's dad had excavated huge, cavernous underground Roman baths that they had all to themselves, huge oblong aquifers scooped out of the midwestern tundra. Every morning they would spend a good hour trying to fling each other into the scalding *caldarium* and the glacial *frigidarium,* which were equally unbearable, and then soaking naked in the *tepidarium.*

Over the course of two weeks Quentin glimpsed Alice's mother exactly once. If anything, she looked even less like Alice than Alice's father did: she was thin and tall, taller than her husband, with a long, narrow, animated face and a dry bunch of blond-brown hair tied back behind her head. She chattered earnestly to him about the research she was doing on fairy music, which was, she explained, mostly scored for tiny bells and inaudible to human beings. She lectured Quentin for almost an hour, with no prompting on his part, and without once asking him who he was or what exactly he was doing in her house. At one point one of her slight breasts wandered out of the misbuttoned cardigan that she wore with nothing under it; she tucked it back in without the slightest trace of embarrassment. Quentin had the impression that it had been some time since she had spoken to anybody.

"So I'm a little worried about your parents," Quentin said that afternoon. "I think they might be completely insane."

They had retreated to Alice's bedroom, where they lay side by side on her enormous bed in their bathrobes, looking up at the mosaic on the ceiling: Orpheus singing to a ram, an antelope, and an assortment of attentive birds.

"Are they?"

"Alice, I think you know they're kind of weird."

"I guess. I mean, *I* hate them, but they're my parents. I don't see them as insane, I see them as sane people who deliberately act like this to torture me. When you say they're mentally ill, you're just letting them off the hook. You're helping them elude prosecution."

"Anyway, I thought you might find them interesting," she said. "I know how mentally excited you get about anything magical. Well, *voila,* for your enjoyment, two career magicians."

He wondered, theoretically, which of them had it worse. Alice's parents were toxic monsters, but at least you could see it. His own parents were more like vampires or werewolves—they passed for human. He could rave about their atrocities all he wanted, he knew the villagers would never believe him till it was too late.

"At any rate I can see where you get your social skills," he said.

"My point is, you don't know what it's like to grow up in a family of magicians."

"Well, I didn't know you had to wear a toga."

"You don't have to wear togas. That's exactly the problem, Q. You don't have to do anything. This is what you don't understand! You don't know any older magicians except our professors. It's a wasteland out there. Out here. You can do nothing or anything or everything, and none of it matters. You have to find something to really care about to keep from running totally off the rails. A lot of magicians never find it."

Her voice was strangely urgent, almost angry. He was trying to catch up to her.

"So you're saying your parents didn't."

"No, they didn't, despite their having had two children, which would have given them a minimum of two good options. Well, I think they might have cared about Charlie, but when they lost him, they lost their way completely. And here they are."

"What about your mom and her fairy orchestras? She seems pretty serious about them."

"That's just to annoy my dad. I'm not even sure they exist."

Suddenly Alice rolled over on top of him, straddling him, hands on his shoulders, pinning him down. Her hair hung straight down at him in a shimmering curtain, tickling his face and giving her the very authoritative appearance of a goddess leaning down from the heavens.

"You have to promise me we'll never be like them, Quentin." Their noses were almost touching. Her weight on top of him was arousing, but her face was angry and serious. "I know you think it's going to be all quests and dragons and fighting evil and whatever, like in Fillory. I know that's what you think. But it's not. You don't see it yet. There's nothing out there.

"So you have to promise me, Quentin. Let's never get like this, with these stupid hobbies nobody cares about. Just doing pointless things all day and hating each other and waiting to die."

"Well, you drive a hard bargain," he said. "But okay. I promise."

"I'm serious, Quentin. It's not going to be easy. It's going to be so much harder than you think. They don't even *know*, Quentin. They think they're happy. That's the worst part."

She undid the drawstring on his pajama bottoms without looking and jerked them down, still staring directly into his eyes. Her robe was already open at the waist, and she had nothing on under it. He knew she was saying something important, but he wasn't grasping it. He put his hands under her robe, feeling her smooth back, the curve of her waist. Her heavy breasts brushed against his chest. They would always have magic. They would have it forever. So what—?

"Maybe they are happy," he said. "Maybe this is just who they are."

"No, Quentin. They aren't, and it isn't." She twined her fingers into his hair and gripped it, hard, so that it hurt. "God, you are such a child sometimes."

They were moving together now, breathing hard. Quentin was inside her, and they couldn't talk anymore, except for Alice just repeating:

"Promise me, Q. Promise me. Just promise."

She said it angrily, insistently, over and over again, as if he were arguing, as if he wouldn't have agreed to absolutely anything at that moment.

GRADUATION

In a way it was a disaster of a vacation. They hardly even went outside except for a few walks (undertaken at a brisk trot) through the freeze-dried Urbana suburbs, so flat and empty it felt like at any moment they could fall off into the immense white sky. But in other ways it was perfect. It brought Alice and Quentin closer together. It helped Quentin understand why she was the way she was. They didn't fight once—if anything the terrifying counterexample of Alice's parents made them feel young and romantic by contrast. And after the first week they'd finished all their homework and were free to lie around and goof off. By the time two weeks were up they were thoroughly stir crazy and ready to start their last semester at Brakebills.

They'd heard almost nothing from the others since last summer. Quentin hadn't really expected to. Of course he was curious about what was going on in the outside world, but he had the idea that Eliot and Josh and Janet were busy ascending to some inconceivable new level of coolness, as far above Brakebills as Brakebills was above Brooklyn or Chesterton, and he would have felt let down if they'd still had the time and inclination to bother keeping in touch with him.

As far as he could deduce from their scattered reports, they were all living together in an apartment in downtown Manhattan. The only decent correspondent among them was Janet, who every couple of weeks sent the cheesiest *I ❤ New York* postcard she could find. She wrote in all caps and kept the punctuation to a minimum:

DEAR Q&A

WHAT IT IS WE 3 WENT TO CHINATOWN LAST WEEK 2 LOOK FOR
HERBS, ELIOT BOUGHT A MONGOLIAN SPELLBOOK ITS IN MONGOLIAN
DUH BUT HE CLAIMS HE CAN READ IT BUT I THINK IT'S MONGOLIAN
PORNO. JOSH BOUGHT A LITTLE GREEN BABY TURTLE HE NAMED IT
GAMERA AFTER THE MONSTER. HE IS GROWING A BEARD JOSH NOT
GAMERA. U GUYS [the rest was in tiny, barely-legible script over-
flowing vertically into the space for the address] HAVE GOT
TO GET HERE BRAKEBILLS IS A SMALL SMALL POND AND NYC IS THE
OCEAN AND ELIOT IS DRINKING LIKE A FISH STOP IT ELIOT STOP IT I
KEEL YOU FOR THIS I KEEL YOU 1000 TIMES . . . [illegible]

SO MUCH LOVE

J✳

Despite widespread popular resistance, or possibly because of it,
Dean Fogg entered Brakebills in an international welters tournament, and
Quentin traveled to overseas magic schools for the first time, though he
didn't see much of them beyond the welters court, and once in a while
a dining hall. They played in the emerald-green courtyard of a medieval
keep in the misty Carpathians, and at a compound bushwhacked out of
the seemingly endless Argentine pampas. On Rishiri Island, off the northern coast of Hokkaido, they played on the most beautiful welters court
Quentin had ever seen. The sand squares were a searing white and perfectly scraped and leveled. The grass squares were lime green and clipped
to a regulation 12 mm. The water squares steamed darkly in the chilly air.
Frowning, uncannily humanoid monkeys watched them play, clinging
to wiggly pine trees, their bare pink faces ringed with nimbi of snowy-
white fur.

But Quentin's world tour was cut short when, to Professor Fogg's acute
embarrassment, the Brakebills team lost all six of its first six matchups
and exited the tournament. Their perfect losing record was preserved forever when they were crushed at home in the first round of the consolation
bracket by a pan-European team captained by a tiny, fiery, curly-haired

Luxembourgeoise on whom Quentin, along with every other boy on the Brakebills team, and some of the girls, developed an instant crush.

The welters season ended on the last day of March, and suddenly, Quentin found himself staring at the end of his Brakebills career across a perilously slender gap of only two months of time. It was like he'd been wending his way through a vast glittering city, zig-zagging through side streets and wandering through buildings and haunted de Chirico arcades and little hidden piazzas, the whole time thinking that he'd barely scratched the surface, that he was seeing just a tiny sliver of one little neighborhood. And then suddenly he turned a corner and it turned out he'd been through the whole city, it was all behind him, and all that was left was one short street leading straight out of town.

Now the most insignificant things Quentin did felt momentous, brimming over with anticipatory nostalgia. He'd be passing by a window at the back of the House, hurrying between classes, and a tiny movement would catch his eye, a distant figure trudging across the Sea in a Brakebills jacket, or a gawky topiary flamingo fussily shedding the cap of snow on its little green head, and he would realize that he would never see that particular movement ever again, or if he did he would see it in some future time as some unimaginably different person.

And then there were the other moments, when he was violently sick of Brakebills and everything and everyone in it, when it felt lame and pokey and claustrophobic and he was desperate to get out. In four years he'd barely even set foot off the Brakebills campus. My God, he was wearing a school uniform. He'd essentially just spent four extra years in high school! Students had a particular way of speaking at Brakebills, an affected, overly precise, quasi-British diction that came from all those vocal exercises, like they were just freshly back from a Rhodes scholarship and wanted everybody to know it. It made Quentin want to lay about him with an edged weapon. And there was this obsession with *naming* things. All the rooms at Brakebills had the same identical desk, a broad-shouldered black-cherrywood hulk that must have been ordered up in bulk sometime in the second half of the nineteenth century. It was honeycombed with little drawers and cubbies and pigeonholes, and each of those drawers and cubbies and pigeonholes had its own precious little name. Every time Quentin

heard somebody drop a reference to "the Ink Chink" and "the Old Dean's Ear" he rolled his eyes at Alice. Sweet Jesus, are they serious? We have *got* to get out of this place.

But where was he going to go, exactly? It was not considered the thing to look panicked or even especially concerned about graduation, but everything about the world after Brakebills felt dangerously vague and underthought to Quentin. The bored, bedraggled specters of Alice's parents haunted him. What was he going to do? What *exactly*? Every ambition he'd ever had in his life had been realized the day he was admitted to Brakebills, and he was struggling to formulate a new one with any kind of practical specificity. This wasn't Fillory, where there was some magical war to be fought. There was no Watcherwoman to be rooted out, no great evil to be vanquished, and without that everything else seemed so mundane and penny-ante. No one would come right out and say it, but the worldwide magical ecology was suffering from a serious imbalance: too many magicians, not enough monsters.

It made it worse that he was the only one who seemed to be bothered by it. Lots of students were already actively networking with established magical organizations. Surendra lectured anybody who would listen about a consortium of wizards—whom he hadn't actually heard from yet, but he was pretty sure they'd basically guaranteed him an internship—who spent their time at suborbital altitudes keeping a weather eye out for stray asteroids and oversize solar flares and other potential planetary-scale disasters. Plenty of students went in for academic research. Alice was looking at a post-graduate program in Glasgow, though the idea of being separated didn't particularly appeal to either of them, nor did the idea of Quentin's aimlessly tagging along with her to Scotland.

It was considered chic to go undercover, to infiltrate governments and think tanks and NGOs, even the military, in order to get oneself into a position to influence real-world affairs magically from behind the scenes. People devoted years of their lives to it. And there were even more exotic paths. A few magicians—Illusionists in particular—undertook massive art projects, manipulating the northern lights and things like that, decadeslong enchantments that might only ever have an audience of one. There was an extensive network of war-gamers who staged annual global conflicts over arbitrary tactical objectives, just for the fun of it, sorcerers against sorcerers, in teams and free-for-all battles royal. They played without safeguards, and it was well known that once in a blue moon someone got killed. But that was half the fun of it, the thrill.

And on and on, and it all sounded completely, horribly plausible. Any one of a thousand options promised—basically guaranteed—a rich, fulfilling, challenging future for him. So why did Quentin feel like he was looking around frantically for another way out? Why was he still waiting for some grand adventure to come and find him? He was drowning—why did he recoil whenever anybody reached down to help him? The professors Quentin talked to about it didn't seem concerned at all. They didn't get what the problem was. What should he do? Why, anything he wanted to!

Meanwhile Quentin and Alice plugged away at their mandatory senior theses with steadily diminishing enthusiasm. Alice was attempting to isolate an individual photon and freeze it in place, halting its headlong light-speed flight. She constructed an intricate trap for it out of wood and glass, interwoven with a hellishly complex spherical tangle of glowing indigo gramarye. But in the end nobody was quite sure whether the photon was in there or not, and they couldn't figure out how to prove it one way or the other. Privately Alice confessed to Quentin that she wasn't totally sure either, and she was genuinely hoping the faculty could settle it one way or the other, because it was driving her insane. After a week of increasingly fractious debate that settled nothing, they voted to give Alice the lowest possible passing grade and leave it at that.

For his project Quentin planned to fly to the moon and back. Distance-wise he figured he could get there in a couple of days, straight shot, and after his Antarctic adventure he was pretty solid on personal warmth spells. (Though they weren't his Discipline either. He'd just about given up on his Discipline.) And the idea had a certain Romantic, lyrical savor to it. He took off from the Sea on a bright, hot, humid spring morning, with Alice and Gretchen and a couple of the more sycophantic new Physical Kids to see him off. The protection spells formed a clear bubble around him. Sounds became distorted, and the green lawn and the smiling faces of his well-wishers took on a surreal fish-eye warp. As he rose, the Earth gradually changed from an infinite matte plain below him to a radiant, bounded blue sphere. Overhead the stars came out and became sharper and steelier and less twinkly.

Six hours into the trip his throat suddenly clamped shut, and iron nails stabbed his eardrums. His eyeballs tried to pry themselves out of their sockets. He had drifted off, and his improvised space bubble had started to fail. Quentin waved his arms like a frantic conductor, *prestissimo,* and the air thickened and warmed again, but by then the fun had gone out of the whole thing. Bouts of shivering and wheezing and nervous laughter rattled him, and he couldn't calm down. Jesus, he thought, was there ever anything less worth risking his life for than this? God knows how much interstellar radiation he'd already absorbed. Space was full of angry little particles.

He reversed course. He considered hiding out for a few days and just pretending he'd gone to the moon. Maybe he could score some moon dust off Lovelady, present it as evidence. The air got warmer again. The sky grew lighter. He relaxed as a cocktail of relief and shame filled him, one generous part of each. The world spread out again underneath him: the fractally detailed coastline, the blue water textured like beaten metal, the beckoning claw of Cape Cod.

The worst part turned out to be walking into the Great Hall for dinner that night, two days early, with a sheepish yeah-I-fucked-up grin plastered on his face, which was sunburned a flaming red. After dinner he borrowed Alice's key and retreated to the Prefects' Common Room, where he drank too much sherry, sipping it alone in front of the darkened window, even though all he could see was his own reflection, picturing the Hudson River moving past in the darkness, sluggish and swollen with cold spring rain. Alice was studying up in her room. Everybody else was asleep except for a lone weeknight party that was racketing on in one wing, spinning off drunk students in pairs and groups. When he was thoroughly smashed on self-pity and alcohol and the dawn was threatening to leap up at him at any moment, Quentin walked gingerly back to his bedroom, climbing the spiral steps past what used to be Eliot's room. He weaved a little bit, swigging directly from the sherry bottle, which he'd liberated on his way out.

He felt his intoxication already turning into a hangover, that queasy neurological alchemy that usually happens during sleep. His abdomen was overfull, swollen with tainted viscera. People he'd betrayed came wandering out from the place in his mind where they usually stayed. His parents. James. Julia. Professor March. Amanda Orloff. Even old dead Mr. What's-his-name, his Princeton interviewer. They all watched him dispassionately. He was beneath their contempt.

He lay down on his bed with the light on. Wasn't there a spell for making yourself happy? Somebody must have invented one. How could he have missed it? Why didn't they teach it? Was it in the library, a flying book fluttering just out of reach, beating its wings against some high window? He felt the bed slipping down and away, down and away, like a film loop of a Stuka sheering down into an attack run, over and over again. He'd been so young when he first came here. He thought about that freezing day in November when he'd taken the book from the lovely paramedic, and the note had blown away into that dry, twisted, frozen garden, and he'd gone blithely running after it. Now he'd never know what it said. Had it contained all the riches, all the good feeling that he was still somehow missing, even after so much goodness had been heaped upon him? Was it the secret revelation of Martin Chatwin, the boy who had escaped into Fillory and never returned to face the misery of this world? Because he was drunk, he thought about his mother, and how she'd held him once when he was little after he'd lost an action figure down a storm drain, and he smooshed his red, smarting face into his cool pillow and sobbed as if his heart were broken.

By then there were only two weeks left until graduation. Classwork ground to a halt. The Maze was a vivid verdant glowing green knot, the air was full of floaty little motes, and siren-like pleasure craft came drifting down the river past the boathouse, laden with oblivious sunbathers. All anybody talked about was how great it would be when they could party and sleep in and experiment with forbidden spells. They kept looking at each other and laughing and slapping each other on the back and shaking their heads. The carousel was slowing down. The music had almost stopped.

Pranks were organized. A decadent, last-days-of-Pompeii vibe swept through the dorms. Somebody thought up a new game involving dice and a lightly enchanted mirror that was basically a magical version of strip poker. Desperate, ill-advised attempts were made to sleep with that one person with whom one had always secretly, hopelessly wanted to sleep.

The graduation ceremony started at six in the afternoon, with the sky still heavy with fading golden light. An eleven-course banquet was served in the dining hall. The nineteen graduating Fifth Years regarded one another with awe, feeling lost and alone at the long, empty dining table. Red wine was served from bottles without labels; it was made, Fogg revealed, using grapes from Brakebills' own tiny pocket vineyard, which Quentin had stumbled on in the fall of his First Year. Traditionally the vineyard's entire output was drunk by the seniors at graduation dinner—had to be drunk, Fogg stressed, hinting darkly at what would happen if a single bottle was left unconsumed. It was a cabernet sauvignon, and it was thin and sour, but they quaffed it lustily anyway. Quentin declaimed a lengthy tribute to its subtle expression of the unique Brakebills *terroir*. Toasts were drunk to the memory of Amanda Orloff, and the glasses hurled into the fireplace to ensure that no lesser toast would ever be drunk from them. When the wind blew, the candles flickered and dropped molten beeswax onto the fresh white tablecloth.

Along with the cheese course they were each presented with a silver bee pin, identical to the ones the prefects wore—Quentin was at a loss to imagine any occasion on which it would be even remotely appropriate to wear it—and a heavy black two-toothed iron key that would permit them to return to Brakebills if they ever needed to. School songs were sung, and Chambers served Scotch, which Quentin had never had before. He tipped his little tumbler of it from side to side, watching the light drift through this mysterious amber fluid. It was amazing that anything in liquid form could taste that much like both smoke and fire.

He leaned over to Georgia and started to explain this fascinating conundrum to her, but as he did so Fogg stood up at the head of the table, strangely grave, dismissed Chambers, and asked the Fifth Years to follow him downstairs.

This was unexpected. Downstairs meant the cellar, where Quentin had almost never been in his whole time at Brakebills—just once or twice to sneak a particularly coveted bottle from the wine cellar, or when he and Alice had been desperate for privacy. But now Professor Fogg led them in a loose, bantering, occasionally singing flock back through the kitchen, through a small, unassuming door in the pantry, and down a flight of worn and dusty wooden stairs that changed midflight into stone. They emerged into a dark, earthy subbasement.

This wasn't where Quentin had thought the party was going. It wasn't a party atmosphere at all. It was cool down here and suddenly quiet. The floor was dirt, the ceilings were low, and the walls were bumpy and unfinished. They devoured sound. Voice by voice the chorus of a traditional Brakebills song—an elaborately euphemistic number entitled "The Prefect Has a Defect"—died away. There was a grave but not unpleasant smell of damp soil.

Fogg stopped at what looked like a manhole cover embedded in the dirt floor. It was brass and densely inscribed with calligraphic writing. Oddly, it looked as shiny and new as a freshly struck coin. The Dean picked up a heavy manhole tool and, with an effort, levered up the brass disk. It was two inches thick, and it took three of the Fifth Years to roll it to one side.

"After you," the Dean said, panting a little. He gestured grandly at the inky black hole.

Quentin went first. He felt around blindly with his Scotch-benumbed feet till he found an iron rung. It was like lowering himself into warm black oil. The ladder took him and the other graduates straight down into a circular chamber large enough for all nineteen of them to stand upright in a circle, which they did. Fogg came down last; they could hear him screwing the manhole cover back into place behind them. Then he descended, too, and with a crash he sent the ladder retracting back up, like a fire escape. After that the silence was absolute.

"No point in losing our momentum," Fogg said. He lit a candle and gamely produced two fifths of bourbon from somewhere and set them going in opposite directions around the circle. Something about this gesture unnerved Quentin. There was a certain amount of sanctioned alcohol consumption at Brakebills—a fairly large amount, really—but this was a bit much. There was something forced about it.

Well, it *was* graduation. They weren't students anymore. They were grown-ups. Just peers, sharing a drink. In a secret underground dungeon, in the middle of the night. Quentin took his swig and passed it on.

Dean Fogg lit more candles in assorted brass candlesticks, making a circle within their larger circle. They couldn't have been more than fifty yards down, but it felt like they were a solid mile beneath the earth, entombed alive, forgotten by the rest of the world.

"In case you're wondering why we're down here," Fogg said, "it's because I wanted to get us outside the Brakebills Protective Cordon. That's a defensive magical barrier that extends out from the House in all directions. That inscribed brass hatch we opened was a gateway through it."

The darkness swallowed his words as soon as he uttered them.

"It's a little unsettling, yes? But it's appropriate, because unlike me you'll be spending the rest of your lives out here. Most years, the point of coming down here is to scare you with ghost stories about the outside world. In your case I don't think that will be necessary. You've witnessed firsthand the destructive power that some magical entities possess.

"It's unlikely you'll ever see anything as bad as what happened on the day of the Beast. But remember that what happened that day can happen again. Those of you who were in the auditorium that day, especially, will carry the mark of it forever. You will never forget the Beast, and you can be sure it won't forget you either.

"Forgive me if I lecture you, but it's the last chance I'm going to get."

Quentin was sitting opposite Fogg in the circle—they had all taken seats on the smooth stone floor—and his mild, clean-shaven face floated in the darkness like an apparition. Both bottles of whiskey reached Quentin simultaneously, and he gamely took a sip from each, one in each hand, and passed them on.

"Sometimes I wonder if man was really meant to discover magic," Fogg said expansively. "It doesn't really make sense. It's a little too perfect, don't you think? If there's a single lesson that life teaches us, it's that wishing doesn't make it so. Words and thoughts don't change anything. Language and reality are kept strictly apart—reality is tough, unyielding stuff, and it doesn't care what you think or feel or say about it. Or it shouldn't. You deal with it, and you get on with your life.

"Little children don't know that. Magical thinking: that's what Freud called it. Once we learn otherwise we cease to be children. The separation of word and thing is the essential fact on which our adult lives are founded.

"But somewhere in the heat of magic that boundary between word and thing ruptures. It cracks, and the one flows back into the other, and the two melt together and fuse. Language gets tangled up with the world it describes.

"I sometimes feel as though we've stumbled on a flaw in the system, don't you? A short circuit? A category error? A strange loop? Is it possible that magic is knowledge that would be better off forsworn? Tell me this: Can a man who can cast a spell ever really grow up?"

He paused. No one answered. What the hell would they say? It was a little late to be scolding them now that they'd already completed their magical education.

"I have a little theory that I'd like to air here, if I may. What is it that you think makes you magicians?" More silence. Fogg was well into rhetorical-question territory now anyway. He spoke more softly. "Is it because you are intelligent? Is it because you are brave and good? Is it because you're special?

"Maybe. Who knows. But I'll tell you something: I think you're magicians because you're unhappy. A magician is strong because he feels pain. He feels the difference between what the world is and what he would make of it. Or what did you think that stuff in your chest was? A magician is strong because he hurts more than others. His wound is his strength.

"Most people carry that pain around inside them their whole lives, until they kill the pain by other means, or until it kills them. But you, my friends, you found another way: a way to use the pain. To burn it as fuel, for light and warmth. You have learned to break the world that has tried to break you."

Quentin's attention wandered to the tiny glimmery points of light here and there on the curved ceiling above them, pricking out the shapes of constellations he didn't recognize, as if they were on another planet, seeing the stars from an alien angle. Someone cleared his throat.

Fogg went on.

"But just in case that's not enough, each one of you will leave this room tonight with an insurance policy: a pentagram tattooed on your back. Five-pointed star, nicely decorative, plus it acts as a holding cell for a demon, a small but rather vicious little fellow. Cacodemon, technically.

"They're tough little scrappers, skin like iron. In fact, I think they may be made of iron. I'll give you each a password that sets him free. Speak the password and he'll pop out and fight for you till he's dead or till whoever's giving you trouble is."

Fogg clapped his hands on his knees and looked at them as if he'd just told them they'd all be receiving a year's supply of attractive and useful Brakebills stationery. Georgia put up her hand tentatively.

"Is . . . is this optional? I mean, is anybody else besides me disturbed by the idea of having an angry demon, you know, trapped inside their skin?"

"If that bothers you, Georgia," Fogg said curtly, "then you should have gone to beauty school. Don't worry, he'll be grateful as hell, so to speak, when you set him free. He's only good for one fight though, so pick your moment.

"That's the other reason we're down here, by the way. Can't conjure a cacodemon inside the Cordon.

"Why we need the bourbon, too, because this is going to hurt like a bitch. Now, who's first? Or shall we go alphabetically?"

The next morning at ten there was a more conventional graduation ceremony in the largest and grandest of the lecture halls. It would be difficult to imagine a more miserable and visibly hungover group of graduating seniors. It was one of the rare occasions when parents were allowed on campus, so no displays of magic, or mentions of same, were allowed. Almost as bad as the hangover was the pain from the tattoo. Quentin's back felt like it was crawling with hungry biting insects that had stumbled on something especially delicious. He was exquisitely conscious of his mother and father sitting a dozen rows behind him.

Quentin's memories of the night before were confused. The Dean had summoned the demons himself, scribbling concentric rings of sigils on the old stone floor with thick chunks of white chalk. He worked quickly and surely, with both hands at once. For the tattooing the guys took off their shirts and jackets and lined up naked to the waist, as did the girls, with varying degrees of modesty. Some of them clutched their crumpled clothes over their chests. A few exhibitionists stripped down proudly.

In the half darkness Quentin couldn't see what Fogg was using to draw on their skin, something slim and glinting. The designs were intricate and had strange, shifting, optical qualities. The pain was astonishing, like Fogg was flaying the skin off their backs and dressing the wounds with salt. But the pain was offset by the fear of what was coming, the moment when he implanted the demon. When they were all ready, Fogg built a low dome of loose glowing embers in the center of the sigil rings, and the room got hot and humid. Blood and smoke and sweat were in the air, and an orgiastic fever. When it was the first girl's turn—going alphabetically that was Alsop, Gretchen—Fogg donned an iron gauntlet and rummaged around in the coals till he got a grip on something.

The red glow lit up Fogg's face from below, and maybe it was just the distortions of memory and alcohol, but Quentin thought he saw something there that he hadn't seen since his first day at Brakebills—something drunken and cruel and unfatherly. When he had hold of what he was looking for he heaved, and out of the embers it came: a demon, trailing sparks, heavy and dog-size and pissed off. In the same motion he crammed it wriggling into Gretchen's slender back; he had to go back and stuff one flailing, sticking-out limb back in. She gasped, her whole body tensed, like she'd had freezing water dumped over her. And then she just looked puzzled, twisting to look over her shoulder, forgetting for a second and letting everyone see her slight, pale-nippled breasts. Because as Quentin discovered when it was his turn, there was no sensation at all.

It all felt like a dream now, though of course the first thing Quentin did that morning was check out his back in the mirror. There it was, a huge five-pointed star in thick black outline, raw and red and slightly off center to the left; he supposed it must be positioned more or less exactly with his heart at its center. Segments of the star were dense with fine squiggly black writing and smaller stars and crescent moons and other less easily identifiable icons—he looked like he hadn't been so much tattooed as notarized, or stamped like a passport. Tired, achy, and hungover as he was, he smiled at it in the mirror. The overall effect was completely badass.

When it was all over, they shuffled out of the auditorium into the old hallway. If they'd had caps, they might have thrown them in the air, but they didn't. There was a low hum of conversation, a couple of whoops, but that was really it; it was over, there was nothing else. If they hadn't been graduated last night, they sure were now. They could go anywhere, do anything they wanted. This was it: the big send-off.

Alice and Quentin drifted out a side door and wandered over to a huge spreading oak, swinging their held hands between them. There was no wind. The sunlight was too bright. Quentin's head throbbed. His parents were in the vicinity, and he'd have to go look for them in a second. Or maybe they could come looking for him for once in their lives. There would be parties tonight, he supposed, but he was already pretty much partied out. He didn't feel like packing up his things, didn't feel like going back to Chesterton, or Brooklyn, or anywhere else for that matter. He didn't feel like staying, and he didn't feel like going. He stole a glance at Alice. She looked peaked. He performed a mental search for the love he was accustomed to feel for her and found it strangely absent. If there was anything he wanted at that moment it was to be alone. But he wasn't going to get that.

These were bad thoughts, but he couldn't or wouldn't stop the flow, stanch the cerebral hemorrhage. Here he was, a freshly licensed and bonded and accredited magician. He had learned to cast spells, seen the Beast and lived, flown to Antarctica on his own two wings, and returned naked by the sheer force of his magical will. He had an iron demon in his back. Who would ever have thought he could do and have and be all those things and still feel nothing at all? What was he missing? Or was it him? If he wasn't happy even here, even now, did the flaw lie in him? As soon as he seized happiness it dispersed and reappeared somewhere else. Like Fillory, like everything good, it never lasted. What a terrible thing to know.

I got my heart's desire, he thought, and there my troubles began.

"We have our whole lives ahead of us and all I want to do is take a nap," Alice said.

There was a soft sound behind them. A soap bubble popping, an intake of breath, a wing beat.

Quentin turned around, and they were all there. Josh with a fringe of blond beard that made him look more than ever like a genial smiling abbot. Janet had gotten her nose pierced, and probably other parts of her. Eliot wore sunglasses, which he had never done at Brakebills, and a shirt of amazing, indescribable perfection. There was somebody else with them, too, a stranger: a serious, slightly older man, tall and darkly, bookishly handsome.

"Get your stuff together," Josh said. He grinned even more widely and spread out his arms like a prophet. "We're going to take you away from all this."

BOOK II

MANHATTAN

Two months later it was November. Not Brakebills November, real November—Quentin had to keep reminding himself that they were on regular real-world time now. He lolled his temple against the cold apartment window. Far below he could see a neat little rectangular park where the trees were red and brown. The grass was threadbare, with dirt patches, like a worn-out rug with the canvas backing showing through the woven surface.

Quentin and Alice lay on their backs on a wide, candy-striped daybed by the window, limply holding hands, looking and feeling like they'd just washed ashore on a raft that had been gently, limply deposited by the surf on the beach of a silent deserted island. The lights were off, but milky-white afternoon sunlight filtered into the room through half-closed blinds. The remains of a game of chess, a sloppy, murderous draw, lay on a nearby coffee table.

The apartment was undecorated and barely furnished except for an eclectic collection they'd trucked in as the need arose. They were squatting: a tiresomely complex magical arrangement had allowed them to secure this particular scrap of underutilized Lower East Side real estate while its rightful owners were otherwise occupied.

A deep, thick silence hung in the still air, like stiff white sheets on a clothesline. Nobody spoke, and nobody had spoken for about an hour, and nobody felt the need to speak. They were in lotus-land.

"What time is it?" Alice said finally.

"Two. Past two." Quentin turned his head to look at the clock. "Two."
The buzzer rang. Neither of them moved.

"It's probably Eliot," Quentin said.

"Are you going over early?"

"Yes. Probably."

"You didn't tell me you were going early."

Quentin sat up slowly, using just his stomach muscles, at the same time
extracting his arm from beneath Alice's head.

"I'm probably going early."

He buzzed Eliot in. They were going to a party.

It was only two months since graduation, but already Brakebills seemed
like a lifetime ago—yet another lifetime, Quentin thought, reflecting
world-wearily that at the age of twenty-one he was already on his third or
fourth lifetime.

When he left Brakebills for New York, Quentin had expected to be
knocked down and ravished by the sheer gritty reality of it all: going from
the jeweled chrysalis of Brakebills to the big, messy, dirty city, where real
people led real lives in the real world and did real work for real money.
And for a couple of weeks he had been. It was definitely real, if by real you
meant non-magical and obsessed with money and amazingly filthy. He had
completely forgotten what it was like to be in the mundane world all the
time. Nothing was enchanted: everything was what it was and nothing
more. Every conceivable surface was plastered with words—concert posters, billboards, graffiti, maps, signs, warning labels, alternate-side parking
regulations—but none of it *meant* anything, not the way a spell did. At
Brakebills every square inch of the House, every brick, every bush, every
tree, had been marinated in magic for centuries. Here, out in the world,
raw unmodified physics reigned, and mundanity was epidemic. It was like
a coral reef with the living vital meaning bleached out of it, leaving nothing
but an empty colored rock behind. To a magician's eyes, Manhattan looked
like a desert.

Though like a desert, it did have some stunted, twisted traces of life, if
you dug for them. There was a magical culture in New York outside the
handful of Brakebills-educated elite who resided there, but it existed on
the city's immigrant margins. The older Physical Kids—a name they had

left behind at Brakebills and would never use again—gave Quentin and Alice the outer-borough subway tour. In a windowless second-story café on Queens Boulevard, they watched Kazakhs and Hasidim construe number theory. They ate dumplings with Korean mystics in Flushing and watched modern-day Isis worshippers rehearse Egyptian street hexes in the back of a bodega on Atlantic Avenue. Once they took the ferry across to Staten Island, where they stood around a dazzlingly blue swimming pool sipping gin and tonics at a conclave of Filipino shamans.

But after a few weeks the energy for those educational field trips had all but evaporated. There was just too much to distract them, and nothing particularly urgent to be distracted from. Magic would always be there, and it was hard work, and he'd been doing it for a long time. What Quentin needed to catch up on was life. New York's magical underground may have been limited, but the number and variety of its drinking establishments was prodigious. And you could get drugs here—actual drugs! They had all the power in the world, and no work to do, and nobody to stop them. They ran riot through the city.

Alice didn't find all this quite as exciting as Quentin did. She had put off the kind of civil service appointment or research apprenticeship that usually ensnared serious-minded Brakebills students so she could stay in New York with Quentin and the others, but inspite of that she showed signs of actual unfeigned academic curiosity, which caused her to spend a good part of every day studying magic instead of, for example, recovering from having gone out the night before. Quentin felt mildly ashamed for not following her example, enough that he even made noises about relaunching his failed lunar expedition, but not so much that he actually did anything about it. (Alice cycled through a sequence of space travel–related nicknames for him—Scotty, Major Tom, Laika—until his lack of progress began to make them more humiliating than funny.) He felt entitled to blow off steam and shake off the Brakebills pixie dust and generally "live." And Eliot felt that way, too ("Ain't that why we got *livers*?" he said in his exaggerated Oregoner accent). It wasn't a problem. He and Alice were just different people. Isn't that what made it interesting?

At any rate Quentin felt interesting. He felt fascinating. For the first year after graduation his financial needs were taken care of by an immense secret slush fund, amassed covertly over the centuries through magically augmented investing, that yielded a regular allowance for all newly minted magicians who needed it. After four cloistered years at Brakebills, cash was like a magic all its own: a way of turning one thing into another thing, producing something out of nothing, and he worked that magic all over town. Money people thought he was artsy, artsy people thought he was money, and everybody thought he was clever and good-looking, and he got invited everywhere: charity social events, underground poker clubs, dive bars, rooftop parties, mobile all-night in-limo narcotics binges. He and Eliot passed themselves off as brothers, and their double act was the hit of the season. It was the revenge of the nerds.

Night after night Quentin would return home toward dawn, alone, deposited in front of his building by a solemn solitary cab like a hearse painted yellow, the street awash with blue light—the delicate ultrasound radiance of the embryonic day. Coming down off coke or ecstasy, his body felt strange and heavy, like a golem fashioned from some ultra-dense star-metal that had fallen from the sky and cooled and congealed into human form. He felt so heavy that he could break through the brittle pavement any second, and plunge down into the sewers, unless he placed his feet gently and precisely in the center of each sidewalk square in turn.

Standing alone amid the still, stately mess of their apartment, his heart would brim over with regret. He felt like his life had gone terribly wrong. He shouldn't have gone out. He should have stayed home with Alice. But he would have been so bored if he'd stayed home! And she would have been bored if she'd come out! What were they going to do? They couldn't go on like this. He felt so grateful to her for not having seen the excesses he had so eagerly indulged in, the drugs he had ingested, the manic flirting and pawing in which he had engaged.

Then he would take off his clothes, which reeked of cigarette smoke, like a toad shedding its skin, and Alice would stir sleepily in the sheets and sit up, the white sheet slipping down off her heavy breasts. She would lean against him, their backs against the cool white wooden curl of their sleigh bed, not speaking, and they would watch as the dawn came up and a garbage truck moved haltingly down the block, its pneumatic biceps gleaming as it greedily consumed whatever its overalled attendants flung into it, ingesting what the city had expectorated. And Quentin would feel a lofty pity for the garbagemen, and for all the straights and civilians. He wondered what they could possibly have in their uncharmed lives that made them think they were worth living.

He heard Eliot try the door, find it locked, and fumble around for his key; Eliot shared an apartment with Janet in Soho, but he was over at Quentin and Alice's so much that it was easier just to give him his own key. Quentin strolled around the open-plan apartment, half-heartedly straightening up, snapping up condom wrappers and underwear and decaying food and depositing them in the trash. It was a beautiful place in a converted factory, all wide-planked, thickly varnished wood floors and arched warehouse windows, but it had seen more considerate tenants. He'd been surprised to discover when they moved in together that while he was an indifferent housekeeper, Alice was the true slob of the relationship.

She retreated to the bedroom to get dressed. She was still in her nightgown.

"Morning," Eliot said, although it wasn't. He loitered just inside the rolling metal freight door, wearing a long overcoat and a sweater that had been expensive before moths got to it.

"Hey," Quentin said. "Just let me grab my coat."

"It's freezing out there. Is Alice coming?"

"I didn't get that impression. Alice?" He raised his voice. "Alice?"

There was no answer. Eliot had already faded back out into the hall. He didn't seem to have much patience for Alice lately, as somebody who didn't share his rigorous dedication to pleasure-seeking. Quentin supposed her unfussy diligence reminded him unpleasantly of the future he was ignoring. Quentin knew it had that effect on him.

He hesitated on the threshold, torn between conflicting loyalties. She would probably be grateful for some quiet time to study.

"I think she's coming later," Quentin said. He called in the direction of the bedroom: "Okay! Bye! I'll see you there!"

There was no answer.

"Bye Mom!" Eliot yelled.

The door closed.

———

Like everything else, Eliot was different in New York. At Brakebills he had always been supremely aloof and self-sufficient. His personal charm and odd appearance and talent for magic had raised him up and set him apart. But since Quentin had joined him in Manhattan, the balance of power between them had shifted somehow. Eliot hadn't survived transplantation unscathed; he no longer floated easily above the fray. His humor was more arch and bitter and childish than Quentin remembered. He seemed to be getting younger as Quentin got older. He needed Quentin more, and he resented Quentin for that. He hated to be left out of anything, and he hated to be included in anything. He spent more time than he should have on the roof of his apartment building smoking his Merits and God knows what else—there wasn't much you couldn't find if you had the money, and they had the money. He was getting too thin. He was depressed and turned nasty when Quentin tried to jolly him out of it. When annoyed he was fond of saying, "God, it's amazing I'm not a dipsomaniac" and then correcting himself: "Oh, wait, that's right . . ." It had been funny the first time. Sort of.

At Brakebills Eliot had started drinking at dinnertime, earlier on weekends, which was fine, because all the upperclassmen drank at dinner, though not all of them bartered their desserts for extra glasses of wine the way Eliot did. In Manhattan, with no professors watching over them, and no classes to be sober for, Eliot was rarely without a glass of something in his hand from one in the afternoon on. Usually it was something relatively innocuous, white wine or Campari or a big dilute tumbler of bourbon and soda clunking with ice. But still. Once when Eliot was nursing a stubborn cold, Quentin remarked lightly that maybe he should consider something more wholesome than a vodka tonic with which to chase his plastic jigger of DayQuil.

"I'm sick, I'm not dead," Eliot snapped. And that was that.

At least one of Eliot's talents had survived graduation: he was still a tireless seeker-out of obscure and wonderful bottles of wine. He was not yet such a lush that he'd abandoned his snobbishness. He went to tastings and chatted up importers and wine-store owners with a zeal that he mustered for nothing else. Once every few weeks, when he had accumulated a dozen or so bottles of which he was especially proud, Eliot would announce that they were having a dinner party. It was one such dinner party that he and Quentin were preparing for today.

They lavished a ridiculous amount of effort on these parties, all out of proportion to any actual fun they might get in return. The venue was always Eliot and Janet's Soho apartment, a vast prewar warren with an implausible profusion of bedrooms, a set ripe for a French farce. Josh was head chef, with Quentin assisting as apprentice chef and kitchen runner. Eliot acted as sommelier, of course. Alice's contribution was to stop reading long enough to eat.

Janet dressed the set: she formulated the night's dress code, chose the music, and hand-wrote and illustrated amazingly beautiful one-off menus. She also confabulated various surreal and sometimes controversial centerpieces. The theme of tonight's party was Miscegenation, and Janet had promised—over objections aesthetic, moral, and ornithological—to deliver Leda and the Swan staged as a pair of magically animated ice sculptures. They would copulate until they melted.

As with all such evenings, the cleverness of the conceit became annoying somewhere around the middle of the afternoon before the party actually started. Quentin had found a grass skirt at an antique store, which he planned to pair with a tuxedo shirt and jacket, but the skirt was so scratchy that he gave up on it. He couldn't think of another idea, so he spent the rest of the afternoon brooding and dodging Josh, who had spent the past week researching recipes that included violently disparate ingredients wedded together—sweet and savory, black and white, frozen and molten, Eastern and Western—and was now frantically slamming oven and cabinet doors and making him taste things and sniping at him over the pastry island. Alice arrived at five thirty, and Quentin and Josh both dodged her as well. By the time the party started everybody was drunk and starving and irritable.

But then, as sometimes happens with dinner parties, everything became mysteriously, spontaneously perfect again. The fabric knitted itself back together. The day before, Josh, who by this time had shaved off his beard ("It's like taking care of a damn pet"), announced that he was bringing a date, which put added pressure on everybody to get their shit together. As the sun set over the Hudson, and sunbeams tinted a delicate rose by their passage through the atmosphere over New Jersey lanced through the apartment's huge common room, and Eliot handed around Lillet cocktails

(Lillet and champagne layered over a velvet hammer of vodka) in chilled martini glasses, and Quentin served miniature sweet-and-sour lobster rolls, everybody suddenly seemed—or maybe they actually were?—wise and funny and good-looking..

Josh had refused to reveal the identity of his date in advance, so when the elevator doors opened—they had the entire floor—Quentin had no idea that he would recognize her: it was the girl from Luxembourg, the curly-haired captain of the European team that had administered the deathblow to his welters career. It turned out (they told the story collaboratively, a set piece they'd evidently been working on) that Josh had bumped into her in a subway station where she was trying to bewitch a vending machine into adding money to her Metrocard. Her name was Anaïs, and she wore a pair of snakeskin pants so ravishing that nobody asked her what if anything they had to do with the theme. She had blond ringlets and a tiny pointy nose, and Josh was obviously besotted with her. So was Quentin. He felt a wild pang of jealousy.

He barely talked to Alice all night anyway, what with ducking in and out of the kitchen warming and plating and serving things. By the time he emerged with the entrées—pork chops dusted with bitter chocolate—it was dark, and Richard was making a speech about magical theory. The wine and the food and the music and the candles were almost enough to make what he was saying seem interesting.

Richard, of course, was the mysterious stranger who turned up with the other former Physical Kids on graduation day. He was a one-time Physical Kid, too, of the generation that preceded Eliot and Josh and Janet, and of them all he was the only one who had actually entered the world of respectable professional wizardry. Richard was tall, with a big head, dark hair, square shoulders, and a big square chin, and he was handsome in a Frankensteinian way. He was friendly enough to Quentin—firm handshake, lots of eye contact with his big, dark eyes. In conversation he liked to address Quentin directly as "Quentin" a lot, which made him feel kind of like they were having a job interview. Richard was employed by the trust that managed the collective financial assets of the magical community, which were vast. He was, in a quiet way, an observant Christian. They were rare among magicians.

Quentin tried to like Richard, since everybody else did, and it would just be simpler. But he was so damn earnest. He wasn't stupid, but he completely lacked any sense of humor—jokes derailed him, so that the whole conversation had to stop while somebody, usually Janet, explained what everybody else was laughing at, and Richard knitted his thick Vulcan eyebrows in consternation at his companions' merely human foibles. And Janet, who could usually be counted on to ruthlessly flense anybody who made the mistake of taking anything seriously, Janet waited on Richard hand and foot! It annoyed Quentin to think that she might look up to Richard the same way he had once looked up to the older Physical Kids. He had the definite sense that Janet must have slept with Richard once or twice back at Brakebills. It was entirely possible that they slept together once in a while now.

"Magic," Richard announced slowly, flushed, "is the tools. Of the Maker." He almost never drank, and two glasses of viognier had put him well over his limit. He looked first left and then right to make sure the whole table was listening. What a fatuous ass. "There's no other way of looking at it. We are dealing with a scenario where there is a Person who built the house, and then He left." He rapped the table with one hand to celebrate this triumph of reason. "And when He left, He left His tools lying around in the garage. Then we found them, and we picked them up, and we started making guesses about how they work. Now we're learning to use them. And that's magic."

"There are so many things wrong with that I don't even know where to start," Quentin distinctly heard himself say.

"So? Start."

Quentin put down the food he was carrying. He had no idea what he was about to say, but he was happy to be publicly contradicting Richard.

"Okay, well, first of all, there's a huge scale problem. Nobody's building universes here. We're not even building galaxies or solar systems or planets. You need cranes and bulldozers to build a house. If there is a 'Maker,' which I frankly don't see much evidence for, that's what He had. What we've got are hand tools. Black and Decker. I don't see how you get from there to what you're talking about."

"If it's a question of scale," Richard said, "I don't see that as insurmountable.

Maybe we're just not"—he searched in his wine glass for the right metaphor—"we're not plugging our tools into the right socket. Maybe there's a much *bigger* socket—"

"I think if you're talking about electricity," Alice put in, "you have to talk about where energy comes from."

That's what I should have said, Quentin thought. Alice relished theoretical arguments as much as Richard, and she was much better at them.

"Any heating spell, you're demonstrably drawing energy from one place and putting it in another. If somebody created the universe, they actually created energy from somewhere. They didn't just push it around."

"Fine, but if—"

"Plus, magic just doesn't *feel* like a tool," Alice went on. "Can you imagine how boring it would be if casting a spell were like turning on an electric drill? But it's not. It's irregular and beautiful. It's not an artifact, it's something else, something organic. It feels like a grown thing, not a made thing."

She looked radiant in a silky black sheath that she knew he liked. Where had she been all night? He seemed to keep forgetting what a treasure she was.

"I bet it's alien tech," Josh said. "Or fourth-dimensional, like, weather or something. From a direction we can't even see. Or we're in some kind of really high-tech multiplayer video game." He snapped his fingers. "So *that's* why Eliot's always humping my corpse."

"Not necessarily," Richard finally broke in. He was still processing Alice's argument. "It's not necessarily irregular. Or I would argue that it partakes of a higher regularity, a higher order, that we haven't been allowed to see."

"Yeah, that's the answer." Eliot was visibly drunk. "That's the answer to everything. God save us from Christian magicians. You sound just like my parents. That is just exactly what my ignorant Christian parents would say. Just, if it doesn't fit with your theory, well, that's just because, oh, it actually does, but God is mysterious, so we can't see it. Because we're so sinful. That's so fucking *easy*."

He fished around in the remnants of Janet's centerpiece with a long serving fork. Leda and the Swan were indistinguishable from each other now, two rounded Brancusi forms still gamely humping away as a tide of slush rose up to drown them.

"Well, heck, we oughta call ourselves the *Meta*-Physical Kids," Josh said.

"And who the fuck is this 'Maker' you're talking about?" Eliot snarled. He was getting vehement and not listening. "Are you talking about God? Because if you're talking about God, just say God."

"All right," Richard said placidly. "Let's say God."

"Is this a moral God? Is He going to punish us for using His holy magic? For being bad little magicians? Is He ["She!" Janet shouted] going to come back and give us a good spanking because we got into the garage and played with Daddy's power tools?

"Because that is just stupid. It's just stupid, and it's ignorant. No one gets punished for anything. We do whatever we want, and that's all we do, and nobody stops us, and nobody cares."

"If He left us His tools, He left them for a reason," Richard said.

"And I suppose you know what that is."

"What's the next wine, Eliot?" Janet asked brightly. She always kept a cool head in difficult moments, maybe because she tended to be so out of control so much of the rest of the time. She looked unusually ravishing tonight, too, in a slinky red tunic that made it to her midthigh, barely, before it gave out. The kind of thing Alice would never wear. Couldn't, not with her figure.

Both Richard and Eliot seemed to want to extend the fight by another round, but Eliot, with an effort of will, allowed himself to be diverted.

"An excellent question." Eliot pressed his hands to his temples. "I am receiving a divine vision from the Almighty Maker of . . . an exquisitely expensive small-batch bourbon . . . which God—or I'm sorry, *the Makeress*—has commanded me to render unto you forthwith."

He stood up unsteadily and lurched in the direction of the kitchen.

Quentin found him sitting red-faced and sweating on a stool by an open window. Icy air was pouring in, but Eliot didn't seem to notice. He stared out unblinking at the city, which receded in perspective lines of lights fanning out into the blackness. He said nothing. He didn't move as Quentin helped Richard manage the individual baked Alaskas—the trick, Richard explained, in his well-practiced explaining tone, was to make sure the meringue, an excellent heat insulator, formed a complete seal over the ice-cream core—and Quentin wondered if they'd lost Eliot for the evening.

It wouldn't be the first time he drank himself out of contention. But a few minutes later he rallied and trailed them back into the dining room with a slender, oddly shaped bottle sloshing with amber-colored whiskey.

Things were winding down. Everyone was treading carefully so as not to trigger another outburst from Eliot or another sermon from Richard. Not long afterward Josh left to take Anaïs home, and Richard retired of his own accord, leaving Quentin, Janet, and Eliot to preside woozily over the empty bottles and crumpled napkins. One of the candles had charred a hole in the tablecloth. Where was Alice? Had she gone home? Or crashed in one of the spare rooms? He tried her cell. No answer.

Eliot had dragged a pair of ottomans over to the table. He reclined on them Roman-style, though they were too low, so he had to reach up to get his drink, and all Quentin could see of him was his groping hand. Janet lay down, too, spooned up contentedly behind him.

"Coffee?" she asked.

"Cheese," Eliot said. "Do we have cheese? I need cheese."

On cue Peggy Lee wandered through the opening verse of "Is That All There Is?" on the stereo. Which would be worse, Quentin wondered. If Richard was right, and there was an angry moral God, or if Eliot was right, and there was no point at all? If magic was created for a purpose, or if they could do whatever they wanted with it? Something like a panic attack came over him. They were really in trouble out here. There was nothing to hang on to. They couldn't go on like this forever.

"There's a Morbière in the kitchen," he said. "It was supposed go with the theme—you know, the two layers, the morning milking, the night milking . . ."

"Yeah, yeah, we get it," Janet said. "Fetch, Q. Go on."

"I'll go," Eliot said, but instead of standing up he just rolled weakly off the couch and fell on the floor. His head made an ominously loud *bonk* as it hit the parquet.

But he was laughing as Quentin and Janet picked him up, Quentin getting his shoulders and Janet taking his feet, all thoughts of cheese extinguished, and maneuvered him out of the dining room and in the direction of his bedroom. On their way out the door Eliot's head hit the door frame with another loud *bonk,* and then it was just too absolutely hilarious, and they all started laughing, and they laughed until they were completely useless, and Janet dropped his feet, and Quentin dropped his shoulders, and his head *bonked* on the floor again, and by this time it was a thousand times more funny than the first two times.

It took Quentin and Janet twenty minutes to get Eliot down the hall to his bedroom, lurching heavily against the walls with their arms around each other as if they were struggling down a flooded steerage-level corridor on the *Titanic*. The world had become smaller and somehow lighter—nothing meant anything, but what was meaning anyway but a burden that weighed them down? Eliot kept saying he was fine, and Quentin and Janet kept insisting they had to pick him up. Janet announced that she had peed herself, actually literally peed herself, she was laughing so hard. As they passed Richard's door Eliot began a loud speech on the order of, "I am the mighty Maker, and I now bequeath to you My Holy Power Tools, because I am too fucking drunk to use them anymore, and good luck to you, because when I get up tomorrow they had better be exactly where I left them, *exactly*, even My . . . no, *especially* My belt sander, because I am going to be so fucking hungover tomorrow, anybody who fucks with My belt sander is going to get a taste of My belt. And it won't taste good. At all."

Finally they heaved him onto his bed and tried to make him drink water and pulled up the covers over his chest. It could have been the sheer domesticity of it—it was as if Eliot were their beloved son, whom they were lovingly tucking in for the night—or maybe it was just boredom, that powerful aphrodisiac, which had never been entirely out of sight even during the party's best moments, but if he was honest with himself Quentin had known for at least twenty minutes, even as they were wrestling Eliot down the hall, that he was going to take Janet's dress off as soon as he had half a chance.

Quentin woke up slowly the next morning. So slowly, over such a long time, that he was never really sure he'd been asleep at all. The bed felt unstable and disconcertingly floaty, and it was weird with two other naked people there. They kept bumping into each other and inadvertently touching and pulling away and then feeling self-conscious about having pulled away.

At first, in the first flush of it, he felt no regret about what happened. It was what you were supposed to do. He was living life to the fullest. Getting drunk and giving in to forbidden passions. That was the stuff of life. Wasn't that the lesson of the foxes? If Alice had any blood in her veins she would have joined them! But no. She had to go to bed early. She was just like Richard. Well, welcome to life in the grown-up magical world, Alice. Magic wasn't going to solve everything. Couldn't she see that? Couldn't she see that they were all dying, that everything was futile, that the only thing to do was to live and drink and fuck whatever and whomever while you still could? She herself had warned him of that, right there in her parents' house in Illinois. And she'd been right!

And then after a while it seemed like a debatable thing—you could really make the case both ways, it was a coin-flip. And then it was an unfortunate lapse, an indiscretion, still within the bounds of the forgivable, but definitely a low point. Not a personal best. And then it was a major indiscretion, a bad mistake, and then, in the last act of the strip tease, it revealed itself to be what it truly was: a terrible, really awful, hurtful betrayal. At some point during this slow, incremental fall from grace Quentin became aware of Alice sitting at the foot of the bed, just her back, facing away from where he and Janet and Eliot lay, resting her chin in her hands. Periodically he imagined that it was just a dream, that she hadn't been there at all. But to be honest he was pretty sure she had. She hadn't looked like a figment. She'd been fully dressed. She must have been up for a while.

Around nine o'clock the room was full of morning light and Quentin couldn't pretend to be asleep anymore. He sat up. He wasn't wearing a shirt, and he couldn't remember where his shirt was. He wasn't wearing anything else either. He would have given anything right then just to have a shirt and some underwear.

With his bare feet on the hardwood floor he felt strangely insubstantial. He couldn't understand, couldn't quite believe what he'd done. It just didn't seem like him. Maybe Fogg was right, maybe magic had inhibited his moral development. Something must have. Maybe that was why he was such a shit. But there had to be a way he could make Alice understand how sorry he was. He dragged a blanket off Eliot's bed—Janet stirred and complained sleepily, then went back to her dreamless, guiltless sleep—and wrapped it around himself and padded out into the silent apartment. The dinner table was like a shipwreck. The kitchen looked like a crime scene. Their little planet was ruined, and there was nowhere left for him to stand. Quentin thought about Professor Mayakovsky, how he'd reversed time, fixed the glass globe, brought the spider back to life. That would be a pretty nice thing to be able to do right about now.

When the elevator doors pinged open, Quentin thought it must be Josh coming back from a successful night with Anaïs. Instead it was Penny, pale and breathing hard from running and so excited he could barely contain himself.

PENNY'S STORY

He had a new mohawk, a proud iridescent green ruff an inch wide and three inches high, like the crest of a centurion's helmet. He had also gained weight—he looked, oddly, younger and softer than he had at Brakebills: less like a lone Iroquois warrior and more like an overfed white suburban gangsta. But it was still Penny who was catching his breath on the Oriental rug and looking around at everything like a curious, judgmental rabbit. He wore a black leather jacket with chrome spikes on it, faded black jeans, and a grubby white T-shirt. Jesus, Quentin thought. Do they even have punks anymore? He must be the last one in New York.

Penny sniffed and wiped his nose on his sleeve. Neither of them spoke. Quentin knew enough to know that Penny would never stoop to petty social pleasantries like saying hello and asking how he'd been and explaining what the hell he was doing here. Just this once Quentin was grateful. He didn't know if he could face it.

"How'd you get in here?" Quentin croaked. His mouth was parched.

"Your doorman was asleep. You should really fire him."

"It's not my doorman." He cleared his throat laboriously. "You must have cast something."

"Just Cholmondeley's Stealth." Penny gave it the correct English pronunciation: *Chumley's.*

"Eliot has a ward on this whole floor. I helped him set it up. Plus you need a key for the elevator."

"We'll need to set a new ward. I unpicked it on the way up."

"Fucking— Okay, first, who's we? We who?" Quentin said. At this moment his dearest wish would have been just a moment's grace to immerse his face in a sinkful of warm water. And maybe to have somebody hold him under till he drowned. "And second, Penny, Jesus, it took us a whole weekend to put up that ward."

He did a quick check: Penny was right, the defensive spells around the apartment were gone, so gone that they hadn't even alerted him when they were going. Quentin couldn't quite believe it. Penny must have taken down their ward from the outside, on the fly, from a standing start, in no more time than it took him to ride up ten floors in an elevator. Quentin kept his face blank—he didn't want to give Penny the satisfaction of seeing how impressed he was.

"What about the key?"

Penny dug it out of his jacket pocket and tossed it to Quentin.

"Took it off your doorman." He shrugged. "Kind of thing you learn on the street."

Quentin was going to say something about how the "street" in question was probably not a street at all but a way or a lane located in some gated community, and anyway it wasn't that hard to steal a key from a sleeping doorman when you were rocking Cholmondeley's Stealth, but it just seemed so unimportant, and the words were just too heavy to get out of his mouth, like they were stone blocks in his stomach that he would have had to physically cough up and regurgitate. Fuck Penny, he was wasting time. He had to talk to Alice.

But by then people had heard Penny's voice. Richard came shambling in from the kitchen where he'd been cleaning up, already awake and irritatingly showered and coiffed and groomed and pressed. Soon Janet came out of Eliot's room, regally swathed in a comforter as if nothing whatsoever unusual had happened the night before. She squeaked when she saw Penny and disappeared into a bathroom.

Quentin realized he would have to get dressed and deal with this. Daylight was here, and with it had come the world of appearances and lies and acting like everything was fine. They were all going to make scrambled eggs and talk about how hungover they were and drink mimosas and Bloody Marys with extra Tabasco and black pepper and act like nothing was wrong, as if Quentin hadn't just broken Alice's heart for no better reason than that he was drunk and felt like it. And as unbelievable, as unthinkable as it seemed, they were going to listen to what Penny had to say.

He was a year behind Quentin and Alice, but by the end of his Fourth Year Penny had decided—he explained, once his audience was assembled and dressed and arranged around him in the living room with drinks and plates, standing or lying full length on couches or sitting cross-legged on the floor as their physical and emotional conditions permitted—that Brakebills had taught him everything it was going to teach him, so he dropped out and moved to a small town in Maine, a few miles north of Bar Harbor. The town was called Oslo, a seedy little resort village with a population that shrank by 80 percent in the off-season.

Penny chose Oslo—not even New Oslo, just Oslo, as if they thought they came up with it first—for its total lack of anything that might distract him. He arrived in mid-September and had no trouble renting a small farmhouse on the outskirts of town on a one-lane rural route. His landlord was a retired schoolteacher who handed him the keys and then fled to his winter home in South Carolina. Penny's nearest neighbors on either side were a congregationless one-shack Pentecostal church and an out-of-session summer camp for disturbed children. It was perfect. He had found his Walden.

He had everything he needed: silence; solitude; a U-haul trailer packed with an enviable library of magical codices, monographs, chapbooks, reference books, and broadsheets. He had a sturdy desk, a well-lit room, and a window with an unscenic view of an unmown backyard that offered no particular temptation to gaze out at it. He had a manageable, intriguingly dangerous research project that showed every sign of maturing into a genuinely interesting line of inquiry. He was in heaven.

But one afternoon a few weeks after he arrived, as he sat at his desk, his watery blue eyes trailing over words of consummate power written centuries ago with a pen made out of a hippogriff feather, Penny found his mind wandering. His large, usually lineless brow crinkled. Something was sapping his powers of concentration. Was he under attack, maybe by a rival researcher? Who would dare! He rubbed his eyes and shook his head and focused harder. But his attention continued to drift.

It turned out that Penny had discovered in himself a weakness, a flaw he never would have suspected himself of in a thousand years, an age to which, with a few careful modifications that he would look into when he had the time, he had every intention of living. The flaw was this: he was lonely.

The idea was outrageous. It was humiliating. He, Penny, was a stone-cold loner, a desperado. He was the Han Solo of Oslo. He knew and loved this about himself. He had spent four interminable years at Brakebills surrounded by idiots—except for Melanie, as he privately referred to Professor Van der Weghe—and now he was finally free of their incessant bullshit.

But now Penny found himself doing things for no reason. Unproductive things. He stood on a concrete dam near his farmhouse and threw down rocks to break up the thin crust of ice that formed on the outflow pond. He walked the mile and a half to the center of town and played video games in the windowless video arcade back behind the pharmacy, stuffing his mouth with stale gumballs from the gumball machine, alongside the no-hope, dead-eyed teenagers who hung out there and did the exact same thing. He made awkward, inexperienced eyes at the underage clerk at the Book Bin, which actually sold mostly stationery and greeting cards, not books. He confided his troubles to the miserable pod of four buffalo who lived on the buffalo farm out on the Bar Harbor road. He thought about climbing over the fence and petting one of their huge, wedge-shaped heads, but he didn't quite have the nerve. They were big buffalo, and you never knew what they were thinking.

That was September. By October he had bought an herb-green Subaru Impreza and was making regular trips to a dance club in Bangor, swigging from a fifth of vodka on the passenger seat (since the club was all ages and didn't serve alcohol) as he drove the forty-five minutes through trackless pine forests. Progress on his research project had dwindled to almost nothing, a couple of hours a day of listless leafing through old notes punctuated by generous breaks for online porn. It was humiliating.

The dance club in Bangor was open only on Friday and Saturday nights, and all he did there was shoot pool in a half-lit lounge area off the main dance floor with other creepy male loners like himself. But it was in that half-lit lounge on one of those Saturday nights that he spotted, to his secret consternation and even more secret relief and gratitude, a familiar face. It was a hard face to like, the face of an emaciated corpse that hadn't been particularly attractive even in life, with a horrible pencil mustache on its upper lip. It belonged to the itinerant salesman Lovelady.

Lovelady was in the dance club in Bangor for approximately the same reason that Penny was there: he had run as far away as he could from the world of Brakebills and magic and then gotten lonely. Over a pitcher of Coors Light and a few games of pool, all of which Lovelady won handily— you don't spend a lifetime trafficking in fake magical items without picking up a few real skills—they exchanged stories.

Lovelady depended heavily for his livelihood on luck and the gullibility of strangers. He spent most of his time trolling the world's junk shops and estate sales the way longline fishermen troll the ocean. He accosted the emotionally vulnerable widows of recently deceased magicians and loitered on the outskirts of the conversations of his wisers and betters, keeping his eye out for anything that had value or that might plausibly be made to appear to have value. He had spent the past few months in northern England, in a studio apartment over a garage in a dreary suburb of Hull, trying his luck in antique stores and secondhand bookshops. His days were spent on buses and, when he was really down on his luck, on an ancient one-speed bicycle he borrowed without permission from the garage, which he wasn't supposed to have access to.

At some point during his stay Lovelady began to receive unwanted attention. Normally he was desperate for anybody to pay attention to him, anybody at all, but this was very different. Strangers on buses stared fixedly at him for no reason. Pay phones rang when he walked by them. When he counted his change, he found only coins from the year he was born. When he watched TV, all he saw was an image of his own face, with a mysterious empty city in the background. Lovelady was neither learned nor particularly intelligent, but he survived on his instincts, and all his instincts told him that something was gravely amiss.

Alone in his apartment, sitting on his pea-soup-colored foam couch, Lovelady took stock. His best guess was this: he had inadvertently acquired an object of genuine power, and something out there coveted it. He was being hunted.

That same night he pulled up stakes. He abandoned his security deposit, donned a rattling array of charms and fetishes, took a bus to London and the Chunnel train to Paris, and from there crossed the Atlantic to throw himself on the already overtaxed mercy of Brakebills. He spent an exhausting afternoon combing the woods north of New York for the school's familiar, comforting compound.

As the sun set through the trees, and the early winter chill gnawed at the tips of his ears, the horrifying truth sank in. He was in the right place, but Brakebills would no longer appear to him. Something, either him or his wares, was objectionable to the school's defensive spells. Whatever he was carrying had rendered him untouchable.

That was when he cut and ran to Maine. It was ironic: for once in his life Lovelady had lucked into something genuinely powerful, a big score. But it was too much luck all at once. He was out of his league. He could have dumped his stock, all of it, right there in the middle of the frozen woods, but after a lifetime of greedy scrimping he didn't quite have the gumption. It would have broken his avaricious heart. Instead he rented a Kozy Kabin in the woods at the off-season rate and conducted a thorough inventory.

He recognized it right away, mixed in with a jumbled consignment of grubby costume jewelry, in a plastic bag tied with a twisty. He didn't know what it was, but its power was obvious even to his untrained eye.

He motioned Penny over to a corner, reached into the pocket of his seedy overcoat, which he hadn't taken off all night, and laid the Baggie on a round particleboard bar table. He grinned his livid, discolored grin at Penny. The buttons were ordinary surplus vintage buttons: two holes, four holes, fake leather, fake tortoiseshell, big angular novelty knobs, and tiny bakelite pinpricks. A few of them were just leftover beads. Penny's eye immediately went to one of them, a flat, otherwise unremarkable pearlescent-white overcoat button about an inch across. It was heavier than it should have been. It practically vibrated with barely contained magical force.

He knew what it was. He knew better than to touch it.

"A magic button?" Janet said. "How weird. What was it?"

Her hair was a disaster, but she was obscenely relaxed, sipping coffee in an armchair, showing off her legs in a short silk bathrobe. She obviously felt triumphant, relishing her conquest, and by extension her victory over Alice. Quentin hated her at that moment.

"You really don't know?" Penny said.

Quentin thought he had a guess, but he wasn't going to say it out loud.

"What did you do?" he said instead.

"I made him come back with me to my house. That night. He wasn't safe where he was, and at least I had a basic security setup. We called the woman who sold him the consignment, but she insisted the buttons weren't in her records. The next day we went and got his stuff and drove to Boston, and I gave him eighty thousand dollars for it. He wouldn't take cash, just gold and diamonds. I practically cleaned out a Harry Winston, but it was worth it. Then I told him to fuck off, and he did."

"Eighty thousand dollars," Eliot said, "wouldn't clear out a display case at a Zales, let alone a Harry Winston."

Penny ignored him.

"That was two days ago. That button attracts attention. I was staying at a hotel in Boston, but last night a fire two floors above me killed a cleaning lady. I never went back to my room. I took the Fung Wah bus from South Station. I had to walk here from Chinatown; whenever I got in a cab the engine would die.

"But what matters is that it's real, and it's ours."

"Ours? Who are 'we'?" Richard asked.

"You," Quentin said coldly, "are a fucking nutjob."

"Quentin gets it," Penny said. "Anybody else?"

"Q, what is he talking about?"

A silent spear of pure, glittering ice entered Quentin's heart. He hadn't heard Alice come in. She stood at the edge of the circle, her hair unwashed and adrift, like a sleepy child who wakes in the middle of the night and appears like an uncertain spirit at the edge of a grown-up party.

"He doesn't know what he's talking about," Quentin muttered. He couldn't look at her. He was drowning in remorse. It almost made him angry at her, how much it hurt to look at her.

"Do you want to explain it or should I?" Penny said.

"You do it. I'm not going to be able to say it without laughing my head off."

"Well, somebody say something, or I'm going back to bed," Eliot said.

"Ladies and gentlemen," Penny said, gravely and grandly, "we are all going to Fillory."

At the end of *The Wandering Dune*—Penny began; it was a lecture he had obviously rehearsed—Helen and Jane Chatwin receive a gift from Highbound, the captain of the rabbit-crewed clipper ship that the girls encounter in the desert. The gift is a little brass-bound oak chest containing five magical buttons, all different shapes and colors, one for each of the Chatwins, each with the power to take the wearer from Earth to Fillory and back again at will.

Everybody in the room had read the Fillory books, in Quentin's case multiple times, but Penny rehearsed the rules anyway. The buttons don't take you directly there: first they move you to a kind of in-between netherworld, an interdimensional layover, and from there you can make the leap to Fillory.

No one knows where this transitional world is. It may be an alternate plane of existence, or a place between planes, interleaved between them like a flower pressed between pages, or a master plane that contains all planes—the spine that gathers the pages and binds them together. To the naked eye it looks like a deserted city, an endless series of empty stone squares, but it serves as a kind of multidimensional switchboard. In the center of each square is a fountain. Step into one of them, the story goes, and you'll be transported to another universe. There are hundreds of different squares, possibly an infinite number, and a corresponding number of alternate universes. The bunnies call this place the Neitherlands—because it's neither here nor there—or sometimes just the City.

But the most important point, Penny said, is that at the end of *The Wandering Dune* Helen hid all the buttons somewhere in her aunt's house in Cornwall. She felt they were too mechanical, they made the journey too easy. Their power was wrong. You shouldn't be able to just go to Fillory whenever you wanted, like catching a bus, she argued. A trip to Fillory had to be earned, that had always been the way. It was a reward for the worthy, bestowed by the ram-gods Ember and Umber. The buttons were a perversion of this divine grace, a usurping of it. They broke the rules. Ember and Umber couldn't control them. Fillory was fundamentally a religious fantasy, but the buttons weren't religious at all, they were magical—they were just tools, with no values attached. You could use them for anything you wanted, good or evil. They were so magical they were practically technological.

So she hid them. Jane was inconsolable, understandably enough, and tore up half the property looking for them, but according to *The Wandering Dune* she never found them, and Plover never wrote any more books.

The Wandering Dune ends in the summer of 1917, or possibly 1918; because of the lack of real-world detail it's impossible to date it precisely. After that the whereabouts of the buttons is unknown. But try a thought experiment, Penny suggested: How long could a box of buttons hidden by a twelve-year-old girl plausibly have stayed hidden? Ten years? Fifty? Nothing stays hidden forever. Wasn't it possible—even inevitable—that in the decades that followed a maid or a real estate agent or another little girl would have found them again? And that from there they would have made their way onto the magical gray market?

"I always thought they were supposed to be lapel buttons," Richard said. "Like a pin. Like 'I Like Ike.'"

"Um, okay, so let's back up for a second?" Quentin said cheerily. He was in the perfect mood for somebody, anybody besides himself, to make an ass of himself, and if that person could be Penny, and if Quentin could help him do it, then ever so much the better. "The Fillory books are fiction? Nothing you're talking about actually happened?"

"Yes and no," Penny said, surprisingly reasonably. "I'll allow that much of Plover's narrative might be fictional. Or fictionalized. But I've come to believe that the basic mechanics of interdimensional travel that Plover describes are quite real."

"Really." Quentin knew Penny well enough to know that he never bluffed, but he kept going anyway out of pigheadedness, urged on by his own inner vileness. "And what makes you think that?"

Penny regarded him with benevolent pity as he prepared the hammer blow.

"Well, I can certainly tell you that the Neitherlands are very real. I've spent most of the past three years there."

No one had an answer to this. The room was silent. Quentin finally dared to glance over at Alice, but her face was a mask. It would almost have been better if she looked angry.

"I don't know if you know this," Penny said, "in fact I'm pretty sure you don't, but I did most of my work at Brakebills on travel between alternate worlds. Or between planes, as we called them. Melanie and I.

"As far as we could determine it was an entirely new Discipline. Not that I was the first person ever to study the subject, but I was the first to have a special aptitude for it. My talents were so unusual that Melanie—Professor Van der Weghe—decided to pull me out of regular classes and give me my own course of study.

"The spellcraft was extremely involved, and I had to improvise a lot of it. I can tell you, a lot of what's in the canon on this stuff is way off base. *Way* off base. They're not seeing the whole picture, and the part of it they are seeing is by far the least important part. You'd think your friend Bigby would have some grasp of this stuff, but he has no idea. I was surprised, I really was. But there were still some issues I couldn't resolve."

"Such as," Eliot said.

"Well, so far I've only been able to travel alone. I can transport my body and clothes and some small supplies, but nothing else and nobody else. Second, I can cross to the Neitherlands, but that's it. I'm stuck there. The wider multiverse is closed to me."

"You mean—?" said Janet. "Wait, so you've been to this amazing magical Interville but that's it?" She actually looked underwhelmed. "I thought you were coming in here this badass multidimensional desperado and all."

"No." Penny could be defensive when he felt like he was under attack, but he was so autistically focused right now that even direct mockery bounced right off him. "My explorations have been limited to the City. It's quite a rich environment in itself, an amazingly complex artifact, to a magically trained eye. There's so little information in the books—*The Wandering Dune* is told through the eyes of a child, and it's not clear to me that either Plover or the Chatwins had any particular command of the techniques they describe. I thought at first that the entire place was a kludge, a virtual environment that functioned as a kind of three-dimensional interface hacked onto a master interdimensional switchboard. Not that it's much of an interface. A maze of identical unlabeled squares? How much help is that? But it was all I could think of.

"The thing is, the more I study it, the more I think it's exactly the opposite—that our world has much less substance than the City, and what we experience as reality is really just a footnote to what goes on there. An epiphenomenon.

"But now that we have the button"—he patted his jeans pocket—"we'll learn so much more. We'll go so much further."

"Have you tried it?" Richard asked.

Penny hesitated. For somebody who so obviously wanted to be hardcore, he was painfully transparent.

"Of course he hasn't," Quentin said, smelling blood. "He's scared shitless. He has no idea what that thing is, only that it's dangerous as hell, and he wants one of us to be a guinea pig."

"That's absolutely not true!" Penny said. His ears were getting red. "An artifact on this level is best faced in the company of allies and observers! With the proper controls and safeguards! No reasonable magician—"

"Look. Penny." Now Quentin could play the reasonable one, and he did it with maximum nastiness. "Slow down. You've gotten so far ahead of yourself, you can't even see how you got there. You've seen an old city, and a bunch of pools and fountains, and you've got a button with some heavy-duty enchantments on it, and you're looking for some framework to fit them all together, and you've latched on to this Fillory thing. But you're grasping at straws. It's crazy. You're cramming a few chance data points into a story that has nothing to do with reality. You need to take a giant step back. Take a deep breath. You're way off the reservation."

Nobody spoke. The skepticism in the room was palpable. Quentin was winning, and he knew it. Penny looked around at his audience beseechingly, unable to believe that he was losing them.

Alice stepped forward into the empty circle around Penny.

"Quentin," she said, "you have always been the most unbelievable pussy."

Her voice broke only a little as she said it. She grabbed Quentin's wrist with one hand and shoved the other one into the left-hand pocket of Penny's baggy black jeans. She fumbled for an instant.

Then they vanished together.

THE NEITHERLANDS

Quentin was swimming. Or he could have been swimming, but in fact he was just floating. It was dark, and his body was weightless, suspended in chilly water. His testicles shrank in on themselves away from the cold. Wavering, heatless sunbeams lanced down through the darkness.

After the first shock the coolness of the water, combined with the weightlessness, felt indescribably good to his dried-out, feverish, unshowered, hungover body. He could have thrashed and panicked, but instead he just let himself hang there, arms out in a dead man's float. Whatever was coming next would come. He opened his eyes, and the water bathed them in moist healing chill. He closed them again. There was nothing to see.

It was a glorious relief. The numbness of it was just magnificent. At the moment when it had been at its most intolerably painful, the world, normally so unreliable and insensitive in these matters, had done him the favor of vanishing completely.

Granted, he would need air at some point. He would look into that in due course. As bad as things were, drowning would still be a hasty course of action. For now all he wanted was to stay here forever, hanging neutrally buoyant in the amniotic void, neither in the world nor out of it, neither dead nor alive.

But an iron manacle was clamped around his wrist. It was Alice's hand, and it was pulling him upward ruthlessly. She wouldn't let him be. Reluctantly, he joined her in kicking toward the surface. Their heads broke water at the same moment.

They were in the center of a still, hushed, empty city square, treading water in the round pool of a fountain. It was absolutely silent: no wind, no birds, no insects. Broad paving stones stretched away in all directions, clean and bare as if they'd just been swept. On all four sides of the square stood a row of stone buildings. They gave off an impression of indescribable age—they weren't decrepit, but they'd been lived in. They looked vaguely Italianate; they could have been in Rome, or Venice. But they weren't.

The sky was low and overcast, and a light rain was falling, almost mist. The droplets dimpled the still surface of the water, which made its way into the pool from the overflowing bowl of a giant bronze lotus flower. The square had the air of a place that had been hastily abandoned, five minutes ago or five centuries, it was impossible to tell.

Quentin treaded water for a minute, then took one long breaststroke over to the stone lip. The pool was only about fifteen feet across, and the rim was scarred and pocked: old limestone. Bracing himself with both hands, he heaved himself up and and flopped out of the water onto dry land.

"Jesus," he whispered, panting. "Fucking Penny. It is real."

It wasn't just because he hated Penny. He really hadn't thought it was true. But now here they were in the City. This was it, the actual Neitherlands, or something that looked uncannily like them. It was unbelievable. The most naïve, most blissfully happy-sappy dream of his childhood was true. God, he'd been so wrong about everything.

He took a deep breath, then another. It was like white light flooding through him. He didn't know he could be this happy. Everything that was weighing him down—Janet, Alice, Penny, everything—was suddenly insubstantial by comparison. If the City was real, then Fillory could be real, too. Last night had been a disaster, an apocalypse, but this was so much more important. It was almost funny now. There was so much joy ahead of them.

He turned to Alice. "This is *exactly*—"

Her fist caught him smack in his left eye. She hit like a girl, without any weight behind it, but he hadn't seen it coming to roll with it. The left half of the world flashed white.

He bent over, half blind, the heel of his hand over his eye. She kicked him in the shins, one and then the other, with dismaying accuracy.

"Asshole! You *ass*hole!"

Alice's face was pale. Her teeth were chattering.

"You bastard. You fucking coward."

"Alice," he managed. "Alice, I'm sorry. But listen . . . look—" He tried to point at the world around them while also verifying that his cornea was still intact.

"Don't you *fucking* speak to me!" She slapped wildly at his head and shoulders with both hands so that he ducked and put up his arms. "Don't you even dare talk to me, you whore! You fucking whore!"

He staggered a few steps away across the stone, trying to escape, his sopping wet clothes flapping, but she followed him like a swarm of bees. Their voices sounded small and empty in the echoless square.

"Alice! Alice!" His orbital ridge was a ring of fire. "Forget about all that for a second! Just for a second!" She'd still been holding the button in her fist when she clocked him. It must be a lot heavier than it looked. "You don't understand. It was just . . . everything—" There was a right way to say this. "I got confused. Life just seemed so empty—I mean out there—it's like what you said, we have to live while we can. Or that's what I thought. But it got out of control. It just got out of control." Why was he talking in clichés? Get to the point. He definitely had one. "We were all just so drunk—"

"Really. Too drunk to fuck?" She had him there. "I could kill you. Do you understand that?" Her face was terrible. There were two white-hot points on her flushed cheeks. "I could burn you to nothing right where you stand. I'm stronger than you. Nothing you could do would stop me."

"Listen, Alice." He had to stop her from talking. "I know it's bad. It's very, very bad. And I'm so sorry. You'll never know how sorry. You have to believe me. But it's so important that you understand!"

"What are you, a child? You got confused? Why didn't you just end it, Quentin? You obviously lost interest a long time ago. You really are a child, aren't you? You're obviously not enough of a man to have a real relationship. You're not even enough of a man to end a real relationship. Do I have to do absolutely everything for you?

"Or you know what it is? You hate yourself so much, you'll hurt anybody who loves you. That's it, isn't it? Just to get even with them for loving you. I never saw that before now."

She stopped at this, shaking her head, lost in a dream of disbelief. Her own words had brought her up short. In the silence the fact that he had cheated on her, and with Janet of all people, hit her all over again, as fully as it had the first time, two hours ago. Quentin could see it: it was like she'd been shot in the stomach.

She held up her hand, palm out, like she was shielding her eyes from his monstrous face. A lock of wet hair was plastered to her cheek. She was gasping for breath. Her lips had gone pale. But they kept moving.

"Was it worth it?" she said. "You always wanted her, you think I didn't see that? You think I'm stupid? Answer me: Do you think I'm stupid? Just tell me! I really want to know if you think I'm stupid!"

She ran at him and slapped his face. He took the full force of the blow.

"No, I don't think you're stupid, Alice." Quentin felt like a boxer who was knocked out standing, out on his feet, crosses for eyes, just wishing to God that he could fall down. She was right, a thousand times right, but if he could just make her see what he saw—if she could only put things in proper perspective. Fucking women. She was walking away now, toward one of the alleys that led to another square, leaving a trail of damp squashing foot prints behind her. "But will you please look around you?" He was begging, trailing after her, his voice ragged with exhaustion. "Will you please acknowledge for a second that something more important than who stuck what body part where is going on around you?"

She wasn't listening, or maybe she was just determined to say what she was going to say.

"You know," she said, almost conversationally, crossing into the next square, "I bet you actually thought fucking her was going to make you happy. You just go from one thing to the next, don't you, and you think it's going to make you happy. Brakebills didn't. I didn't. Did you really think Janet would? It's just another fantasy, Quentin."

She stopped and hugged her arms over her midsection, like the pain was a gastric ulcer, and sobbed bitterly. Her wet clothes clung to her; a little pool was forming around her. He wanted to comfort her, but he didn't dare touch her. The stillness of the square was almost tangible around them. The Fillory books had described them as all exactly identical, but he could see they weren't, far from it. They shared the same crypto-Italian style, but this one had a colonnade on one side, and the fountain in the center was rectangular, not round like the one they'd come in through. At one end a white marble face vomited water into it.

Footsteps on stone. Quentin thought he would have welcomed any interruption, anything, especially if it was carnivorous and would eat him alive.

"Kind of a reunion, isn't it?"

Penny came stepping briskly across the flagstones toward them. The gray facade of a stone piazza loomed above them, with heraldic inlays: an anchor and three flames. Penny looked as happy and relaxed as Quentin had ever seen him. He was in his element and glowing with pride. His clothes were dry.

"Sorry. I've spent so much time here, but I've never had anybody to show it to. You wouldn't think that would matter, but it does. When I first came through there was a corpse lying right there on the ground. Right over there."

He pointed like a campus tour guide.

"Human, or close to it, anyway. Maybe Maori, he had a tattoo on his face. He could only have been dead a few days. He must have gotten trapped here—came in, but the pools wouldn't let him out somehow. I think he died of starvation. The next time I came the body was gone."

Penny studied their two faces and took in the situation for the first time: Alice's tears, Quentin's rapidly darkening black eye, their toxic body language.

"Oh." His face softened slightly. He made a gesture, and suddenly their clothes were warm and dry and pressed, too. "Look, you have to forget about all that stuff here. This place can be dangerous if you're not paying attention. I'll give you an example: Which way would you go to get back to our home square?"

Alice and Quentin looked around obediently, Penny's reluctant students. In their running fight they had cut an angle through the second square into a third. Or a fourth? Their footprints had already faded. There was an alley on each side of the square, and through each alley you could catch a glimpse of other irregular alleys and fountains and squares, more and more, diminishing to infinity. It was like a trick with mirrors. The sun was hidden, if there even was a sun. Penny was right: they had no idea which one led back to Earth, or even which general direction they'd come from.

"Don't worry, I marked it. You only came about a quarter mile. One up and one over." Penny pointed in exactly the opposite direction Quentin would have guessed. "In the book they just wander at random, and it always comes out all right, but we have to be more careful. I use orange spray paint to mark a path. I have to do it fresh every time I come here. The paint disappears."

Penny headed back in the direction he'd pointed. Tentatively, without looking at each other, Quentin and Alice fell in behind him. Their clothes were getting damp all over again from the rain.

"I have strict operating procedures when I'm here. There are no directions, so I've had to invent new ones. I named them after the buildings in the Earth square, one for each side: palace, villa, tower, church. Can't be a real church, but that's what it looks like. This is churchward, the way we're going now."

They were back at the fountain, which Penny had circled with big sloppy X's of fluorescent orange paint. A little way off there was a crude shelter, a tarp with a cot and a table underneath. Quentin wondered how he'd missed it before.

"I set up a base camp here for a while, with food and water and books." He was so excited, like a rich, unpopular kid the first time he brings home friends to see his fancy toys. He didn't even notice that Quentin and Alice weren't saying anything. "I always thought it would be Melanie who came here the first time, but she could never quite work the spells. I tried to teach her, but she's not quite strong enough. Almost, though. In a way I'm happy it's you guys. You know you were the only friends I ever had at Brakebills?"

Penny shook his head as if there was something amazing about the fact that more people didn't like him. Only twelve hours ago, Quentin thought, he and Alice would have barely been able to keep from cracking up with conspiratorial laughter at the suggestion that they had ever been friends with Penny.

"Oh, I almost forgot: no light spells here. They go crazy. When I first came here, I tried to do a basic illumination. I couldn't see for two hours afterward. It's like the air here is hyperoxygenated, only with magic. One spark and everything goes up."

There were two stone steps leading up to the fountain. Quentin sat down on the top one and leaned his back against the rim. The water looked unnaturally black, like ink. There was no point in fighting anymore. He would just sit here and listen to Penny talk.

"You wouldn't believe how far I've walked in this place. Hundreds of miles! Way farther than the Chatwins ever went. Once I saw a fountain that had overflowed like a plugged-up toilet and flooded its square a foot deep, and half the squares around it. Twice I've seen ones that were capped. Sealed over with a bronze cover like a well, like they were keeping people out. Or in. Once I found fragments of white marble on the pavement. I think it was a broken sculpture. I tried to piece it back together, to see what it was a statue of, but I never could.

"You can't get into the buildings. I've tried every way you can think of. Lock picks. Sledgehammers. Once I brought an acetylene cutting torch. And the windows are too dark to see in, but once I brought a flashlight— you know, one of those high-intensity rescue flashlights, that the Coast Guard uses? When I turned it all the way up I could see inside, just a little bit.

"I'll tell you something: they're full of books. Whatever they look like on the outside, on the inside every one of these buildings is really a library."

Quentin had no idea how long they'd been there, but it was a while. Hours maybe. They'd walked through square after square, like lost tourists, the three of them. Everything they saw shared a common style, and the same weathered, ancient look, but nothing ever quite repeated. Quentin and Alice couldn't look at each other, but they couldn't resist the seductions of this grand, melancholy place either. At least the rain had let up.

They passed through a tiny square, a quarter the size of the others and paved in cobblestones, where if they stood in the center it seemed like they could hear the ocean, the breaking and withdrawing of waves. In another square Penny pointed out a window with ghostly scorch marks above it, as if it had been the scene of a fire. Quentin wondered who had built this place, and where they'd gone. What had happened here?

Penny described in great technical detail his elaborate but ultimately unsuccessful campaign to rappel up the side of one of the buildings to get a view above the rooftops. The one time he'd managed to secure a line, on a piece of decorative masonry, he'd been overcome by dizziness halfway up, and when he recovered he found himself turned around, rappeling down the same wall he'd been trying to ascend.

At different times all three of them saw, in the farthest possible distance, a verdant square that seemed to contain a garden, with rows of what might have been lime trees in it. But they could never reach it—as they approached it always lost itself in the shifting perspectives of the alleyways, which were slightly out of alignment with one another.

"We should get back," Alice said finally. Her voice sounded dead. It was the first time she'd spoken since she screamed at him.

"Why?" Penny asked. He was having the time of his life. He must have been terribly lonely here, Quentin thought. "It doesn't matter how much time we spend here, you know. No time passes on Earth. To the others it'll be like we popped out and popped right back, just like that, bing-bang. They won't even have time to be surprised. I spent a whole semester here once and nobody noticed."

"I'm sure we wouldn't have noticed anyway," Quentin said, because he knew Penny would ignore him.

"I'm actually probably a year or so older than you guys, subjectively, because of all the time I spent here. I should have kept closer track."

"Penny, what are we doing here?"

Penny looked puzzled.

"Isn't it obvious? Quentin, we're going to Fillory. We have to. This is going to change everything."

"Okay. Okay." Something nagged at him about this, and he was going to put it into words. He had to force his weary brain to grind out thoughts. "Penny, we have to slow down. Look at the big picture. The Chatwins got to go to Fillory because they were chosen. By Ember and Umber, the magic sheep. Rams. They were there to do good, to fight the Watcherwoman, or whatever."

Alice was nodding.

"They only got to go when something was going on," she said. "The Watcherwoman, or the wandering dune, or that ticking watch thing in *The Flying Forest*. Or to find Martin. That was what Helen Chatwin was saying. We can't just go barging in without an invitation. That's why she hid the buttons in the first place—they were a mistake. Fillory wasn't like the real world, it was a perfect universe where everything was organized for good. Ember and Umber are supposed to control the borders.

"But with the buttons anybody could get in. Random people who weren't part of the story. Bad people. The buttons weren't part of the logic of Fillory. They were a hole in the border, a loophole."

The mere fact that Alice knew her Fillory lore cold, no hesitation, added another high-powered exponent to Quentin's guilty, bankrupt longing for her. How could he have gotten so confused that he thought he wanted Janet instead of her?

Penny was nodding and rocking his whole body forward and backward semi-autistically.

"But you're forgetting something, Alice. We're not bad people." The zeal light came on behind Penny's eyes. "We're the good guys. Has it occurred to you that maybe that's why we found the button in the first place? Maybe this is it, we're getting the call. Maybe Fillory needs us."

He waited expectantly for a reaction.

"It's thin, Penny," Quentin said finally, weakly. "This is all really thin."

"So what?" Penny stood up. "*So. What.* So what if Fillory doesn't work out? Which it will? So we end up somewhere else. It's another world, Quentin. It's a million other worlds. The Neitherlands are the place where all worlds meet! Who knows what other imaginary universes might turn out to be real? All of human literature could just be a user's guide to the multiverse! Once I marked off a hundred squares straight in one direction and never saw the edge of this place. We could explore for the rest of our lives and never begin to map it all. This is it, Quentin! It's the new frontier, the challenge of our generation and the next fifty generations after that!

"It all starts here, Quentin. With us. You just have to want it.

"What do you say?"

He actually stuck out his hand, as if he expected Quentin and Alice to put theirs on top of his, and they would all do a football cheer. Go team! Quentin was sorely tempted to leave him hanging, but finally he let Penny give him a limp low-five. His eye still throbbed.

"We should get back," Alice said again. She looked exhausted. She couldn't have slept much last night.

Alice produced the oddly weighty pearl button from her pocket. It looked ridiculous—it had sounded reasonable enough in the books, but that was the books, and the Chatwins had used the buttons only the one time. In real life it was like they were playing some children's game. It was a little kid's idea of a magical object. Though what did you expect from a bunch of talking bunnies?

Back in their home square they lined up on the edge of the fountain, holding hands, balancing precariously on the rim. The prospect of getting wet again was unspeakably depressing. In a corner of the square Quentin saw that a sapling had broken its way up through one of the paving stones from below. It was gnarled and bent, twisted almost into the shape of a helix, but it was alive. It made him wonder what had been paved over to build the City, and what would be there if it should ever fall. Had there been woods here? Would there be again? This too shall pass.

Alice stood on Penny's other side so she wouldn't have to touch Quentin. They stepped off the edge together, right foot first, in sync.

The crossing was different this time. They fell down through the water like it was air, then through darkness, then it was like they were falling out of the sky, down toward Manhattan on a gray Friday morning in winter—brown parks, gray buildings, yellow taxis waiting on stripy white cross-walks, black rivers studded with tugboats and barges—down through the gray roof and into the living room where Janet and Eliot and Richard were still caught in mid–double take, as if Alice had just now grabbed the button in Penny's pocket, as if the past three hours hadn't even happened.

"Alice!" Janet said gleefully. "Get your hand out of Penny's pants!"

UPSTATE

Of course after that everybody had to go. They barely even said anything about Quentin's swollen eye. ("The natives were restless," he ad-libbed dryly.) Moments after he and Alice returned Josh came in—he'd spent the night with Anaïs after all—and they had to tell him the whole story all over again. Then they went through in threes. Josh went through with Penny and Richard. Penny took Janet and Eliot through. Josh called Anaïs and made her come over, and she went through with him and Penny.

Of them all only Janet had a bad reaction. The moment they surfaced, apparently, she heaved and threw up her breakfast right into the cold, clear magical water. Then she panicked. Eliot came back with a dead-on impression of the frantic way she'd clutched Penny's arm and said:

"Button! Button now!"

Quentin was unmoved by her discomfort. She was a vampire, he thought. She preyed on other people's healthy love and made it sick and crippled.

The mood in the room was serious and sober. Everybody gave each other long, searching looks heavy with significance. Nobody could seem to put into words how important it was, but they all agreed that this was a major thing. *Major.* And it had to be their thing, for now at least, they had to contain it. Nobody else could know. At Penny's insistence they sat down in a big circle on the rug in the living room and rewove the wards on the apartment, right then and there, working together. Richard's taste for authority, which so often made his presence all but unendurable, turned out to come in handy now. He directed the group casting in an efficient, businesslike fashion, like a seasoned conductor leading a chamber orchestra through a difficult passage of Bartók.

It took twenty minutes to finish the spell, and then ten more to add some fancy extra defensive and concealment layers—prudent, given the level of interest the button was evidently attracting in the at-large magical ecosystem. When they were done, when everything was checked out and double-checked, a hush settled over the room. They all sat still and just let the magnitude of what was happening here marinate in their minds. Josh rose quietly and went to the kitchen to make sandwiches for lunch. Eliot threw open a window and lit a cigarette. Janet regarded Quentin with cool amusement.

Quentin lay back on the rug and stared up at the ceiling. He needed sleep, but this was no time for sleep. Wild emotions competed for possession of his brain, like rival armies taking and retaking the same hill: excitement, remorse, anticipation, foreboding, grief, anger. He tried to focus on Fillory, to make the good feeling come back. This would change everything. Yes, his universe had just expanded times a million, but Fillory was the key to it all. That creeping, infectious sense of futility that had been incubating in his brain even since before graduation had met its magic bullet. Alice didn't see it yet, but she would. This was what they'd been waiting for. This is what her parents had never found. A bleary grin kept smearing itself across his face, and the years fell away from him like layers of dead skin. They weren't wasted years exactly, he could never say that, but they were years in which, in spite of all his amazing gifts, he'd been conscious of somehow not quite getting the gift he wanted. Enough to get by on, maybe. Sure. But this, this was everything. Now the present had a purpose, and the future had a purpose, and even the past, their whole lives, retroactively, had meaning. Now they knew what it was for.

If only it hadn't happened now. If Penny could just have shown up a day earlier. Fucking Penny. Everything had been completely ruined and then completely redeemed in such rapid succession that he couldn't tell which state ultimately applied. But if you looked at it a certain way, what happened between him and Janet wasn't about him and Janet at all, or even him and Alice. It was a symptom of the sick, empty world they were all in together. And now they had the medicine. The sick world was about to be healed.

The others stayed sitting on the floor, leaning back on their elbows, lounging with their backs against the couch, glancing at one another every once in a while and breaking out in incredulous giggles. It was like they were stoned. Quentin wondered if they were feeling what he was feeling. This was what they'd been waiting for, too, without knowing it, he thought. The thing that was going to save them from the ennui and depression and meaningless busywork that had been stalking them ever since graduation, with its stale, alcoholic breath. It was finally here, and not a moment too soon. They couldn't go on like this, and now they wouldn't have to.

It was Eliot who finally took control of the situation. He almost seemed like his old self again. Calendars were cleared. Nobody had any serious obligations pending, not compared to this, nothing that couldn't be delayed or sicked out of or blatantly welched on. He clapped his hands and gave orders, and everybody seemed to enjoy being serious and efficient for a change.

Nobody knew Anaïs especially well—not even Josh, really—but she turned out to be a highly useful individual. Her circle of acquaintance included somebody who knew somebody who owned a place upstate, a comfortable old farmhouse on a hundred acres, somewhere private enough and defensible enough to use as a staging area for whatever it was they were going to do next. And that first somebody was also a magician senior enough to open a portal to get them there. She would come by later that afternoon, as soon as the Nets game was over.

They had to do it on the roof, because the very effective and thorough triple-triple wards they'd just that morning set up (and were now about to abandon) prevented any magical transport directly in or out of the apartment. By five thirty that afternoon they were looking out over the crowded cocktail-tray skyline of lower Manhattan. No one else was up there in winter. The roof was littered with windblown, overturned plastic lawn furniture and char-encrusted barbecue implements. A lonely wind chime burbled to itself from the eaves of a utility shed.

They hugged themselves against the cold and scuffed the gravel with their feet as they watched a hale, gray-haired Belgian sorceress with nicotine-stained fingers and a rather sinister wicker fetish on a string around her neck pull open the portal. It was a five-sided portal, the bottom edge running parallel to the ground, and its vertices shed tiny sputtering actinic blue-white sparks—a purely cosmetic touch, Quentin suspected, but they gave the scene an air that was both melancholy and festive at the same time.

There was a sense of momentous occasion. They were embarking on a grand adventure on the spur of the moment. Isn't that what it means to be alive, Goddamn it? When the portal was finished and stable, the gray-haired witch kissed Anaïs on both cheeks, said something in French, and left hurriedly, but not before Janet made her take a picture of all of them together with their trunks and bundles and bags full of groceries piled up behind them, using a disposable camera.

The group, all eight of them now, stepped through together onto a vast, frost-burnt front lawn. The serious mood on the roof was instantly broken as Janet and Anaïs and Josh raced one another inside and squealed and bounced on the sofas and ran around arguing over the bedrooms. Anaïs had been mostly right about the house: it was certainly large and comfortable, and at least a few bits of it were old. Apparently it was once a generously proportioned Colonial farmhouse, but somebody with progressive architectural ideas had gotten hold of it and remixed its old timber and fieldstone with glass and titanium and poured cement and added flat-screen TVs and a high-end audio system and an Aga range.

Alice went directly and silently up to the master bedroom, which took up almost half the third floor, and closed the door, glaring away any rival claimants with burning, red-rimmed eyes. Suddenly exhausted after his mostly sleepless night, followed by his magically extended day, Quentin found a small guest bedroom at the back of the house. Its hard, antiseptic twin bed felt like all he deserved.

It was dark when he woke up. The cool blue digits of the clock radio said 10:27. In the darkness they could have been phosphorescent squiggles on the side of a deep-sea fish. He couldn't find the light switch, but his groping hands encountered the door to a small half bath and managed to turn on the light over the mirror. Quentin splashed water on his face and wandered out into the strange house.

He found the others, except for Alice and Penny, in the dining room, where they had already made and demolished a meal of heroic proportions, the remains of which lay spread out on a stupendous table that looked like it was built from the beams of the True Cross, handsomely varnished and nailed together with authentic iron spikes. Large pieces of modern art the color and texture of dried, crusted blood hung on the walls.

"Q!" they shouted.

"Where's Alice?"

"Came and went," Josh said. "What's going on? You guys fighting or what?"

He shadowboxed a jab or two. He obviously didn't know what had happened. Anaïs, sitting next to him, delivered a mock knockout punch to his stubbly chin. They were all drunk again, same as last night, same as every night. Nothing had changed.

"Seriously," Janet said. "Did she give you that shiner? Seems like somebody's always punching you in the face, Q."

Her manner was as bright and toxic as ever, but her eyes were rimmed with red. Quentin wondered if she'd come out of last night's holocaust quite as unscathed as he'd thought.

"It was Ember and Umber," he said. "The magic rams. Didn't Alice tell you? They punished me for being sinful."

"Yeah?" Josh said. "Did you kick their woolly asses?"

"I turned the other cheek." Quentin didn't feel like talking, but he was hungry. He got a plate from the kitchen and sat down at the far end of the table and served himself leftovers.

"We were talking about what to do next," Richard said. "Making up an actions list."

"Right." Josh pounded authoritatively on the heavy table. "Who's got some action items for me? We need to enumerate our deliverables!"

"Food," Richard said, straight-faced. "And if we're really going to Fillory, we all need to reread all the books."

"Gold," Anaïs chipped in gamely. "And trade items. What do Fillorians want? Cigarettes?"

"We're not going to Brezhnev-era Russia, Anaïs. Steel?"

"Gunpowder?"

"My God," Eliot said. "Listen to you people. I am not going to be the man who brought the gun to Fillory."

"We should bring overcoats," Richard said. "Tents. Cold-weather gear.

We have no idea what season it is there. We could be walking into deep winter."

Yesterday—meaning before his nap—Fillory was going to make everything all right. Now it was hard to focus on it: it seemed like a dream again. Now the mess with Janet and Alice was the real thing. It would drag everything else down with it.

He pulled himself together with an effort.

"How long are we talking about going for?"

"A couple of days? Look, we can just come back if we forget something," Eliot said. "With the button it's a snap. We'll just stay till it gets boring."

"What should we do when we get there?"

"I think they'll probably give us a quest," Penny said. "That's what always happened to the Chatwins."

Heads turned. Penny was standing in the doorway in a T-shirt and sweatpants, blinking like an owl, looking like he'd just woken up, too.

"I don't know if we can count on that, Penny." For some reason it annoyed Quentin, how starry-eyed and optimistic Penny was being about this. "It's not like the rams summoned us. It might not even be like the books. Maybe there never were any quests. Plover probably just put that stuff in so there would be a good story. Maybe we'll just suck around Fillory like we're sucking around here."

"Don't be a killjoy," Josh said, "just because your girlfriend beats you up."

Penny was shaking his head. "I just don't see Plover coming up with all that stuff on his own. It's not rational. He was a gay dry-cleaning magnate with a background in practical chemistry. He didn't have a creative bone in his body. No way. It's Occam's razor. It's much more likely that he was writing it as it happened."

"So what do you think," Eliot said, "we're going to meet a damsel in distress?"

"We might. Not necessarily a damsel, but . . . you know, a nymph maybe. Or a dwarf, or a pegasus. You know, that needs help with something." Everybody was laughing, but Penny kept on going. It was almost touching. "Seriously, it happens in the books, every time."

Josh pushed a tiny doll glass of something clear and alcoholic in front of Quentin, and he took a sip. It was some kind of fiery fruit eau-de-vie, and it tasted like a vital nutrient that his body had been chronically deprived of his entire life.

"Sure, but real life's not actually like that," Quentin went on, fumbling after what he was sure was an important insight. "You don't just go on fun adventures for good causes and have happy endings. You're not going to be a character in a story, there's nobody arranging everything for you. The real world just doesn't work like that."

"Maybe your world doesn't, Earth man," Josh said. He winked. "We're not in your world anymore."

"And I don't want to turn this into a theological discussion," Richard added, with towering dignity, "but there is room for disagreement on that score."

"And even if you don't believe that this world has a god," Penny finished up, "you must admit that Fillory has one. Two even."

"This does bring us back, albeit in an insane way, to what is actually a pretty reasonable question," Eliot said. "Which is what do we do when we get there?"

"We should go after that magic flower," Josh suggested. "You know, the one that when you smell it it automatically makes you happy? Remember that? That thing would be worth bank here."

While nobody was watching, Janet caught Quentin's eye and waggled her eyebrows and did something lewd with her tongue. Quentin eyed her back, unblinking. She was actually enjoying this, he thought. She'd sabotaged him and Alice, and she was loving it. Little montage flashes of last night—it couldn't possibly have just been last night—cycled through his brain, snapshots that had stubbornly survived the merciful angel of alcoholic erasure. Everything about sex with Janet had been so different from Alice. The smell, the feel of her skin, her businesslike know-how. The shame and the fear had caught up with him even before it was over, before he came, but he hadn't stopped.

And had Eliot really been awake for the whole thing? His brain dealt out a sloppy fan of mental Polaroids, out of sequence: an image of Janet kissing Eliot, of her hand working diligently between Eliot's legs. Had she really been weeping? Had *he* kissed Eliot? A vivid sense memory of somebody else's stubble, surprisingly scratchy, chafing his cheek and upper lip.

Good God, he thought wearily. What goes on.

He had reached the outer limits of what Fun, capital *F*, could do for him.

The cost was way too high, the returns pitifully inadequate. His mind was dimly awakening, too late, to other things that were as important, or even more so. Poor Alice. He needed a hair shirt, or ashes, or a scourge—there should be some ritual that he could perform to show her how desperately sorry he was. He would do anything, if she would just tell him what to do.

He shoved the pictures back down wherever they came from, back into the mental shuffle, speeding them on their way with some more of that yummy eau-de-vie. An idea was germinating in his tired, bruised brain.

"We could find Martin Chatwin," Richard volunteered. "The way the other children were always trying to."

"I'd like to bring something back for Fogg," Eliot said. "Something for the school. An artifact or something."

"That's it?" Josh said. "You're going to Fillory to bring back an apple for teacher? God, you're so unbelievably lame sometimes."

Oddly, Eliot didn't take the bait. This was affecting them all in different ways.

"Maybe we could find the Questing Beast," Quentin said quietly.

"The what?" Josh wrinkled his forehead. No Fillory scholar he.

"From *The Girl Who Told Time*. Remember? The beast that can't be caught. Helen chases it."

"What do you do with it if you do catch it? Eat it?"

"I don't know. Maybe it leads you to treasure? Or gives you some secret wisdom? Or something?" He hadn't thought this through completely. It had seemed important to the Chatwins, but now he couldn't remember why.

"You never find out," Penny said. "Not in the books. They never catch it, and Plover never mentions it again. It's a good idea. But I was thinking, you know, maybe they'll make us kings. Kings and queens. The way the Chatwins were."

As soon as Penny said it, Quentin wondered why he hadn't thought of it himself. It was so obvious. They'd be kings and queens. Of course they would. If the City was real, why not all the rest of it, even that? They could live in Castle Whitespire. Alice could be his queen.

God, he was agreeing with Penny. That was a danger sign if there ever was one.

"Huh." Janet mulled this over, her ever-alert brain ticking over. She was actually taking it seriously, too. "Would we have to marry each other?"

"Not necessarily. The Chatwins didn't. Then again, they were all siblings."

"I don't know," said Anaïs. "It sounds like a big job, being queen. There is probably bureaucracy. Administration."

"Lucrative though. Think of the perks."

"If the books are even accurate," Eliot said. "And if the thrones are vacant. That's two big ifs. Plus there's seven of us and only four thrones. Three people get left out."

"I'll tell you what we need," Anaïs said. "We need war magic. Battle magic. Offense, defense. We need to be able to hurt people if we have to."

Janet looked amused.

"Shit's illegal, babe," she said, obviously impressed despite herself. "You know that."

"I don't care if it is." Anaïs shook her precious blond curls. "We need it. We have *no idea* what we will be seeing when we cross over. We have to be ready. Unless any of you big strong men knows how to use a sword?" There was silence, and she smirked. *"Alors."*

"Did they teach you that stuff where you went?" Josh asked. He looked a little afraid of her.

"We are not so pure in Europe as you Americans, I guess."

Penny was nodding. "Battle magic isn't illegal in Fillory."

"Out of the question," Richard said crisply. "Do you realize the kind of heat you'd bring down on us? Who here besides me has dealt with the Magicians' Court? Anybody?"

"We're already in the shit, Richard," Eliot said. "You think that button would be legal if the court knew about it? If you want out, get out now, but Anaïs is right. I'm not going over there with just my dick in my hand."

"We can get a dispensation for small arms," Richard went on primly. "There are precedents for that. I know the forms."

"Guns?" Eliot made a sour face. "What is wrong with you? Fillory is a pristine society. Have you ever even *watched Star Trek*? This is basic Prime Directive stuff. We have a chance to experience a world that has not yet been fucked up by assholes. Do any of you get how important that is? Any of you?"

Quentin kept expecting Eliot to declare himself too cool for the whole Fillory project and start making snarky jokes about it, but he was turning out to be surprisingly focused and unironic about it. Quentin couldn't remember the last time Eliot had been openly enthusiastic about anything. It was a relief to see that he could still admit that he cared about something.

"I do *not* want to be around Penny with a gun," Janet said firmly.

"Look, Anaïs is right," Eliot said. "We'll work up some basic attack spells, just in case. Nothing too insane. We'll just have a couple of aces in the hole. And we have those cacodemons in our backs, don't forget. And the button."

"And our dicks in our hands." Anaïs giggled.

The next day Richard, Eliot, Janet, and Anaïs drove into Albany to shop for supplies; Janet, being from L.A., was the only one who had a driver's license. Quentin, Josh, Alice, and Penny were supposed to be researching battle magic, but Alice wouldn't speak to Quentin—he had knocked on her door that morning, but she wouldn't come out—and the technicalities were beyond Josh, so it came down to Alice and Penny working together.

Soon the big dining room table was covered with books from Penny's U-haul stash and sheets of butcher paper crawling with flow charts. They were deep into it. As the two biggest magic nerds of the group, Alice and Penny were completely absorbed in each other, speaking some ad hoc technical jargon they came up with on the fly, Penny scribbling reams of archaic notations and Alice nodding seriously over his shoulder and pointing. They were doing original work, building spells from scratch; it wasn't fantastically difficult stuff, but any prior art in the area had been thoroughly suppressed.

Watching them work, Quentin was consumed with jealousy. Thank God it was Penny—anybody else and he would have been seriously suspicious. He and Josh spent the afternoon in the den with some beer and Smart Food watching cable on a flat-screen TV the size of a billboard. There had been no TV at Brakebills, or in their Manhattan apartment, and it felt exotic and forbidden.

Around five o'clock Eliot came and roused them.

"Come on," he said. "You're missing Penny's big show."

"How was Buffalo?"

"Like a vision of the apocalypse. We bought parkas and hunting knives."

They trailed Eliot out to the backyard. Seeing him happy and excited and reasonably sober restored Quentin's faith in the possibility that they were on the right track, that everything broken was fixable. He grabbed a scarf and a bizarre Russian hat with earflaps that he found in a closet.

The sun was setting behind the Adirondacks in the distance, cold and red and desolate through the haze. The others were grouped at the bottom of the lawn, which sloped down to a row of bare, decorative lindens. Penny was sighting down his arm at one of the trees while Alice paced off distance in long, even steps. She jogged over to Penny and they whispered, then she paced off the distance again. Janet stood to one side with Richard, looking adorable in a pink parka and a woolly watch cap.

"All right!" Penny called. "Stand back, everybody."

"How much farther back can we stand?" Josh asked. Sitting on a broken white marble balustrade, a random architectural element dropped in by the landscaper, he took a nip from a bottle of schnapps and passed it to Eliot.

"Just so you're standing back. Okay, fire in the hole."

Like a sequined assistant, Alice stepped up to an end table on the green, placed an empty wine bottle on it, and stepped away.

Facing the bottle, Penny took a quick breath and spoke a rapid sequence of clipped syllables under his breath, ending with a one-handed flicking gesture. Something—a spray of three somethings, steely gray and tightly grouped—shot out of his fingertips, too fast to follow, and flickered across the lawn. Two of them missed, but one of them snapped the bottle's neck off cleanly, leaving the base standing headlessly upright.

Penny grinned. There was scattered applause.

"We call it 'Magic Missile,'" he said.

"Magic Missile, baby!" Josh's breath steamed in the cold air. His face was radiant with excitement. "That's straight up Dungeons & Dragons shit!"

Penny nodded.

"We actually based some of this on old D & D spells. There's a lot of practical thinking in those books."

Quentin wasn't smiling. Wasn't anybody going to say anything? This was dark magic. God knows he wasn't a prude, but this was a spell meant to break up flesh, to physically wound. They were crossing so many lines it was hard to figure out where they were anymore. If they ever actually had to cast this stuff, it would already be too late.

"God, I hope we don't have to use that," was all he said out loud.

"Oh, come on, Quen*tina*. We're not looking for trouble. We just want to be ready if it comes." Josh could hardly contain himself. "Dungeons & Dragons, motherfucker!"

Next Alice whisked the card table away so that Penny stood alone, facing the dark line of lindens. The others stood and sat scattered behind him, under the empty sunset sky. The sun was almost down now. Their noses were running and their ears were red, but the cold didn't seem to bother Penny, who was still wearing only a T-shirt and sweatpants. They were really in the middle of nowhere. Quentin was used to the background blare and hum of Manhattan, and even at Brakebills there were so many people around, there had always been someone somewhere yelling or knocking something over or blowing something up. Here, when the wind wasn't sighing moodily in the trees, there was nothing. The whole world was on mute.

He tied down the earflaps of his Russian hat with a string.

"If this doesn't work—" Penny began.

"Just do it already!" Janet said. "It's cold out here!"

Penny did a deep knee-bend and spat on the gray-brown grass. Then he executed a grotesque, wild-armed flailing movement, at odds with what Quentin had seen of his otherwise highly disciplined style. Violet light sputtered in his cupped hands in the darkness so that the bones in his fingers were visible through the skin. He shouted something and finished with an overarm pitching motion.

A small, dense, orange spark left Penny's palm and flew across the grass, dead level. At first it looked absurdly inoffensive, silly, like a toy, or an insect. But as it sailed toward the trees it grew, blooming into a fiery sparking comet the size of a beach ball, veined and roiling and snapping. It was almost stately, spinning slowly backward as it moved through the cold dusk air. Shadows wound across the lawn, shifting with the fast-moving light source. The heat was intense; Quentin felt it on his face. When it hit a linden, the whole tree went up at once with a single loud crackling *woof.* A gout of flame ascended into the sky and vanished.

"Fireball!" Penny called out unnecessarily.

It was an instant bonfire. The tree burned fast and merrily. Sparks flew up impossibly high into the twilight sky. Janet whooped and jumped up and down and clapped her hands like a cheerleader. Penny smiled thinly and took a theatrical bow.

They stayed at the house upstate for a few more days, lounging around, grilling on the back patio, drinking up all the good wine, going through the DVD collection, all cramming into the hot tub and then not cleaning it afterward. The fact was, Quentin realized, after all the buildup, all the hasty preparation and rush-rush-rush, they were stalling, vamping, waiting for something to push them into pulling the trigger. They were so excited they didn't see how terrified they were. And when he thought about all the happiness waiting for him in Fillory, Quentin almost felt like he didn't deserve it. He wasn't ready. Ember and Umber would never have summoned someone like him.

In the meantime Alice had somehow figured out a way of never being in the same room as Quentin at the same time. She'd developed a sixth sense about him—he'd catch a glimpse of her out a window, or a flash of her feet as she vanished upstairs, but that was as close as they came. It was almost like a game; the others played it, too. When he did spot her in the open— sitting up on the kitchen counter, kicking her legs and chatting with Josh, or hunched over the dining room table with Penny and his books, like everything was fine—he didn't dare intrude. That would be against the rules of the game. Seeing her there, so close and at the same time so infinitely removed, was like looking through a doorway into another universe, a warm, sunny, tropical dimension that he had once inhabited, but from which he was now banished. Every night he left flowers outside her bedroom door.

It was a shame: he probably never even had to know what happened. He could easily have missed it. Though maybe they would have stayed there forever if he had. He stayed up late one night, playing cards with Josh and Eliot. Playing cards with magicians always degenerated into a meta-contest over who was better at warping the odds, so that practically every hand came up four aces against a couple of straight flushes. Quentin was, tentatively, feeling better. They were drinking grappa. The twisted knot of shame and regret in his chest that had been there since the night with Janet was gradually coming undone, or at least scarring over. It wasn't nothing, but it wasn't everything either. There was so much right between him and Alice. They could get past this.

Maybe it was time he helped her see that. He knew she wanted to. He'd screwed up, he was sorry, they would get past it. QED. They just needed to get it into perspective. She was probably just waiting for him to say it. He excused himself and headed up the stairs to the third floor, where the master bedroom was. Josh and Eliot gamely rooted him on his way:

"Q! Q! Q! Q!"

When he was almost at the top of the stairs, he stopped. Quentin would have known it anywhere, the sound that Alice made when she was having sex. Now here was a conundrum for his drunken mind to reflect on: she was making it now, but it wasn't Quentin who was making her make it. He stared down at the burnt-orange natural-weave fibers of the runner that ran down the middle of the stairs. He could not be hearing that sound. It came in through his ears and made spots appear in his vision. His blood fizzed like a science experiment and turned to acid. The acid propagated through his body and made his arms and legs and brain burn. Then it made its way to his heart, like a deadly blood clot that had broken loose and was drifting free, bringing death with it. When it reached his heart, his heart turned white hot.

She was with Penny or Richard, obviously. He had just left Josh and Eliot, and they would never do that to him anyway. He walked stiff-legged back down the stairs and down the hall to Richard's room and kicked open the door and slapped the light on. Richard was there in bed, alone. He sat bolt upright, blinking in an asinine Victorian nightshirt. Quentin turned off the light and slammed the door shut again.

Janet came out into the hall in pajamas, frowning.

"What's going on?"

He shouldered roughly past her.

"Hey!" she yelled after him. "That hurt!"

Hurt? What did she know about hurt? He snapped on the lamp in Penny's room. Penny's bed was empty. He picked up the lamp and threw it on the floor. It flashed and died. Quentin had never felt like this before. It was kind of amazing: his anger was making him superpowered. He could do anything. There was literally nothing he could not do. Or almost. He tried to rip down Penny's curtains, but they wouldn't come, even when he hung on them with all his weight. Instead he opened the window and ripped the clothes off the bed and stuffed them out through it. Not bad, but not enough. He spiked the alarm clock, then started pulling books off the shelves.

Penny had a lot of books. It was going to take a while to get them all off the shelves. But that was okay, he had all night, and he had all the energy in the world. Wasn't even sleepy. It was like he was on speed. Except that after a while it got harder to pull the books off the shelves because Josh and Richard were holding his arms. Quentin thrashed insanely, like a toddler having a tantrum. They dragged him out into the hall.

It was so stupid, really. So obvious. Certainly you couldn't call it clever. He fucked Janet; she fucks Penny. They should be even now. But he'd been drunk! How did that make them even? He barely knew what he was doing! How did that make them even? And Penny—Jesus. He wished it *had* been Josh.

They confined him to the den, gave him the bottle of grappa and a stack of DVDs and figured he'd knock himself out. Josh stayed there to make sure Quentin didn't try any magic, as worked up as he was, but he nodded off right away, his round cheek on the hard arm of the couch, like a sleepy apostle.

As for Quentin, sleep didn't interest him right now. The pain was a falling feeling. It was a little like coming off the ecstasy, that long descent. He was like a cartoon character who falls off a building. *Pow,* he hits an awning, but he punches straight through it. *Pow,* he hits another one. And another one. Surely one of them will catch him and sproing him back up, or just fold up and embrace him like a canvas cradle, but it doesn't, it's just one flimsy busted awning after another. Down and down and down. After a while he longs to stop, even if it means hitting the sidewalk, but he doesn't, he just keeps falling, down through awning after awning, deeper and deeper into the pain. Turtles all the way down.

Quentin didn't bother with the DVDs, just flipped channels on the huge TV and slugged straight from the bottle until sunlight came bleeding up over the horizon, like more acid blood oozing out of his sick ruptured heart, which felt—not that anybody cared—like a rotten drum of biohazardous waste at the very bottom of a landfill, leaching poison into the groundwater, enough poison to kill an entire suburb full of innocent and unsuspecting children.

He never did fall asleep. The idea came over him around dawn, and he waited as long as he could, but it was just too damn good to keep to himself. He was like a kid on Christmas morning who couldn't wait for the grown-ups to waken. Santa was here, and he was going to fix everything. At seven thirty, still half drunk, he busted out of the den and went down the hallways banging on doors. What the hell, he even climbed the stairs and kicked open Alice's door, caught a glimpse of Penny's bare white plump rump, which he didn't really need to see. It made him wince and turn away. But it didn't shut him up.

"Okay!" he was shouting. "People! Get up, get up, get up! It's time! Today's the day! People, people, people!"

He sang a verse of James's stupid middle school song:

> *In olden times there was a boy*
> *Young and strong and brave-o*

He was a cheerleader now, waving his pom-poms, jumping up and down, doing splits on the parquet, shouting as loud as he could.

"We! Are! Going! To!

"Fill!

"O!

"Reeeeeee!"

BOOK III

FILLORY

They held hands in a circle in the living room, packs on their backs. It felt like a dorm stunt, like they were all about to drop acid or sing an a cappella show tune or set some kind of wacky campus record. Anaïs's face blazed with excitement. She hopped up and down despite the load on her back. None of last night's drama had registered on her at all. She was the only person in the room who looked happy to be there.

The funny thing was that it had worked. Quentin wouldn't let it alone, he kept hounding them, and eventually, with surprisingly little resistance, they gave in. Today would be the day. Partly they were afraid of him, with his scary glittering pain-eyes, but partly it was because they had to admit he was right: it was time to go, and they'd just been waiting for somebody, even somebody as obviously drunk and demented as Quentin was, to stand up and call it.

Looking back, in a philosophical frame of mind, it occurred to Quentin that he'd always thought this would be a happy day, the happiest day of his life. Funny how life had its little ways of surprising you. Little quirks of fate.

If he wasn't happy, he did feel unexpectedly liberated. At least he wasn't hunched over with shame anymore. This was pure emotion, unalloyed with any misgivings or caveats or qualifications. Alice was no longer the alabaster saint here. It was not so hard to meet her eyes across the circle. And was that a flicker of embarrassment he saw in hers? Maybe she was learning a little something about remorse, what that felt like. They were down in the muck together now.

They had spent the morning gathering up and packing the gear and the supplies that were already basically gathered up and packed anyway, and rounding up whoever was in the bathroom or dithering over which shoes or had just wandered off out onto the lawn for no obvious reason. Finally they were all together in the living room in a circle, shifting their weight from foot to foot and looking at each other and saying:

"Okay?"

"Okay?"

"Everybody okay?"

"Let's do it."

"Let's do this!"

"Okay!"

"Okay!"

"Let's—"

And then Penny must have touched the button, because they were all rising up together through clear, cold water.

Quentin was first out of the pool, his pack weighing him down. He was sober now, he was pretty sure, but still angry, angry, angry, and brimming over with self-pity. Let it flow. He didn't want to touch anybody or have anybody touch him. He liked being in the Neitherlands though. The Neitherlands had a calming effect. Quiet and still. If he could just lie down for a minute, just right here on the old worn stones, just for a minute, maybe he could sleep.

The expensive Persian rug they'd been standing on floated up after them in the water. Somehow it had come through by accident. Had the button mistaken it for their clothing? Funny how these things worked.

Quentin waited while the others straggled out of the fountain one by one. They bunched up at the edge, treading water and hanging on to each other, then heaving their backpacks out and crawling up after them over the stone rim. Janet looked pale. She was stuck in the water, with Josh and Eliot on either side helping her stay afloat. She couldn't get over the lip of the fountain. Her eyes were unfocused, and her face was chalk.

"I don't know, I just—" She kept shaking her head and repeating it over and over again: "I don't know what's wrong—"

Together they dragged her up out of the water, but there was no strength in her limbs. Her knees buckled and she dropped to all fours, and the weight of her pack tugged her over onto her side on the paving stones. She lay there wet and blinking. It's not like Quentin had never seen Janet incapacitated before, but this was different.

"I don't know if I wanna throw up or if I don't," she said slowly.

"Something's wrong," Alice said. "The City. She's having an allergic reaction, something like that."

Her voice was not overburdened with sympathy.

"Is anybody else getting it?" Eliot looked around quickly, assuming command of the operation. "Nobody else, okay. Let's go to phase two. Let's hurry."

"I'm okay, just let me rest. I just—Jesus, don't you feel it?" Janet looked up helplessly at the others, gulping air. "Doesn't anybody else feel it?"

Anaïs kneeled down next to her in sisterly solidarity. Alice regarded her inscrutably. Nobody else was affected.

"This is interesting," Penny said. "Now why doesn't anybody else—?"

"Hey. Asshole." Quentin snapped his fingers in Penny's face. He had no problem with naked hostility right now. He was feeling very uninhibited. "Can't you see she's in pain? Phase two, asshole, let's go."

He hoped Penny would come after him, maybe they could have a rematch of their little fight club. But Penny just gave Quentin a calm assessing look and turned away. He was taking full advantage of the opportunity to rise above, to be the bigger man, the gracious winner. He rattled a spray can of industrial-orange paint and circled the fountain with it, marking the ground with crosses, then set off in the direction he called palaceward, after the lavish white palazzo on that side of the square. It was no mystery where they were going: the scene in the book was written in Plover's characteristically clear, unambiguous prose. It had the Chatwins walking three more squares palaceward and then one to the left to get to the fountain that led to Fillory. The rest of the group straggled after him, squelching in their wet clothes. Janet had her arms around Quentin's and Eliot's shoulders.

The last jog took them across a stone bridge over a narrow canal. The layout of the city reminded Quentin of a welters board, but writ large. Maybe the game reflected some distant, barely legible rumor of the Neitherlands that had filtered down to Earth.

They halted in a tidy square that was smaller than the one they'd started in, and dominated by a large, dignified stone hall that might have been the mayoral seat of a medieval French village. The clock set at the peak of its facade was frozen at noon, or midnight. The rain was getting heavier. In the center of the square was a round fountain, a figure of Atlas half crushed beneath a bronze globe.

"Okay!" Penny spoke unnecessarily loudly. The big ringmaster. He was nervous, Quentin could see. Not so tough now, loverman. "This is the one they use in the books. So I'm going through to check weather conditions."

"What do you want, a drum roll?" Janet snapped through clenched teeth. "Go!"

Penny took the white button out of his pocket and gripped it in his fist. Taking a deep breath, he mounted the lip of the pool and stepped off, straight-legged, into the still water. At the last moment he reflexively held his nose with one hand. He dropped into the dark water and disappeared. It had swallowed him up.

There was a long hush. The only sound was Janet's hoarse panting and the splashing of the fountain. A minute passed. Then Penny's head broke the surface, sputtering and blowing.

"It worked!" he shouted. "It's warm! It's summer! It's summer there!"

"Was it Fillory?" Josh asked.

"I don't know!" He dog-paddled over to the lip of the pool, breathing hard. "It's a forest. Rural. No signs of habitation."

"Good enough," Eliot said. "Let's go."

"I'm okay," Janet said.

"No, you're not. Let's go, everybody."

Richard was already going through the packs, tossing out the winter gear, the brand-new parkas and woolly hats and electric socks, in an expensive multicolored heap.

"Line up sitting along the edge," he said over his shoulder. "Feet in the water, holding hands."

Quentin wanted to say something sarcastic but couldn't think of anything. There were heavy rusted iron rings set into the edge of the pool. They had stained the stone around them a dark ferrous brown. He lowered his feet into the inky water. The water felt slightly thinner than real water, more the consistency of rubbing alcohol. He stared down at his submerged shoes. He could barely make them out.

Some tiny sane part of him knew he was out of control, but that wasn't the part of him that had its hands on the wheel. Everything anybody said sounded to him like a nasty double entendre calculated to remind him of Alice and Penny. Atlas appeared to be leering at him. He was dizzy from lack of sleep. He closed his eyes. His head felt huge and diffuse and empty, like a puff of cloud hanging above his shoulders. The cloud began to drift away. He wondered if he was going pass out. He would dearly love to pass out. There was a dead spot in his brain, and he wanted the dead spot to spread and metastasize over the whole of it and blot out all the painful thoughts.

"Body armor?" Eliot was saying. "Jesus, Anaïs, have you even *read* the books? We're not walking into a firefight. We're probably going to be eating scones with a talking bunny."

"Okay?" Penny called. "Everybody?"

They were all sitting, all eight of them, in an arc around the edge of the fountain, scooched forward so they could drop in without using their hands, which were tightly clasped. Janet lolled on Eliot's shoulder, her white neck exposed. She was out cold; she looked terribly vulnerable. To Quentin's right, Josh was studying him with concern. His huge hand squeezed Quentin's.

"It's okay, man," he whispered. "Come on. You're okay. You got this."

Probably everybody took a last look around, locked eyes, felt a frisson. Eliot quoted Tennyson's "Ulysses" about seeking new worlds and sailing beyond the sunset. Somebody whooped—maybe Anaïs, the whoop had a Francophone quality. But Quentin didn't whoop, and he didn't look. He just stared at his lap and waited for each successive second to impose itself on him in turn like an uninvited guest the way the previous one had. On Penny's signal they dropped into the fountain together, not quite in sync but almost—it had a Busby Berkeley feel to it. Janet more or less face-planted forward into the water.

It was a falling down, a plunge: outbound from the Neitherlands meant descending. It was like they were parachuting, only it was too rapid for that, somewhere between parachuting and straight free-falling, but with no rushing wind. For a long silent moment they could see everything: a sea of flourishing leafy canopies extending all the way to the horizon, pre-industrially verdant, giving way to square meadows in one direction that Quentin tentatively tagged as north, as reckoned by a pallid sun in a white sky. He tried to keep an eye on it as they went in. The ground rushed up to slam them.

Then, just like that, they were down. Quentin flexed his knees instinctively, but there was no impact or sense of momentum absorbed. All at once they were just standing there.

But where was there? It wasn't a clearing exactly. It was more like a shallow ditch, a trench running through a forest, the bottom clogged with dead leaves and loam and twiggy arboreal detritus. Quentin steadied himself with one hand on the sloping bank. Light trickled down thinly through the massed branches overhead. A bird chattered and then left off. The silence was deep and thick.

They had been scattered by the transition, like a freshly deployed stick of paratroopers, but they were still in sight of one another. Richard and Penny were fighting their way out of a huge dead bush. Alice and Anaïs were seated on the trunk of a colossal tree that had fallen athwart the ditch, as if they'd been carefully placed there by a giant child arranging dolls. Janet was sitting on the ground with her hands on her thighs, taking deep breaths, the color flooding back into her face.

The whole scene had a deeply uncurated feel to it. This was not a forest that had been culled or thinned. This was primeval. This was the way trees lived when they were left to their own devices.

"Penny?" Josh stood on the edge of the ditch, gazing down at the rest of them, hands in pockets. He looked incongruously natty in a jacket and a nice shirt, no tie, even though they were all soaked to the bone. "It's cold, Penny. Why the fuck is it cold?"

It was true. The air was dry and bitter; their clothes were freezing fast. Their breath puffed out white in the frigid stillness. Fine light snow sifted down from the white sky. The ground was hard under the fallen leaves. It was deep winter.

"I don't know." Penny looked around, frowning. "It was summer before," he said a little petulantly. "Just a second ago! It was hot!"

"Will someone please help me down, please?" Anaïs was looking down at the ground dubiously from her perch on the giant tree trunk. Josh gallantly took her by her narrow waist and lifted her down; she gave a pleased little squeak.

"It's the time thing," Alice said. "I just thought of it. It could be six months since Penny was here, in Fillory time. Or more like sixty years, the way the seasons work. This always happens in the books. There's no way to predict it."

"Well, I predict that I'm going to freeze my tits off in five minutes," Janet said. "Somebody go back for the jackets."

They all agreed that Penny should go back and get the parkas, and he was an instant away from touching the button when Eliot suddenly lunged at him and grabbed his arm. He pointed out, as calmly as possible, that if the time streams of Fillory and the Neitherlands moved at different speeds, then if Penny went back by himself, it could easily be days, or years, before he got back to Fillory with the gear, at least from the Fillorian point of view, by which time they could have frozen to death or died of old age or accumulated countless other equally serious problems. If they were going to go, they would all have to go together.

"Forget it." Janet shook her head. She still looked green. "I can't go back there. Not yet. I'd rather freeze my tits off than puke my guts out."

Nobody argued. Nobody wanted to leave quite yet anyway, not now that they were finally here in Fillory, or wherever they were. They weren't going anywhere without at least poking around. Penny began making the rounds with his clothes-drying spell.

"I think I can see a way to go," said Alice, who was still perched up on the tree trunk. Snow had begun to settle in her dark hair. "On the other side. It sort of turns into a path through the forest. And there's something else, too. You're going to want to see this for yourselves."

If they took off their packs, there was enough space at the bottom of the ditch to scramble under the huge trunk on all fours, single file, their hands and knees sinking into the thick layer of frostbitten leaves. Eliot came through last, passing the packs ahead of him. They stood up on the other side, slapping dirt off their hands. Penny rushed to hand Alice down from where she sat, but she ignored him and jumped down herself, although it meant crashing down on her hands and knees and picking herself up again. She didn't seem to be particularly relishing her adventure of the night before, Quentin thought.

To one side of the path was a small spreading oak. Its bark was dark gray, almost black, and its branches were gnarled and wiggly and all but empty of leaves. Embedded in its trunk at head height, as if the tree had simply grown up around it, was a round ticking clock face a foot across.

One by one, without speaking, they all scrambled up the sloping bank to get a closer look. It was one of the Watcherwoman's clock-trees.

Quentin touched the place where the tree's hard rough bark met the smooth silver bezel around the clock face. It was solid and cold and real. He closed his eyes and followed the curve of it with his finger. He was really here. He was in Fillory. There was no question about it now.

And now that he was here it would finally be all right. He didn't see how yet, but it would. It had to be. Maybe it was the lack of sleep, but hot tears poured helplessly down his cheeks, leaving cold tracks behind them. Against all his own wishes and instincts he got down on his knees and put his head in his hands and pushed his face into the cold leaves. A sob clawed its way out of him. For a minute he lost himself. Somebody, he would never know who, not Alice, put their hand on his shoulder. This was the place. He would be picked up, cleaned off, and made to feel safe and happy and whole again here. How had everything gone so wrong? How could he and Alice have been so stupid? It barely even mattered now. This was his life now, the life he had always been waiting for. It was finally here.

And it flashed into his head with sudden urgency: Richard was right. They had to find Martin Chatwin, if he was somehow still alive. That was the key. Now that he was here, he wasn't going to give it up again. He must know the secret of how to stay here forever, make it last, make it permanent.

Quentin got to his feet, embarrassed, and blotted his tears on his sleeve.

"Welp," Josh said finally, breaking the silence. "I guess that pretty much tears it. We're in Fillory."

"These clock-trees are supposed to be the Watcherwoman's thing," Quentin said, still sniffling. "She must still be around."

"I thought she was dead," Janet said.

"Maybe we're in an earlier time period," Alice suggested. "Maybe we went back in time. Like in *The Girl Who Told Time*."

She and Janet and Quentin didn't look at each other when they spoke.

"Maybe. I think they left some of these still growing, though, even after they got rid of her. Remember they even see one in *The Wandering Dune*."

"I could never finish that book," Josh said.

"I wonder." Eliot eyed it appraisingly. "Think we could get this thing back to Brakebills? That would make a hell of a present for Fogg."

Nobody else seemed inclined to pursue that line of speculation. Josh made double pointy-fingers at Eliot and mouthed the word *douche*.

"I wonder if that's the correct time," Richard said.

Quentin could have stood there and stared at the clock-tree all day, but the chill wouldn't let them stand still. The girls were already wandering away. He followed them reluctantly, and soon they were all trooping off together in a ragged group along the ditch-cum-path, deeper into Fillory. The sound of their feet shuffling through the dry leaves was deafening in the quiet.

No one spoke. For all their careful practical preparations there had been very little discussion of strategy or objectives, and now they were here it was obvious anyway. Why bother planning an adventure? This was Fillory—adventure would find them! With every step they took they half expected a marvelous apparition or revelation to come trotting out of the woods. But nothing much presented itself. It was almost anticlimactic—or was this just the buildup to something *really* amazing? The remains of ragged stone walls trailed off into the underbrush. The trees around them remained still and stubbornly inanimate, even after Penny, in the spirit of exploration and discovery, formally introduced himself to several of them. Here and there birds chirped and flitted and perched, high up in the trees, but none of them offered them any advice. Every little detail looked superbright and saturated with meaning, as if the world around them were literally composed of words and letters, inscribed in some magical geographical script.

Richard took out a compass but found the needle stuck, pinned down against its cardboard backing, as if Fillory's magnetic pole were deep underground, straight down beneath their feet. He flung it away into a bush. Janet hopped up and down as she walked, her hands crammed under her armpits against the cold. Josh speculated about the hypothetical contents of an imaginary porn magazine for intelligent trees that would be entitled *Enthouse*.

They walked for twenty minutes, half an hour at most. Quentin alternately blew into his hands and withdrew them into the sleeves of his sweater. He was wide awake now, and sober, at least for the moment.

"We need to get some fauns up in this piece," Josh said, to nobody. "Or some swordfights or whatever."

The path meandered and then faded out. They were expending more and more effort just to push their way through the foliage. There was some internal disagreement as to whether or not there had ever been an actual path, or whether it was just a strip of thin forest, or even whether—this was Penny's take—the trees had begun subtly, imperceptibly shifting themselves to get in their way. But before they could arrive at a consensus they came across a stream percolating through the woods.

It was a lovely little winter stream, wide and shallow and perfectly clear, twinkling and lapping along as if it were delighted to have just found this twisty channel. Wordlessly, they gathered at its edge. The rocks were capped with round dollops of snow, and the quieter eddies along the banks had iced over. A branch poking up in the middle of the stream was hung with fabulous Gothic-sculpted icy drops and buttresses all along its length. There was nothing overtly supernatural about it, but it temporarily satisfied their appetite for wonder. On Earth it would have been a charming little rill, nothing more, but the fact that they were seeing it in Fillory, in another world, possibly the first Earth beings ever to do so, made it a glittering miracle.

They had stared at it for a full minute in rapt silence before Quentin realized that right in front of them, emerging from the deepest part of the stream, was a woman's naked head and shoulders.

"Oh my God," he said. He took a clumsy, numb step backward, pointing. "Shit. You guys."

It was surreal. She was almost certainly dead. The woman's hair was dark and wet and thick with clumped ice. Her eyes—she appeared to be looking right at them—were midnight blue and didn't move or blink, and her skin was a pale pearlescent gray. Her shoulders were bare. She looked sixteen at most. Her eyelashes were clotted with frost.

"Is she—?" Alice didn't finish the question.

"Hey!" Janet called. "Are you all right?"

"We should help her. Get her out of there." Quentin tried to get closer, but he slipped on a frozen rock and went in up to his knee. He scrambled back onto the bank, his foot burning with cold. The woman didn't move. "We need rope. Get the rope, there's rope in one of the packs."

The water didn't even look deep enough to submerge her that far, and Quentin actually wondered, horribly, if they were looking at a body that had been severed at the waist and then dumped in the water. Rope, what was he thinking? He was a damn magician. He dropped the pack he was rifling through and began a simple kinetic spell to lift her out.

He felt the premonitory warmth of a developing spell in his fingertips, felt the weight and tug of the body in his mind. It felt good to do magic again, to know that he could still focus despite everything. As soon as he started he realized that the Circumstances were scrambled here—different stars, different seas, different everything. Thank God it was a simple spell. The grammar was a shambles—Alice corrected him in a clipped voice as he worked. Gradually the woman rose up dripping out of the water. She was whole, thank God, and naked—her body was slim, her breasts slight and girlish. Her nails and nipples were pale purple. She looked frozen, but she shuddered as the magic took hold. Her eyes focused and came awake. She frowned and raised one hand, somehow halting the spell before he was finished, with her toes still trailing in the freezing water.

"I am a naiad. I cannot leave the stream." By her voice she could have been in junior high. Her eyes met Quentin's.

"Your magic is clumsy," she added.

It was electrifying. Quentin saw now that she wasn't human, her fingers and toes were webbed. To his left he heard a shuffling noise. It was Penny. He was getting down on his knees on the snowy bank.

"We humbly apologize," he said, head bowed. "We most humbly seek your pardon."

"Jesus Christ!" Josh stage-whispered. "Dork!"

The hovering nymph shifted her attention. Stream water rilled down her bare skin. She tilted her head girlishly.

"You admire my beauty, human?" she asked Penny. "I am cold. Would you warm me with your burning skin?"

"Please," Penny went on, blushing furiously. "If you have a quest to bestow upon us, we would gladly undertake it. We would gladly—"

Mercifully Janet cut him off.

"We're visitors from Earth," she said firmly. "Is there a city around here that you could direct us to? Maybe Castle Whitespire?"

"—we would gladly undertake to do your bidding," Penny finished.

"Do you serve the rams?" Alice asked.

"I serve no false gods, human girl. Or goddesses. I serve the river, and the river serves me."

"Are there other humans here?" Anaïs said. "Like us?"

"Like you?" The nymph smiled saucily, and the tip of a startling blue tongue appeared for an instant between her rather sharp-looking front teeth. "Oh, no. Not like you. None so cursed!"

At that moment Quentin felt his telekinetic spell cease to exist. She'd abolished it, though he didn't catch how, without a word or a gesture. In the same instant the naiad flipped head down and dived, her pale periwinkle buttocks flashing in the air, and vanished into dark water that looked too shallow to contain her.

Her head poked up again a moment later.

"I fear for you here, human children. This is not your war."

"We're not children," Janet said.

"What war?" Quentin called.

She smiled again. Between her lavender lips her teeth were pointy and interlocking like a fighting fish's. She held something dripping in her webbed fist.

"A gift from the river. Use it when all hope is lost."

She tossed it at them overhand. Quentin caught it one-handed; he was relieved out of all proportion to its actual importance that he didn't bobble it. Thank God for his old juggling reflexes. When he looked up again, the nymph was gone. They were alone with the chattering brook.

Quentin was holding a small ivory horn chased with silver.

"Oh-*kay!*" Josh shouted. He clapped his hands and rubbed them together. "We are *definitely* not in Kansas anymore!"

The others gathered around to look at the horn. Quentin handed it to Eliot, who turned it over a few times, peered into one end, then the other.

"I don't feel anything on it at all," Eliot said. "Looks like something you'd buy in an airport gift shop."

"You wouldn't necessarily feel it," Penny said proprietarily. He took it and stowed the horn in his pack.

"We should have asked her if this is Fillory," Alice said quietly.

"Of course it's Fillory," Penny said.

"I'd like to be sure. And I'd like to know why we're cursed."

"And what's this war?" Richard asked, his heavy brows knotted. "This raises a lot of questions."

"And I didn't like those teeth," Alice added.

"Jesus," Josh said. "Jesus! That was a naiad, people! We just saw a river nymph! How cool is that? How cool are we? Huh? Fuckin' Fillory, people!"

He grabbed Quentin's shoulders and shook him. He ran at Richard and made him bump chests.

"Can I just say that she was pretty hot?" said Janet.

"Shyeah! I'll take that over a faun any day," Josh said. Anaïs swatted him.

"Hey, that's Penny's girlfriend you're talking about," Janet said. "Show some respect."

The tension faded, and for a minute they all chattered among themselves, giving one another shit and just geeking out on the sheer alien magic of it all. Was she corporeal? Did she become fluid once she entered the stream? How else could she submerge herself in such shallow water? And how had she canceled Quentin's spell? What was her function in the magical ecosystem? And what about the horn? Alice was already paging through her worn Fillory paperbacks for references to it—didn't Martin find a magic horn in the first book . . . ?

After a while it began to sink in that they'd been outside for forty-five minutes in deep winter wearing nothing but jeans and sweaters. Even Janet admitted it was time to head back to the City. Eliot corralled the stragglers and chatterers, and they all linked hands on the bank of the stream.

They stood in a circle, still a little giddy, and for a moment happy conspiratorial glances flew between them. There was some bad personal stuff going down, but that didn't have to ruin everything, did it? They were doing something really important here. This was what every one of them had been waiting for, looking for, their whole lives—what they were meant to do! They'd found the magic door, the secret path through the hidden garden. They'd gotten ahold of something new, a real adventure, and it was only just beginning.

It was in that hush that they heard it for the first time—a dry, rhythmic ticking sound. It was almost lost in the twittering of the brook, but it grew louder and more distinct. One by one they stopped talking to listen. It was snowing more heavily now.

Out of context it was hard to place. Alice was the first to twig.

"It's a clock," she said. "That's a clock ticking."

She searched their faces impatiently.

"A clock," she repeated, panicky now. "Watcherwoman, that's the Watcherwoman!"

Penny fumbled hastily for the button. The *tick-tock* grew even louder, like a monstrous heart beating, right on top of them, but it was impossible to tell what direction it was coming from. And then it didn't matter, because they were floating up through cold, clear water to safety.

This time it was all business. Back in the City they gathered up the cold-weather gear—all except for Janet, who lay limply on the ground doing yoga breathing—and then got back in the fountain, where they linked hands along the edge with what was becoming practiced ease. Janet found the strength to make a joke about Anita Ekberg in *La Dolce Vita*. They nodded once all around and slipped back in in unison.

They were in Fillory again, set down by the stream they'd just left, but the snow was gone. It was an early fall day now, the air full of lukewarm mist. The temperature felt like high sixties. It was like time-lapse photography: the branches of trees that had been bare five minutes ago now swarmed with turning leaves. One golden leaf floated tinily, impossibly high in the gray sky on some fluky updraft. The grass was littered with glassy puddles from a torrential autumn rain that must have ended only minutes earlier. They stood around in the mild air, hugging their bundles of parkas and woolly gloves and feeling foolish.

"Overdressed again," Eliot said. He dropped his bundle in disgust. "Story of my life."

No one could think of a reasonable alternative to just leaving the winter gear lying there on the wet grass. They could have gone back to the Neitherlands to store it, but then it might have been winter all over again when they got back. It seemed ridiculous, a bug in the system, but it didn't matter, they were energized now. They filled their canteens from the stream.

A bridge spanned the creek fifty yards downstream, a gentle arch made of intricate, curly Fillorian ironwork. Quentin was sure it couldn't have been there before, but Richard insisted they just hadn't seen it through the snow-laden branches. Quentin looked at the flowing, burbling water. There was no sign of the nymph. How much time had passed since they were last here? he wondered. Seasons in Fillory could last a century. Or had they gone back in time? Was this the same adventure, or were they starting a new one?

On the far side of the bridge there was a wide, neat path through the forest, dusted with leaves and pine needles but definitely a path in good standing this time, an official path. They made good time, their spirits buoyed up by the perfect weather and a constant, low-level adrenaline drip. It was really on now. No more false starts. It wasn't that Fillory could wipe out what happened last night—but maybe it could, for all he knew. Anything could happen here. A brown deer ambled out of the forest and walked ahead of them for a stretch, looking back over its shoulder with an air of genuinely exceptional intelligence, they all agreed, but if it could speak it declined to address them. They tried to follow it—maybe it was leading them somewhere? was it a messenger from Ember and Umber?—but it bounded away exactly the way an ordinary non-magical deer would have.

Josh practiced a spell that uncurled Anaïs's hair from a distance. She kept looking around, annoyed but unable to pinpoint the source. Janet linked arms with Quentin and Eliot and made them do a "Follow the Yellow Brick Road" skipping dance. He couldn't be sure, but he didn't think Eliot had had a drink all day. When was the last time that had happened?

The forest seemed to go on forever. Once in a while the sun appeared long enough to shoot some long, dusty beams down between the trees, then disappeared again.

"This is right," Penny said, looking around. His eyes were glazed. He had entered a daze of ecstatic certainty. "This feels right to me. We're supposed to be here."

Janet rolled her eyes.

"What do you think, Q?" Penny said. "Doesn't this feel right to you?"

Without knowing how it happened Quentin had Penny's ratty T-shirt bunched in his fists. Penny weighed more than he'd counted on, but Quentin still managed to get him off balance and push him backward until his head clunked against the damp trunk of a pine tree.

"Never speak to me," Quentin said evenly. "Do you understand? You do not address me directly, ever. You do not speak to me."

"I don't want to fight you," Penny said. "That's exactly what the Watcherwoman wants—"

"Did you not just hear what I said?" Quentin clunked Penny's head against the tree again, hard this time. Somebody said his name. "You lardy little fucking nub? Did you not just fucking hear what I fucking said? Was I unclear in any way?"

He walked away without waiting for an answer. Fillory had better give him something to fight soon or he was going to lose it completely.

The novelty of actually, physically being in Fillory was wearing thin. In spite of everything a mood of general grumpiness was growing, a spoiled-picnic mood. Every time a bird perched overhead for more than a few seconds Josh would say, "Okay, this is the one," or "I think it's trying to tell us something," or eventually, "Hey asshole, fly away from me, please. Okay, thanks."

"At least the Watcherwoman hasn't shown up," Eliot said.

"If that even was the Watcherwoman before," Josh said. "Supposedly they got her in the first book, right? So."

"Yeah, I know." Eliot had a handful of acorns and was chucking them at trees as they walked. "But something's a little off here. I don't understand why that nymph wasn't boring us about Ember and Umber. They're always so pushy about Them in the books."

"If there's a war between the rams and the Watcherwoman still going on, we're going to want to get with Ember and Umber stat," Alice said.

"Oh, yeah," Janet said. She made quotey-fingers. "'Stat.'"

"If They want us on Their side, They will find us," Penny intoned. "We need have no fear on that score."

No one answered him. It was becoming increasingly clear that Penny's encounter with the nymph had put him in an altered state. That was how he was dealing with Fillory. He'd undergone a conversion experience, flipped into full-on Renaissance Faire role-playing mode.

"Watch it, *watch it!*" Richard yelled. They registered the drumming thuds of hooves on soft earth almost too late. A carriage drawn by two horses tore past them at a full gallop, scattering them into the trees on either side of the road. The carriage was closed and dark; on its side it bore what looked like a coat of arms that had recently been painted over in black.

The coachman was bundled up in a black cloak. He—she? it was impossible to tell—signaled the horses to slow to a walk, then a stop, a hundred feet ahead of them down the road.

"The thick plottens," Eliot said dryly.

It was about damn time something happened. Quentin, Janet, and Anaïs walked boldly toward it, all competing to be the reckless one, the hero, the one who pushed things forward. In his present state of mind Quentin felt fully prepared to go right up and knock on the shutters, but he found himself pulling up a few yards away. So did the others. The black coach did look ominously funereal.

A muffled voice spoke from inside the carriage.

"Do they bear the Horns?"

This was evidently directed not at them but at the coachman, who had the better vantage point. If the coachman replied, he/she did so inaudibly.

"Do you bear the horns?" This voice was louder and clearer.

The advance party exchanged looks.

"What do you mean, Horns?" Janet called. "We're not from around here."

This was ridiculous. It was like talking to the Once-ler in Dr. Seuss.

"Do you serve the Bull?" Now the voice sounded shriller to his ears, with high, twittering overtones.

"Who's the bull?" Quentin said, loudly and slowly, as if he were talking to somebody who didn't speak English or was mildly retarded. There was no bull in the Plover books, so—? "We are *visitors to your land*. We do not *serve the bull*, or *anybody else for that matter.*"

"They're not deaf, Quentin," Janet said.

Long silence. One of the horses—they were black, too, as was the tackle, and everything else—whickered. The first voice said something inaudible.

"What?" Quentin took a step closer.

A trapdoor banged open on top of the carriage. The sound was like a gunshot. A tiny expressionless head and a long green insect torso popped up out of it—it could only have been a praying mantis, but grown grotesquely to human size. It was so skinny and it had so many long emerald-colored legs and graceful whip antennae that at first Quentin didn't notice that it was holding a green bow with a green arrow nocked.

"Shit!" Quentin yelped reflexively. His voice cracked. It was close range, and there was no time to run. He cringed violently and fell down.

The horses took off like a shot the moment the mantis released. The trapdoor banged shut again. Dust and twigs spun up into the air in the carriage's wake, its four big wheels fitting neatly in the ruts in the road.

When Quentin dared to look up again, Penny was standing over him. He held the arrow in one hand. He must have used a spell to speed up his reflexes, Fillorian Circumstances be damned, then plucked it out of the air in midflight. It would have neatly speared Quentin's kidney.

The others came straggling up to watch the carriage recede into the distance.

"Wait," Josh said sarcastically. "Stop."

"Jesus, Penny," Janet breathed. "Nice catch."

What, was she going to fuck him now? Quentin thought. He stared at the arrow in Penny's hand, panting. It was a yard long and fletched in black and yellow like a hornet. The tip had two angry curly steel barbs welded to it. He hadn't even had time to panic.

He took a shaky breath.

"That all you got?" he yelled after the dwindling carriage, too late for it to be funny.

Slowly he got to his feet. His knees were water and wouldn't stop shaking.

Penny turned and, in an odd gesture, offered him the arrow. Quentin snorted angrily and walked away, slapping leaf junk off his hands. He didn't want Penny to see him trembling. It probably would have missed anyway.

"Wow," Janet said. "That was one angry bug."

The day wore on. Light was leaking out of the sky, and the fun was leaking out of the afternoon. Nobody wanted to admit they were frightened, so they took the only other option, which was to be irritable instead. If they didn't go back soon, they'd have to find somewhere to make camp for the night in the woods, which maybe wasn't such a good idea if they were going to get shot at by giant bugs. None of them had enough medical magic to handle a barbed shaft to the small intestine. They stood and argued on the dirt road. Should they go back to Buffalo, maybe pick up some Kevlar after all? There were only so many arrows Penny could catch. Would Kevlar even stop an arrow?

And what kind of political situation were they walking into here? Bugs and bulls, nymphs and witches—who were the good guys and who were the bad guys? Everything was much less entertaining and more difficult to organize than they'd counted on. Quentin's nerves were thoroughly jangled, and he kept touching the place on his stomach under his sweater where the arrow would have gone in. What, was it mammals vs. insects now? But then why would a praying mantis be fighting for a bull? The nymph had said this wasn't their war. Maybe she had a point.

Quentin's feet were killing him breaking in his brand-new hiking boots. He'd never dried off the foot he'd soaked in the stream before, and now it felt hot and blistered and mildewy. He imagined painful fungal spores taking root and flourishing in the warm wetness between his toes. He wondered how far they'd walked. It had been about thirty hours since he'd slept.

Both Penny and Anaïs were adamantly against turning back. What if the Chatwins had turned back? Penny said. They were part of a story now. Had anybody actually ever read a story? This was the hump, the hard part, the part they'd be rewarded for later. You just had to get through it. And not to go on, but who are the good guys here? We are the good guys. And the good guys always survive.

"Wake up!" Alice said. "This isn't a story! It's just one fucking thing after another! Somebody could have died back there!" She obviously meant Quentin but didn't want to say his name.

"Maybe Helen Chatwin was right," Richard said. "Maybe we're not supposed to be here."

"You don't get it, do you?" Janet stared them down. "It's supposed to be confusing at the beginning. The situation will get explained *in time.* We just have to keep moving. Keep picking up clues. If we leave now and come back it'll be like five hundred years from now and we'll have to start all over again."

Quentin looked from one to the other of them: Alice smart and skeptical, Janet all action and thoughtless exuberance. He turned to Anaïs to ask her how far she thought they'd walked, on the vague theory that a European person might have a more accurate sense of these things than a bunch of Americans, when he realized he was the only one of the party who wasn't staring off into the forest to their right. Passing them through the darkening trees, on a parallel course, was the strangest thing Quentin had ever seen.

It was a birch tree, striding along through the forest. Its trunk forked a meter from the ground to form two legs on which it took stiff, deliberate steps. It was so thin that it was hard to keep track of in the half-light, but its white bark stood out from the dark trunks around it. Its thin upper branches whipped and snapped against the trees it pushed past. It looked more like a machine or a marionette than a person. Quentin wondered how it kept its balance.

"Holy crap," said Josh.

Without speaking they began to trail after it. The tree didn't hail them, but for a moment its crown of branches twisted in their direction, as if it were glancing over a shoulder it didn't have. In the stillness they could actually hear it creaking as it foraged along, like a rocking chair. Quentin got the distinct impression it was ignoring them.

After the first five minutes of magical wonderment passed it began to be socially awkward, blatantly following the tree-spirit-thing like this, but it didn't seem to want to acknowledge them, and they weren't about to let it go. As a group they clung to it. Maybe this thing was going to put them in the picture, Quentin thought. If it didn't turn around and beat them all to death with its branches.

Janet kept a close eye on Penny and shushed him whenever he looked like he might be about to say something.

"Let it make the first move," she whispered.

"Freak show," Josh said. "What is that thing?"

"It's a dryad, idiot."

"I thought those were girl-trees."

"They're supposed to be *sexy* girl-trees," Josh said plaintively.

"And I thought dryads were oaks," Alice said. "That's a birch."

"What makes you think it's not a girl-tree?"

"Whatever it is," Josh said under his breath, "it's pay dirt. Fuckin' tree-thing, man. Pay fuckin' dirt."

The tree was a fast walker, almost bouncing along on its springy, knee-less legs, to the point where soon they would have to break into a half jog to keep up with it. Just when it looked like they were either going to lose their only promising lead so far or segue into an undignified chase scene, it became obvious where it was heading anyway.

HUMBLEDRUM

Ten minutes later Quentin was sitting in a booth in a dimly lit bar with a pint of beer on the table in front of him, as yet untasted. Though unexpected, this felt like a good development for him. Bar, booth, beer. This was a situation where he knew how to handle himself, whatever world he was in. If he'd been training for anything since he left Brakebills, it was this.

Identical pints stood in front of the others. It was late afternoon, five thirty or so, Quentin guessed, though how could you know? Were there even twenty-four hours in a day here? Why would there be? Despite Penny's insistence that the tree had been "leading" them here, it was pretty clear they would have found the inn on their own. It was a dark, low-roofed log cabin with a sign outside featuring two crescent moons; a delicate little clockwork mechanism caused the two moons to revolve around each other when the wind blew. The cabin was backed up against, and appeared almost to emerge from, a low hillock that humped up out of the forest floor.

Cautiously pushing inside, through swinging doors, they discovered what could have passed for a period room in a museum of Colonial America: a long narrow chamber with a bar against one wall. It reminded Quentin of the Historick Olde Innes he'd wandered through when he was visiting his parents in Chesterton.

Only one other booth was occupied, by a family(?)—a tall, white-haired old man; a high-cheekboned woman who might have been in her thirties; and a serious little girl. Obviously locals. They sat perfectly silent and erect, staring balefully at the empty cups and saucers in front of them. The little girl's hooded eyes expressed a precocious acquaintance with adversity.

The walking birch tree had disappeared, presumably into a back room. The bartender wore a curious old-fashioned uniform, black with many brass buttons, something like what an Edwardian policeman might have worn. He had a narrow, bored face and heavy black five o'clock shadow, and he slowly polished pint glasses with a white cloth in the manner of bartenders since time immemorial. Otherwise the room was empty, except for a large brown bear wearing a waistcoat sitting slumped in a sturdy armchair in one corner. It wasn't clear whether the bear was conscious or not.

Richard had brought along several dozen small gold cylinders in the hope that they would work as a kind of universal interdimensional currency. The bartender accepted one without comment, weighed it expertly in his palm, and returned a handful of change: four dented, wobbly coins stamped with an assortment of faces and animals. Two of them bore mottos in two different unreadable scripts; the third was a well-worn Mexican peso from the year 1936; the fourth turned out to be a plastic marker from a board game called Sorry. He set about filling pewter tankards.

Josh stared into his dubiously and took a fastidious sniff. He was as fidgety as a third-grader.

"Just drink it!" Quentin hissed irritably. God, people were such losers sometimes. He lifted his own tankard. "Cheers."

He swished the liquid around in his mouth. It was bitter and carbonated and alcoholic and definitely beer. It filled him with confidence and a renewed sense of purpose. He'd had a scare, but it's funny how it—and the beer—were now focusing his mind wonderfully. Quentin shared his booth with Richard, Josh, and Anaïs—he had successfully avoided sitting next to either Alice or Janet, or Penny—and they exchanged multiple transverse glances over their foamy pints. They were a long way from where they'd started out that morning.

"I don't think that bear is stuffed!" Josh whispered excitedly. "I think that's a real bear!"

"Let's buy it a beer," Quentin said.

"I think it's asleep. And anyway it doesn't look that friendly."

"Beer might help with that," Quentin said. He felt punchy. "This could be the next clue. If it's a talking beer, I mean a talking bear, we could, you know, talk to it."

"About what?"

Quentin shrugged and took another sip.

"Just get a feel for what's going on around here. I mean, what else are we doing here?"

Richard and Anaïs hadn't touched their drinks. Quentin took another big gulp just to spite them.

"We're playing it safe, is what we're doing," Richard said. "This is strictly reconnaissance. We're avoiding any unnecessary contact."

"You're kidding me. We're in Fillory, and you don't want to talk to anybody?"

"Absolutely not." Richard sounded shocked, shocked, at the very idea. "We've made contact with another plane of existence. What, that's not enough for you?"

"As a matter of fact, it's not. A giant praying mantis tried to kill me earlier today, and I'd like to know why."

Fillory had yet to give Quentin the surcease from unhappiness he was counting on, and he was damned if he was leaving before he got what he wanted. Relief was out there, he knew it, he just needed to get deeper in, and he wasn't about to let Richard slow him down. He had to jump the tracks, get out of his Earth-story, which wasn't going so well, and into the Fillory-story, where the upside was infinitely higher. Anyway, the mood he was in, Quentin was willing to take any position on any subject with anybody if it meant he could pick a fight.

"Barkeep!" Quentin said, louder than necessary. As an afterthought he gave himself a thick Wild West drawl. If it feels right, go with it. He jerked his thumb at the bear. " 'Nother round fer mah friend the bar there in the corner."

A bar in a bar. Clever. In the other booth Eliot, Alice, Janet, and Penny all turned around in unison to look at him. The man in the uniform just nodded wearily.

The bear, it emerged, drank only peach schnapps, which it sipped from delicate thimble-size glasses. Given its bulk, Quentin guessed it could consume a more or less unlimited amount of it. After two or three it ambled over on all fours and joined them, dragging over the heavy armchair, the only piece of furniture in the room capable of supporting its weight, by hooking its claws into the chair's much-abused upholstery and pulling. It looked way too big to be moving around in a confined space.

The bear was named Humbledrum, and it was, as its name suggested, a very modest bear. It was a brown bear, it explained in deep sub-subwoofer tones, a species larger than the black bear but much much smaller than the mighty grizzly bear, though the grizzly was in fact a variety of brown bear. It was not, Humbledrum reiterated periodically, half the bear that some of those grizzlies were.

"But it's not just about who's the biggest bear," Quentin offered. They were bonding. He wasn't sure exactly what he wanted from the bear, but this seemed like a good way to get it. He was drinking Richard's beer, having finished his own. "There's other ways to be a good bear."

Humbledrum's head bobbed enthusiastically.

"Oh yes. Oh yes. I am a good bear. I never meant to say that I'm a bad bear. I'm a good bear. I respect territories. I'm a respectful bear." Humbledrum's terrifyingly huge paw fell on the table emphatically, and it put its black muzzle very close to Quentin's nose. "I am a very. Respectful. Bear."

The others were conspicuously silent, or talked among themselves, elaborately play-acting that they were unaware of the fact that Quentin was conversing with a drunk magic bear. Richard had bailed out early, swapping places with the always-game Janet. Josh and Anaïs huddled together, looking trapped. If Humbledrum noticed any of this, it didn't seem to bother it.

Quentin understood that he was operating outside most of the group's comfort level. He could see out of the corner of his eye that Eliot was trying to shoot him warning glances from the other table, but he avoided them. He didn't care. He had to push things forward; he was afraid of staying still. This was his play, and he was playing it, and he was going to play it his way till it was played out. Everybody else could either get on board or button their candy asses on back to Drop City.

It wasn't like what he was doing was easy. The range of Humbledrum's interests was suffocatingly narrow, and its depth of knowledge in those areas abysmally profound. Quentin still vaguely remembered being a goose, how laser-focused he'd been on air currents and freshwater green-ery, and he realized now that all animals were probably, at heart, insuffer-able bores. As a hibernating mammal Humbledrum had far more than the layman's familiarity with cave geology. When it came to honey, it was the subtlest and most sophisticated of gastronomes. Quentin learned quickly to steer the conversation away from chestnuts.

"So," Quentin said, flatly interrupting a disquisition on the stinging habits of the docile Carniolan honeybee (*Apis mellifera carnica*) as con-trasted with those of the slightly more excitable German honeybee (*Apis mellifera mellifera*, aka the German black bee). "Just to be clear, this is Fil-lory we're in, right?"

The lecture ground to a halt. Under its fur Humbledrum's massive brow furrowed, producing a vivid equivalent of human befuddlement.

"What is, Quentin?"

"This place we're in, right now," Quentin said. "It's called Fillory."

A long moment passed. Humbledrum's ears twitched. It had impossibly cute, round, furry teddy-bear ears.

"Fillory," it said slowly, cautiously. "That is a word I have heard." The giant bear sounded like a kid at the blackboard hedging his bets against what might or might not be a trick question.

"And this is it? We're in Fillory?"

"I think it . . . may once have been."

"So what do you call it now?" Quentin coaxed.

"No. No. Wait." Humbledrum held up a paw for silence, and Quentin felt a tiny pang of pity. The enormous hairy idiot really was trying to think. "Yes, it is. This is Fillory. Or Loria? Is this Loria?"

"It has to be Fillory," Penny said, leaning over from the other booth. "Loria is the evil country. Across the eastern mountains. It's not like there's no difference. How can you not know where you live?"

The bear was still shaking its heavy muzzle.

"I think Fillory is somewhere else," it said.

"But this *definitely* isn't Loria," Penny said.

"Look, who's the talking bear here?" Quentin snapped. "Is it you? Are you the talking fucking bear? All right. So shut the fuck up."

Outside the bar the sun had set, and a few other creatures trailed in. Three beavers sipped from a common dish at a round café table in the company of a fat, green, oddly alert-looking cricket. In one corner, by itself, a white goat lapped at what looked like pale yellow wine in a shallow bowl. A slender, shy-looking man with horns jutting through his blond hair sat at the bar. He wore round glasses, and the lower half of his body was covered in thick bushy hair. The whole scene had a dreamlike quality, like a Chagall painting come to life. In passing, Quentin noted how disturbing it was to see a man with goat's legs. Those backward-bending knees reminded him of the crippled or the gravely deformed.

As the inn filled up the silent family rose as one and shuffled out of their booth, their expressions still somber. Where could they be going? Quentin wondered. He'd seen no sign of a village nearby. It was getting late, and he wondered if they had a long walk ahead of them. He pictured them trudging down the grooved dirt road in the moonlight, the little girl riding on the old man's narrow shoulders and then later, when she was too tired even for that, drooling drowsily on his lapel. He felt chastened by their gravity. They made him feel like a bumptious tourist, rattling drunkenly around what was, he kept forgetting, their country, a real country with real people in it, not a storybook at all. Or was it? Should he run after them? What secrets were they taking with them? When she reached to open the door, Quentin saw that the woman with the elegant cheekbones had lost her right arm below the elbow.

After another round of schnapps and scintillating persiflage with Humbledrum, the little silver birch sapling emerged from wherever it had been concealing itself and threaded its way through the room toward them, padding on feet of matted roots which still had clods of dirt clinging to them.

"I am Farvel," it said chirpily.

It looked even stranger in the full light of the bar. It was a literal stick figure. There were talking trees in the Fillory books, but Plover was never very precise in describing their appearance. Farvel spoke through what looked like a lateral cut in its bark, the kind of wedge that a single hatchet blow might have left. The remainder of its features were sketched out by a spray of thin branches covered in fluttering green leaves, which roughly limned the outlines of two eyes and a nose. He looked like a Green Man carving in a church, except that his flat little mouth gave him a comically sour expression.

"Please pardon my rudeness earlier, I was disconcerted. It is so rare to meet travelers from other lands." It had brought a stool from the bar, and now it bent itself into a rough sitting position. It looked a little like a chair itself. "What brings you here, human boy?"

At last. Here we go. The next level.

"Oh, I don't know," Quentin began, casually throwing an arm over the back of the booth. Obviously, he was emerging as the designated point person, the team's natural first-contact specialist. The bartender joined them as well, having been replaced at his station by a solemn, dignified chimp with a hangdog face. "Curiosity mostly, I guess. We found this button? That let us travel between worlds? And we were all sort of at loose ends on Earth anyway, so we just . . . came over here. See what we could see, that kind of a thing."

Even half drunk, that sounded a lot lamer than he'd hoped. Even Janet was looking at him with concern. God, he hoped Alice wasn't listening. He smiled weakly, trying to play it cool. He wished he hadn't had quite so much beer on quite such an empty, weary stomach.

"Of course, of course," Farvel said companionably. "And what have you seen so far?"

The bartender watched Quentin steadily. He sat back-to-front on a cane chair, his arms resting on the seat back.

"Well, we ran into a river nymph who gave us a horn. A magic horn, I think. And then this bug—this insect, in a carriage, I guess it was a praying mantis—it shot an arrow at me, that almost hit me."

He knew he should probably be playing this closer to the vest, but which part should he be leaving out exactly? How did those calculations work? The rigors of keeping pace with Humbledrum had left him a shade less than razor-keen. But Farvel didn't seem put off, he just nodded sympathetically. The chimp came out from behind the bar to place a lighted candle on their table, along with another round of pints, this time on the house.

Penny leaned over the back of the booth again.

"You guys don't work for the Watcherwoman, do you? Or I mean, like, secretly? Not like you want to, but you have to?"

"Jesus, Penny." Josh shook his head. "Smooth."

"Oh my, oh dear," Farvel said. A charged glance passed between him and the bartender. "Well, I suppose you could say . . . but no, one shouldn't say. Oh dear, oh dear."

Its composure thoroughly disrupted, the little treelet, the picture of arboreal distress, let its branches droop a little, and its green birch leaves fluttered anxiously.

"I like a touch of lavender in my honey," Humbledrum observed, apropos of nothing. "You want the bees to nest near a good-size field of it. Downwind, if you can manage it. That's the real trick of it. In a nutshell."

Farvel wrapped one slender twig-hand around its glass and tipped some beer into its mouth. After a visible struggle with itself, the tree-spirit began again.

"Young human," Farvel said. "What you suppose is true, in a sense. We do not love her, but we fear her. Everybody does, who knows what's good for them.

"She has not yet succeeded in slowing the advance of time, not yet." It glanced at the humid green twilight forest visible through the open doorway, as if to reassure itself that it was still there. "But she hungers to. We see her sometimes, from far away. She moves through the forest. She lives in the treetops. She has lost her wand, they say, but she will find it again soon, or fashion a new one.

"And then what? Can you imagine it, that eternal sunset? All will be confused. With no boundaries to separate them, the day animals and the night creatures will go to war with each other. The forest will die. The red sun will bleed out over the land until it is as white as the moon."

"But I thought the Witch was dead," Alice said. "I thought the Chatwins killed her."

So she was listening. How could she sound so calm? Another glance passed between Farvel and the bartender.

"Well, that's as may be. It was long ago, and we are far from the capital here. But the rams have not shown themselves here for many a year, and here in the country living and dead are not such simple things. Especially when witches come into it. And she has been seen!"

"The Watcherwoman has." Quentin was trying to follow. This was it, they were getting into it, the sap was starting to flow.

"Oh yes! Humbledrum saw her. Slender she was, and veiled."

"We heard her!" Penny said, getting into the spirit of it. "We heard a clock ticking in the woods!"

The bear just stared into his glass of schnapps with small, watery eyes.

"So the Watcherwoman," Penny said eagerly. "Is this a problem we can, you know, help you with?"

All of a sudden Quentin felt supremely tired. The alcohol in his system, which had thus far been acting as a stimulant, without warning flipped to a chemical isomorph of itself and became a sedative instead. Where before he'd been burning it like rocket fuel, now it was gumming up the works. It was dragging him down. His brain began to shut down nonessential operations. Somewhere in his core the self-destruct countdown had begun.

He sat back in the booth and allowed his eyes to glaze over. This was the moment that should have galvanized him into action, the moment that all those years at Brakebills had been leading up to, but instead he was letting go, sinking down into dysphoria. Whatever, if Penny wanted to take this over, let it be his show from now on. He had Alice, why shouldn't he have Fillory, too? The time for clever thinking had passed anyway. The tree was clearly taking their bait, or they were taking its bait, or both. Either way, here it was, the adventure had arrived.

There was a time when this had been his most passionate hope, when it would have ravished him with happiness. It was just so weird, he thought sadly. Why now, when it was actually happening, did the seductions of Fillory feel so crude and unwanted? Its groping hands so clumsy? He thought he'd left this feeling behind long ago in Brooklyn, or at least at Brakebills. How could it have followed him here, of all places? How far did he have to run? If Fillory failed him he would have nothing left! A wave of frustration and panic surged through him. He had to get rid of it, break the pattern! Or maybe this was different, maybe there really was something off here. Maybe the hollowness was in Fillory, not in him?

He slid warily out of the booth, rubbing up against Humbledrum's huge scratchy thigh on his way out, and visited the restroom, a malodorous pit-style affair. He thought for a second that he might be sick into it, and that maybe that wouldn't be the worst idea in the world, but nothing happened.

When he got back, Penny had taken his seat. He took Penny's place in the other booth and rested his chin in his hands and his hands on the table. If only they had drugs. Getting high in Fillory, that would really be the ultimate. Eliot had moved to the bar and appeared to be chatting up the horned man.

"What this land needs," Farvel was saying, leaning into the table conspiratorially and inviting the others to do likewise, "is kings and queens. The thrones in Castle Whitespire have been empty for too long, and they can only be filled by the sons and daughters of Earth. By your kind. But"—he cautioned them, stirringly—"only the stout of heart could hope to win those seats, you understand. Only the *stoutest* of heart."

Farvel looked on the verge of squeezing out a viscous, sappy tear. Jesus, what a speech. Quentin could practically have recited his lines for him.

Humbledrum farted mournfully, three distinct notes.

"So what would this involve, exactly?" Josh asked, in a tone of studied skepticism. "Winning, as you say, those seats?"

What it involved, Farvel explained, was a visit to a perilous ruin called Ember's Tomb. Somewhere within the tomb was a crown, a silver crown that had once been worn by the noble King Martin, centuries ago, when the Chatwins reigned. If they could recover the crown and bring it to Castle Whitespire, then they could occupy the thrones themselves—or four of them could anyway—and become kings and queens of Fillory and end the threat of the Watcherwoman forever. But it wouldn't be easy.

"So do we absolutely need this crown?" Eliot asked. "Otherwise what? It won't work?"

"You must wear the crown. There is no other way. But you will have help. There will be guides for you."

"Ember's Tomb?" Quentin roused himself for a final effort. "Waitaminnit. Does that mean Ember's dead? And what about Umber?"

"Oh, no-no-no!" Farvel said hastily. "It is just a name. A traditional name, it means nothing. It has just been so long since Ember was seen in these parts."

"Ember is the eagle?" Humbledrum rumbled.

"The ram." The uniformed bartender corrected him, speaking for the first time. "One of them. Widewings was the eagle. He was a false king."

"How can you not know who Ember is?" Penny asked the bear disgustedly.

"Oh dear," the tree said, hanging its vernal, garlanded face sadly down toward the table. "Do not judge the bear too harshly. You must understand, we are very far from the capital here, and many have ruled these green hills, or tried, since the last time you children of Earth walked them.

The silver years of the Chatwins are long ago now, and the years since have been forged from baser metals. You cannot imagine the chaos we have suffered through. There was Widewings the Eagle, and after him the Wrought Iron Man, the Lily Witch, the Spear-Carrier, the Saint Anselm. There was the Lost Lamb, and the vicious depredations of the Very Tallest Tree.

"And you know," he finished, "we are so very far from the capital here. And it is very confusing. I am only a birch, you know, and not a very large one."

A leaf fluttered to the table, a single green tear.

"I have a question," Janet said, unintimidated as ever. "If this crown is so damn important, and Ember and Umber and Amber or whatever are so powerful, why don't they just go get it themselves?"

"Ah, well, there's Laws," Farvel sighed. "They can't, you see. There's Higher Laws that even such as They are bound by. It must be you who retrieve the crown. It can only be you."

"We have lived too long," the bartender said glumly, to no one. He'd been putting away his own wares with impressive efficiency.

Quentin supposed it all made sense. Ember and Umber absent, a power vacuum, an insurgent Watcherwoman emerging from whatever witchy quasi-death she'd suffered at the Chatwins' hands. Penny had been right after all: they'd gotten a quest. Their role was clear. It had a pat, theme-park quality to it, like they were on some fantasy-camp role-playing vacation, but it did make sense. He could still hope. But let's be sure.

"I don't want to sound crass," he said out loud. "But Ember and Umber are the big shots around here, right? I mean, of all those people, things, whatever you mentioned, They're the most powerful? And morally righteous or whatever? Let's be clear on this for a second. I want to be sure we're backing the right horse. Or ram. Whatever."

"Of course! It would be folly to think otherwise!"

Farvel shushed him, looking worriedly over at the table of beavers, who didn't seem to be paying them any attention, but you couldn't be too careful. Bizarrely, Farvel produced a cigarette from somewhere and lit it from the candle on the table, careful not to ignite any part of itself. It protruded jauntily from the tree's little cleft mouth. The thing must have a death wish. Aromatic smoke rose up through the leafy corona of its face.

"Only do not judge us too harshly. The rams have been absent for many years. We have had to carry on without them. Make our own way. The forest must live."

Eliot and the horned man had vanished, presumably together. Incorrigible, that man; it cheered Quentin up by a scintilla that somebody at least was having a good time. The white goat slurped its yellow wine loudly in its corner. Humbledrum just gazed sorrowfully into its schnapps. Quentin reminded himself, as if he had almost forgotten the fact, that he was very far from home, in a room full of animals drinking alcohol.

"We have lived too long," the bartender announced again, sullenly. "The great days are past."

They stayed at the inn that night. The rooms were carved hobbit-style into the hill behind the main cabin. They were comfortable, windowless, and silent, and Quentin slept like the dead.

In the morning they sat at a long table in the bar, eating fresh eggs and toast and drinking cold water out of stone jugs, their backpacks piled up in a heap in one of the booths. Apparently Richard's gold cylinders went a long way in the Fillorian economy. Quentin felt clear-eyed and miraculously un-hungover. His restored faculties appreciated with a cold new keenness the many painful aspects of his recent personal history, but they also allowed him to really appreciate almost for the first time the reality of his physical presence in actual Fillory. It was all so detailed and vivid compared to his cartoonish fantasies. The room had the seedy, humiliated look of a bar seen in direct sunlight, sticky and thoroughly initialed by knife- and claw-wielding patrons. The floor was paved with old round millstones lightly covered with a scattering of straw, the chinks between them filled in with packed dirt. Neither Farvel nor Humbledrum nor the bartender were anywhere in sight. They were served by a brusque but otherwise attentive dwarf.

Also in the dining room were a man and a woman who sat opposite each other by a window, sipping coffee and saying nothing and glancing over at the Brakebills table every once in a while. Quentin had the distinct impression that they were just killing time, waiting for him and the others to finish their breakfast. That proved to be the case.

When the table was cleared, the pair introduced themselves as Dint— the man—and Fen. Both were fortyish and weather-beaten, as if they spent a lot of time outdoors in a professional capacity. They were, Dint explained, the guides. They would take the party to Ember's Tomb, in search of King Martin's crown. Dint was tall and skinny, with a big nose and huge black eyebrows that together took up most of his face; he was dressed all in black and wore a long cape, apparently as an expression of the extreme seriousness with which he regarded himself and his abilities. Fen was shorter and denser and more muscular, with close-cropped blond hair. With a whistle around her neck she could have been a gym teacher at a private school for girls. Her clothes were loose-fitting and practical, evidently designed for ease of movement in unpredictable situations. She projected both toughness and kindness, and she wore high boots with fascinatingly complex laces. She was, to the best of Quentin's ability to gauge these things, a lesbian.

Cool autumn sunlight slotted through the narrow windows cut in the heavy log walls of the Two Moons. Sober, Quentin felt more eager than ever to get on with it. He looked hard at his beautiful, despoiled Alice—his anger at her was a hard nugget he didn't know if he could ever digest, a kidney stone. Maybe when they were kings and queens. Maybe then he could have Penny executed. A palace coup, and definitely not a bloodless one.

Penny proposed that they all swear an oath together, to celebrate their shared high purpose, but it seemed like overkill, and anyway he couldn't muster a quorum. They were all shrugging into their packs when Richard abruptly announced that they could go if they wanted, but he would be staying behind at the inn.

No one knew how to react. Janet tried to joke him out of it, then when that didn't work she pleaded with him.

"But we've come this far together!" she said, furious and trying not to show it. Of all of them she hated this kind of disloyalty to the group the most. Any crack in their collective facade was an attack on her personally. "We can always turn back if things get sketchy! Or in an emergency we can use the button as a rip cord! I think you're way overreacting."

"Well, and I think you're underreacting," Richard said. "And I think you can count on the authorities to overreact when they find out about how far you're taking this."

"If they find out about it," Anaïs put in. "Which they will not."

"*When* they find out about it," Janet said hotly, "this is going to be the discovery of the century, and we are going to make history, and you're missing out on it. And if you can't see that, I frankly have no idea why you came along in the first place."

"I came along to keep you people from doing anything stupid. Which is what I'm trying to do right now."

"Whatever." She put a hand in his face, then walked away, her own face crumpling. "Nobody cares if you come or not. There are only four thrones anyway."

Quentin half expected Alice to join Richard—she looked like she was hanging on to her nerve by the very tips of her fingers. He wondered why she hadn't bolted already; she was way too sensible for a random lark like this. Quentin felt the opposite way. The danger would be going back, or staying still. The only way out was through. The past was ruins, but the present was still in play. They would have to tie him down to keep him from going to Ember's Tomb.

Richard would not be dislodged, so in the end they set off in a loose pack without him, with Dint and Fen walking ahead. They followed yesterday's carriage path for only a short while before striking out at an angle into the woods. For all the glory of their high and noble purpose, it felt like they were going on a summer-camp nature hike, or a junior high field trip, with the kids goofing off and the two counselors looking dour and superior and grown-up and glaring them back into line when they strayed too far. For the first time since they came to Fillory everybody was relaxing and being themselves instead of playing intrepid explorer-heroes. Low stone walls traversed the forest floor, and they took turns balancing along them. Nobody knew who had built them, or why. Josh said something about where was the damn Cozy Horse when you needed it. Before long they emerged from the forest into a maze of sunlit meadows, and then into open farmland.

It would not have been hard to get Alice alone. But whenever Quentin rehearsed what he wanted to say, however well it began, he got to a point where he had to ask her what happened with Penny, and then the dream sequence just went white, like a film of a nuclear blast. Instead, he made conversation with the guides.

Neither of them was very talkative. Dint did show a flicker of interest when he learned that the visitors were magicians, too, but they turned out not to have much in common. His entire expertise was in battle magic. He was barely aware that there were other kinds.

Quentin had the impression he was loath to give away any trade secrets. But he did open up about one thing.

"I sewed this myself," he said, a little shyly, pulling his cape to one side to show Quentin a bandolier-like vest underneath with many small pockets on it in rows. "I keep herbs in here, powders, whatever I might need in the field. If I'm casting something with a material component I can just . . . like this"—he executed a series of rapid pinching-and-dispensing motions that he'd obviously spent a lot of time practicing—"and I'm ready to go!"

Then the dour facade descended again, and he went back to his silent brooding. He carried a wand, which almost nobody at Brakebills did. It was considered slightly embarrassing, like training wheels, or a marital aid.

Fen was more overtly friendly but at the same time harder to read. She wasn't a magician, and she carried no obvious weapons, but it was understood that of the two of them she was the muscle. As far as Quentin could make out she was some kind of martial artist—she called the discipline she practiced *inc aga,* an untranslatable phrase from a language Quentin had never heard of. She kept to a strict regimen: she couldn't wear armor or touch silver or gold, and she ate practically nothing. What *inc aga* looked like in practice was impossible for Quentin to fathom—she would talk about it only in high-flown, abstract metaphors.

She and Dint were both adventurers by profession.

"There aren't many of us now," Fen said, her short sturdy legs somehow devouring distance faster than Quentin's long skinny ones. She never looked at him as she talked, her bulgy eyes continuously searching the horizon for potential threats. "Humans, I mean. Fillory is a wild place, and getting wilder. The forest is spreading, getting deeper and darker. Every summer we cut down the trees, burn them down sometimes, and then mark the borders of the woods. The next summer the borders are buried a hundred yards deep. The trees eat the farms, and the farmers come to live in the towns. But where will we live when all of Fillory is forest? When I was a girl, the Two Moons was in open country.

"The animals don't care," she added bitterly. "They like it this way."

She lapsed into silence. Quentin thought it might be a good time to change the subject. He felt like a green-as-grass PFC from Dubuque, Iowa, trading banter with the hardened South Vietnamese regular attached to his unit.

"So, I don't mean to sound crass," he said, "but are we paying you for this? Or is somebody?"

"If we succeed, that will be payment enough."

"But why would you want somebody from our world to be king anyway? Who you don't even know? Why not somebody from Fillory?"

"Only your kind can sit the thrones of Castle Whitespire. It's the Law. Always has been."

"But that makes no sense. And this is speaking as the beneficiary of the Law here."

Fen grimaced. Her protuberant eyes and full lips gave her face a fishy cast.

"Our people have been slaughtering and betraying one another for centuries, Quentin," she said. "How can you be any worse? The rule of the Chatwins is the last peaceful time anyone can remember. You don't know anyone here; you have no history, no scores to settle. You belong to no faction." She stared fixedly at the road ahead of them, biting off her words. The bitterness in her tone was bottomless. "It makes perfect political sense. We have reached the point where ignorance and neglect are the best we can hope for in a ruler."

They hiked through slow-rolling hills for the rest of the day, their thumbs hooked in the straps of their backpacks, sometimes along chalk roads, sometimes cutting across fields, crickets jumping up out of the long grass to get out of their way. The air was cool and clean.

It was an easy hike, a beginner's hike. There was singing. Eliot pointed out a ridge that he said was "positively screaming" to have pinot grapes planted on it. At no point did they see a town or another traveler. The rare tree or fence post they passed cast a crisp shadow on the ground, straight and clear, like it was etched there. It made Quentin wonder how Fillory really worked. There was hardly any central government, so what would a king actually do? The entire political economy appeared to be frozen in the feudal Middle Ages, but there were elements of Victorian-level technology as well. Who had made that beautiful Victorian carriage? What craftsmen wove the innards of the clockwork mechanisms that were so ubiquitous in Fillory? Or were those things done by magic? Either way, they must keep Fillory in its pre-industrial, agrarian state on purpose, by choice. Like the Amish.

At noon they witnessed one of Fillory's famous daily eclipses, and they observed something that was described in none of the books: instead of being a sphere, the moon of Fillory was formed in the shape of an actual, literal crescent, an elegant silvery arc that sailed through the sky, rotating slowly around its empty center of gravity.

They made camp at sunset in a ragged square scrap of meadow. Ember's Tomb, Dint told them, was in the next valley over, and they wouldn't want to spend the night any closer to it. He and Fen divided the watches between them; Penny volunteered to take one, but they declined. They ate some roast-beef sandwiches they'd been saving since the house upstate and unrolled sleeping bags and slept in the open, their bodies pressing flat the tough, coarse green grass underneath.

EMBER'S TOMB

The hill was smooth and green. Set into its base was a simple post-and-lintel doorway: two enormous rough stone slabs standing upright with a third slab laid across them. In the space between them was darkness. It reminded Quentin of a subway entrance.

It was just dawn, and the door was on the western face of the hill, so the hill's shadow fell over them. The grass was frosted with pale dew. There was no sound at all. The shape of the hill was a pure emerald-green sine wave against the lightening sky. Whatever was going to happen was going to happen here.

They stopped and huddled a hundred yards away, miserable and unshowered, to pull themselves together. The morning was chilly. Quentin rubbed his hands together and tried a warmth spell that only left him feeling feverish and slightly queasy. He couldn't seem to get oriented to Fillory's Circumstances. He had slept heavily the night before, with vivid dreams, the weight of his fatigue sinking him down into dark, primal realms haunted by roaring winds and tiny furry beasts, early mammals hiding fearfully in the long grass. He wished he could just stand here a little longer and look at the pink light on the dew. Everybody had a heavy hunting knife, which back on Earth had seemed beyond overkill but now felt pathetically inadequate.

The shape of the hill tugged at something in his deep memory. He thought of the hill they'd seen in that enchanted mirror, in that musty little storeroom back at Brakebills, where he and Alice and Penny had studied together, so long ago. It looked like the same hill. But so did a thousand hills. It was just a hill.

"So just to be clear," Eliot was saying to Dint and Fen. "It's called Ember's Tomb, but Ember isn't buried here. And he's not dead."

He sounded exactly as relaxed and unworried as he ever had back at Brakebills. Just dotting the *i*'s, clearing up the details, the way he would have insouciantly picked apart one of Bigby's problem sets, or decoded a closely written wine label. He was in control. The deeper they rolled into Fillory, the shakier Quentin felt, but Eliot was the opposite: he just got calmer and more sure of himself, exactly the way Quentin had thought that he, Quentin, would, and exactly the way that he wasn't.

"Every age finds a use for this place," Fen was saying. "A mine, a fortress, a treasure house, a prison, a tomb. Some dug it deeper. Others walled up the parts they didn't need or wished to forget. It is one of the Deep Ruins."

"So you've been here before?" Anaïs asked. "I mean, in there?"

Fen shook her head. "Not this one. A hundred places like it."

"Except that the crown is in this one. And how did it get there exactly?"

Quentin had wondered that same thing. If the crown really had belonged to Martin, maybe that was where he went when he disappeared. Maybe he died down there.

"The crown is there," Dint snapped. "We will go in and get it. Enough questions."

He swirled his cape impatiently.

Alice was standing very near Quentin. She looked small and still and cold.

"Quentin, I don't want to go in there," she said softly, without looking at him.

Over the past week Quentin had devoted literally hours to fantasizing about what he would say to Alice if she ever spoke to him again. But all his carefully planned speeches fell away at the sound of her voice. She wasn't going to get a speech. It was so much easier to be angry. Being angry made him feel strong, even though—and this contradiction did nothing to diminish his anger—he was angry only because his position was so weak.

"So go home," was all he said.

That wasn't right either. But it was too late, because somebody was running toward them.

———

The weird thing was that the entrance to the tomb was still a hundred yards off, and Quentin could see the creatures coming the whole way, two of them, running flat out across the wet grass for at least a minute, like they were out doing early-morning wind sprints. It was almost funny. They weren't human, and they didn't seem to belong to the same species as each other either, but they were both cute. One was something like a giant hare, squat and covered in gray-brown fur, maybe four feet tall and about that wide. It hopped toward them determinedly, its long ears flattened back. The other one was more like a ferret—or maybe a meerkat? A weasel? Quentin tried to think what the closest equivalent furry animal would be. Whatever it was it ran upright and it was tall, seven feet at least, most of it long silky torso. Its face was chinless, with prominent front teeth.

This odd couple came charging at them across the green grass silently, no battle cry, no sound track, in the still early-morning air. At first it looked like they might be running to greet them, but Bunny had short, stubby swords in both its front paws, held out steady in front of him as he ran, and Ferret was hefting a quarterstaff.

They closed to within fifty yards. The Brakebills crowd shrank back involuntarily, as if the newcomers exerted an invisible force field. This was it: they had come to the end of what was conceivable. Something was about to give. It had to. Dint and Fen didn't move. Quentin realized there wasn't going to be any parley or rock-paper-scissors. This was going to be about stabbing. He had thought he was ready, but he wasn't. Somebody had to stop it. The girls were hanging on to each other as if in a howling wind, even Alice and Janet.

Oh my God, Quentin thought, this is really happening. This is really happening.

Ferret arrived first. It stutter-stepped to a jittery stop, breathing hard. Its huge eyes blinked as it smoothly spun its staff two-handed in a figure-eight pattern. It whickered in the still air.

"Hup!" yelled Fen.

"Ha!" Dint answered.

They set themselves side by side, as if they were getting ready to lift something heavy. Then Dint stepped back, ceding first blood.

"Jesus," Quentin heard himself say. "Jesus jesus jesus." He wasn't ready for this. This wasn't magic. This was the opposite of magic. The world was ripping open.

Ferret feinted once and snapped a nasty jab at Fen's face. The two ends of the quarterstaff were now glowing an ominous enchanted orange, like the tip of a cigarette. Somebody shrieked in the silence.

Even as one end of the staff whipped forward, Fen turned away from it, bowing forward at the waist, ducking the jab and turning seamlessly, almost lazily, into a graceful spinning roundhouse kick. She seemed to be moving slowly, but her foot clocked Ferret's weak chin hard enough to spin its head around a quarter turn.

Ferret grinned, with blood in its big teeth, but it had more bad news coming. Fen was still spinning, and her next kick connected low and hard with the side of its knee. The knee bent in, sideways, wrongly. Ferret staggered and aimed the same jab at Fen's face, whereupon Fen caught the flashing quarterstaff barehanded—the smack of it hitting her open palm was like a rifle shot. She dropped her slick martial arts elegance and tussled savagely, messily for control.

For a second they froze, vibrating with isometric strain while Ferret, with agonizing, comical slowness, stretched its neck forward to try to bite Fen's bare throat with its big rodent incisors. But she had it outmuscled. Fen slowly forced the staff up under its chin, right into where its Adam's apple would be, while her right foot stamped pneumatically on the outside of its hurt knee, over and over again. It gagged and twisted away.

Just as Quentin thought he couldn't watch anymore, Ferret made its last mistake. It took its paw off the quarterstaff for an instant—it looked like it was going for a knife strapped to its thigh. With the extra leverage Fen flung it down hard on the turf, and the wind huffed out of it.

"Ha!" she barked, and stamped twice on its thickly furred throat, hard. A long, gargling rattle followed, the first sound Quentin had heard it make.

Fen popped up, visibly amped, her face red under her blond buzz cut. She picked up the quarterstaff, braced herself, and broke it over her knee in one try. Throwing the broken pieces aside, she leaned down and screamed in Ferret's face.

"Haaaaaaaaaaa!"

The broken ends of the staff spat out a few feeble burnt-orange sparks on the grass. Sixty seconds had passed, maybe not even that.

"Jesus jesus jesus," Quentin said, hugging himself. Someone was throwing up on the grass. It had never once even occurred to him to try to help. He wasn't ready for this. This wasn't what he'd come here for.

Meanwhile the other assassin, the squat muscular Bunny, had never arrived on the scene. Dint had done something to the ground beneath its long rabbit feet, or maybe to its sense of balance, so that it couldn't seem to stand up. It was scrabbling around helplessly on the grass like it was wet ice. Fen, on a roll, stepped over Ferret's body toward him, but Dint stopped her.

He turned back to the Brakebills crowd.

"Can any of you take him from here? Bow and arrow maybe?" Quentin couldn't tell if he was pissed that they weren't helping or if he was just being polite, offering them a taste of the action. "Anybody?"

Nobody answered. They stared at him like he was speaking gibberish. Every time the muscle-bound hare tried to get up its paws kept flying out from under it. Chittering and weeping, the hare shouted a guttural cry and threw one of its swords at them, but it slipped again and the sword landed safely short and off to one side.

Dint waited for an answer from the group, then turned away disgustedly. He made a quiet tapping gesture with his wand, like he was ashing a cigar, and a bone in the hare's upper thigh snapped audibly. It screamed in falsetto.

"Wait!" It was Anaïs, pushing her way forward, past a waxwork Janet. "Wait. Let me try."

The fact that Anaïs could even walk and talk right now was incomprehensible to Quentin. She began a spell but stuttered a few times, rattled, and had to start over. Dint waited, obviously impatient. On her third try she completed a sleep spell that Penny had taught them. Bunny's grunting struggles ceased. It sagged onto its side on the grass, looking alarmingly sweet. Ferret was still gagging weakly, eyes open and staring at the sky, red foam pouring from its mouth, but nobody paid any attention to it. No part of it below its neck was moving.

Anaïs went over and picked up the short sword the hare had thrown.

"There," she said to Dint proudly. "Now we kill it, no problem!"

She hefted the sword happily in one hand.

———

As a teenager in Brooklyn Quentin had often imagined himself engaging in martial heroics, but after this he knew, as a cold and immutable fact, that he would do anything necessary, sacrificing whatever or whomever he had to, to avoid risking exposure to physical violence. He wasn't even ashamed. Shame never came into it. He embraced his new identity as a coward. He would run in the other direction. He would lie down and cry and put his arms over his head or play dead. It didn't matter what he had to do, he would do it and be glad.

They trailed after Dint and Fen—and what kind of retarded names were those anyway, Dint and Fen? he thought numbly—through the doorway and into the hill. He barely noticed his surroundings. A square stone corridor opened out into a huge open chamber that looked almost as big as the hill that contained it, which must have been mostly hollow. Green-tinted light filtered down through a circular oculus at the room's apex. The air was full of stone dust. The ruins of an enormous brass orrery stood in the center of the room, its skinny arms stripped of its planets. It looked like a broken, defoliated Christmas tree, the smashed spheres lying at its base like fallen ornaments.

Nobody noticed a large—ten-feet-long large—green lizard standing frozen amid the remains of shattered tables and benches until it abruptly unfroze and skittered off into the shadows, claws skritching on the stone floor. The horror was almost pleasant: it wiped away Alice and Janet and everything else except itself, like a harsh, abrasive cleanser.

They wandered from room to empty room, down echoing stone hallways. The floor plan was beyond chaotic. The stonework changed styles and patterns every twenty minutes as a new generation of masons took over. They took turns putting light spells on their knives, their hands, various inappropriate body parts in an effort to break the tension.

Having tasted blood, Anaïs now tagged after Dint and Fen like an eager puppy, lapping up whatever observations she could get out of them about personal combat.

"They never had a chance," Fen said, with professional disinterest. "Even if Dint hadn't taken the second one, even if I had been alone, the quarterstaff is not a collaborative weapon. It simply takes up too much room. Once the tall one is into a form, those tips are flying left and right, up and down. He can't afford to worry about his friend. You face them one-on-one, and you move on.

"They should have fallen back, waited for us together in that big chamber. Taken us by surprise."

Anaïs nodded, obviously fascinated.

"Why didn't they?" she asked. "Why did they come running straight at us?"

"I don't know." Fen frowned. "Could've been an honor thing. Could've been a bluff, they thought we'd run. Could be they were under a spell, they couldn't help it."

"Did we have to kill them?" Quentin burst out. "Couldn't we have just, I don't know—"

"What?" Anaïs turned on him, sneering. "Maybe we could have taken them prisoner? We could have rehabilitated them?"

"I don't know!" he said helplessly. This wasn't how it was supposed to work. "Tied them up? Look, I guess I just wasn't that clear on what it would actually be like. Killing people."

It made him think of the day the Beast appeared—that same bottomless feeling, all bets off, like the cable had snapped and they were in free fall.

"Those are not people," Anaïs said. "Those were not people. And they tried to kill us first."

"We were breaking into their home."

"Glory has its price," Penny said. "Did you not know that, before you sought it?"

"Well, I guess they paid the price for us, huh?"

To Quentin's surprise Eliot rounded on him, too.

"What, you're going to back out? You?" Eliot laughed a bitter, barking laugh. "You need this almost as badly as I do."

"I'm not backing out! I'm just saying!"

Quentin had time to wonder why exactly Eliot did need this before Anaïs cut them off.

"Oh, God. Please, can we not?" She shook her curly head in disgust. "Can we all just not?"

Four hours and three flights of stairs and one mile of empty corridor later Quentin was examining a door when it opened suddenly, hard, smacking him in the face. He took a step backward and put a hand to his upper lip. In his half-stunned state he was more preoccupied with whether or not his nose was bleeding than with who or what had just slammed the door into it. He raised the back of his hand to his upper lip, checked it, raised it again, then checked it again. Yep, definitely bleeding.

An elfin being stuck its narrow, angry face around the edge of the door and glared at him. Purely by reflex Quentin kicked it shut.

He'd been about to point out the door to the others, who were busy surveying a wide, low-ceilinged room with a dry basin in the center. A creeping ivy-like plant had grown out of the basin and halfway up the walls and then died. Daylight was a months-ago memory. There were twinkly lights going off behind Quentin's eyes, and his nose felt like a warm, melting gob of something salty and throbbing. With melodramatic slowness the door creaked open again, gradually revealing a slight, pointy-featured man wearing black leather armor. He didn't look particularly surprised to see Quentin. The man, elf, whatever, whipped a rapier out of his belt and snapped into a formal fencing stance. Quentin backed away, gritting his teeth with fear and resignation. Just like that, Fillory had vomited out another one of its malignant menagerie.

Maybe fatigue had dulled the edge of his fear, but almost unbeknownst to himself Quentin was enunciating the words to Penny's Magic Missile spell. He'd practiced it back in New York, and now he backpedaled as he cast it because the Black Elf—as Quentin tagged him—was advancing on him using a poncey sideways fencing shuffle, his free hand held aloft, wrist limp. Quentin was getting the spell right, he could feel it, and he was loving himself for getting it right. Terror and physical pain sharpened and simplified Quentin's moral universe. He snapped the magical darts straight into the elf's chest.

The Black Elf coughed and sat down hard, looking dismayed. His face was the perfect height for kung-fu kicking, so Quentin, in what felt like an act of consummate bravery, kicked him savagely in the face. The rapier clattered to one side.

"Haaaaaaa!" Quentin shouted. It was like when he'd fought Penny, when the fear had left him. Was this battle rage at last? Was he going to become a berserker like Fen? It felt so good to stop being afraid.

Nobody else in the room had noticed what was going on, not until he yelled. Now the scene tilted and slid into nightmare. Four more Black Elves scrambled through the open door carrying an assortment of weapons, followed by two goat-legged men and two terrifying flying giant bumblebees the size of basketballs. Also present was something fleshy and headless that scrambled along on four legs, and a silent, wispy figure composed of white mist.

With the two teams arranged on their respective sides of the room, a staring match ensued. It all reminded Quentin powerfully of the opening moments of a game of dodgeball. His body seethed. He wanted to cast the missile spell again. He'd gone from feeling frail and vulnerable and cowardly to feeling badass and supercharged and armor-plated. The two mercenaries were whispering and pointing, choosing up targets.

Fen picked up a pebble and tossed it lightly, sidearm, at one of the fauns (they had evil fauns now?), who let it bounce off a round leather buckler strapped to his forearm. He looked pissed.

"The grimling's the problem," Quentin heard Fen say to Dint.

"Yeah. Leave the pangborn, though, I have something for that."

Dint withdrew a wand from his cape and appeared to write something in the air with it. He said a couple of words into the tip, like it was a microphone, then he indicated one of the fauns with it, a conductor cuing a soloist. The faun burst into flame.

It was like it was made of magnesium soaked in gasoline and had just been waiting for an errant spark to set it off. No part of it was not on fire. It took a step backward, then turned to the goat-man next to it as if to say something. Then it fell down, and Quentin couldn't look at it anymore. As all hell broke loose he tried to hang on to the gleeful bloodlust he'd felt so clearly a moment ago, to fan it back into life, but he'd lost it, fumbled it in the confusion.

Fen was thriving. This was evidently what she trained for. Quentin had missed it before, but she was actually mixing in a little magic as she fought—her *inc aga* was a hybrid technique, a martial art fully integrated with some highly specialized spellcasting style. Her lips moved, and there were white flashes where her fist- and hand-strikes landed. Meanwhile Dint addressed himself to the ghostly, misty figure, saying something inaudible that caused it to struggle and then be dispersed by an invisible, soundless roaring gale.

Quentin took a quick inventory of his brave company. Eliot had made himself useful by casting a kinetic spell on the second satyr, pinning it safely to the ceiling. Anaïs had her short sword out—it had a moonlight shimmer to it now, which meant she'd put a sharpness charm on it—and was looking eagerly around for somebody to stick it into. Janet was hugging herself against the back wall, her face wet and shining with tears. Her eyes were blank. She was gone.

Too many things were happening at once. Quentin's stomach clenched when he realized an elf had singled Alice out and was advancing across the dry basin toward her, twirling a long straight knife—were they called poniards?—in each hand. It was obvious from Alice's face that every spell she'd ever learned had just now slipped her mind. She turned away, dropped to one knee, and locked her hands behind her head. Nobody in the history of all the conflicts in the world had ever looked more defenseless.

He only had time to feel all the tenderness he had ever felt for her surge up in one infinitely concentrated instant—and to be surprised that it was all still there, moist and intact beneath the unsightly scorched layer of his anger—before the back of Alice's blouse tore wide open and a small leathery biped clawed its way vigorously out of the skin of her back. It was a party trick, a showgirl bursting out of a cake. Alice had loosed her cacodemon.

No question, the cacodemon was instantly the happiest being in the room. This was exactly the party it wanted to be at. Facing the elf, it bounced on its toes like a wiry little tennis pro preparing for return of service, with triple match point on its side. Its leap was evidently several beats faster than its opponent had counted on. In a moment it was past the poniards and had fastened its wiry grip on the elf's upper arms and buried its horrible face in the soft hollow of the elf's throat. The elf gagged and sawed futilely at the demon's shark-skinned back with its knives. Quentin reminded himself for at least the hundredth time never to underestimate Alice again.

And just like that it was over. They were out of opponents. The elves and the bees were down. The room was full of acid smoke from the burned satyr. Fen owned most of the body count; she was already running through a post-combat warm-down ritual, stepping backward through the forms she'd executed in the brief battle and whispering their names to herself. Penny was carefully casting a sleep spell on the satyr that Eliot had stuck to the ceiling, while Anaïs watched, impatient to administer the coup de grace. Quentin noted, with the pettiest possible annoyance, that they had the satyr without the buckler, which meant that Dint had burned the satyr with the buckler, which meant that he couldn't loot the buckler for himself. He had a crusty dried mustache from his bloody nose.

That wasn't so bad, he told himself. This wasn't such a nightmare. He risked a shuddering sigh of relief. Was that really it? Had they gotten everything?

Janet had finally thawed from her frozen state and was busy with something. Unlike everything else they'd seen, the fleshy, headless four-legged creature was neither humanoid nor obviously related to any terrestrial fauna. It was radially symmetrical, like a starfish, with no obvious front or back or face. It stood unreadable in a dark corner, taking sudden scary little hops in unexpected directions. It had a large faceted gem embedded in its back. Decoration? Or was that its eye? Its brain?

"Hey." Fen snapped her fingers in Janet's direction. "Hey!" Evidently she'd forgotten Janet's name. "Leave that. Leave the grimling to us."

Janet ignored her. She continued to take wary steps toward it. Quentin wished she wouldn't. She was in no kind of emotional state to be working magic.

"Janet!" he shouted.

"Shit," Dint said distinctly.

It was a businesslike "shit"—another damn mess for him to clean up. He brought his wand back out from wherever he'd stashed it.

But before he could act Janet reached carefully behind her back and brought out something small but heavy. Gripping it with both hands, she made a small adjustment and then fired five shots into the creature at close range. The pistol bounced upward with each shot, and each time she carefully re-aimed it. The sound was shattering in the low-ceilinged chamber. One shot struck sparks off the jewel in the grimling's back. It sank to the floor, shivering and deflating like a parade balloon, still expressionless. It made a high urgent whistling sound. By the fifth shot it was visibly dead.

Nothing and nobody in the room moved. Janet turned around. The tears she had shed earlier were already dry.

She glared at them.

"What the fuck are you looking at?" she said.

It got colder the deeper they went. At six stories underground Quentin was shivering in his heavy sweater and thinking nostalgically about the warm puffy parkas they'd abandoned way back by the sunny little stream. They broke for a rest in a circular room with a beautiful lapis lazuli spiral inlaid in the floor. Dark green ambient light emanated from somewhere, like the light in an aquarium. Dint sat in the lotus position, wrapped his cape around him, and meditated. A gap of about six inches separated him from the floor. Fen did calisthenics. The break was clearly not for their benefit; they were like professional mountaineers impatiently shepherding a herd of rich fat cats up the slopes of Mount Everest. The Brakebills party was a package they were contractually obligated to deliver.

Alice sat by herself on a stone bench, her back against a pillar, looking blankly at a mosaic on the wall depicting a sea monster, a creature like an octopus but much larger and with many more than eight legs. Quentin straddled the bench at the other end, facing her. Her eyes flicked over to his for a long moment. There was not a hint of either contrition or forgiveness in them. He made sure his eyes looked the same.

They watched the mosaic. The little squares that made up the sea creature were moving very slowly, rearranging themselves on the wall. The crude blue waves rolled along very gradually. It was easy decorative magic. There was a bathroom floor at Brakebills that had much the same effect. Alice felt like a black hole that was trying to pull him in, rip the flesh clean off him with its sheer toxic gravity.

Finally she took out her canteen and used it to wet a spare white sock.

"Let's do something about your nose," she said.

She reached out to dab at his face, but at the last minute he realized he didn't want her to touch him. He took the sock himself, carefully. It turned pink as he wiped at his upper lip.

"So what was it like," Quentin said. "When you let the demon out."

Now that the high of combat was gone, and she was no longer in danger, his anger came creeping back. The anesthetic was wearing off. It was an effort not to say anything vicious. She hiked her foot up onto the bench and started undoing the laces on her sneakers.

"It felt good," she said carefully. "I thought it would hurt, but it was kind of a relief. Like sneezing. I never felt like I could really breathe with that thing inside me."

"Interesting. Did it feel as good as fucking Penny?"

He'd actually thought he was going to be civil, but it was too hard. The words came out of his mouth of their own malevolent volition. He wondered what else he would say. I've got all kinds of demons inside of me, he thought. Not just the one.

If he'd managed to hurt Alice, she didn't let it show. She carefully peeled off a sock. A nasty white blister covered the entire ball of her foot. They watched the mosaic some more. A little boat had floated into the scene, a lifeboat maybe, or a launch from a whaler. It was crowded with tiny people. It looked pretty much like a done deal that the sea creature was going to crush the little boat in its many long green arms.

"That was—" She stopped and started over. "That wasn't good."

"So why did you do it."

Alice tilted her head, thoughtfully, but her face was white.

"To get back at you. Because I was feeling like shit about myself. Because I didn't think you would care. Because I was drunk, and he came on pretty strong—"

"So he raped you."

"No, Quentin, he did not—"

"Never mind. Stop talking."

"I don't think I understood how much it would hurt you—"

"Just stop talking, I can't talk to you anymore, I can't hear anything you're saying!"

He'd started that little speech speaking normally and he ended it shouting. In a way fighting like this was just like using magic. You said the words, and they altered the universe. By merely speaking you could create damage and pain, cause tears to fall, drive people away, make yourself feel better, make your life worse. Quentin leaned forward, all the way forward, until he had placed his forehead on the cool marble of the bench in front of him. His eyes were closed. He wondered what time it was. His head felt a little spinny. He could fall asleep right there, he thought. Just like this. He wanted to tell Alice he didn't love her, but he couldn't, because it wasn't true. It was the one lie he couldn't quite tell.

"I wish this were over," Alice quietly.

"What."

"This mission, this adventure, whatever you want to call it. I want to go home."

"I don't."

"This is bad, Quentin. Somebody's going to get hurt."

"Good, I hope they do. If I die doing this, at least I'll have done something. Maybe you'll do something one of these days instead of being such a pathetic little mouse all the time."

She said something he didn't catch.

"What?"

"I said, don't talk to me about death. You don't know anything about it."

For no reason, and against his express conscious wishes, some very tight elastic band of muscle around Quentin's chest relaxed very slightly. Something between a laugh and a cough escaped him.

He sank back against his pillar.

"God, I am literally losing my fucking mind."

Across the room Anaïs sat with Dint, talking intently and going over a handmade map of their progress so far that he'd sketched on what looked suspiciously like graph paper. Anaïs seemed more like a part of the guides' gang than the Brakebills gang now. As he watched she bent over the map, deliberately smooshing her tit into Dint's shoulder as she did so. Josh was nowhere to be seen. Penny and Eliot were dozing on the floor in the center of the room, their heads resting on their packs. Eliot had hectored Janet about the gun until he extracted a promise from her to dispose of it responsibly.

"Do you even want this anymore, Quentin?" Alice asked. "I mean, what we're doing here? This kings and queens idea?"

"Of course I do." He'd almost forgotten why they were here. But it was true. A throne was exactly what he needed right now. Once they were ensconced in Castle Whitespire, wreathed in glory and every possible physical comfort, then maybe he could find the strength to come to grips with all this. "You'd have to be an idiot not to."

"You know the funny thing though?" She sat up straight, suddenly animated. "I mean the really hilarious thing? You actually don't. You don't even want it. Even if this whole thing came off without a hitch, you wouldn't be happy. You gave up on Brooklyn and on Brakebills, and I fully expect you to give up on Fillory when the time comes. It makes things very simple for you, doesn't it? Well, and of course you were always going to give up on us.

"We had problems, but we could have fixed them. But that was too easy for you. It might actually have worked, and then where would you be? You would have been stuck with me forever."

"Problems? We had problems?" People looked up. He dropped his voice to a furious whisper. "You fucked fucking Penny! I'd say that's a fucking problem!"

Alice ignored this. If he didn't know better, he would have said that the tone of her voice almost resembled tenderness.

"I will stop being a mouse, Quentin. I will take some chances. If you will, for just one second, look at your life and see how perfect it is. Stop looking for the next secret door that is going to lead you to your real life. Stop waiting. This is it: there's nothing else. It's here, and you'd better decide to enjoy it or you're going to be miserable wherever you go, for the rest of your life, forever."

"You can't just decide to be happy."

"No, you can't. But you can sure as hell decide to be miserable. Is that what you want? Do you want to be the asshole who went to Fillory and was miserable there? Even in Fillory? Because that's who you are right now."

There was something true about what Alice was saying. But he couldn't grasp it. It was too complex, or too simple. Too something. He thought of that first week he'd spent at Brakebills, when he and Eliot had gone sculling, and they'd watched the other rowers hunching and shivering in what to Quentin was a warm summer day. That was what he looked like to Alice. It was strange: he'd thought that doing magic was the hardest thing he would ever do, but the rest of it was so much harder. It turned out that magic was the easy part.

"Why did you come here, Alice?" he said. "If you don't even want this?"

She looked at him evenly.

"Why do you think, Quentin? I came because of you. I came here because I wanted to take care of you."

Quentin looked around at the others. He saw Janet sitting with her back against one wall with her eyes closed, though Quentin didn't get the sense that she was asleep. The revolver was cradled in her lap. She wore a red T-shirt with a white star on it and khaki pants. She must be cold, he thought. As he watched she sighed and licked her lips without opening her eyes, like a little girl.

He didn't want to be cold. Alice was still watching him. Behind her the mosaic was a swirl of green tentacles and whitecaps and floating fragments. He slid down the stone bench to her end and kissed her and bit her lower lip until she gasped.

After a certain point it was no longer possible to ignore the fact that they were lost. The hallways wound fiendishly and branched frequently. They were in a maze, and they were not solving it. Dint had become obsessive about his map, which now stretched to half a dozen sheets of graph paper that he shuffled and scribbled on intently whenever they turned a corner. At Brakebills they'd learned a spell that would leave glowing footprints behind them, but Dint thought it would just lead predators straight to them. The walls were carved with ranks of crude marching figures in profile, thousands of them, each one holding a different totem: a palm leaf, a torch, a key, a sword, a pomegranate.

It was darker here. They kept piling on light spells to anything that would take one, but the glow just didn't seem to go as far. They fast-walked down the corridor, double-time now. The mood was that of a picnic threatened by lightning. The corridor branched and branched again and intermittently dead-ended, forcing them to backtrack. Quentin's feet hurt in his brand-new hiking boots; a stray spur of something hard stabbed him in the same spot on his left ankle every time he took a step.

He risked a glance back the way they'd come. There was a red glow back there—something somewhere in the maze was throwing off a deep crimson light. He felt a deep-seated lack of interest in finding out what it was.

Ten minutes later they got hung up at a fork in the passageway, Dint vigorously supporting the right fork, Josh making the case, admittedly largely on intangibles, that the other fork looked "*way* more promising" and just "feels more like what we want." The walls were painted with oddly

convincing trompe-l'oeil landscapes now, crowded with tiny dancing figures. Doors slammed open and shut in the distance.

The hallway was brightening behind them. They all saw it now. It was
like a subterranean sun was rising. Discipline was getting ragged. They
broke into a half run, and it was too dark for Quentin to be absolutely sure
that nobody lagged behind. He focused on Alice. She was panting. The
back of her blouse gaped palely open where the demon had torn its way out;
he could see her black bra strap, which had somehow survived the operation. He wished he had a jacket to give her.

He caught up with Dint.

"We should slow down," Quentin panted. "We're going to lose
somebody."

Dint shook his head. "They're tracking us now. If we stop, they'll
mob us."

"What the fuck, man! Didn't you plan for this?"

"This *is* the plan, Earth child," Dint snarled back. "You don't like it, go
home. We need kings and queens in Fillory. Is that not a thing worth dying
for?"

Not really, Quentin thought. Asshole. That slutty nymph was right.
This is not your war.

They bulled through a door into a tapestry that was apparently concealing it from the other side. Behind the tapestry was a candle-lit banquet hall
set with food, fresh and steaming. They were alone; it was as if the waiters
who placed the dishes there had just moments earlier scampered out of
sight. The table stretched out in both directions with no end points. The
tapestries were rich and detailed, the silverware gleaming, the crystal gob-
lets full of wine, deep gold and arterial purple.

They stopped and stared in both directions, blinking. It was like they
had stumbled into the dream of a starving man.

"Nobody eats!" Dint called. "Don't touch it! Nobody eats, nobody
drinks!"

"There are too many entrances," Anaïs said, her pretty green eyes flicking in all directions. "They can attack us."

She was right. A door opened farther down the hall, admitting two
large, rangy individuals of the monkey family, though Quentin couldn't
have said exactly what to call them. Their glazed simian eyes looked bored.

In perfect synchrony they dipped their hands into pouches slung over their shoulders and came up with golf-size lead balls. With a practiced windup of their overdeveloped shoulders and overlong arms, they whipped the balls at the group at big-league fastball speeds.

Quentin grabbed Alice's hand, and they cowered back behind a heavy tapestry, which caught one of the balls. The other one clipped a candlestick on the table and then spectacularly vaporized four wineglasses in a row. Under other circumstances, Quentin thought, that would actually have been cool. Eliot touched his forehead, where he'd been hit by a shard of glass. His fingers came away bloody.

"Would somebody please kill those things, please!" Janet said disgust-edly. She was crouched under the table.

"Seriously," Josh complained through clenched teeth. "This shit isn't even mythological. We need some unicorns or something up in this piece."

"Janet!" Eliot said. "Do your demon!"

"I already did!" she yelled back. "I did it the night after graduation! I felt sorry for it!"

Huddling behind the rough fabric of the tapestry, Quentin watched a pair of legs stroll by, unhurriedly. While the rest of them hunkered down, Penny strode confidently toward the two ball throwers as they wound up again, no expressions on their stiff monkey faces. He was gesturing fast with both hands and singing an incantation in a high, clear tenor. Calm and serious in the shifting candlelight, wearing just a T-shirt and jeans, he looked much less like a puffy wannabe than he used to. He looked like a hardened young battle-mage. Was that how he'd looked to Alice, Quentin wondered, the night she slept with him?

With one hand Penny stopped a lead ball in midair, then a second. They hovered there unsupported for a moment like surprised humming-birds before they recovered their weight and dropped to the floor. With the other hand Penny lobbed back a fiery seed that grew and expanded like an unfurling parachute. The tapestries on either side of the hall blazed where the fireball brushed them. It engulfed the two monkeys, and when it dis-sipated they were simply gone, and a ten-foot section of the banquet table was a roaring bonfire.

"Yeah!" Penny yelled, momentarily forgetting his Fillory-speak. "Boom, bitches!"

"Amateur," Dint muttered.

"If my hairline is messed up," Eliot said weakly, "I will bring those things back to life and kill them all over again."

They retreated along the banquet hall in the opposite direction, awkwardly shuffling past the straight-backed wooden chairs. The hall was just too narrow—with the table in the center there wasn't enough room for them to form up properly. The setup had a zany *Scooby Doo* feeling. Quentin took a running step and half leaped, half slid across the banquet table, clearing dishes as he went, feeling like an action hero sliding across the firebird-emblazoned hood of his muscle car.

A curious Alice in Wonderland menagerie was crowding into the hall from either side. As military order broke down in the room so did taxonomical order. Species and body parts were mashed up seemingly at random. Had everything collapsed after the Chatwins left, to the point where humans and animals interbred? There were ferrets and rabbits, giant mice and loping monkeys and a vicious-looking fisher, but there were also men and women with the heads of animals: an astute-looking fox-headed man who appeared to be preparing a spell; a woman with a thick-necked lizard head with huge independent eyes; an oddly dignified pike-bearer upon whose shoulders swayed the sinuous neck and tiny head of a pink flamingo.

Fen plucked a sharp knife off the banquet table, gripped the blade carefully between her thumb and forefinger, and threw it spinning so that it took the fox-man point-first in the eye socket.

"Move," she barked. "Everybody. Fall back. Don't let them bog us down. We have to be close now."

They fell back along the length of the banquet hall. The basic idea was to try to keep a coherent line of scrimmage between them and their attackers, but the line kept getting disrupted. One of their party would get hung up—the chairs kept getting in the way—or the tomb dwellers would group together and make a charge, or worse, one of them would blunder in from the side through a hidden door straight into the center of their party. He and Alice managed to hold hands for the first ten seconds, but after that it just wasn't possible. This wasn't like the earlier fights. The whole thing kept degenerating into the running of the bulls. The hall seemed to go on forever; possibly it did. The candles and mirrors and food gave the whole scene an incongruously festive air. Even if they decided to take the button home, at this point it would be hard to muster everybody in one place to actually do it.

Quentin jogged along with his knife out, though he didn't know if he was capable of using it. He felt like he had in gym class, trying to look like part of the team while at the same time desperately hoping nobody would pass him the ball. A giant house cat popped out from behind a tapestry right in front of him, and Fen almost certainly saved Quentin's life by cannoning fearlessly into the thing so that they rolled together on the floor, grappling and thrashing, until she knocked it out with a furious *inc aga* head-butt. Quentin gave her a hand up and they ran on.

Dint was putting on a show. He'd hopped spryly up onto the banquet table and was striding along it, rapping out percussive syllables with astonishing speed and fluency, his wand tucked back behind his ear. His long black hair crackled, and crazy energies flashed out from the tips of his long fingers; sometimes he actually had two different spells going simultaneously, Quentin noticed, a primary attack in one hand and a second, lesser piece of witchery simmering in his off hand. At one point he made his arms swell up hugely, picked up two chairs in each giant hand and clubbed down a half dozen opponents with them in three businesslike swings—left, right, left.

Penny managed to persuade a section of the table to rear up like an angry centipede and attack the Fillorians until they chopped it to pieces. Even Quentin got off a couple of sweaty-palmed Magic Missiles into the press. Fen's tunic was soaked with sweat. She closed her eyes and placed her palms together, whispering, and when she parted them they gleamed with a terrible white phosphorescence. The next foe she met—a sinewy scimitar-wielder who was either wearing a leopard skin or was half leopard from the waist up—she shouted and punched her fist through its chest up to her shoulder.

But the close calls were getting closer. The situation was disintegrating, and they needed an exit strategy. The corridor was filling with bodies and smoke. Quentin's breath whistled through his teeth, and in his head he was singing a psychotic nonsense song.

Somewhere along the line Quentin left his knife in a furry Fillorian stomach. He never saw the creature's face—it was a creature, not a person, not a person, not a person—but later he would remember the sensation of jamming it in, how the blade punched through the tough rubbery muscles of the diaphragm and then slid easily into the underlying viscera, and how the muscles gripped the blade after it was in. He snatched his hand away from the hilt like it was electrified.

Quentin registered first Josh, then Eliot, hunching their shoulders and letting loose their cacodemons. Eliot's was particularly awesome-looking, banded from head to foot in horizontal yellow and black danger stripes. It slid sideways across the smooth table, scrabbling like a flung cat, then charged into the fray with unself-conscious glee, clinging and tearing and leaping and clinging again.

"Goddamn it!" Janet was screaming. "What else? What the fuck else?"

"This is bullshit," Eliot yelled hoarsely. "Side door! Pick a side door and go through it!"

There was a moment of premonitory silence, as if some of the creatures actually sensed what was going to happen next. Then the floor jolted, and a giant man made of glowing red-hot iron shouldered his way sideways through the wall.

He took the whole wall down with him. A flying brick nicked Fen's head, and she dropped like she'd been shot. Waves of heat poured off the giant, warping the air around him, and anything he touched burned. He stood bent over, hands on the floor—he was about a third again too tall for the confined space of the banquet hall. His eyes were molten gold, with no pupils. Dust filled the air. The giant put his foot on Fen's prostrate body, and she burst into flames.

Everybody ran. Anybody who fell was trampled. The heat coming off the man's smooth red skin was unbearable. Quentin would have done anything to put distance between it and himself. There were pileups at the nearest exits; Quentin pushed past them and farther down the hall. He looked around for Alice and couldn't even find anybody human until he risked a look back and saw Josh standing in the middle of the hallway, all alone.

He seemed to be undergoing one of his freakish power surges. He'd summoned another of his miniature black holes, the way he'd done that day on the welters pitch. It had nearly swallowed a tree that day; now as Quentin watched an entire length of tapestry wavered toward it and then flowed into it all at once, ripping free of its curtain rod with a sound like a fusillade of pistol shots. The light in the hall dimmed and became amber. The red giant was momentarily stalled by this. He was squatting down, studying the apparition, apparently fascinated by it. He was bald, and his expression was blank. His huge, hairless, glowing-red cock and balls swung loose between his thighs like the clapper of a bell.

Then Quentin was alone and running along a cool, dark side corridor. It was silent—the noise switched off like a TV. He was sprinting flat out, and then he was running, then jogging, and then, after a while, he was just walking. It was over. He couldn't run anymore. The air scorched his lungs. He bent over and put his hands on his knees. His back itched painfully, behind his right shoulder, and when he reached back to scratch he found an arrow dangling from the hump of muscle there. Unthinkingly, he pulled it out, and a freshet of blood trickled down his back, but there wasn't much pain. It had only gone in an inch, probably not even that far. He was almost glad it hurt. The pain was something to hang on to. He held the wooden shaft, grateful to have something solid in his hands. The silence was amazing.

He was safe again. For a few minutes he allowed himself to luxuriate in the simple joys of breathing cool air, of not running, of being alone in the semidarkness and not in immediate danger of dying. But the gravity of the situation kept seeping through, messily, until he could no longer blot it up. He could be the last one alive for all he knew. He had no idea how to get back up to the surface. He could die down here. He felt the weight of the dirt and rock over his head. He was buried alive. Even if he made it out, he didn't have the button. He had no way to get back to Earth.

Footsteps in the darkness. Somebody was coming, walking. The figure's hands were glowing with a light charm. Wearily, Quentin started in on yet another Magic Missile spell, but before he could finish he realized it was just Eliot. He let his hands drop and sagged to the floor.

Neither of them spoke, they just leaned together against the wall, side by side. The cold stone soothed the little divot of pain the arrow had punched in Quentin's back. Eliot's shirt was untucked. His face was all smudged with soot on one side. He would have been furious if he'd known.

"You all right?"

Eliot nodded.

"Fen's dead," Quentin said.

Eliot took a deep breath and ran his glowing hands through his thick wavy hair.

"I know. I saw."

"I don't think there's anything we could have done," Eliot said. "Big Red back there was just out of our league, that's all."

They fell silent. It was like the words had spun off into some void where they had no meaning. They'd lost any connection with the world; or maybe it was the world that had peeled away from the words. Eliot passed him a flask with something strong in it, and he drank and passed it back. It seemed to restore some link between him and his body.

Quentin drew his knees up and hugged them.

"I got hit by an arrow," he said. It felt like a stupid thing to say. "In my back."

"We should go," Eliot said.

"Right."

"Backtrack. Try to meet back up with the others. Penny's got the button." It was amazing that Eliot could still be so practical after everything that had happened. He was so much stronger than Quentin was.

"That big glowing guy though."

"Yeah."

"Maybe he's still back there."

Eliot shrugged.

"We have to get to the button."

Quentin was thirsty, but there was no water. He couldn't remember when he'd dropped his pack.

"I'll tell you something funny," Eliot said after a while. "I think Anaïs hooked up with Dint."

"What?" In spite of himself Quentin smiled. He felt his dry lips crack. "When did they even have time?"

"Bathroom break. After that second fight."

"Wow. Tough break for Josh. But you have to applaud their initiative."

"Definitely. But hard cheese on Josh."

"Hard cheese."

It was the kind of thing they used to say back at Brakebills.

"I'll tell you something else funny," Eliot went on. "I don't regret coming here. Even now that it's all gone to shit, I'm still glad I came. Could that possibly be the stupidest thing I've ever said to you? But it's the truth. I think I was going to drink myself to death back on Earth."

It was true. For Eliot there hadn't been any other way. Somehow that made it a little bit better.

"You could still drink yourself to death here."

"At this rate I won't have the chance."

Quentin stood up. His legs were stiff and achy. He did a deep knee-bend. They started back the way they came.

Quentin didn't feel any fear anymore. That part of it was over, except that he was worried about Alice. The adrenaline was gone, too. Now he was just thirsty, and his feet hurt, and he was covered in scratches he couldn't remember having gotten. The blood on his back had dried, sticking his shirt to the arrow wound. It tugged uncomfortably every time he took a step.

It became apparent pretty soon that he didn't have anything to worry about anyway, because they couldn't even find their way back to the banquet hall. They must have taken a wrong turn somewhere, maybe several. They stopped and tried some basic path-finding magic, but Quentin's tongue felt thick and clumsy, and neither of them could seem to get the words quite right, and anyway they really needed a dish of olive oil to make it work properly.

Quentin couldn't think of anything to say. He waited while Eliot took a piss against the stone wall. It felt like they'd come to the end, but they had no choice but to keep walking. Maybe this is still part of the story, he thought numbly. The bad part right before everything comes out all right. He wondered what time it was on the surface. He felt like he'd been up all night.

The masonry of the walls was older now, crumblier. For short stretches it was just dusty unworked cave rock. They were at the very outer fringes of this subterranean universe, wandering among badly eroded planets and dim, decaying stars. The hallway had ceased to branch now. It contented itself with curving gently to the left, and Quentin thought he could feel the curve getting gradually tighter, like it was spiraling inward, like the interior corridors of a nautilus shell. He figured it stood to reason, what little reason was left in the world, that there was a geometrical limit to how far it could keep curving in on itself before they came to something. Pretty soon it turned out he was right.

THE RAM

Just like that, there they all were.

Quentin and Eliot stood at the edge of a large round underground chamber, blinking at bright torchlight. It was different from the rooms they'd already seen in that it appeared to be naturally occurring. The floor was sandy, the ceiling craggy and irregular and unworked, with stalactites and other rocky excrescences poking down that you wouldn't want to hit your head on. The air was chilly and damp and still. Quentin could hear an underground stream gurgling somewhere, he couldn't see where. The sound had no origin or direction.

The others were here, too, all of them except for poor Fen. Josh and Alice were in an entrance a little ways over. Janet stood in another archway looking lost and bedraggled, Dint and Anaïs were in the next one over, and Penny was alone in the one after that. They stood in the doorways like contestants framed in the spangled, lightbulbed archways of a game show.

It was a miracle. It even looked like they'd all just arrived at the exact same moment. Quentin took a deep breath. Relief flooded through him like a warm liquid transfusion. He was just so fucking glad to see every last one of them. Even Dint—good old Dint, you hound dog! Even Penny, and only partly because he still had his pack, presumably with the button still inside. The story's outcome was still in play after all. Even after everything that had gone wrong it could still all turn out basically okay—it was a disaster, but a mitigated disaster. It was still possible that five years from now, when they were more or less over their post-traumatic stress disorder, they'd all get a big kick out of getting together and talking about it. Maybe the real Fillory wasn't that different from the Fillory he'd always wanted after all.

Kings and queens, Quentin thought. Kings and queens. *Glory has its price. Did you not know that?*

A block of stone stood in the center of room. On it was a large shaggy sheep—or no, it had horns, so that made it a ram. It lay with its eyes closed, its legs folded under it, its chin resting on a crown, a simple golden circlet snuggled between its two shaggy front knees. Quentin wasn't sure if it was asleep or dead or just a very lifelike statue.

He took a tentative, exploratory step into the room, feeling like a man setting foot on shore after a long and grievous afternoon on a storm-tossed yacht. The sandy floor felt reassuringly solid.

"I didn't know—" he called hoarsely to Alice. "I wasn't sure if you were still alive or not!"

Josh thought Quentin was talking to him. His comical face was ashen. He looked like a ghost seeing a ghost.

"I know." He coughed wetly into his fist.

"What the hell happened? Did you fight that thing?"

Josh nodded shakily. "Sort of. I felt a big spell coming on, so I just went with it. I think I finally felt what you guys feel. I called up one of those swirly black holes. He looked at it, then he looked at me with those freaky gold eyes, then it just sucked him in. Headfirst. Just ate him. I saw his big red legs sticking out kicking, and I just booked it out of there.

"Did you check out his dick though? That guy was hung!"

Quentin and Alice embraced without speaking. The others made their way over. Stories were exchanged. It was a reunion. Somehow everybody had managed to make it out of the banquet hall unscathed, or at least not too badly scathed. Anaïs showed everybody where her golden curls got crisped off in the back as she ran. Janet was the only one who hadn't escaped out a side door; instead she ran all the way to the end of the hall, which it turned out did have an end after all, though it took her an hour to get there ("Three years of cross country," she said proudly). She'd even had a glass of the wine with no ill effects, apart from mild intoxication.

They all shook their heads. What they'd all been through. Nobody would ever believe it. Quentin was so tired he could hardly think, except to think: we did it, we really did it. Eliot passed the flask, and everybody drank. It had been a game at first, and then it all got horribly real, but now it was starting to feel like a game again, something like what they'd been imagining on that terrible, wonderful morning back in Manhattan. Good fun. A real adventure. After a while they ran out of things to say, just stood in a circle looking at each other and shaking their heads with silly punch-drunk smiles on their faces.

A deep, dry cough interrupted them.

"Welcome."

It was the ram. He had opened His eyes.

"Welcome, children of Earth. Welcome, too"—here he acknowledged Dint—"you valiant child of Fillory. I am Ember."

He was sitting up. He had the strange, horizontal, peanut-shaped pupils that sheep have. His thick wool was the color of pale gold. His ears stuck out comically beneath the heavy horns that curled back magnificently from His forehead.

Of them all, only Penny knew what to do. He dropped his backpack and walked over to stand in front of the ram. He got down on his knees in the sand and bowed his head.

"We sought a crown," he said grandly, "but we have found a king. My lord Ember, it is my honor and privilege to offer You my fealty."

"Thank you, My child."

The ram's eyes half closed, gravely and joyfully. Thank God, was all Quentin could think. Literally, thank God. It was really Him. It was the only explanation. It wasn't like they'd done anything especially heroic to deserve this re-reversal of fortune. Ember must have brought them here. He had saved them. This was it, the closing credits. They'd won. The coronation could begin.

He looked from Penny to the ram and back. He could hear feet shuffling on the sandy floor. Somebody else besides Penny was kneeling, Quentin didn't turn to see who. He stayed standing. For some reason he wasn't ready to kneel down, not yet. He would in a minute, but somehow this didn't feel like the moment. Though it would have been nice—he'd been walking for so long. He wasn't sure what to do with his hands, so he clasped them together over his crotch.

Ember was talking, but Quentin's mind glossed over the words. They had a certain boilerplate quality—he'd always skipped over Ember's and Umber's speeches in the books, too. Come to think of it, if this was Ember, where was Umber? Normally you never saw them apart.

". . . with your help. It is time We resumed our rightful stewardship over this land. Together We shall go forth from this place and restore glory to Fillory, the glory of the old days, the great days . . ."

The words washed over him. Alice could fill him in later. In the books Ember and Umber had always come off as slightly sinister, but in person Ember didn't seem that bad at all. He was nice, even. Warm. Quentin could see why the Fillorians didn't mind Him that much. He was like a kindly, crinkly-eyed department-store Santa. You didn't take Him too seriously. He didn't look any different from an ordinary ram, except that He was larger and better groomed, and He gave off more of an air of alert, alien intelligence than you would expect from your average sheep. The effect was unexpectedly funny.

Quentin found it hard to focus on what Ember was saying. He was drunk on exhaustion and relief and Eliot's flask. He would be happy to stipulate to any big speeches. He just wished he knew where that tantalizing, tinkling, trickling sound was coming from, because he was perishing of thirst.

There was the crown right there, between Ember's hooves. Should somebody ask for it? Or would he just give it to them when He was ready? It was ridiculous, like a question of dinner-party etiquette. But he supposed the ram would give it to Penny now, as a reward for his prompt display of sycophancy, and they'd all have to be his underlings. Maybe that was all it took. Quentin didn't particularly want to see Penny crowned as High King of Fillory. After all this, was Penny going to turn out to be the hero of this little adventure?

"I have a question."

A voice interrupted the old ram midstream. Quentin was surprised to find that it was his own.

Ember paused. He was quite a large animal, easily five feet at the withers. His lips were black, and His wool looked pleasantly soft and cloudlike. Quentin would have liked to bury his face in that wool, to weep in it and then fall asleep in it. Penny craned his neck around and bulged his eyes warningly at Quentin.

"I don't mean to sound overly inquisitive, but if You're, you know, Ember, how come You're down here in this dungeon, and not up there on the surface helping Your people?"

In for a penny. It wasn't that he wanted to make a huge point about it. He just wanted to know why they'd all had to go through so much. He wanted to square it away before they went any further.

"I mean—and this is already coming out more dramatically than I meant it to—You are a god, and things are really falling apart up there. I mean, I think a lot of people are wondering where You've been all this time. That's all. Why would You let Your people suffer like that?"

This would have worked better with a big ballsy shit-eating grin attached to it, but instead it was coming out shivery and a little teary. He was saying "I mean" too much. But he wasn't backing down. Ember made an odd, nonverbal bleating sound. His mouth worked more sideways than a human mouth would. Quentin could see His thick, stiff, pink ram's tongue.

"Show some respect," Penny muttered, but Ember raised one black hoof.

"We should not have to remind you, human child, that We are not your servant." Ember spoke less gently than He had before. "It is not your needs that We serve, but Our own. We do not come and go at your whim.

"It is true, We have been here under the Earth for some time. It is difficult to know how long, this far from the sun and his travels, but some months at least. Evil has come to Fillory, and evil must be fought, and there is no fighting without cost. We have suffered, as you see, an embarrassment to our hindquarters."

He turned His long, golden head half a degree. Quentin now saw that one of the ram's hind legs was in fact lame. Ember held it stiffly, so that the hoof only just brushed the stone. It wouldn't take His weight.

"Well, but I don't understand," Janet spoke up. "Quentin's right. You're the god of this world. Or one of them. Doesn't that make You basically all-powerful?"

"There are Higher Laws that are past your understanding, daughter. The power to create order is one thing. The power to destroy is another. Always they are in balance. But it is easier to destroy than to create, and there are those whose nature it is to love destruction."

"Well, but why would You create something that had the power to hurt You? Or any of Your creatures? Why don't You help us? Do You have any idea how much we hurt? How much we suffer?"

A stern glance. "I know all things, daughter."

"Well, okay, then know this." Janet put her hands on her hips. She had struck an unexpected vein of bitterness in herself, and it was running away with her. "We human beings are unhappy all the time. We hate ourselves and we hate each other and sometimes we wish You or Whoever had never created us or this shit-ass world or any other shit-ass world. Do You realize that? So next time You might think about not doing such a half-assed job."

A ringing silence followed her outburst. The torches guttered against the walls. They'd left streaks of black soot all the way up to the domed ceiling. It was true, what she was saying. It made him angry. But there was something about it that made him nervous too.

"You are incensed, daughter." Ember's eyes were full of kindness.

"I'm not Your daughter." She crossed her arms. "And yeah, no shit I'm incensed."

The great old ram sighed deeply. A tear formed in His great liquid eye, spilled over, and was absorbed into the golden wool on his cheek. In spite of himself, Quentin thought of the proud Indian in the old anti-littering commercials. From behind him Josh leaned into Quentin's shoulder and whispered: *Dude! She made Ember cry!*

"The tide of evil is at the full," the ram was saying, a politician staying relentlessly on message. "But now that you have come, the tide will turn."

But it wouldn't. Suddenly Quentin knew it. It all came to him in one sick flash.

"You're here against Your will," he said. "You're a prisoner down here. Aren't You?"

This wasn't over after all.

"Human, there is so much you do not understand. You are still but a child."

Quentin ignored him. "That's it, isn't it? That's why You're down here? Somebody put You down here, and You can't get out. This wasn't a quest, this was a rescue mission."

Next to him Alice had both her hands over her mouth.

"Where's Umber?" she asked. "Where is Your brother?"

Nobody moved. The ram's long muzzle and black lips were still and unreadable.

"Mmmm." Eliot rubbed his chin, calmly assessing. "It is possible."

"Umber's dead, isn't He?" Alice said dully. "This place isn't a tomb, it's a prison."

"Or a trap," Eliot said.

"Human children, listen to Me," Ember said. "There are Laws that go far beyond anything in your understanding. We—"

"I've heard pretty much enough about my understanding," Janet snapped.

"But who did it?" Eliot stared down at the sand, thinking fast. "Who even has the muscle to do this to Ember? And why? I suppose it was the Watcherwoman, but this is all very odd."

Quentin felt a prickling in his shoulders. He looked around at the dark corners of the cave they were in. It wouldn't be long before whatever had broken Ember's leg turned up, and they would have to fight again. He didn't know if he could take another fight. Penny was still on his knees, but the back of his neck as he looked up at Ember was flushed crimson.

"Maybe it's time to hit the ol' panic button," Josh said. "Back to the Neitherlands."

"I have a better idea," Quentin said.

They had to get control of the situation. They could quit now, but the crown was right there, right in front of them. They were so close. They were almost home, they could win it all if they could just figure out a way to push through to the end of the story. If they could gut it out through one more scene.

And he realized he knew how.

Penny had dropped his pack on the sandy floor. Quentin bent down and rummaged through it. Of course Penny had webbed and bungeed the fucking thing to within an inch of its life, but in among the Power Bars and the Leatherman and the spare tighty whiteys, wrapped in a red bandanna, he found what he was looking for.

The horn was smaller than he remembered it.

"Right? Remember what the nymph said?" He held it up. "'When all hope is lost'? Or something like that?"

"I wouldn't say *all* hope is lost . . ." Josh said.

"Let me see that," Dint said imperiously. He had been conspicuously silent since Ember woke up. Anaïs clung to his arm.

Quentin ignored him. Everybody was talking at once. Penny and the ram were locked in some kind of intense lover's quarrel.

"Interesting," Eliot said. He shrugged. "It might work. I'd rather try that than go back to the City. Who do you think will come?"

"Human child," the ram said loudly. "Human child!"

"Go for it, Q," Janet said. She looked paler than she should have. "It's time. Go for it."

Alice just nodded gravely.

The silver mouthpiece tasted metallic against his lips, like a nickel or a battery. The breath he took was so deep that pain lanced hotly into his arrow-stuck shoulder as his ribs expanded. He wasn't sure exactly what to do—purse his lips like a trumpeter, or just blow into it like a kazoo?—but the ivory horn produced a clear, even, high note as gentle and round as a French horn winded by a seasoned symphony player in a concert hall. Everybody stopped talking and turned to look at him. It wasn't loud, exactly, but it made everything else quiet around it, so that it was instantly the only sound in the room, and everything resonated with its pure, simple strength. It was natural and perfect, a single note that sounded like a grand chord. It went on and on. He blew until his lungs were empty.

The sound echoed and faded away, gone as if it had never been. The cavern was still. For a moment Quentin felt ridiculous, like he'd just blown a noisemaker. What was he expecting, anyway? He really didn't know.

There was a snuffling sound from Ember's pedestal.

"O child," came the ram's deep voice. "Don't you know what you have done?"

"I just got us out of this mess. That's what I've done."

The ram drew Himself up.

"I am sorry you came here," Ember said. "Children of Earth. No one asked you to come. I am sorry that our world is not the paradise you were looking for. But it was not created for your entertainment. Fillory"—the old ram's jowls shook—"is not a theme park, for you and your friends to play dress-up in, with swords and crowns."

He was visibly mastering some powerful emotion. It took Quentin a moment to recognize it. It was fear. The old ram was choking on it.

"That's not why we came here, Ember," Quentin said quietly.

"Is it not?" Ember said, basso profundo. "No, of course it is not." His alien eyes were hard to meet, with their molten yellow whites and black pupils like figure eights on their sides, symbols of infinity. "You came here to save us. You came here to be our King.

"But tell me something, Quentin. How could you hope to save us when you cannot even save yourself?"

Quentin was spared the necessity of answering, because that was when the catastrophe began.

A small man in a neat gray suit appeared in the cave. His face was obscured by a leafy branch that hung in front of it in midair. He looked exactly the way Quentin remembered. The same suit, the same club tie. His face was no less illegible. He held his pink, manicured hands clasped urbanely in front of him. It was as if Quentin had never left the classroom where he first appeared. In a way he supposed he never had. The terror was so absolute, so all-encompassing, that it was almost like calm: not a suspicion but the absolute certainty that they were all about to die.

The Beast spoke.

"I believe that was my cue." His tone was mild, his accent patrician English.

Ember roared. The sound was colossal. It shook the room, and a stalactite fell and shattered. The inside of Ember's mouth was mottled pink and black. At that moment the ram no longer looked quite so ridiculous. There were great humps of muscle under all that fluffy wool, like boulders under moss, and His ribbed horns were thick and stony—they curled all the way around so that the two sharp tips pointed forward. Head down, He surged down off the stone plinth at the man in the gray suit.

The Beast slapped Him aside with a smooth, unhurried backhand motion. The gesture was almost casual. Ember shot sideways like a rocket and hit the rock wall with a sickening, boneless smack. The physics of it looked wrong, as if the ram were as light as a leaf and the Beast as dense as dwarf star matter. Ember dropped motionless to the sandy floor.

He lay where He fell. The Beast flicked woolly fluff off one immaculate gray sleeve with the backs of his fingers.

"It's a funny thing about the old gods," he said. "You think that just because they're old they must be difficult to kill. But when the fighting starts, they go down just like anybody else. They aren't stronger, they're just older."

There was a sandy shuffling from behind Quentin. He risked a glance: Dint had turned on his heel and walked out of the room. The Beast did nothing to stop him. Quentin suspected the rest of them wouldn't get off that easily.

"Yes, he was one of mine," the Beast said. "Farvel was, too, if you want to know the whole truth. The birch tree, you remember him? They mostly are. The rams' time is over. Fillory is my world now."

It wasn't a boast, just a statement of fact. Fucking Dint, Quentin thought. And I pretended to like his stupid vest.

"I knew you'd come for me. It's hardly a surprise. I've been waiting for you for ages. But is this really all of you? It's a bad joke, you know." He gave an incredulous snort. "You've no chance at all."

He sighed.

"I suppose I won't be needing this anymore. I'd almost gotten used to it."

Almost absentmindedly the Beast plucked the branch that hung in front of his face with a thumb and forefinger, as if he were taking off a pair of sunglasses, and tossed it lightly aside.

Quentin cringed—he didn't want to see its real face—but it was too late. And it turned out he had nothing to worry about, because it was an utterly ordinary face. It could have been the face of an insurance adjuster: round, mild, soft-chinned, boyish.

"Nothing? You don't recognize me?"

The Beast strode over to the stone plinth, picked up the crown that still lay there, and placed it on his graying temples.

"My God," Quentin said. "You're Martin Chatwin."

"In the flesh," the Beast announced cheerfully. "And my, how I've grown!"

"I don't understand," Alice said shakily. "How can you be Martin Chatwin?"

"But surely you knew? Isn't that why you're here?" He searched their faces but got no answer. They were frozen in place—not magically this time, just paralyzed the regular way, with fear. He frowned. "Well, I don't suppose it matters. But I would have thought that was the whole point. It's a little insulting, really."

He pouted for show, a sad clown. It was disturbing to see a middle-aged man with the mannerisms of a little English schoolboy. It really was him. He hadn't grown up at all. He even had a curiously miniature, asexual quality, as if he'd stopped growing the moment he'd run away into that forest.

"What happened to you?" Quentin asked.

"What happened?" The Beast spread his arms triumphantly. "Why, I got what I wanted. I went to Fillory, and I never came back!"

It was all becoming clear. Martin Chatwin hadn't been stolen by monsters, he had become one. He had found what Quentin thought he wanted, a way to stay in Fillory, to leave the real world behind forever. But the price had been high.

"I wasn't going to go back to Earth after I'd seen Fillory. I mean, you can't show a man paradise and then snatch it back again. That's what gods do. But I say: down with gods."

"It's amazing what you can accomplish if you put your mind to it. I made some very interesting friends in the Darkling Woods. Very helpful chaps." He spoke genially, expansively, like a toastmaster at a dinner party. "Mind you, the kinds of things you have to do to work that kind of magic—well, your humanity is the first thing to go. You don't stay a man once you've done the things I've done. Once you know the things I know. I hardly miss it now."

"Friends," Quentin said dully. "You mean the Watcherwoman."

"The Watcherwoman!" Martin seemed to find this hilarious. "Oh, my! That is amusing. Sometimes I forget what's in those books. I've been here a *very* long time, you know. I haven't read them in centuries.

"No, not the Watcherwoman. Goodness, the crowd I run with make her look like—well, they make her look like you. Amateurs.

"But enough chit-chat. Who's got the button?"

The button was, of course, in Penny's bag, which lay right at Quentin's feet. I did this, he thought, with a pang that ran all the way through him. This is twice. Twice I've summoned the Beast. I'm a curse on everyone around me.

"Button, button, who's got the button? Who's got it?"

Penny began backing away from the thing in the gray suit, at the same time starting up a spell—another secret weapon, maybe, Quentin didn't recognize it. But Martin moved invisibly fast, like a poisonous fish striking. In a blur he had both of Penny's wrists in the grip of one hand. Penny struggled wildly; he bent at the waist and kicked Martin in the stomach, then braced his legs against his chest and pushed to try to get free, grunting with the effort. The Beast barely seemed to notice.

"I'm afraid not, dear boy," he said.

He opened his mouth wide, too wide, as if his jaw were unhinging like a snake's, and placed both of Penny's hands in his mouth. He bit them off at the wrists.

It wasn't a clean bite. Martin Chatwin had blunt human teeth, not fangs, and it took an extra shake of his calm, middle-aged head to fully crush the wrist bones and detach Penny's hands. Then the Beast dropped him, chewing busily, and Penny fell back on the sand. Arterial blood sprayed crazily from the stumps, then he rolled over and they were underneath him. His legs thrashed like he was being electrocuted. He didn't scream, but frantic snuffling noises came from where his face was pushed into the sandy floor. His sneakers scrabbled in the dirt.

The Beast swallowed once, twice, his Adam's apple bobbing. He grinned, almost embarrassed, holding up one finger while he chewed: give me a moment. His eyes narrowed with pleasure.

"Shit shit shit shit shit . . ." somebody wailed, high and desperate. Anaïs.

"Now," Martin Chatwin said, when he could speak again. "I'd like the button, please."

They stared at him.

"Why," Eliot said numbly. "What are you?"

Martin took out his handkerchief and dabbed Penny's blood from the corner of his mouth.

"Why, I'm what you thought *that* was." He indicated Ember's motion-less body. "I'm a god."

Quentin's chest was so tight that he kept taking tense irregular little breaths, in and out.

"But why do you want it?" he asked.

Talking was good. Talking was better than killing.

"Just tying up loose ends," Martin said. "I would have thought it was obvious. The buttons are the only things I know of that could force me to return to Earth. I've got almost all of them rounded up. Just one more after this. Goodness knows where the bunnies got them. I still haven't figured that out.

"Do you know, when I first ran away, they hunted me like an animal? My own siblings? They wanted to bring me home. Like an animal!" His urbane manner cracked for an instant. "Later Ember and Umber came looking for me, too, to try to deport me, but by then it was much too late for that. Much too late. I was too strong even for them.

"That bloody cunt of a Watcherwoman is still at it, with her damned clock-trees. Mucking about with time. Even now their roots go halfway through this bloody world. She's next after you, she's still got a button. The last one. Once I've got hers I really don't think there'll be any way to get rid of me at all."

Penny rolled over onto his side. He looked up at Quentin, his face strangely ecstatic, though paler than ever and covered in sand. His eyes were closed. He had the stumps of his wrists pressed tight against his chest. His shirt was wringing wet with blood.

"Is it bad, Q?" Penny asked. "I'm not going to look. You tell me. How bad is it?"

"You're all right, man," Quentin muttered.

Martin could not suppress a joyless clubman's chuckle at that. He went on.

"I've been back once or twice, of course, by myself. Once to kill the old bugger, Plover." His smooth brow crinkled, and he looked thoughtful. "He earned that. That and more. I wish I had him to kill again.

"And I nipped through once when your Professor March bungled a spell. Just to keep an eye on things. I thought somebody at Brakebills might be planning something—I get a sort of sense of the future sometimes. It appears that I was right. Though I must have eaten the wrong student."

Martin clapped his hands together and rubbed them in anticipation.

"Well, that's all bygones," he said, perking up. "Let's have it."

"We hid it again," Alice said. "Like your sister Helen. We buried the button. Kill us and you'll never find it."

My brave Alice. Quentin gripped her hand. I brought this on us. His knees were trembling uncontrollably.

"Oh, well played, my girl. Shall I start ripping people's heads off, one by one? I think you'll tell me before it comes to that."

"Wait, why would you kill us at all?" Quentin asked. "Fuck it, we'll just give you the button. Just leave us alone!"

"Oh, I wish I could do that, Quentin. I truly do. But you see, this place changes you." Martin sighed and waggled his extra fingers, his hands like pale spiders. "It's why the rams didn't like humans staying here too long. As it is, I've almost gone too far. I've got quite a taste for human flesh now. Don't you go anywhere, William," he added, nudging Penny's twitching body with the toe of his shoe. "Fauns just don't have the same savor."

William, Quentin thought. That must be Penny's real name. He never knew it before.

"And you know, I can't have you lot running around trying to overthrow me. Treason, that is. Everybody notice that I've crippled your principal spellcaster? You got that?"

"You pathetic fucker." Quentin said evenly. "It wasn't even worth it, was it? That's the funny part. You came here for the same reason we did. And are you happy now? You found out, didn't you? There's no getting away from yourself. Not even in Fillory."

Martin snarled and made an enormous bound forward, covering the thirty feet that separated them in a single leap. At the last second Quentin turned to run, but the monster was already on his back, his teeth in Quentin's shoulder, his arms hugging Quentin's chest. The Beast's jaws were like a huge hungry pliers gripping his collarbone. It bent and cracked sickeningly.

The jaws regripped, getting a better hold on him. Quentin heard himself make an involuntary groan as the air was crushed out of his lungs. He was so afraid of the pain, but when it came down to it it wasn't so much the pain as the pressure, the incredible, unbearable pressure. He couldn't breathe. Quentin thought for an instant he might be able to manage some magic, maybe something grand and strange like he had that first day at Brakebills, in his Examination, but he couldn't speak to cast a spell. He reached back with his hands—maybe he could find Martin's eyes with his thumbs, or rip his ears—but all he could do was pull Martin's thin gray English hair.

Martin's panting breath roared in Quentin's ear like a lover's. He still looked mostly human, but at this range he was pure animal, snuffling and growling and reeking of alien musk. Tears started from Quentin's eyes. It was all ending now, this was the big finale. Eaten alive by a Chatwin, for the sake of a button. It was almost funny. He'd always assumed he'd survive, but everybody assumes that, don't they? He thought it would all be so different. There must have been a better way. What had been his first mistake? There were so many.

But then the pressure was gone, and his ears were ringing. Alice had her pale fingers wrapped in a double fist around Janet's blue-black revolver. Her face was white, but her hands were steady. She fired two more shots, broadside, into Martin's ribs, then he turned to face her and she fired straight into his chest. Pulverized bits of the Beast's suit and tie spun and floated in the air.

Quentin thrashed forward, a primordial fish heaving itself up onto a sandy bank, sucking wind, anything to get away. Now the real pain was coming. His right arm was numb and dragging and not quite as firmly attached to him as he was used to. He tasted blood in his mouth. He heard Alice fire twice more.

When he thought he was far enough away, he risked a look back. His peripheral vision was going gray around the edges. It was closing in in a circle, like the final moments of a Porky Pig cartoon. But he could see Alice and Martin Chatwin facing each other across ten empty paces of sand.

Out of bullets. She tossed the revolver backhand back to Janet.

"All right," she said quietly. "Let's see what else your friends taught you."

Her voice sounded very small in the silent cave, but not afraid. Martin regarded her with bemused curiosity. He cocked his head at an angle.

What was she thinking? Was she really going to try to fight him? Ten long, still seconds ticked by.

When he rushed her, Alice was ready. She was the only one. There was no warning: he went at her from a standing start—first he was still, then he was a blur. Quentin didn't know how she could react so fast, when he could barely track Martin's movements, but before the Beast was even halfway to her she had him up in the air, his legs churning pathetically, gripped in an iron kinetic spell. She slammed him to the ground so hard he bounced.

He was on his feet again almost at once, smoothing out his suit, and he came at her again without even seeming to set himself. This time she stepped to one side like a matador, and he blew past her. Alice was moving like the Beast now—she must have sped up her own reaction time, the way Penny had with the arrow. With a massive effort Quentin pushed himself up till he was half sitting, then something gave in his chest and he collapsed back down again.

"Are you following this?" Alice asked Martin. There was a growing confidence in her voice, as if she were trying bravado on for size and finding that she liked it. "You didn't see it coming, did you? And this is just straight Flemish praxis. Nothing else. I haven't even gotten to any Eastern material yet."

With a crack the Beast snapped off a stalagmite at the base and whipped it sidearm at Alice, but the stone spear burst in midair before it reached her. Fragments whined away in all directions. Quentin wasn't tracking it all, but he didn't think she'd done that. The others must be backing her up, a phalanx with Alice at the head.

Though Alice was way ahead of them. Maybe poor Penny could have followed what she was doing, but Alice was in a place Quentin hadn't known she could go. He was a magician, but she was something else, a true adept. He had no idea she was so far beyond him. There was a time when he might have felt envious of her, but now he felt only pride. That was his Alice. Sand rushed hissing from the floor in a shroud, like a swarm of enraged bees, and wrapped itself around Martin's head, trying to penetrate his mouth and nose and ears. He twisted and flailed his arms frantically.

"Oh, Martin." A smile played at the corners of her mouth. It was almost wicked. "That's the trouble with monsters. No theoretical rigor. No one ever made you iron out your fundamentals, did they? If they had, you certainly wouldn't fall for this . . ."

In his blinded state Martin walked straight into a fireball *à la* Penny that burst over him. But Alice didn't wait. She couldn't afford to. Her lips never stopped moving, and her hands never stopped their fluid, unhurried motions, one spell rolling right over into the next. It was high-stakes blitz chess. The fireball was followed by a glimmering spherical prison, then by a toxic hail of Magic Missiles—she must have taken apart that spell and supercharged it so that it yielded a whole flock of them. The sand she'd whipped up from the floor gathered and fused into a faceless glass golem, which landed two jabs and a roundhouse punch before Martin shattered it with a counterpunch. But he seemed disoriented. His round English face was an ominous flustered red. A colossal, crushing weight seemed to settle on his shoulders, some kind of invisible yoke that took him down to one knee.

Anaïs projected an ocher lightning strike at Martin that left behind a bloodshot afterimage on Quentin's retinas, and Eliot and Josh and Janet had joined hands and were sending a hail of rocks that beat on his back. The room was full of a babel of incantations, but Martin didn't seem to notice. Alice was the only one he saw.

From a half crouch he lunged at her across the sand, and some kind of phantasmal armor materialized around her, like nothing Quentin had ever seen before, silvery and translucent—it flickered in and out of visibility. The Beast's fingers slid off it. The armor came with a shimmery pole arm that Alice spun in one hand, then set and thrust at Martin's stomach. Sparks flew between them.

"Fergus's Spectral Armory!" she shouted. She was breathing hard. His eyes were red and fixed on her grimly. "Like it? Do you? Very basic principles. Second Year stuff! But then you never bothered with school, did you, Martin? You wouldn't have lasted an hour at Brakebills!"

Seeing her fight alone like this was intolerable. Quentin lifted his cheek from the sandy floor and tried to speak a spell, anything, even to create a distraction, but his lips wouldn't shape words. His fingers were going numb. He beat his hands against the ground in frustration. He had never loved Alice more. He felt like he was sending her his strength, even though he knew she couldn't feel it.

Alice and Martin sparred savagely for a solid minute. The armor spell must have come with a bonus of martial arts savvy, because Alice whipped her faerie glaive around in a complicated pattern, two-handed now; it had a small, vicious spike on its butt end that drew blood. Sweat matted her hair to her forehead, but she never lost focus. After another minute the armor vanished—the spell must have expired—and she did something that froze the air around the Beast into an intricate frostwork mummy. Even his clothes froze and fell to pieces in shards, leaving him naked and fish-belly white.

But by then he was close enough to seize her arm. Suddenly she was a girl again, small and vulnerable.

But not for long. She spat out a ferocious sequence of syllables and transformed into a tawny lioness with a white scruff of beard under her chin. She and Martin went down grappling, mouths gaping, trying to get their teeth into each other. Alice worked with her huge back legs to scratch and disembowel, caterwauling angrily.

Janet was circling the fight, trying to cram bullets into the revolver and dropping them freely on the sand, but there was nowhere to aim anyway. They were all tangled up together. The next moment the Beast was in the coils of a massive spotted anaconda, then Alice was an eagle, then a huge brindled bear, then a horrific man-size scorpion with pincing legs and its venomous sting, the size of a crane hook, lodged in Martin Chatwin's back. Light flashed and crackled around them as they fought, and their struggling bodies rose from the ground. The Beast was on top of her, and Alice expanded hugely to become a limber, sinuous white dragon on its back, her enormous wings slapping the sand and sending everybody scrambling. The Beast grew with her, so that she was wrestling a giant. She gripped him in her talons and screamed a torrent of blue fire like jet exhaust straight into his face.

For a minute he writhed in Alice's grip. His eyebrows were gone, and his face was comically blackened. Quentin could hear the Alice-dragon panting raggedly. The Beast shuddered and was still for a moment. Then he appeared to compose himself, and he punched Alice once, hard, in the face.

Instantly she was human again. Her nose was bleeding. Martin rolled neatly to one side and got to his feet. Naked though he was, he produced a clean handkerchief from somewhere and used it to dab some of the soot from his face.

"Dammit," Quentin rasped. "Somebody do something! Help her!"

Janet got one last bullet in and fired, then she threw the pistol overhand. It bounced off the back of Martin Chatwin's head without mussing his hair.

"Fuck you!" she shouted.

Martin took a step toward Alice. No. This had to end.

"Hey, asshole!" Quentin managed. "You forgot one thing."

He spat blood and switched to his best *Cubano* accent, his voice cracking hysterically: *"Say hello to my leel friend!"*

Quentin whispered the catchword Fogg had given him the night of graduation. He'd imagined it in his head a hundred times, and now as he pronounced the final syllable something big and hard was struggling and thrashing under his shirt, scrabbling at the skin of his back.

Looking up at it, Quentin noticed that his cacodemon was wearing a little pair of round spectacles hooked over its pointy ears. What the fuck, his cacodemon had glasses? It stood over him, uncertain, looking learned and thoughtful. It didn't know whom to fight.

"The naked guy," Quentin said in a hoarse whisper. "Go! Save the girl!"

The demon skidded to a stop ten feet from its prey. It feinted left, then left again, like it was playing one-on-one with Martin, trying to break his ankles, before it gathered itself and sprang directly for his face. Wearily, as if to express to them the unfairness of the trouble they were putting him through, Martin put up a hand to catch it in flight. The demon tore at his fingers, hissing. Martin began slowly stuffing it into his mouth, like a gecko eating a spider, while it pulled his hair and gouged at his eyes.

Quentin waved at Alice frantically to run—maybe if they all split up?—but she wasn't looking at him. She licked her lips and tucked her hair behind her ears with both hands. She got to her feet.

Something had changed in her face. She had made a decision. She began to work with her hands, the preliminaries to something very advanced. At the sound both Martin and the cacodemon looked at her. Martin took the opportunity to break the demon's neck and push the rest of its body into his mouth.

"So," she said. "So you think you're the biggest monster in this room?"

"Don't," Janet said, but Alice didn't stop. She was trying something. Everybody seemed to get it except Quentin.

"No, no, no!" Eliot said angrily. "Wait!"

"You're not even a magician at all, are you, Martin?" Alice said quietly. "You're just a little boy. That's all you are. That's all you ever were." She bit back a sob. "Well, I'm sorry."

She closed her eyes and began to recite. Quentin could see it all in Alice's face, everything they'd been through, everything they'd done to each other, everything they'd gotten past. She was letting it all come out. It was a big spell, Renaissance, very academic magic. Big energies. He couldn't imagine what good it would do, but a moment later he realized the spell wasn't the point. The side effects were the point.

He began scratching his way toward her, anything he could do to get closer. He didn't care if it killed him.

"No!" he shouted. "No!"

The blue fire began in her fingertips and spread, inexorably, through her hands and up her wrists. It lit up her face. Alice opened her eyes again. She regarded it with fascination.

"I'm on fire," she said, almost in her normal voice. "I didn't think—I'm burning." And then in a rising shriek that could have been agony or could have been ecstasy: "I'm burning! Oh, God! Oh, Quentin, I'm burning! It's burning me!"

Martin halted his slow advance to observe as Alice became a *niffin*. Quentin couldn't see his expression. Alice took a step backward and sat down, still staring at her arms. They were now blue fire up to the shoulders. They were like two highway flares; her flesh was not consumed but, strangely, replaced by the fire that was chewing through it. She stopped speaking, just moaned on an ever-higher, ever-louder note. Finally as the blue fire rose up her neck she threw back her head and opened her mouth wide, but no more sound came out.

The fire left behind it a new Alice, one that was smaller and made of something like blue glowing glass, fresh and hot from the furnace. The process flooded the cavern with blue light. Even before the transformation was complete Alice had left the ground. She was pure fire now, her face full of that special madness belonging to things that are neither living nor dead. She floated above the floor as easily as if she were floating in a swimming pool.

The spirit that had replaced Alice, the *niffin*, regarded them neutrally with furious, insane, empty sapphire eyes. For all her power she looked delicate, like she was blown from Murano glass. From where he lay Quentin watched with detached, academic interest through a red haze of agony. The capacity for terror or love or grief or anything but pain had gone along with his peripheral vision.

She was not Alice. She was a righteous destroying angel. She was blue and nude and wore an expression of irrepressible hilarity.

Quentin had stopped breathing. For a moment Alice hovered before the Beast, incandescent with anticipation. At the last instant he appeared to sense that the odds had shifted and began a step backward, then he bolted in a blur. But even then he was too slow. The angel had him by his gray, conservatively cut hair. Bracing her other hand on his shoulder, she tore Martin Chatwin's head off his neck with a crisp, dry ripping sound.

All of this action had become too exhausting for Quentin to watch. He clung to it like a faltering radio signal, but it was so hard to maintain clear reception. He rolled languorously over onto his back.

His mind had become a loopy parody of itself, stretched thin as taffy, translucent as cellophane. Something unspeakable had happened, but he couldn't keep hold of it. Somehow the world as he knew it was no longer there. He'd managed to find a reasonably soft, sandy patch of floor to recline on—it was thoughtful of Martin, really, to have brought them to a room where the sand was so deliciously fine and cool. Although it was a shame that this clean white sand was now almost entirely saturated with blood, his and Penny's. He wondered if Penny was still alive. He wondered if it would be at all possible to pass out. He wanted to fall asleep and never wake up.

Quentin heard the scuff of a fine leather shoe, and Eliot loomed into the patch of ceiling directly above him, then passed by.

From somewhere ambiguous in space and time, Ember's voice reached Quentin. Not dead yet, he thought. Tough bastard. Or maybe he was just imagining it.

"You have won," the ram's voice bleated from the shadows. "Take your prize, hero."

Eliot picked up the golden crown of the High King of Fillory. With an inarticulate cry he threw it like a discus off into the darkness.

The last dream was broken. Quentin either fainted or died, he didn't know which.

BOOK IV

THE RETREAT

Quentin woke up in a beautiful white room. For a second—or was it an hour? a week?—he thought it was his room in Brakebills South, that he was back in Antarctica. But then he saw that the window was open and heavy green curtains were puffing in, and out, and in again with the coming and going of a warm summer wind. So definitely not Antarctica.

He lay looking up at the ceiling, letting himself drift and spin along on spacey, narcotic mental currents. He didn't feel even remotely curious about where he was or how he'd gotten there. He blissed out on insignificant details: the sunlight, the smell of clean linens, a splinter of blue sky in the window, the gnarly whorls of the dark chocolate brown timbers that crossed the whitewashed ceiling. He was alive.

And those nice, surprisingly Pottery Barn-y curtains, the color of the stems of plants. They were coarse-woven, but it wasn't the familiar, depressing fake-authentic coarseness of high-end Earth housewares, which merely imitated the real coarseness of fabrics that were woven by hand out of genuine necessity. As he lay there Quentin's uppermost thought was that these were *authentically coarse-woven curtains,* woven by people who didn't know any other way of making curtains, who didn't even know that their way was special, and whose way was therefore not discounted and emptied of meaning in advance. This made him very happy. It was as if he'd been looking for these curtains forever, as if he'd been waiting his whole life to wake up one morning in a room in which those coarse-woven, stem-green curtains hung over the windows.

From time to time a horsy clippety-clopping could be heard from the hall outside. This mystery solved itself when a woman with the body of a horse stepped partway into the room. The effect was surprisingly unsurprising. She was a sturdy, sun-kissed woman with short brown hair who just happened to be attached to the chassis of a sleek black mare.

"You are conscious?" she asked.

Quentin cleared his throat. He couldn't get it all the way clear. It was horribly dry, too dry to speak, so he just nodded.

"Your recovery is nearly complete," the centauress said, with the air of a busy senior resident doing rounds who didn't have time to waste rejoicing over medical miracles. She began the slow process of reversing herself, daintily, purposefully, back out into the hall.

"You have been asleep for six months and two days," she added before she disappeared.

Quentin listened to her clippety-clop away. It was quiet again. He did his best to hang on to the blissful feeling. But it didn't last.

The six months of his recovery were practically a blank—just a quickly evaporating impression of blue depths and complex, enchanted dreams. But Quentin's memories of what happened in Ember's Tomb were very clear. He might reasonably have expected that day (or had it been night?) to fall in a blackout period, or at least be veiled in merciful post-traumatic haziness. But no, not at all. He could remember it with perfect fidelity, deep focus, full force, from any angle, right up until the moment he lost consciousness.

The shock of it snapped his chest flat. It emptied out his lungs the way the Beast's jaws had, not just once but over and over again. He was helpless against it. He lay in his bed and sobbed until he choked. His weak body spasmed. He made noises he'd never heard a human being make. He ground his face into his flat, prickly straw pillow until it was wet with tears and snot. She had died for him, for all of them, and she was never coming back.

He couldn't think about what happened, he could only play it back again and again, as if there were a chance it could come out differently, or even just hurt a little less, but every time he played it back he wanted to die. His half-healed body ached all over, as if it were bruised right down to his skeleton, but he wanted it to hurt even more. He didn't know how to operate in a world that would allow this to happen. It was a shit world, a fraud and a con, and he wanted nothing more to do with it. Whenever he slept, he woke up trying to warn somebody of something, but he never knew what, or who, and it was always too late.

With the sorrow came anger. What had they been thinking? A bunch of kids walking into a civil war in an alien world? Alice was dead (and Fen, and probably Penny, too) and the worst part was that he could have saved them all, and he hadn't. He was the one who told them it was time to go to Fillory. He'd blown the horn that summoned the Beast. Alice had come because of him, to take care of him. But he hadn't taken care of her.

The centaurs watched him weep with alien unconcern, like fish.

He learned over the next few days that he was in a monastery, or something like it, or that was as much as he could gather from the centaurs who ran the place. It wasn't a place of worship, they explained, with a note of whinnying condescension, but a community devoted to the most absolute possible expression, or incarnation—or perhaps realization was an even better word—of the incomprehensibly complex but infinitely pure sylvan values of centaurhood, which Quentin's fallen human brain could never hope to grasp. There was something distinctly German about the centaurs.

It came out, not very tactfully, that they considered humans to be inferior beings. It wasn't the humans' fault. They were simply cripples, severed by an unhappy accident of birth from their rightful horse halves. The centaurs regarded Quentin with pity nicely tempered by a near-total lack of interest. Also, they seemed to be constantly afraid that he was going to tip over.

None of them had any exact memory of how Quentin had gotten here. They didn't pay close attention to the backstory of the occasional damaged human who fetched up in their midst. When pressed, Quentin's doctor, a terrifyingly earnest individual whose name was Alder Acorn Agnes Allison-fragrant-timber, said she vaguely remembered some humans, unusually filthy and bedraggled specimens, now that you mention it, bringing Quentin in on a makeshift litter. He'd been unconscious and deep in shock, with his rib cage crushed and one of his forelimbs badly dislocated, practically detached. Such anatomical disorder was distasteful to the centaurs. And they were not insensible of the service the humans had rendered to Fillory in ridding it of Martin Chatwin. They did their best to render assistance.

The humans lingered in the area for a month, maybe two, while the centaurs wove deep webs of wood-magic around Quentin's torn, bruised, insulted body. But they thought it unlikely that he would ever wake up. And in time, as Quentin showed no signs of recovering consciousness, the humans reluctantly departed.

He supposed he could have been angry that they had left him there, in Fillory, with no way of returning to his own world. But all he felt was warm, cowardly relief. He didn't have to face them. The sight of their faces would have burned the skin right off him with shame. He wished he had died, and if he couldn't have death, at least he had this, the next best thing: total isolation, lost forever in Fillory. He was broken in a way that magic could never fix.

His body was still weak, and he spent a lot of time in bed, resting his atrophied muscles. He was an empty shell, roughly hollowed out by some crude tool, gutted and left there, a limp, raw, boneless skin. If he tried, he could summon up old sense-memories. Nothing from Fillory or Brakebills, just the really old stuff, the easy stuff, the safe stuff. The smell of his mother's oil paints; the lurid green of the Gowanus Canal; the curious way Julia pursed her lips around the reed of her oboe; the hurricane that blew through when they took that family vacation in Maine, he must have been about eight, when they went out on the lawn and threw their sweaters in the air and watched them sail away over the neighbor's fence and then fell down laughing. A beautiful blossoming white cherry tree stood outside his window in the warm afternoon sunlight. Every part of it moved and swayed in a slightly different rhythm from every other part. He watched it for a long time.

If he was feeling daring, he thought about the time he'd spent as a goose flying south, wingtip to wingtip with Alice, buoyed up by pillowy masses of empty air, gazing coolly down at looping, squiggly, switchbacked rivers. If he did it now, he thought, he would remember to look out for the Nazca Lines in Peru. He wondered if he could go back to Professor Van der Weghe and have her change him back, and he would just stay that way, live and die as a stupid goose and forget that he'd ever even been a human. Sometimes he thought of a day he'd spent with Alice on the roof of the Cottage. They had a joke that they were going to play on the others when they got back from somewhere, but the others never came home, and he and Alice had just lain up there on the warm shingles all afternoon, looking at the sky and talking about nothing.

A few days of this went a long way. His body was healing fast and getting restless, and his brain was waking up and needed new diversions to distract it. It wouldn't leave him alone for long.

Onward and upward. He couldn't stop himself from getting better. Soon Quentin was out and about and exploring the grounds, a walking skeleton. Severed from his past, and from everything and everyone he knew, he felt as insubstantial and semi-existent as a ghost. The monastery—the centaur name for it was the Retreat—was all stone colonnades and towering trees and wide, well-maintained paths. Despite himself, he was ravenously hungry, and although the centaurs were strict vegetarians they turned out to be wizards with salad. At mealtimes they set out huge heaping wooden troughs full of spinach and lettuce and arugula and sharp dandelion greens, all delicately oiled and spiced. He discovered the centaur baths, six rectangular stone pools of varying temperatures, each one large enough that he could do three long, deep breaststrokes from one edge to the other. They reminded him of the Roman baths in Alice's parents' house. And they were deep, too: if he dove in and kicked downward with enough vigor, until the light dimmed and his hindbrain complained and the water pressure forced its fingers into his ears, he could still just barely brush the rough stone bottom with his fingers.

His mind was an icy pond constantly in danger of thawing. He trod on it only lightly—its surface was perilously slick and who knew how thin. To break through would mean immersion in what was below: cold, dark anaerobic water and angry, toothy fish. The fish were memories. He wanted to put them away somewhere and forget where he'd put them, but he couldn't. The ice gave way at the oddest moments: when a fluffy talking chipmunk looked up at him quizzically, when a centaur nurse was inadvertently kind to him, when he caught a glimpse of his face in a mirror. Something hideous and saurian would rise up and his eyes would flood and he would wrench himself away.

The grief he felt for Alice kept unfolding new dimensions he hadn't known were there. He felt like he'd only seen and loved her, really loved her, all of her, for those last few hours. Now she was gone, broken like the glass animal she'd made that first day they'd met, and the rest of his life lay in front of him like a barren, meaningless postscript.

For the first few weeks after his resurrection Quentin still felt deep aches in his chest and shoulder, but they faded as more weeks piled on top of those first few. He was at first shocked and subsequently kind of fascinated to discover that the centaurs had replaced the skin and muscle tissue he'd lost to the Beast with something that looked very much like dark fine-grained wood. Two-thirds of his collarbone, and most of his right shoulder and biceps, now appeared to be composed of a smooth, highly polished fruit-wood—cherry maybe, or possibly apple. The new tissue was completely numb—he could rap on it with his knuckles and not feel a thing—but it was perfectly able to flex and bend when and where he needed it to, and it merged gracefully with the flesh around it, without a seam. He liked it. Quentin's right knee was wooden now, too. He couldn't actually remember having injured that particular part of him, but whatever, maybe something untoward had happened to it on the way back.

And there was another change: his hair had gone completely white, even his eyebrows, like the man in Poe's "Descent into the Maelstrom." He looked like he was wearing an Andy Warhol wig.

He would do anything to keep from sitting still. He practiced with a bow and arrow on a wide, disused, weed-grown archery range. When he could get his attention, he had one of the younger centaurs teach him the rudiments of riding and fencing with a saber, in the name of physical therapy. Sometimes he pretended his sparring partner was Martin Chatwin, sometimes he didn't; either way, he never once landed a hit. A small contingent of talking animals had discovered Quentin's presence at the Retreat, a badger and some oversize talking rabbits. Excited by the sight and smell of a human, and from Earth at that, they had gotten it into their heads that he was the next High King of Fillory, and when he angrily insisted that he wasn't, and that he'd lost all interest in that particular ambition, they dubbed him the Reluctant King and left tributes of nuts and cabbages outside his windows, and constructed pathetic handmade (or pawmade) crowns for him woven out of twigs and adorned with worthless quartz pebbles. He tore them apart.

A small herd of tame horses roamed the wide lawns of the Retreat at will. At first Quentin thought they were just pets, but the arrangement turned out to be slightly more complex than that. Centaurs of both sexes frequently copulated with the horses, publicly and loudly.

Quentin had found his few meager possessions stacked in little piles along one wall of his room. He stowed them in a dresser; they took up exactly half of one of its five drawers. His room also held a battered old Florida-style writing desk, painted white and pale green, and one day Quentin went rummaging through its warped, poorly fitted drawers to see what previous inmates might have left behind. It had occurred to him to attempt some written magic, a basic scrying technique, to try to learn something about what had happened to the others. It almost certainly wouldn't work between planes, but you never knew. Along with an assortment of odd buttons and dried-out chestnuts and exotic Fillorian insect corpses he found two envelopes. Also in the desk was a dry, tough, leafy branch.

The envelopes were thick and made of the coarse bleached-white paper the centaurs made. On the first his name was written in an elegant calligraphic handwriting that Quentin recognized as Eliot's. His vision swam; he had to sit down.

Inside it was a note. It was rolled around the flattened, dehydrated remains of what was once a single Merit Ultra Light cigarette, and it read as follows:

DEAR Q,

HELL OF A THING GETTING YOU OUT OF THAT DUNGEON. RICHARD SHOWED UP, FINALLY, FOR WHICH I SUPPOSE WE SHOULD BE GRATEFUL, THOUGH G-D KNOWS HE DOESN'T MAKE IT EASY.

WE WANTED TO STAY, Q, BUT IT WAS HARD, AND GETTING HARDER EVERY DAY. THE CENTAURS SAID IT WASN'T WORKING. BUT IF YOU'RE READING THIS THEN YOU WOKE UP AFTER ALL. I'M SORRY ABOUT EVERYTHING. I KNOW YOU ARE TOO. I KNOW I SAID I DIDN'T NEED A FAMILY TO BECOME WHO I WAS SUPPOSED TO BE, BUT IT TURNED OUT THAT I DID. AND IT WAS YOU.

WE'LL MEET AGAIN.

—E

The other envelope contained a notebook. It was thick and old-looking and squashed around the corners. Quentin recognized it instantly, even though he hadn't seen it since a chilly November afternoon six years ago.

With a cold, clear mind he sat down on his bed and opened *The Magicians.*

The book was disappointingly short, maybe fifty handwritten pages, some of them smudged and water-damaged, and it was not written in Christopher Plover's usual plain, simple, open-hearted prose. It was cruder, funnier, more arch, and it showed signs of having been scribbled in haste, with a generous assortment of misspellings and missing words. This was because it wasn't written by Christopher Plover at all. It was—the author explained in the first paragraph—the first book of *Fillory and Further* by somebody who had actually been there. That person was Jane Chatwin.

The story of *The Magicians* picked up immediately after the end of *The Wandering Dune,* after Jane, the youngest, and her sister Helen ("that dear, self-righteous busybody") quarreled over Helen's hiding of the magic buttons that could take them to Fillory. Having failed to unearth them herself, Jane was forced to wait, but no further invitations to Fillory arrived. She and her siblings seemed fated to live out the rest of their lives on Earth as ordinary children. She supposed it was all right—after all, most children never got to go to Fillory at all—but it hardly seemed fair. The others had all gone to Fillory at least twice, and she'd only gotten to go once.

And there was the matter of Martin: he was still missing after all this time. Their parents had long since given up hope, but the children hadn't. At night Jane and the other little Chatwins crept into each other's bedrooms and whispered about him, wondering what adventures he was getting up to in Fillory, and when he would finally come home to them, as they knew he one day would.

Years passed. Jane was thirteen, no longer a girl, as old as Martin was when he'd disappeared, when the call finally came. She was visited by a cooperative and industrious hedgehog named Prickleplump, who helped her recover an old cigar box containing the buttons from the old dry well down which Helen had dropped it. She could have enlisted one of the others to come with her, but instead Jane returned to Fillory alone, by way of the City, the only Chatwin ever to enter the other world without a sibling to keep her company.

She found Fillory beset by a powerful wind. It blew and blew and never stopped blowing. At first it was amusing, and everybody flew kites, and a craze for flowy clothing that billowed out on the breeze swept through the royal court at Whitespire. But over time the wind became relentless. The birds were exhausted from struggling with it, and everybody's hair was getting tangled. The leaves were being stripped from the forest, and the trees were complaining. Even when you went inside and closed the door you could still hear it groaning, and feel it blowing on your face for hours afterward. Castle Whitespire's wind-powered clockwork heart threatened to spin out of control, and had to be decoupled from its windmills and halted for the first time in living memory.

A group of eagles and griffins and pegasi allowed themselves to be borne away on the wind, convinced that it would blow them away to a fantastical land, one even more magical than Fillory. They returned a week later coming from the other direction, hungry and disheveled and windburned. They refused to discuss what they had seen.

Jane belted on a rapier, put her hair up in a tight bun, and set off into the Darkling Woods alone, resolute, bent forward against the gale, heading upwind in search of its source. Soon she came across Ember, alone in a clearing. He was injured and distraught. He told her of Martin's transformation, and his efforts to expel the child, which had ended with the death of Umber. They held a council of war.

With a bellowing bleat Ember summoned the Cozy Horse, and together they mounted its broad velvet back and set off to see the dwarves. Swing players at the best of times, the dwarves could never be relied upon to cooperate with anybody, but even they were convinced that Martin was dangerous, and besides, all that wind was blowing the topsoil off their beloved underground warrens. They fashioned for Jane a silver pocket watch, a work of consummate horological mastery, so dense with tiny gears and cams and glorious spiral springs that its interior was a solid teeming mass of gleaming clockwork. With it, the dwarves explained, Jane could control the flow of time itself— turn it forward, turn it back, speed it up, slow it down—as she liked.

Jane and Ember left with the pocket watch, shaking their heads. Honestly, there was never any telling what the dwarves were capable of. If they could build a time machine, you wondered why they didn't run the whole kingdom. Except, she supposed, that they couldn't be bothered.

Quentin turned the last page. The book ended there. It was signed on the bottom of the last page by Jane herself.

"Well, that was anticlimactic," Quentin said out loud.

"The truth doesn't always make a good story, does it? But I think I tied up most of the loose threads. I'm sure you can fill in the rest, if you really think about it."

Quentin practically jumped out of what was left of his skin. Sitting on top of his desk on the other side of the room, very still, long legs crossed, was a small, pretty woman with dark hair and pale skin.

"At least I try to make a good entrance."

She had gone native: she wore a light brown cloak over a practical gray traveling dress that was slit up the sides far enough to show some leg. But it was unmistakably her. The paramedic, and the woman who'd visited him in the infirmary. And yet that wasn't who she was at all.

"You're Jane Chatwin, aren't you?"

She smiled brightly and nodded.

"I autographed it." She pointed to the manuscript. "Imagine what it would be worth. Sometimes I think about turning up at a Fillory convention just to see what would happen."

"They'd probably think you were a cosplayer," Quentin said, "and getting a little old for it."

He set aside the manuscript on the bed. He had been very young when he met her for the first time, but he wasn't young anymore. As her brother Martin would have said: My, how he'd grown. Her smile was not as irresistible as it used to be.

"You were the Watcherwoman, too, weren't you?"

"Was and am." Still sitting, she sketched a curtsy. "I suppose I could retire now that Martin is gone. Though really, I've only just started to enjoy myself."

He expected himself to smile back at her, but the smile did not materialize. He didn't feel like smiling. Quentin couldn't have said exactly what he was feeling.

Jane remained very still, studying him as she had that first day they met. Her presence was so laden with magic and meaning and history that she almost glowed. To think she had spoken to Plover himself, and told him the stories Quentin had grown up on. The circularity of it all was dizzying. The sun was setting, and the light stained Quentin's white bedspread a dusky orange-pink. The edges of everything were softening in the twilight.

"This doesn't make any sense," he said. He had never felt less tempted by a pretty woman's charms. "If you were the Watcherwoman, why did you do all those things? Stop time and all that?"

She smiled wryly.

"This item"—she produced a silver pocket watch as thick and round as a pomegranate from somewhere in her cloak—"did not come with an instruction manual. It took a bit of experimenting before I got the hang of it, and some of those experiments weren't so successful. There was one long afternoon in particular . . ." She grimaced. Her accent was the twin of Martin's. "People took it the wrong way. And anyhow, Plover embroidered all that stuff. What an imagination that man had."

She shook her head, as if Plover's flights of fancy were the most incredible part of all this.

"And you know, I was only thirteen when I started out. I had no training in magic at all. I had to figure everything out on my own. I suppose I'm a bit of a hedge witch that way."

"So all those things the Watcherwoman did—"

"A lot of it did actually happen. But I was careful. The Watcherwoman never killed anyone. I cut corners, sometimes at other people's expense, but I had other things on my mind. My job was to stop Martin, and I did what I had to. Even those clock-trees." She snorted ruefully. "Brilliant idea those were. They never did a bloody thing. The funniest part is that Martin was terrified of them! He couldn't figure them out."

For a moment her face lost its composure, just for a moment. Her eyes welled with tears, and she blinked rapidly.

"I keep telling myself that we lost him that first night, when he walked away into the forest. It was never him after that, not really. He died a long time ago. But I'm the only Chatwin left now. He was a monster, but he was the last family I had."

"And we killed him," Quentin said coldly. His heart was palpitating. The feeling he'd had trouble identifying earlier was clarifying itself: it was rage. This woman had used him, used them all like toys. And if some of the toys got broken, oh well. That had been the real point of the whole story all along. She had manipulated him, sent him and the others into Fillory to find Martin. She had made sure he got there. For all he knew she'd planted the button for Lovelady to find in the first place. It didn't matter now. It was over, and Alice was dead.

He stood up. A cool, grassy evening breeze stirred the green curtains.

"Yes," Jane Chatwin said carefully. "You killed him. We won."

"We won?" He was incredulous. He couldn't hold back anymore. All the grief and guilt he'd been salting away so carefully was coming back to him as anger. The ice was cracking. The pond was boiling. "We won? You have a damn time machine in your pocket, and that's the best you could do? You set us up, Jane, or whoever the fuck you are. We thought we were going on an adventure, and you sent us on a suicide mission, and now my friends are dead. Alice is dead." Here he had to swallow hard before he could go on. "Is that really the best you could do?"

She dropped her eyes to the floor. "I am sorry."

"You're sorry." The woman was unbelievable. "Good. Show me how sorry you are. Take me back. Use the watch, we'll go back in time. We'll do it all again. Let's go back and fix this."

"No, Quentin," she said gravely. "We can't go back."

"What do you mean, no? We can go back. We can and we will!"

He was talking at her louder and louder, staring at her, as if by talking and staring he could force her into doing what he needed her to do. She had to! And if talking wouldn't do it, he could make her. She was a small woman, and apart from that watch he was willing to bet that he was twice the magician she'd ever be.

She was shaking her head sadly.

"You have to understand." She didn't back away. She spoke softly, as if she could soothe him, placate him into forgetting what she'd done. "I'm a witch, I'm not a god. I've tried this so many ways. I've gone down so many different timelines. I've sent so many other people to fight Martin. Don't make me lecture you on the practicalities of chronological manipulation, Quentin. Change one variable and you change them all. Did you think you were the first one to face Martin in that room? Do you think that was even the first time *you* faced him? That battle has been fought again and again. I've tried it so many different ways. Everyone always died. And I always wound back the clock.

"As bad as it was, as bad as it is, this is by far the best outcome I've ever achieved. No one ever stopped him but you and your friends, Quentin. You were the only ones. And I'm sticking with it. I can't risk losing everything we've gained."

Quentin folded his arms. Muscles were jumping in his back. He was practically vibrating with fury. "Well, then. We'll go back all the way. To before *The World in the Walls*. Stop him before it all starts. Find a timeline where he doesn't even go to Fillory."

"I've tried, Quentin! I've tried!" She was pleading with him. "He always does! I've tried it a thousand times. There is no world where he doesn't.

"I'm tired. I know you lost Alice. I lost my brother. I'm tired of fighting that thing that used to be Martin."

Suddenly she did look very tired, and her eyes lost their focus, as if she were seeing into some other world, one she would never get to. It made it hard for him keep up his high-pressure rage. It kept bleeding away even as he stoked it.

This wasn't over. He lunged, but she saw it coming. He was quick, but she was quicker. Maybe they'd played this scene already, in another timeline, or maybe he was just that obvious. Before he was halfway across the room she spun on her heel and threw the silver watch as hard as she could at the wall.

It was hard enough. The wall was stone, and the watch squashed like an overripe fruit. It made a sound like a bag of nickels. The delicate crystal face shattered, and tiny gears and wheels skittered away across the floor like pearls from a broken necklace.

Jane turned back to him defiantly, breathing hard. He stared down at the corpse of the broken timepiece.

"No more," she said. "Put an end to it. It's time to live with what we have and mourn what we lost. I wish I could have told you more before it was too late, but I needed you too much to tell you the truth."

In a curious gesture she placed her hands on his cheeks, drew his face down to hers, and kissed him on the forehead. The room was almost dark now. The door creaked in the quiet spring evening as she opened it.

"Try not to judge Martin too harshly," she said from the doorway. "Plover used to diddle him whenever he could get him alone. I think that's why he went to Fillory in the first place. Why else would he try to crawl into a grandfather clock? He was looking for somewhere to hide."

With that she was gone.

Quentin didn't go after her, just stared at the doorway for a long minute. When he walked over to the door to close it, pieces of the broken watch scrunched under his feet.

It just went down and down. Had he finally gotten to the bottom of it? In the last of the dying light he looked down at the notebook on the hard centaur bed. There was a note tucked into the pages, the same one the wind had snatched away from him the first time he tried to read it. But all it said was:

SURPRISE!

He sat back down. In the end he and Alice had just been bit players, extras who had the bad luck to wander into a battle scene. A brother and sister at war with each other in their nightmare nursery fantasyland. No one cared that Alice was dead, and no one cared that he wasn't.

Now he had answers, but they weren't doing what answers were supposed to do: they weren't making things simpler or easier. They weren't helping. Sitting there on his bed, he thought about Alice. And poor, stupid Penny, and miserable Eliot. And that poor bastard Martin Chatwin. He got it now, of course, finally. He'd been going about this all wrong. He should never have come here at all. He should never have fallen in love with Alice. He should never even have come to Brakebills. He should have stayed in Brooklyn, in the real world. He should have nursed his depression and his grudge against the world from the relative safety of mundane reality. He never would have met Alice, but at least she would be alive, somewhere. He could have eked out his sad wasted life with movies and books and masturbation and alcohol like everybody else. He would never have known the horror of really getting what he thought he wanted. He could have spared himself and everybody else the cost of it. If there was a moral to the story of Martin Chatwin, that was it in a nutshell. Sure, you can live out your dreams, but it'll only turn you into a monster. Better to stay home and do card tricks in your bedroom instead.

It was partly Jane's fault, of course. She had lured him on at every turn. Well, he wouldn't get fooled again. He wouldn't give anybody the chance. Quentin felt a new attitude of detachment descend on him. His molten anger and grief were cooling into a glossy protective coating, a hard transparent lacquer of uncaring. If he couldn't go back, he would just have to do things differently going forward. He felt how infinitely safer and more sound this attitude was. The trick was just not wanting anything. That was power. That was courage: the courage not to love anyone or hope for anything.

The funny thing about it was how easy everything got, when nothing mattered. Over the next few weeks the new Quentin, with his white Warhol hair and his wooden Pinocchio shoulder, took up his magical studies again. What was wanted now was control. He wanted to be untouchable.

In his little cell Quentin practiced things he'd never had time to master before, or never dared to try. He went back to the most advanced Popper exercises—gruesomely difficult, only theoretically executable etudes that he'd faked his way through back at Brakebills. Now he repeated them over and over again, smoothing out the rough edges. He invented new, even crueler versions and mastered them as well. He relished the pain in his hands, ate it up. His enchantments took on a power and precision and fluency they'd never had before. His fingertips left tracks of fire and sparks and neon indigo smears in the air, that buzzed and whined, too bright to look at directly. His brain glowed with cold, brittle triumph. This was what Penny had been looking for when he went to Maine, but Quentin was actually doing it. Only now, he thought, now that he had killed off his human emotions, only now that he didn't care anymore, could he wield truly superhuman power.

As the sweet spring air drifted through his room, and then the oven-hot summer air, and sweat poured down his face, and the centaurs trotted by outside his door, lofty and incurious, he came to see how Mayakovsky had performed some of the feats Quentin had found so baffling. In an empty meadow he carefully reverse-engineered Penny's flashy Fireball spell. He found and corrected the mistakes he'd made in his senior project, the trip to the moon, and he finished Alice's project, too, in memoriam, isolating and capturing a single photon and even observing it, Heisenberg be damned: an infinitely furious, precious, incandescent little wave-spark.

Seated in the lotus position on top of the sun-faded Florida desk, he allowed his mind to expand until it encompassed one, then three more, then six field mice in all as they went about their tiny urgent business in the grass outside his window. He summoned them to sit before him and, with a thought, gently extinguished the electrical current that lived within each of them. Their little fluffy bodies went still and cold. Then, just as easily, he touched each of them with magic, instantly relighting their tiny souls as if he were touching a match to the pilot light of a stove.

Panicked, they scrambled in all directions. He let them go. Alone in his room, he smiled at his secret greatness. He felt lordly and munificent. He had tampered with the sacred mystery of life and death. What else was there in this world that could engage his attention? Or in any world?

June ripened into July, then burst and withered and dried and became August. One morning Quentin woke up early to find a cool mist hanging low over the lawn outside his first-floor window. Standing there in plain view, looking huge and ethereal, was a white stag. It bent to crop the grass with its small mouth, tilting its grand, top-heavy rack of antlers, and he could see the muscles working in its neck. Its ears were bigger and floppier than he would have expected. It raised its head again when Quentin appeared in the window, conscious of being observed, then sauntered off across the lawn and disappeared unhurriedly from view. Frowning, Quentin watched it go. He went back to bed but couldn't sleep.

Later in the day he sought out Alder Acorn Agnes Allison-fragrant-timber. He found her working an elaborate, room-size loom built to harness both the pumping power of her muscular back legs and the delicate manipulations of her human fingers.

"The Questing Beast," she said, breathing hard, still pumping, her hands still weaving. "It is a rare sight. Undoubtedly it was drawn here by the positive energies radiated by our superior values. You are fortunate that it offered itself to some centaur's sight while you happened to be watching."

The Questing Beast. From *The Girl Who Told Time*. So that was what it looked like. Somehow he'd expected something more ferocious. Quentin patted Agnes on her glossy black hindquarters and left. He knew what he had to do.

That night he took out the leafy branch he had found in the writing desk. It was the branch that had hung in front of the Beast's face, which it had tossed aside right before their battle. The branch was dead and dried now, but its leaves were still olive and rubbery. He stuck its hard stem in the moist turf and mounded up some dirt to make sure it stayed upright.

The next morning Quentin woke to find a fully grown tree outside his window. Set into its trunk was the face of a softly ticking clock.

He put his hand on the tree's hard gray trunk, feeling its cool, dusty bark, then let it drop. His time here was over. He packed a few possessions, abandoned others, stole a bow and a quiver of arrows from the shed by the archery range, liberated a horse from the centaurs' feral sex-herd, and left the Retreat.

THE WHITE STAG

The hunt for the Questing Beast took him to the edge of the vast Northern Marsh, then back south, skirting the edge of the Great Bramble, then north again, angling west through the Darkling Woods as far as the vast, gently gurgling expanse of the Lower Slosh. It was like visiting places he'd seen in dreams. He drank from streams and slept on the ground and ate fire-roasted game—he had become a passable archer, and when he couldn't hit something on his own he used magic to cheat.

He rode his horse hard; she was a gentle bay who didn't seem very sorry to leave the centaurs behind. Quentin's mind was as empty of thoughts as the woods and fields were of people. The pond in his head was frozen again, a foot thick this time. On his best days he could go hours without thinking about Alice.

If he thought of anything it was the white stag. He was on a quest, but it was his quest now, nobody else's. He scanned the skyline for the prickle of its antlers and thickets for the flash of its pale flank. He knew what he was doing. This was what he'd dreamed about all the way back in Brooklyn. This was the primal fantasy. When he had finished it, he could close the book for good.

The Questing Beast led him even farther west, through the hills of the Chankly Bore, over a pass in a bitterly sharp mountain range, beyond anything he recognized or had ever heard of from the Fillory books. He was in virgin territory now, but he didn't stop to explore, or name the peaks. He descended a blazing white chalk cliff to a strip of volcanic black sand on the shore of a great, undiscovered western sea. When it spotted him still in pursuit, the stag bounded out onto the surf as if it were dry land. It leaped from breaker to breaker and swell to swell, like it was jumping from crag to crag, antlers erect, shaking its head and snuffing sea foam from its nostrils.

Quentin sighed. The next day he sold the gentle bay and booked passage across the western sea.

He managed to hire a nimble sloop named, embarrassingly enough, the *Skywalker*, crewed by an efficient foursome of three taciturn brothers and their burly, suntanned sister. Without speaking they swarmed through *Skywalker*'s fiendishly idiosyncratic rigging, which consisted of two dozen small lateen sails that required constant minor adjustments. They were awed by his wooden prosthetics. Two weeks out they put in at a jolly tropical archipelago—a sun-drenched scatter pattern of mango swamps and sheep meadows—to take on fresh water, then they pushed on.

They passed an island inhabited by angry, bloodthirsty giraffes, and a floating beast that offered them an extra year of life in exchange for a finger (the sister took the beast up on it, times three). They passed an ornate wooden staircase that spiraled down into the ocean, and a young woman adrift on an open book the size of a small island, in which she scribbled tirelessly. None of these adventures inspired in Quentin anything resembling wonder or curiosity. All that was over for him.

Five weeks out they made landfall on a scorched black rock, and the crew threatened to mutiny if they didn't turn back. Quentin stared them down, then bluffed about his magical powers, then finally quintupled their pay. They sailed on.

Being brave was easy when you would rather die than give up. Fatigue meant nothing when you actually wanted to suffer. Before this Quentin had never been on a sailboat big enough to have a jib, but now he was as lean and brown and salty-skinned as his crew. The sun became huge, and the seawater grew hot against the *Skywalker*'s gunwales. Everything felt electrically charged. Ordinary objects gave off strange optical effects, flares and sunspots and coronas. The stars were low, burning orbs, visibly spherical, pregnant with illegible meaning. A powerful golden light shone through everything, as if the world were only a thin scrim behind which a magnificent sun was shining. The stag kept bounding on ahead of them.

At last an unknown continent filled the horizon. It was wrapped in a magical winter and thickly wooded with fir trees that grew right up to the shore, so that the salt water lapped at their tangled roots. Quentin dropped anchor and told the crew, who were shivering in their thin tropical clothes, to wait a week and then leave without him if he wasn't back. He gave them the rest of the gold he'd brought, kissed the seven-fingered sister goodbye, lowered the sloop's caïque, and rowed himself to shore. Strapping his bow to his back, he pushed his way into the snow-choked forest. It was good to be alone again.

The Questing Beast showed itself on the third night. Quentin had made camp on a low bluff overlooking a clear, spring-fed pool. Just before dawn he woke to find it standing at the water's edge. Its reflection shivered as it lapped the cold water. He waited for a minute, on one knee. This was it. He strung his bow and slipped an arrow from his quiver. Looking down from the low bluff, with the early-morning air almost dead, it wasn't even a difficult shot. At the moment of release he thought: I'm doing what even the Chatwins failed to do, Helen and Rupert. He didn't feel the pleasure he thought he would. He put his shaft through the tough meat of the white stag's muscular right thigh.

He winced. Thank God he hadn't hit an artery. It didn't try to flee, just sat stiffly on its haunches like an injured cat. He had the impression, from its resigned expression, that the Questing Beast had to go through this kind of thing once a century or so. The cost of doing business. Its blood looked black in the pre-dawn twilight.

It showed no fear as Quentin approached. It reached back with its supple neck and grasped the arrow firmly in its square white teeth. With a jerk the shaft came free. It spat out the arrow at Quentin's feet.

"Hurts, that," the Questing Beast said matter-of-factly.

It had been three days since Quentin had spoken to anybody.

"What now," he said hoarsely.

"Wishes, of course. You get three."

"My friend Penny lost his hands. Fix them."

The stag's eyes defocused momentarily in thought.

"I cannot. I am sorry. He is either dead or not in this world."

The sun was just beginning to come up over the dark, massed fir forest. Quentin took a deep breath. The cold air smelled fresh and turpentiney.

"Alice. She turned into some kind of spirit. A *niffin*. Bring her back."

"Again I cannot."

"What do you mean you can't? It's a wish."

"I don't make the rules," the Questing Beast said. It lapped at the blood that still trickled down its thigh. "You don't like it, find some other magic stag and shoot it instead."

"I wish that the rules were different."

The stag rolled its eyes. "No. And I'm counting those three together as your first wish. What's number two?"

Quentin sighed. He hadn't really allowed himself to hope.

"Pay off my crew. Double what I promised them."

"Done," the Questing Beast replied.

"That's ten times their base salary, since I already quintupled it."

"I said 'done,' didn't I? What's number three?"

Years ago Quentin had worked out exactly what he would wish for if anybody ever gave him the chance. He would wish to travel to Fillory and to be allowed to stay there forever. But that was years ago.

"Send me home," he said.

The Questing Beast closed its round brown eyes gravely, then opened them. It dipped its antlers toward him.

"Done," it said.

Quentin supposed he could have been more specific. By rights the Questing Beast could have sent him back to Brooklyn, or to his parents' house in Chesterton, or to Brakebills, or even to the house upstate. But the stag went the literal way with it, and Quentin wound up in front of his last semipermanent residence, the apartment building in Tribeca that he'd shared with Alice. Nobody noticed as he abruptly came into being in the middle of the sidewalk in the late morning of what appeared to be an early-summer day. He walked away quickly. He couldn't even look at their old doorway. He left his bow and arrows in a trash can.

It was a shock to suddenly be surrounded by so many of his fellow human beings again at such close quarters. Their mottled skins and flawed physiognomies and preening vanities were less easy to ignore. Maybe some of that centaur snobbery had rubbed off on him. A revolting stew of fragrances both organic and inorganic invaded his nose. The front page of a newspaper, acquired at the corner deli, informed him that he'd been gone from Earth for a little over two years.

He would have to call his parents. Fogg would have kept them from fretting too much, but still. It almost made him smile to think of seeing them now. What the hell would they say about his hair? Soon, but not yet. He walked around, getting reacclimated. The spells involved in retrieving cash from an ATM were child's play now. He got a shave and a haircut and bought some clothes that weren't made by centaurs and hence didn't look like a Renaissance Faire costume. He babied himself. He had lunch at a fancy steakhouse and nearly died with pleasure. By three o'clock he was drinking Moscow Mules in a long, dark, empty basement bar in China-town where he used to go with the Physical Kids.

It had been a long time since he'd drunk alcohol. It had a dangerous thawing effect on his frozen brain. The ice that kept his feelings of guilt and sorrow under control creaked and groaned. But he kept on with it, and soon a deep, pure, luxurious sadness came over him, as heady and decadent as a drug. The place started filling up at five. By six the after-work drinkers were jostling Quentin at the bar. He could see that the light falling down the stairs out front had changed. He was on his way out when he noticed a slender, pretty girl with blond curls nuzzling a man who looked like an underwear model in a corner booth. Quentin didn't know the underwear model from Adam, but the pretty girl was definitely Anaïs.

It wasn't the reunion he would have wanted, nor was she the person he would have chosen to reunite with. But maybe it was better this way, with somebody he didn't care too much about, who didn't care too much about him, either. And he had those trusty Moscow Mules to carry some of the load for him. Baby steps. They sat outside on the stairway. She put her hand on his arm and goggled at his white hair.

"You would not have believed *eet,*" she said. Oddly, her pan-European accent had deepened and her English grammar worsened since he'd seen her last. Possibly it played better in the bar scene. "The time we 'ad getting out. It was quiet for a while, and then they rush us again. Josh was very good, you know. Very good. I had never seen him work magic like that. There was a thing that swam in the floor, under the stones—like a shark, I think, but it swam in the stones. It got hold of your leg."

"That might explain this," Quentin said. He showed her his wooden knee, and she goggled all over again. The alcohol was making all this much easier than expected. He was braced for a torrent of emotion, a cavalry charge of grief on his defenseless peace of mind, but if it was coming it hadn't yet.

"And there was a thing—a spell in the walls, I think—so that we went around in circles. We ended up in Amber's room again."

"Ember's."

"What did I say? Anyhow we 'ad to break the spell—" She stopped to wave through the window at her buff boyfriend in the bar. She sounded as if she'd told this story many times already, to the point where she was quite bored of it. For her it all happened two years ago, to people she'd barely known anyway. "And we carried you the whole way. My God. I don't think we would have made it if Richard"—ree-SHARD—"'adn't found us.

"It almost makes you like him, you know? He had a way of making us invisible to the monsters. He practically carried us out of that place. Still I have a scar."

She flounced up the hem of her skirt, which was none too long to begin with. A thick, bumpy keloid strip six inches long stood out from her smooth, tanned thigh.

Amazingly, Penny had survived, she told him, or at least he had for a while. The centaurs were unable to reconstruct his hands, and without them he could no longer cast spells. When they reached the Neitherlands Penny walked away from the rest of the party, as if he were searching for something. When he came to a tall, narrow stone palazzo, unusually old and worn, he stopped in front of it and spread out his handless arms as if in supplication. After a minute the doors of the palazzo opened. The others caught a glimpse of ranks of bookcases—the warm, secret paper heart of the City. Penny stepped inside and the doors closed behind him.

"Can you believe it even all happened?" she kept saying. "It is like a *cauchemar*. But it is all over now."

It was strange: Anaïs didn't seem to blame him, or herself. She had found some way of mourning what had happened. Or maybe it hadn't touched her to begin with. It was hard to guess what went on under those blond curls.

Throughout the story she kept looking over his shoulder at the underwear model, and after a while he took pity on her and let her go. They said goodbye—kiss, kiss. Neither party promised to keep in touch. What was the point of lying now, at this late stage in the game? Like she said, it was all over now. He stayed sitting outside on the steps, in the warm early hours of the summer evening, until it crossed his mind how much he didn't want to run into Anaïs again on her way out.

It was getting dark, and he would need somewhere to sleep tonight. He could find a hotel, but why bother? And why wait? He had abandoned almost everything he owned back in Fillory, but one thing Quentin had hung on to was the iron key Fogg had given him when he graduated. It hadn't worked from Fillory—he'd tried—but now, standing by himself on a trash-littered street in Tribeca, breathing the soupy, sun-warmed city air, he took it out of the pocket of his brand-new jeans. It felt reassuringly hefty. On a hunch he held it up to his ear. It gave off a high, constant musical ringing tone, like a struck tuning fork. He'd never noticed that before.

Feeling grandly lonely, and only a little frightened, he gripped the key with both hands, closed his eyes, relaxed, and let it tug him forward. It was like riding the rope tow at a ski slope. The key parted an invisible seam in the air and drew him swiftly forward and with a delightful sense of acceleration through some highly convenient sub-dimension back to the stone terrace out behind the house at Brakebills. The pain of going back was great, but the necessity was greater. He had one last piece of business to take care of, and then it really would all be over forever.

KINGS AND QUEENS

As the junior member of the PlaxCo account team, associate management consultant Quentin Coldwater had few actual responsibilities beyond attending the occasional meeting and being civil to whatever colleagues he happened to bump into in the elevator. On the rare occasions when actual documents managed to make their way into his in-box or onto his desk, he rubber-stamped them *(Looks good to me!!!—QC)* without reading them and sent them on their way.

Quentin's desk was, as it happened, unusually large for a new hire at his level, especially one as youthful as he appeared to be (though his startling white hair lent him a certain gravitas beyond his years), and whose educational background and previous work history were on the sketchy side. He just appeared one day, took possession of a corner office recently vacated by a vice president three times his age, and started drawing a salary and piling up money in his 401(k) and receiving medical and dental benefits and taking six weeks of vacation a year. In return for which he didn't seem to do much of anything beyond play computer games on the ultra-flat double-wide-screen monitor the outgoing veep had left behind.

But Quentin didn't inspire any resentment in his new colleagues, or even any particular curiosity. Everybody thought somebody else knew the story on him, and if it turned out that they didn't, they definitely knew for a fact that somebody over in HR had the scoop. And anyway, supposedly he'd been a superstar at some high-flying European school, fluent in all kinds of languages. Math scores through the roof. The firm was lucky to have him. *Lucky.*

And he was affable enough, if a little mopey. He seemed smart. Or at least he looked smart. And anyway, he was a member of the PlaxCo account team, and here at the consulting firm of Grunnings Hunsucker Swann everybody was a team player.

Dean Fogg had advised Quentin against it. He should take more time, think it over, maybe get some therapy. But Quentin had taken enough time. He had seen enough of the magical world to last him the rest of his life, and he was erecting a barrier between himself and it that no magic could breach. He was going to cut it off and kill it dead. Fogg had been right after all, even if he didn't have the guts to make good on his own argument: people were better off without magic, living in the real world, learning to deal with it as it came. Maybe there were people out there who could handle the power a magician could wield, who deserved it, but Quentin wasn't one of them. It was time he grew up and faced that fact.

So Fogg set him up with a desk job at a firm with large amounts of magician money invested in it, and Quentin took the subway and rode the elevator and ordered in lunch like the rest of humanity, or at any rate the most privileged 0.1 percent of it. His curiosity about the realms invisible had been more than satisfied, thanks tremendously much. At least his parents were pleased. It was a relief to be able to tell them what he did for a living and not lie.

Grunnings Hunsucker Swann was absolutely everything Quentin had hoped it would be, which was as close to nothing at all as he could get and still be alive. His office was calm and quiet, with climate control and tinted floor-to-ceiling windows. Office supplies were abundant and top-notch. He was given all the balance sheets and org charts and business plans to review that he could possibly have wanted. To be honest, Quentin felt superior to anybody who still messed around with magic. They could delude themselves if they liked, those self-indulgent magical mandarins, but he'd outgrown that stuff. He wasn't a magician anymore, he was a man, and a man took responsibility for his actions. He was out here working the hard flinty bedrock face of it all. Fillory? He'd been there and done that, and it hadn't done him or anybody else any good. He was damn lucky he got out alive.

Every morning Quentin put on a suit and stood on an old elevated subway platform in Brooklyn, raw cement stained with rust by the bits of iron rebar poking out of it. From the uptown end he could just barely see the tiny, hazy, aeruginous spike of the Statue of Liberty out in the bay. In the summertime the thick wooden ties sweated aromatic beads of liquid black tar. Invisible signals caused the tracks to shift and shunt the trains left and right, as if (as if, but not actually) directed by unseen hands. Nearby unidentifiable birds swirled in endless cyclonic circles above a poorly maintained dumpster.

Every morning when the train arrived it was full of young Russian women riding in from Brighton Beach, three-quarters asleep, swaying in unison to the rocking of the car, their lustrous dark hair dyed a hideous unconvincing blond. In the marble lobby of the building where Quentin worked, elevators ingested pods of commuters and then spat them out on their respective floors.

When he left work every day at five, the entire sequence repeated itself in reverse.

As for his weekends, there was no end to the multifarious meaningless entertainments and distractions with which the real world supplied Quentin. Video games; Internet porn; people talking on their cell phones in bodegas about their stepmothers' medical conditions; weightless supermarket plastic bags snagged in leafless trees; old men sitting on their stoops with no shirts on; the oversize windshield wipers on blue-and-white city buses slinging huge gouts of rainwater back and forth, back and forth, back and forth.

It was all he had left, and it would have to be enough. As a magician he had been among the world's silent royalty, but he had abdicated his throne. He had doffed his crown and left it lying there for the next sucker to put on. *Le roi est mort.* It was a kind of enchantment in itself, this new life of his, the ultimate enchantment: the enchantment to end all enchantments forever.

One day, having leveled up three different characters in three different computer games, and run through every Web site he could plausibly and even implausibly want to surf, Quentin noticed that his Outlook calendar was telling him that he was supposed to be at a meeting. It had started half an hour ago, and it was on a fairly remote floor of GHS's corporate monolith, necessitating the use of a different elevator bank. But throwing caution to the wind he decided to attend.

The purpose of this particular meeting, Quentin gathered from some hastily harvested context clues, was a joint post-mortem of the PlaxCo restructuring, which had apparently been triumphantly wrapped up some weeks earlier, though Quentin had somehow missed that crucial detail till now. Also on the agenda was a new, related project, just kicking off, to be conducted by another team consisting of people Quentin had never met before. He found himself sneaking glances at one of them.

It was hard to say what stood out about her, except that she was the only person besides Quentin who never spoke once during the entire meeting. She was some years older than him and not notably attractive or unattractive. Sharp nose, thin mouth, chin-length mousy brown hair, with an air of powerful intelligence held in check by boredom. He wasn't sure how he knew, maybe it was her fingers, which had a familiar muscular, overdeveloped look. Maybe it was her features, which had a mask-like quality. But there was no question what she was. She was another one like him: a former Brakebillian in deep cover in the real world.

The thick plottens.

Quentin buttonholed a colleague afterward—Dan, Don, Dean, one of those—and found out her name. It was Emily Greenstreet. The one and only and infamous. The girl Alice's brother had died for.

Quentin's hands shook as he pressed the elevator buttons. He informed his assistant that he would be taking the rest of the afternoon off. Maybe the rest of the week, too.

But it was too late. Emily Greenstreet must have spotted him, too—maybe it really was the fingers?—because before the day was over he had an e-mail from her. The next morning she left him a voice mail and attempted to remotely insert a lunch date into his Outlook calendar. When he got online she IMed him relentlessly and finally—having gotten his cell phone number off the company's emergency contact list—she texted him:

Y POSTPONE THE INEVITABLE?

Y not? he thought. But he knew she was right. He didn't really have a choice. If she wanted to find him, then sooner or later she would. With a sense of defeat he clicked ACCEPT on the lunch invitation. They met the following week at a grandly expensive old-school French restaurant that had been beloved of GHS executives since time immemorial.

It wasn't as bad as he thought. She was a fast-talking woman, so skinny and with such erect posture that she looked brittle. Seated across from each other, almost alone in a hushed circle of cream tablecloths and glassware and heavy, clinking silverware, they gossiped about work. He hardly knew enough of the names to keep up, but she talked enough for both of them. She told him about her life—nice apartment, Upper East Side, roof deck, cats. They found that they had a funny kind of black humor in common. In different ways they had both discovered the same truth: that to live out childhood fantasies as a grown-up was to court and wed and bed disaster. Who could possibly know that better than they—the man who watched Alice die, and the woman who'd essentially killed Alice's brother? When he looked at her he saw himself eight years down the line. It didn't look all that bad.

And she liked a drink or five, so they had that in common, too. Martini glasses, wine bottles, and whiskey tumblers piled up between them, a miniature metropolis of varicolored glass, while their cell phones and Black-Berries plaintively, futilely tried to attract their attention.

"So tell me," Emily Greenstreet said, when they'd both imbibed enough to create the illusion of a comfortable, long-standing intimacy between them. "Do you miss it? Doing magic?"

"I can honestly say I never think about it," he said. "Why? Do you?"

"Miss it, or think about it?" She rolled a lock of her mousy, chin-length hair between two fingers. "Of course I do. Both."

"Are you ever sorry you left Brakebills?"

She shook her head sharply.

"The only thing I regret is not leaving that place sooner." She leaned forward, suddenly animated. "Just thinking about that place now gives me the howling fantods. They're just kids, Quentin! With all that power! What happened to Charlie and me could happen again to any one of them, any day, any minute. Or worse. Much worse. It's amazing that place is still standing." He noticed that she never said "Brakebills," just "that place." "I don't even like living on the same coast with it. There's practically no safe-guards at all. Every one of those kids is a nuclear bomb waiting to go off!

"Somebody needs to get control of that place. Sometimes I think I should blow their cover, get the real government in there, get it properly regulated. The teachers will never do it. The Magician's Court will never do it."

She chattered on in that vein. They were like two recovering alcoholics, hopped up on caffeine and Twelve Step gospel, telling each other how glad they were to be sober and then talking about nothing but drinking.

Though unlike recovering alcoholics they could and did drink plenty of alcohol. Temporarily revived by a molten *affogato*, Quentin went to work on a bitter single malt Scotch that tasted like it had been decanted through the stump of an oak tree that had been killed by lightning.

"I never felt safe in that place. Never, not for a minute. Don't you feel safer out here, Quentin? In the real world?"

"If you want to know the truth, these days I don't feel much of anything."

She frowned at that. "Really. Then what made you give it all up, Quentin? You must have had a good reason."

"I would say my motives were pretty much unimpeachable."

"That bad?" She raised her thin eyebrows, flirtatiously. "Tell me."

She sat back and let the restaurant's fancy easy chair embrace her. Nothing a recovering addict likes more than a tale of how bad it had been in the old days, and how low a fellow addict had sunk. Let the one-downsmanship begin.

He told her just how low he'd sunk. He told her about Alice, and their life together, and what they had done, and how she had died. When he revealed the specifics of Alice's fate, Emily's smile vanished, and she took a shaky slurp from her martini glass. After all, Charlie had become a *niffin*, too. The irony was quite comprehensively hideous. But she didn't ask him to stop.

When he was finished, he expected her to hate him as much as he hated himself. As much, perhaps, as Quentin suspected she hated herself. But instead her eyes were brimming over with kindness.

"Oh, Quentin," she said, and she actually took his hand across the table. "You can't blame yourself, truly you can't." Her stiff, narrow face shone with pity. "You need to see that all this evil, all this sadness, it all *comes* from magic. It's where all your trouble began. Nobody can be touched by that much power without being corrupted. It's what corrupted me, Quentin, before I gave it up. It's the hardest thing I ever did."

Her voice softened.

"It's what killed Charlie," she said quietly. "And it killed your poor

Alice, too. Sooner or later magic always leads to evil. Once you see that then you'll see how to forgive yourself. It will get easier. I promise you."

Her pity was like a salve for his raw, chafed heart, and he wanted to accept it. She was offering it to him, it was right there across the table. All he had to do was reach out for it.

The check arrived, and Quentin charged the astronomical sum to his corporate card. In the restaurant's foyer they were both so drunk that they had to help each other into their raincoats—it had been pissing rain all day. There was no question of going back to the office. He was in no shape for that, and anyway it was already getting dark. It had been a very long lunch.

Outside under the awning they hesitated. For a moment Emily Greenstreet's funny, flat mouth came unexpectedly close to his.

"Have dinner with me tonight." Her gaze was disarmingly direct. "Come to my apartment. I'll cook for you."

"Can't do it tonight," he said blurrily. "I'm sorry. Next time maybe."

She put a hand on his arm. "Listen, Quentin. I know you think you're not ready for this—"

"I know I'm not ready."

"—but you'll *never* be ready. Not until you decide to be." She squeezed his forearm. "Enough drama, Quentin. Let me help you. It's not the worst thing in the world, admitting you need help. Is it?"

Her kindness was the most touching thing he'd seen since he left Brakebills. And he hadn't had sex, good God, since the time he'd slept with Janet. It would be so easy to go with her.

But he didn't. Even as they stood there he felt something tingle in his fingertips, under his fingernails, some residue left by the thousands of spells that had flowed through them over the years. He could still feel them there, the hot white sparks that had once come streaming so freely from his hands. She was wrong: blaming magic for Alice's death wasn't going to help him. It was too easy, and he'd had enough of doing things the easy way. It was all well and good for Emily Greenstreet to forgive him, but people were responsible for Alice's death. Jane Chatwin was, and Quentin was, and so was Alice herself. And people would have to atone for it.

In that instant he looked at Emily Greenstreet and saw a lost soul, alone in a howling wasteland, not so different from the way her one-time lover

Professor Mayakovsky had looked standing alone at the South Pole. He wasn't ready to join her there. But where else could he go? What would Alice have done?

Another month went by, and it was November, and Quentin was sitting in his corner office staring out the window. The building across the street was considerably shorter than the Grunnings Hunsucker Swann building, so he had a clear view of its rooftop, which consisted of a neat beige gravel walkway running around a gray grid of massive, complicated air-conditioning and heating units. With the coming of the bitter late fall weather the air-conditioning had gone silent and the heaters had sprung into life, and huge nebulae of steam curled off them in abstract whorls: hypnotic, silent, slowly turning shapes that never stopped and never repeated themselves. Smoke signals sent by no one, to no one, signifying nothing. Lately Quentin spent a lot of time watching them. His assistant had quietly given up attempting to schedule appointments for him.

All at once, and with no warning, the tinted floor-to-ceiling window that made up one entire wall of Quentin's office shattered and burst inward. Quentin's ultra-modern, narrow-wale Venetian blinds went crazily askew. Cold air and raw unfiltered sunlight came flooding in. Something small, round, and very heavy rolled across the carpet and bumped into his shoe.

He looked down at it. It was a bluish marble sphere: the stone globe they used to use to start a welters match.

Three people were floating in midair outside his window, thirty stories up.

Janet looked older somehow, which of course she was, but there was something else different about her. Her eyes, the irises, radiated a seething violet mystical energy like nothing Quentin had ever seen before. She wore a tight black leather bustier that she was in imminent danger of spilling out of. Silver stars were falling all around her.

Eliot had acquired a pair of immense white feathery wings somewhere that spread out behind him, with which he hovered on an intangible wind. On his head was the golden crown of Fillory that Quentin had last seen in Ember's underground chamber. Between Janet and Eliot, her arms wrapped in black silk, floated a tall, painfully skinny woman with long wavy black hair that undulated in the air as if she were underwater.

"Hello, Quentin," Eliot said.

"Hi," Janet said.

The other woman didn't say anything. Neither did Quentin.

"We're going back to Fillory," Janet said, "and we need another king. Two kings, two queens."

"You can't hide forever, Quentin. Come with us."

With the tinted window gone and the afternoon sunlight pouring into his office, Quentin couldn't read his monitor anymore. The climate control was howling trying to fight off the cold air. Somewhere in the building an alarm went off.

"It could work this time," Eliot said. "With Martin gone. And besides, we never figured out what your Discipline was. Doesn't that bother you?"

Quentin stared at them. It was a few seconds before he found his voice.

"What about Josh?" he croaked. "Go ask him."

"He's got another project." Janet rolled her eyes. "He thinks he can use the Neitherlands to get to Middle-earth. He honestly believes he's going to bone an elf."

"I thought about being a queen," Eliot added. "Turns out they're very open-minded about that kind of thing in Fillory. But at the end of the day rules is rules."

Quentin put down his coffee. It had been a long time since he'd experienced any emotion at all other than sadness and shame and numbness, so long that for a moment he didn't understand what was happening inside him. In spite of himself he felt sensation coming back to some part of him that he'd thought was dead forever. It hurt. But at the same time he wanted more of it.

"Why are you doing this?" Quentin asked slowly, carefully. He needed to be clear. "After what happened to Alice? Why would you go back there? And why would you want me with you? You're only going to make it worse."

"What, worse than this?" Eliot asked. He tilted his chin to indicate Quentin's office.

"We all knew what we were doing," Janet said. "You knew it, we knew it. Alice certainly knew it. We made our choices, Q. And what's going to happen? Your hair's already white. You can't look any weirder than you already do."

Quentin swiveled around to face them in his ergonomic desk chair. His heart felt like it was burning with relief and regret, the emotions melting and running together and turning into bright, hot, white light.

"The thing is," he said. "I'd hate to cut out right before bonus season."

"Come on, Quentin. It's over. You've done your time." Janet's smile had a warmth in it that he'd never seen before, or maybe he'd just never noticed it. "Everybody's forgiven you but you. And you are *so* far behind us."

"You might be surprised about that."

Quentin picked up the blue stone ball and studied it.

"So," he said, "I'm gone for five minutes and you have to bring in a hedge witch?"

Eliot shrugged.

"She's got chops."

"Fuck you," said Julia.

Quentin sighed. He unkinked his neck and stood up.

"Did you really have to break my window?"

"No," Eliot said. "Not really."

Quentin walked to the floor's edge. Sprays of smashed window glass crunched on the carpet under his fancy leather shoes. He ducked under the broken blinds. It was a long way down. He hadn't done this for a while.

Loosening his tie with one hand, Quentin stepped out into the cold clear winter air and flew.

Also from bestselling author
Lev Grossman

The epic second and third installments to the #1 *New York Times* bestselling Magicians trilogy, now an original series on Syfy

"If the Narnia books were like catnip for a certain kind of kid, these books are like crack for a certain kind of adult." —*The New York Times*

CHAPTER 1

Quentin rode a gray horse with white socks named Dauntless. He wore black leather boots up to his knees, different-colored stockings, and a long navy-blue topcoat that was richly embroidered with seed pearls and silver thread. On his head was a platinum coronet. A glittering side-sword bumped against his leg—not the ceremonial kind, the real kind, the kind that would actually be useful in a fight. It was ten o'clock in the morning on a warm, overcast day in late August. He was everything a king of Fillory should be. He was hunting a magic rabbit.

By King Quentin's side rode a queen: Queen Julia. Up ahead were another queen and another king, Janet and Eliot—the land of Fillory had four rulers in all. They rode along a high-arched forest path littered with yellow leaves, perfect little sprays of them that looked like they could have been cut and placed by a florist. They moved in silence, slowly, together but lost in their separate thoughts, gazing out into the green depths of the late summer woods.

It was an easy silence. Everything was easy. Nothing was hard. The dream had become real.

"Stop!" Eliot said, at the front.

They stopped. Quentin's horse didn't halt when the others' did— Dauntless wandered a little out of line and halfway off the trail before he persuaded her for good and all to quit walking for a damn minute. Two years as a king of Fillory and he was still shit at horseback riding.

"What is it?" he called.

They all sat for another minute. There was no hurry. Dauntless snorted once in the silence: lofty horsey contempt for whatever human enterprise they thought they were pursuing.

"Thought I saw something."

"I'm starting to wonder," Quentin said, "if it's even possible to track a rabbit."

"It's a hare," Eliot said.

"Same difference."

"It isn't, actually. Hares are bigger. And they don't live in burrows, they make nests in open ground."

"Don't start," both Julia and Janet said, in unison.

"Here's my real question," Quentin said. "If this rabbit thing really can see the future won't it know we're trying to catch it?"

"It can see the future," Julia said softly, beside him. "It cannot change it. Did you three argue this much when you were at Brakebills?"

She wore a sepulchral black riding dress and an actual riding hood, also black. She always wore black, like she was in mourning, even though Quentin couldn't think of anyone she should have been in mourning for. Casually, like she was calling over a waiter, Julia summoned a tiny songbird to her wrist and raised it up to her ear. It chipped, chirruped something, and she nodded back and it flew away again.

Nobody noticed, except for Quentin. She was always giving and getting little secret messages from the talking animals. It was like she was on a different wireless network from the rest of them.

"You should have let us bring Jollyby," Janet said. She yawned, holding the back of her hand against her mouth. Jollyby was Master of the Hunt at Castle Whitespire, where they all lived. He usually supervised this kind of excursion.

"Jollyby's great," Quentin said, "but even he couldn't track a hare in the woods. Without dogs. When there's no snow."

"Yes, but Jollyby has very well-developed calf muscles. I like looking at them. He wears those man-tights."

"I wear man-tights," Quentin said, pretending to be affronted. Eliot snorted.

"I imagine he's around here somewhere." Eliot was still scanning the trees. "Discreet distance and all that. Can't keep that man away from a royal hunt."

"Careful what you hunt," Julia said, "lest you catch it."

Janet and Eliot looked at each other: more inscrutable wisdom from Julia. But Quentin frowned. Julia made her own kind of sense.

Quentin hadn't always been a king, of Fillory or anywhere else. None of them had. Quentin had grown up a regular non-magical, non-royal person in Brooklyn, in what he still in spite of everything thought of as the real world. He'd thought Fillory was a fiction, an enchanted land that existed only as the setting of a series of fantasy novels for children. But then he'd learned to do magic, at a secret college called Brakebills, and he and his friends had found out that Fillory was real.

It wasn't what they expected. Fillory was a darker and more dangerous place in real life than it was in the books. Bad things happened there, terrible things. People got hurt and killed and worse. Quentin went back to Earth in disgrace and despair. His hair turned white.

But then he and the others had pulled themselves together again and gone back to Fillory. They faced their fears and their losses and took their places on the four thrones of Castle Whitespire and were made kings and queens. And it was wonderful. Sometimes Quentin couldn't believe that he'd lived through it all when Alice, the girl he loved, had died. It was hard to accept all the good things he had now, when Alice hadn't lived to see them.

But he had to. Otherwise what had she died for? He unslung his bow and stood up in the stirrups and looked around. Bubbles of stiffness popped satisfyingly in his knees. There was no sound except for the hush of falling leaves slipping through other leaves.

A gray-brown bullet flickered across the path a hundred feet in front of them and vanished into the underbrush at full tilt. With a quick fluid motion that had cost him a lot of practice Quentin nocked an arrow and drew. He could have used a magic arrow, but it didn't seem sporting. He aimed for a long moment, straining against the strength of the bow, and released.

The arrow burrowed into the loamy soil up to the feathers, right where the hare's flashing paws had been about five seconds ago.

"Almost," Janet said, deadpan.

There was no way in hell they were going to catch this thing.

"Toy with me, would you?" Eliot shouted. "Yah!"

He put the spurs to his black charger, which whinnied and reared obligingly and hoofed the empty air before lunging off the path into the woods after the hare. The crashing sound of his progress through the trees faded almost immediately. The branches sprang back into place behind him and were still again. Eliot was not shit at horseback riding.

Janet watched him go.

"Hi ho, Silver," she said. "What are we even doing out here?"

It was a fair question. The point wasn't really to catch the hare. The point was—what was the point? What were they looking for? Back at the castle their lives were overflowing with pleasure. There was a whole staff there whose job it was to make sure that every day of their lives was absolutely perfect. It was like being the only guests at a twenty-star hotel that you never had to leave. Eliot was in heaven. It was everything he'd always loved about Brakebills—the wine, the food, the ceremony—with none of the work. Eliot loved being a king.

Quentin loved it too, but he was restless. He was looking for something else. He didn't know what it was. But when the Seeing Hare was spotted in the greater Whitespire metropolitan area, he knew he wanted a day off from doing nothing all day. He wanted to try to catch it.

The Seeing Hare was one of the Unique Beasts of Fillory. There were a dozen of them—the Questing Beast, who had once granted Quentin three wishes, was one of them, as was the Great Bird of Peace, an ungainly flightless bird like a cassowary that could stop a battle by appearing between the two opposing armies. There was only one of each of them, hence the name, and each one had a special gift. The Unseen Monitor was a large lizard who could turn you invisible for a year, if that's what you wanted.

People hardly ever saw them, let alone caught them, so a lot of guff got talked about them. No one knew where they came from, or what the point of them was, if any. They'd always been there, permanent features of Fillory's enchanted landscape. They were apparently immortal. The

Seeing Hare's gift was to predict the future of any person who caught it, or so the legend went. It hadn't been caught for centuries.

Not that the future was a question of towering urgency right now. Quentin figured he had a pretty fair idea of what his future was like, and it wasn't much different from his present. Life was good.

They'd picked up the hare's trail early, when the morning was still bright and dewy, and they rode out singing choruses of "Kill the Wabbit" to the tune of "Ride of the Valkyries" in their best Elmer Fudd voices. Since then it had zigzagged them through the forest for miles, stopping and starting, looping and doubling back, hiding in the bushes and then suddenly zipping across their paths, again and again.

"I do not think he is coming back," Julia said.

She didn't speak much these days. And for some reason she'd mostly given up using contractions.

"Well, if we can't track the hare we can track Eliot anyway." Janet gently urged her mount off the track and into the trees. She wore a low-cut forest-green blouse and men's chaps. Her penchant for mild cross-dressing had been the scandal of the season at court this year.

Julia didn't ride a horse at all but an enormous furry quadruped that she called a civet, which looked like an ordinary civet, long and brown and vaguely feline, with a fluidly curving back, except that it was the size of a horse. Quentin suspected it could talk—its eyes gleamed with a bit more sentience than they should have, and it always seemed to follow their conversations with too much interest.

Dauntless didn't want to follow the civet, which exuded a musky, un-equine odor, but she did as she was told, albeit at a spiteful, stiff-legged walk.

"I haven't seen any dryads," Janet said. "I thought there'd be dryads."

"Me neither," Quentin said. "You never see them in the Queenswood anymore."

It was a shame. He liked the dryads, the mysterious nymphs who watched over oak trees. You really knew you were in a magical fantasy otherworld when a beautiful woman wearing a skimpy dress made of leaves suddenly jumped out of a tree.

"I thought maybe they could help us catch it. Can't you call one or summon one or something, Julia?"

"You can call them all you want. They will not come."

"I spend enough time listening to them bitch about land allocation," Janet said. "And where are they all if they're not here? Is there some cooler, magical-er forest somewhere that they're all off haunting?"

"They are not ghosts," Julia said. "They are spirits."

The horses picked their way carefully over a berm that was too straight to be natural. An old earthwork from an ancient, unrecoverable age.

"Maybe we could make them stay," Janet said. "Legislate some incentives. Or just detain them at the border. It's bullshit that there's not more dryads in the Queenswood."

"Good luck," Julia said. "Dryads fight. Their skin is like wood. And they have staves."

"I've never seen a dryad fight," Quentin said.

"That is because nobody is stupid enough to fight one."

Recognizing a good exit line when it heard one, the civet chose that moment to scurry on ahead. Two sturdy oak trees actually leaned aside to let Julia pass between them. Then they leaned back together again, leaving Janet and Quentin to go the long way around.

"Listen to her," Janet said. "She has so totally gone native! I'm tired of her more-Fillorian-than-thou bullshit. Did you see her talking to that fucking bird?"

"Oh, leave her alone," Quentin said. "She's all right."

But if he was being honest, Quentin was fairly sure that Queen Julia wasn't all right.

Julia hadn't learned her magic the way they had, coming up through the safe, orderly system of Brakebills. She and Quentin had gone to high school together, but she hadn't gotten into Brakebills, so she'd become a hedge witch instead: she'd learned it on her own, on the outside. It wasn't official magic, institutional magic. She was missing huge chapters of lore, and her technique was so sloppy and loopy that sometimes he couldn't believe it even worked at all.

But she also knew things Quentin and the others didn't. She hadn't had the Brakebills faculty standing over her for four years making sure she colored inside the lines. She'd talked to people Quentin never would have talked to, picked up things his professors would never have let him touch. Her magic had sharp, jagged edges on it that had never been filed down.

It was a different kind of education, and it made her different. She talked differently. Brakebills had taught them to be arch and ironic about magic, but Julia took it seriously. She played it fully goth, in a black wedding dress and black eyeliner. Janet and Eliot thought it was funny, but Quentin liked it. He felt drawn to her. She was weird and dark, and Fillory had made the rest of them so damn light, Quentin included. He liked it that she wasn't quite all right and she didn't care who knew it.

The Fillorians liked it too. Julia had a special rapport with them, especially with the more exotic ones, the spirits and elementals and jinnis and even more strange and extreme beings—the fringe element, in the hazy zone between the biological and the entirely magical. She was their witch-queen, and they adored her.

But Julia's education had cost her something, it was hard to put your finger on what, but whatever it was had left its mark on her. She didn't seem to want or need human company anymore. In the middle of a state dinner or a royal ball or even a conversation she would lose interest and wander away. It happened more and more. Sometimes Quentin wondered exactly how expensive her education had been, and how she'd paid for it, but whenever he asked her, she avoided the question. Sometimes he wondered if he was falling in love with her. Again.

A distant bugle sounded—three polished sterling silver notes, muffled by the heavy silence of the woods. Eliot was sounding a recheat, a hunting call.

He was no Jollyby, but it was a perfectly credible recheat. He wasn't much for drafting legislation, but Eliot was meticulous about royal etiquette, which included getting all the Fillorian hunting protocol exactly right. (Though he found any actual killing distasteful, and usually managed to avoid it.) His bugling was good enough for Dauntless. She trembled, electrified, waiting for permission to bolt. Quentin grinned at

Janet, and she grinned back at him. He yelled like a cowboy and kicked and they were off.

It was insanely dangerous, like a full-on land-speeder chase, with ditches opening up in front of you with no warning, and low branches reaching down out of nowhere to try to clobber your head off (not literally of course, though you could never tell for sure with some of these older, more twisted trees). But fuck it, that's what healing magic is for. Dauntless was a thoroughbred. They'd been starting and stopping and dicking around all morning, and she was dying to cut loose.

And how often did he get a chance to put his royal person at risk? When was the last time he even cast a spell? His life wasn't exactly fraught with peril. They lay around on cushions all day and ate and drank their heads off all night. Lately whenever he sat down some unfamiliar interaction had been happening between his abdomen and his belt buckle. He must have gained fifteen pounds since he took the throne. No wonder kings looked so fat in pictures. One minute you're Prince Valiant, the next you're Henry VIII.

Janet broke trail, guided by more muffled bugle notes. The horses' hooves made satisfyingly solid beats on the packed loam of the forest floor. Everything that was cloying about court life, all the safety and the relentless comfort, went away for a moment. Trunks and spinneys and ditches and old stone walls whipped and blurred past. They dodged in and out of hot sun and cool shade. Their speed froze the falling sprays of yellow leaves in midair. Quentin picked his moment, and when they hit open meadow he swung out wide to the right, and for a long minute they were side by side, coursing wildly along in parallel.

Then all at once Janet pulled up. Quickly as he could Quentin slowed Dauntless to a walk and brought her around, breathing hard. He hoped her horse hadn't pulled up lame. It took him another minute to find his way back to her.

She was sitting still and straight in the saddle, squinting off into the midday gloom of the forest. No more bugle calls.

"What is it?"

"Thought I saw something," she said.

Quentin squinted too. There was something. Shapes.

"Is that Eliot?"

"The hell are they doing?" Janet said.

Quentin dropped down out of the saddle, unslung his bow again and nocked another arrow. Janet led the horses while he walked in front. He could hear her charging up some minor defensive magic, a light ward-and-shield, just in case. He could feel the familiar staticky buzz of it.

"Shit," he said under his breath.

He dropped the bow and ran toward them. Julia was down on one knee, her hand pressed against her chest, either gasping or sobbing, he couldn't tell which. Eliot was bent over talking to her quietly. His cloth-of-gold jacket had been yanked half off his shoulder.

"It's okay," he said, seeing Quentin's white face. "That fucking civet threw her and bolted. I tried to hold it but I couldn't. She's okay, she just got the wind knocked out of her."

"You're all right." That phrase again. Quentin rubbed Julia's back while she took croaking breaths. "You're okay. I always said you should get a regular horse. I never liked that thing."

"Never liked you, either," she managed.

"Look." Eliot pointed off into the twilight. "That's what made it bolt. The hare went in there."

A few yards away a round clearing began, a still pool of grass hidden in the heart of the forest. The trees grew right up to its edge and then stopped, like somebody had cleared it on purpose, nipping out the border precisely. It could have been ruled with a compass. Quentin picked his way toward it. Lush, intensely emerald-green grass grew over lumpy black soil. In the center of the clearing stood a single enormous oak tree with a large round clock set in its trunk.

The clock-trees were the legacy of the Watcherwoman, the legendary—but quite real—time-traveling witch of Fillory. They were a magical folly, benign as far as anyone could tell, and picturesque in a surreal way. There was no reason to get rid of them, assuming you even could. If nothing else they kept perfect time.

But Quentin had never seen one like this. He had to lean back to see its crown. It must have been a hundred feet tall, and it was massively thick, at least fifteen yards around at its base. Its clock was stupendous. The face was taller than Quentin was. The trunk erupted out of the green grass and burst into a mass of wiggly branches, like a kraken sculpted in wood.

And it was moving. Its black, nearly leafless limbs writhed and thrashed against the gray sky. The tree seemed to be caught in the grip of a storm, but Quentin couldn't feel or hear any wind. The day, the day he could perceive with his five senses, was calm. It was an invisible, intangible storm, a secret storm. In its agony the clock-tree had strangled its clock—the wood had clenched it so tightly that the bezel had finally bent, and the crystal had shattered. Brass clockwork spilled out through the clock's busted face and down onto the grass.

"Jesus Christ," Quentin said. "What a monster."

"It's the Big Ben of clock-trees," Janet said behind him.

"I've never seen one like that," Eliot said. "Do you think it was the first one she made?"

Whatever it was, it was a Fillorian wonder, a real one, wild and grand and strange. It was a long time since he'd seen one, or maybe it was just a long time since he'd noticed. He felt a twinge of something he hadn't felt since Ember's Tomb: fear, and something more. Awe. They were looking the mystery in the face. This was the raw stuff, the main line, the old, old magic.

They stood together, strung out along the edge of the meadow. The clock's minute hand poked out at a right angle from the trunk like a broken finger. A yard from its base a little sapling sprouted where the gears had fallen, as if from an acorn, swaying back and forth in the silent gale. A silver pocket watch ticked away in a knot in its slender trunk. A typically cute Fillorian touch.

This was going to be good.

"I'll go first."

Quentin started forward, but Eliot put a hand on his arm.

"I wouldn't."

"I would. Why not?"

"Because clock-trees don't just move like that. And I've never seen a broken one before. I didn't think they *could* break. This isn't a natural place. The hare must have led us here."

"I know, right? It's classic!"

Julia shook her head. She looked pale, and there was a dead leaf in her hair, but she was back on her feet.

"See how regular the clearing is," she said. "It is a perfect circle. Or at least an ellipse. There is a powerful area-effect spell radiating out from the center. Or from the foci," she added quietly, "in the case of an ellipse."

"You go in there, there's no telling where you'll end up," Eliot said.

"Of course there isn't. That's why I'm going."

This, this was what he needed. This was the point—he'd been waiting for it without even knowing it. God, it had been so long. This was an adventure. He couldn't believe the others would even hesitate. Behind him Dauntless whickered in the stillness.

It wasn't a question of courage. It was like they'd forgotten who they were, and where they were, and why. Quentin retrieved his bow and took another arrow from his quiver. As an experiment, he set his stance, drew, and shot at the tree trunk. Before it reached its target the arrow slowed, like it was moving through water instead of air. They watched it float, tumbling a little end over end, backward, in slow motion. Finally it gave up the last of its momentum and just stopped, five feet off the ground.

Then it burst, soundlessly, into white sparks.

"Wow." Quentin laughed. He couldn't help it. "This place is enchanted as *balls!*"

He turned to the others.

"What do you think? This looks like an adventure to me. Remember adventures? Like in the books?"

"Yeah, remember them?" Janet said. She actually looked angry. "Remember Penny? We haven't seen him around lately, have we? I don't want to spend the rest of my queenhood cutting up your food for you."

Remember Alice, she could just as well have said. He remembered Alice. She had died, but they'd lived, and wasn't this what living was about? He bounced on his toes. They tingled and sweated in his boots, six inches from the sharp edge of the enchanted meadow.

He knew the others were right, this place practically reeked of weird magic. It was a trap, a coiled spring that was aching to spring shut on him and snap him up. And he wanted it to. He wanted to stick his finger in it and see what happened. Some story, some quest, started here, and he wanted to go on it. It felt fresh and clean and unsafe, nothing like the heavy warm lard of palace life. The protective plastic wrap had been peeled off.

"You're really not coming?" he said.

Julia just watched him. Eliot shook his head.

"I'm going to play it safe. But I can try to cover you from here."

He began industriously casting a minor reveal designed to suss out any obvious magical threats. Magic crackled and spat around his hands as he worked. Quentin drew his sword. The others made fun of him for carrying it, but he liked the way it felt in his hand. It made him feel like a hero. Or at least it made him look like a hero.

Julia didn't think it was funny. Though she didn't laugh at much of anything anymore. Anyway, he'd just drop it if magic was called for.

"What are you going to do?" Janet said, hands on her hips. "Seriously, what? Climb it?"

"When it's time I'll know what to do." He rolled his shoulders.

"I do not like this, Quentin," Julia said. "This place. This tree. If we attempt this adventure it will mean some great change of our fortunes."

"Maybe a change would do us good."

"Speak for yourself," Janet said.

Eliot finished his spell and made a square out of his thumbs and forefingers. He closed one eye and squinted through it, panning around the clearing.

"I don't *see* anything . . ."

A mournful bonging came from up in the branches. Near its crown the tree had sprouted a pair of enormous swaying bronze church bells. Why not? Eleven strokes: it still kept time, apparently, even though the works were broken. Then the silence filled back in, like water that had been momentarily displaced.

Everybody watched him. The clock-tree's branches creaked in the soundless wind. He didn't move. He thought about Julia's warning: some great change of our fortunes. His fortunes were riding high right now, he had to admit. He had a goddamned castle, full of quiet courtyards and airy towers and golden Fillorian sunlight that poured like hot honey. Suddenly he wasn't sure what he was wagering that against. He could die in there. Alice had died.

And he was a king now. Did he even have the right to go galloping off after every magic bunny that wagged its cottontail at him? That wasn't his job anymore. All at once he felt selfish. The clock-tree was right there in front of him, heaving and thrashing with power and the promise of adventure. But his excitement was slipping away. It was becoming contaminated with doubt. Maybe they were right, his place was here. Maybe this wasn't such a good idea.

The urge to go into the meadow began to wear off, like a drug, leaving him abruptly sober. Who was he kidding? Being king wasn't the beginning of a story, it was the end. He didn't need a magic rabbit to tell him his future, he knew his future because it was already here. This was the happily ever after part. Close the book, put it down, walk away.

Quentin stepped back a pace and replaced his sword in its sheath in one smooth gesture. It was the first thing his fencing master had taught him: two weeks of sheathing and unsheathing before he'd even been allowed to cut the air. Now he was glad he'd done it. Nothing made you look like more of a dick than standing there trying to find the end of your scabbard with the tip of your sword.

He felt a hand on his shoulder. Julia.

"It is all right, Quentin," she said. "This is not your adventure. Follow it no further."

He wanted to lean his head down and rub his cheek back and forth against her hand like a cat.

"I know," he said. He wasn't going to go. "I get it."

"You're really not going?" Janet sounded almost disappointed. Probably she'd wanted to watch him blow up into glitter too.

"Really not."

They were right. Let somebody else be the hero. He'd had his happy ending. Right then he couldn't even have said what he was looking for in there. Nothing worth dying for, anyway.

"Come on, it's almost lunchtime," Eliot said. "Let's find some less exciting meadow to eat in."

"Sure," Quentin said. "Cheers to that."

There was champagne in one of the hampers, staying magically chilled, or something like champagne—they were still working on a Fillorian equivalent. And those hampers, with special leather loops for the bottles and the glasses—they were the kind of thing he remembered seeing in catalogs of expensive, useless things he couldn't afford back in the real world. And now look! He had all the hampers he could ever want. It wasn't champagne, but it was bubbly, and it made you drunk. And Quentin was going to get good and drunk over lunch.

Eliot climbed back into the saddle and swung Julia up behind him. It looked like the civet was gone for good. There was still a large patch of damp black earth on Julia's rump from the fall. Quentin had a foot in Dauntless's stirrup when they heard a shout.

"Hi!"

They all looked around.

"Hi!" It was what Fillorians said instead of "hey."

The Fillorian saying it was a hale, vigorous man in his early thirties. He was striding toward them, right across the circular clearing, practically radiating exuberance. He broke into a jog at the sight of them. He totally ignored the branches of the broken clock-tree that were waving wildly over his head; he couldn't have cared less. Just another day in the magic forest. He had a big blond mane and a big chest, and he'd grown a big blond beard to cover up his somewhat moony round chin.

It was Jollyby, Master of the Hunt. He wore purple-and-yellow striped tights. His legs really were pretty impressive, especially considering that he'd never even been in the same universe as a leg press or a StairMaster or whatever. Eliot was right, he must have been following them the whole time.

"Hi!" Janet shouted back happily. "Now it's a party," she added to the others, sotto voce.

In one huge leather-gloved fist Jollyby held up a large, madly kicking hare by its ears.

"Son of a bitch," Dauntless said. "He caught it."

Dauntless was a talking horse. She just didn't talk much.

"He sure did," Quentin said.

"Lucky thing," Jollyby called out when he was close enough. "I found him sitting up on a rock, happy as you please, not a hundred yards from here. He was busy keeping an eye on you lot, and I got him to bolt the wrong way. Caught him with my bare hands. Would you believe it?"

Quentin would believe it. Though he still didn't think it made sense. How do you sneak up on an animal that can see the future? Maybe it saw other people's but not its own. The hare's eyes rolled wildly in their sockets.

"Poor thing," Eliot said. "Look how pissed off it is."

"Oh, Jolly," Janet said. She crossed her arms in mock outrage. "You should have let us catch it! Now it'll only tell *your* future."

She sounded not at all disappointed by this, but Jollyby—a superb all-around huntsman but no National Merit Scholar—looked vexed. His furry brows furrowed.

"Maybe we could pass it around," Quentin said. "It could do each of us in turn."

"It's not a bong, Quentin," Janet said.

"No," Julia said. "Do not ask it."

But Jollyby was enjoying his moment as the center of royal attention.

"Is that true, you useless animal?" he said. He reversed his grip on the Seeing Hare and hoisted it up so that he and the hare were nose to nose.

It gave up kicking and hung down limp, its eyes blank with panic. It was an impressive beast, three feet long from its twitching nose to its tail, with a fine gray-brown coat the color of dry grass in winter. It wasn't cute. This was not a tame hare, a magician's rabbit. It was a wild animal.

"What do you see then, eh?" Jollyby shook it, as if this were all its idea and therefore its fault. "What do you see?"

The Seeing Hare's eyes focused. It looked directly at Quentin. It bared its huge orange incisors.

"Death," it rasped.

They all stood there for a second. It didn't seem scary so much as inappropriate, like somebody had made a dirty joke at a child's birthday party.

Then Jollyby frowned and licked his lips, and Quentin saw blood in his teeth. He coughed once, experimentally, as if he were just trying it out, and then his head lolled forward. The hare dropped from his nerveless fingers and shot away across the grass like a rocket.

Jollyby's corpse fell forward onto the grass.

"Death and destruction!" the hare called out as it ran, in case it hadn't made itself clear before. "Disappointment and despair!"